CIRCUS OF WONDERS

CIRCUS OF WONDERS

A Novel

ELIZABETH MACNEAL

THORNDIKE PRESS
A part of Gale, a Cengage Company

Thorndike Press® Large Print Core.
The text of this Large Print edition is unabridged.
Other aspects of the book may vary from the original edition.
Set in 16 pt. Plantin.

LIBRARY OF CONGRESS CIP DATA ON FILE.
CATALOGUING IN PUBLICATION FOR THIS BOOK
IS AVAILABLE FROM THE LIBRARY OF CONGRESS.

ISBN-13: 978-1-4328-9695-9 (hardcover alk. paper)

Published in 2022 by arrangement with Emily Bestler Books/Atria Books, a Division of Simon & Schuster, Inc.

Printed in Mexico
Print Number: 01   Print Year: 2022

For Mum and Dad, with all my love

■ ■ ■ ■

PART ONE:
MAY 1866

■ ■ ■ ■

The river
where you set
your foot just now
is gone —
those waters
giving way to this,
now this.
— HERACLITUS, *Fragments*

We are unfashioned creatures, but half
made up.
— MARY SHELLEY, *Frankenstein,* 1823

NELL

It begins with an advertisement, nailed to an oak tree.

"Jasper Jupiter's Circus of Wonders!" someone shouts.

"What is it?"

"The greatest show on earth!"

Everyone is shuffling forward, tutting, shouting. A woman shrieks, "Watch your wings!"

Through a gap between armpits, Nell glimpses a fragment of the handbill. The color sings, bright red edged in gold. An illustration of a bearded woman, dressed in a red doublet, golden wings clipped to her boots. *"Stella the Songbird, Bearded Like a Bear!"* Nell leans closer, straining to see the whole of the advertisement, to read the looping words. *"Minnie, the Famed Behemoth"* — a huge gray creature, long snouted — *"Brunette, the Welsh Giantess. The World's Smallest Museum of Curious Objects"* — a

9

sketch of a white crocodile in a jar, the sloughed skin of a snake.

At the top of the handbill, three times the size of any of the other acts, is a man's face. His mustache is curled into two sharp brackets, cane held like a thunderbolt. *"Jasper Jupiter,"* she reads, *"showman, presents a dazzling troupe of living curiosities —"*

"What's a living curiosity?" Nell asks her brother.

He doesn't answer.

As she stands there, she forgets the endless cutting and tying of violets and narcissi, the numerous bee stings that swell her hands, the spring sun that bakes her skin until it looks parboiled. Wonder kindles in her. The circus is coming here, to their small village. It will pin itself to the salt-bleached fields behind them, stain the sky with splashes of exquisite color, spill knife jugglers and exotic animals and girls who strut through the streets as if they own them. She presses closer to her brother, listens to the racket of questions. Gasps, exclamations.

"How do they make the poodles dance?"

"A monkey, dressed as a tiny gallant!"

"Does that woman really have a beard?"

"Mouse pelts. It will be mouse pelts, fixed with glue."

Nell stares at the handbill — its scrolled

10

edges, its fierce colors, its shimmering script — and tries to burn it into her mind. She wishes she could keep it. She would like to sneak back when it is dark and pull loose the nails — gently, so as not to rip the paper — and look at it whenever she wants, to study these curious people as carefully as she pores over the woodcuts in the Bible.

Tent shows have often pitched in nearby towns, but never in their village. Her father even visited Sanger's when it set up in Hastings. He told stories about boys with painted lips, men who rode horses upside down and fired pistols at pint pots. *Marvels you wouldn't believe. And the doxies — oh, as cheap as —* He broke off, winked at Charlie. In the fields, news of circus disasters passed gleefully from mouth to mouth. Tamers eaten by lions, girls who tiptoed across high wires and tumbled to their deaths, fires that consumed the tent whole and roasted the spectators inside, boiled whales in their tanks.

There is a lull in the shouting, and into that a voice calls, "Are you in it?"

It is Lenny, the crate builder, his red hair falling into his eyes. He is grinning as if he expects everyone to join in. Those around him fall silent and, encouraged, he speaks more loudly. "Show us a handstand! Before

11

the other wonders arrive."

From the way her brother flinches, at first Nell thinks Lenny is talking to him. But it is impossible; there is nothing unusual about Charlie, and it is her who Lenny watches, his gaze sliding over her hands and cheeks. The silence hangs, broken only by whispers.

"What did he say?"

"I didn't hear!"

A shuffling, fidgeting.

Nell can feel the familiar burn of eyes on her. When she glances up, they startle, focus too intently on their fingernails, at a stone on the ground. They mean to be kind, she knows, to spare her the humiliation. Old memories split open. How, two years ago, the storm cast salt onto the violets and shriveled them, and her father pointed at her with a wavering finger. *She's a bad omen, and I said it the day she was born.* How her brother's sweetheart, Mary, is careful not to brush her hand by mistake. *Is it catching?* The bare stares of passing travelers, the mountebanks who try to sell her pills and lotions and powders. A life of being both intensely visible and unseen.

"What did you say, Lenny?" her brother demands, and he is poised, taut as a ratting terrier.

"Leave him," Nell whispers. "Please."

She is not a child, not a scrap of meat to be fought over by dogs. It is not their fight; it is *hers*. She feels it like a fist in her belly. She covers herself with her hands as if she is naked.

The crowd moves back as Charlie pounces, his arm pounding like the anvil of a machine, Lenny pinned beneath him. Somebody tries to pull him off, but he is a monster, swiping, kicking, flailing.

"Please," she begs, reaching for her brother's shirt. "Stop it, Charlie."

She looks up. Space has opened around her. She is standing alone, fidgeting with the hem of her cap. A jewel of blood glints in the dust. Sweat circles the armpits of her dress. The minister hovers his hand over her shoulder as if to pat it.

Her bee stings throb, her hands bruised purple with sap.

Nell forces her way through the crowd. Behind her, the grunt of fighting, fabric tearing. She starts to walk toward the cliffs. She craves a swim, that low ache as her limbs fight the current. She will not run, she tells herself, but her footsteps soon hammer the ground and her breath is hot in her throat.

TOBY

Toby should be riding back to camp, careering down these twisted hedgerows before dusk sets in. But he never can resist the way people watch him as he puts up the advertisements, nails held between his lips. He takes longer than he should, as if this is part of the show. His brother would laugh at his theatrical wielding of the hammer, how he steps to one side as if he might be whisking away a cape. *Ta-da.* But the villagers look at him as if he is important, as if he is *somebody,* and he pulls back his shoulders, straightens the dandelion crown he made for his horse.

As soon as he arrives back at the camp, he will seep into the background. He is a mere enabler of others, his brute strength the only way to repay the debt he owes his brother. He lifts hay and ferries king poles and oils ratchets. He is tall, but not tall enough. He is wide, but not fat enough. His strength is

14

useful, but it quails compared to those who make a living from it — Violante, the Spanish Hercules, who can lift an iron cannon weighing four hundred pounds by the hair on his head.

As Toby stands by the inn, and people eye the handbills poking from his saddlebag, sweat dampens his collar. The day is too clear, too hot, to be real. It hovers, as still and perfect as a glass bauble, as if it is about to break.

He watches a blond-haired girl as she runs toward the sea, dust rising behind her like smoke. A freckled boy limps round the corner of the inn, blood on his nose and mouth. *They were so excited about the show that a fight broke out.* That is what he will tell his brother, Jasper, tonight. At least news of such frenzied anticipation will do something to ease Jasper's temper, which will surely come as soon as he sets foot in this — well, even *village* would be generous. Rib-thin dogs and timber cottages hunched like dowagers. Toby thinks of Sevastopol and the burnt husks of dwellings, and the scent of flowers cloys. His fingers shake, the reins clinking. The gulls scream like mortars. A reek of stale bodies, of dried manure. He rubs his cheek.

He clambers onto his horse (Grimaldi,

named after the clown), digs his spurs into its side, and begins to head back to their current pitch, an hour's ride away. Tonight, they will pack up the wagons, yoke the zebras, and begin their slow procession to this settlement. He has arranged a field where they will set up their tent, instructed the grocer to provide cabbages and old vegetables for the animals.

Just past the turnpike, Toby decides to take the longer coastal lane, where the girl ran. As he rides toward the cliffs, he passes tiny walled gardens carpeted with violets and realizes that this village is a flower farm. He hears his first cuckoo of the year, canters past a wheatear settled on a branch.

The sea is gin clear, rocks as sharp as bayonets. Sea meets sky in a pale blur. He stops, turns his fingers into a rough square, as if he might capture the scene with his photography machine. He lowers his hands. Pristine images have held no charm for him since the Crimean War. Instead, he draws out a cigar and a pack of lucifers.

It is in that moment, as he strikes a match and inhales its fresh scent — camphor, sulfur — that he sees the girl poised on a rock, as though she is about to walk onto a stage. The drop to the water must be six, ten feet high. He cries out, "No!," as she

16

throws herself forward, toes pointed, pale hair streaming behind her like a flame. The sea swallows her, gargles. She rises briefly, arms high, fighting. He loses sight of her. Waves thunder.

She is, he is quite sure, drowning. She has been under for too long already. Toby tumbles from his horse, charges forward. Down the steep cliff path, stones skittering, ankle twisting beneath him, Grimaldi staggering behind. No sign of her. Pain like a blade. Her hand appears as if grown from the sea itself. He tugs at his shirt and crashes into the shallows. It is cold but he does not care.

And then, she surfaces, and her arms slice the waves. She twists with the sea, basking as easily as a seal. She kicks her legs, dives down, and then breaks the water, hair stuck to her face. It feels private, somehow, as if Toby is intruding; but he finds himself arrested by the quiet ecstasy of her movements, how she carves through the water as smoothly as a hot knife in butter. She cuts her way to the boulder she jumped from, waits for a swell, and clings to it, dress stuck to her. He half expects a scaled tail to emerge, not legs.

When she is on the rock, she notices him, and he sees himself as she must, calfskin jerkin half off, water soaking his trousers. His shirt is open, his belly so large and pale. A foolish bear of a man. He blushes, shame spreading up his neck.

"I-I thought you were drowning," he says.

"No."

She cups her chin in her hands and glares at him, her face half shadowed. But he realizes that something lies beneath her anger; a yearning, as if this place is too small for her, as if she wants more. He feels a corresponding tug in his own chest.

He is surprised to realize that she is so small and unkempt, her clothes unraveling, her salt-lightened hair so knotted. There is an unconscious poise in the way she sits, a smoothness to her movements when she wrings the water from her sleeves. She looks away from him, toward the horizon, and there is something about her that he cannot explain. The shadow, he notices, has fallen on the wrong cheek. He must be mistaken. He peers more closely. A crackle of electricity seizes him. He steps forward, waves swilling around his knees.

It is as if someone has taken a paintbrush and run it from her cheekbone to her chin, splashed tiny flecks of brown paint across the rest of her face and neck. He should look away, but he can't. He cannot believe that this quiet village could contain someone so extraordinary. Here, among the nettles and the dirt and the crumpled cottages.

"Have a long look, why don't you?" she says. There is challenge in her eyes, as if waiting for him to flinch.

Her words rip a hole in him. He flushes. "I-I . . ." he stammers. "I-I didn't . . ."

Silence takes over. The waves spit at him and thunder over the stones. The sea sits between them, as if protecting her. He should leave. Already the sun is lowering, and he will have to ride an hour in the dark. He doesn't know these parts. He touches the knife at his thigh where it waits, ready to sink itself into any brigand who might pounce from a tree.

There is a shout from the cliffs, a man's voice. "Nell-ie! Nell-ie!"

She slips behind the rock, out of sight.

The man might be her husband; she looks old enough to be married. He wonders if they have argued, if this is why she is hiding down here.

"Well, good-bye," Toby says, but she does not reply.

He moves toward the shore. Sea anemones flaunt themselves in rock pools. He mounts Grimaldi and, as he crests the path, he comes across the man calling her name. He raises his cap.

"Did you see a girl down there?" he asks.

Toby pauses, and the lie is easy. "No."

As soon as he is at the top, he glances back, but she is gone. Slipped into the water, perhaps, or still crouched behind the boulder. Spray lifts from that small hip of rock. He shakes his head and presses his horse into a gallop.

He races as if pursued. He races as if to outrun himself, his own thoughts, as if to open up the distance between him and her. Little flies lodge in his throat. The saddle creaks. He wants to leave her there, like a child who has lifted a stone and replaces it without killing the wood louse beneath it. He wants to forget her. But she lingers, as though pressed onto glass.

Have a long look, why don't you?

He blinks, rides faster. He misses his brother with a sudden ache, a need to be with him, to winch himself back in, to be assured of his silence and protection.

Scutari, Scutari, Scutari.

Those cold nights, the screech of bullets. Soldiers shivering beneath ripped tarpaulins.

That is the past, he tells himself; nobody knows what he has done except Jasper. *Nobody knows.* But his heart is racketing, and he leans closer to the horse for fear he will tip himself off. A gull eyes him, shrieks as if to say, *I know — I know — I know —*

He is a coward, a liar, and a man died because of him. A thousand more might have perished by his hand.

Sparrows dash from low branches. He passes a single carriage. A hare is almost caught under Grimaldi's hooves. Toby, who is usually so cautious, has never ridden so fast in his life.

He will bring his brother news about the girl, and Jasper's face will crease into simple delight. It will ease his debt, just a little. That is the first thing he will do when he arrives back at the camp. If he doesn't, he knows his brother will guess anyway. Sometimes, it feels as if Jasper holds Toby's mind in a jar. He is a book to be read, a plain machine whose parts Jasper can easily assemble. He ducks to miss a low branch, his thighs burning. He has a memory of Jasper, prizing silver rings off dead soldiers, gripping a bagful of Russian crucifixes. *I snatches whatever I sees! This will make our circus!*

If he tells Jasper about the girl, about *Nellie,* what then?

Others could appreciate her worth too. She'd earn far more than she does here.

But as a pheasant scrabbles out of his path, he has an image of himself as a wide-eyed bloodhound, fetching his brother a dead bird in his mouth.

NELL

"Nell-ie, Nell-ie."

Her brother is calling her name, but Nell does not reply. It is the man she watches, galloping across the clifftops, neck bent to his horse's mane. She has a contrary urge to beckon him to return, to have him look at her as he did before. The sight of him, water crashing around his knees, his startled horse with its saddlebag of handbills. *I thought you were drowning.* The memory is so acute it is a surprise when she looks at the beach and finds it empty. And then she digs her knuckles into her thighs, remembers how he watched her fooling around in the water. He might be laughing at her even now, just as Lenny did.

Show us a handstand! Before the other wonders arrive.

It is only her here, only her and a thousand barnacles and a rock pool of scuttling crabs as transparent as fingernails. Her brother's

23

shouts fade. The brine has made her birth-marks itch, and she lifts up her sodden skirts and inspects them, longing to rake them with her fingernails. Some are the size of freckles, others so large she can span them with her fingers. They cover her torso, her back, her arms. She has never thought of them as *blots* or *stains* as her father calls them. Instead, she likes to think of them as rocks and pebbles, tiny grains of sand, a whole seashore dimpling her body.

Nell remembers the fair in the next town when she was a young child — the cart heavy with flowers, her and Charlie whoop-ing as they bounced over potholes, the rattle of those tall metal wheels. Her brother was five; she must have been almost four. It was when they drew into the marketplace that she began to notice murmurings around her, stares, sudden drawings-back. Towns-folk she didn't recognize and who didn't know her. Hissed questions. Her father pulled to one side. *What's wrong with her? It's a tragedy* — she thought perhaps she was dying and nobody had told her. She asked her brother, her voice high in panic, and he shook his head. "It's these," he said, pressing his fingers to her hands. "Only these. I hardly see them." But still, she did not understand, did not see her birthmarks

24

as any particular sadness, any problem that needed to be fixed. A small crowd gathered, fingers pointing. Someone reached out and flicked her cheek. Her brother's hand in hers, his fast breath. "Don't listen to them," he whispered. But after that, she started to notice it more, to imagine her friends regarding her with mockery or confusion, until she began to isolate herself from the other children, to choose solitude.

When they were a little older and had been taught to read by their minister, they found a battered copy of *Fairy Tales and Other Stories* on the shelves at the inn. She and Charlie read it carefully together. The Brothers Grimm and Hans Christian Andersen. They read about Hans My Hedgehog, half boy, half beast; about the Maiden without Hands; about Beast and his elephant trunk and his body glittering with fish scales. It was the stories' endings that always silenced her, that made her pull her dress over her fingers. Love altered each character — Hans shucked his hedgehog spines like a suit, the maiden's hands grew back, Beast became a man — and Nell pored over the woodcuts so carefully, staring at those plain, healed bodies. Would her birthmarks disappear if somebody loved her? Each time, Charlie nestled closer to her and raised his hands as if he were casting a spell to rid her of them, and it made her tearful in a way she could neither understand nor explain.

She slips into the water. The cold stabs at her, so sharp it feels like a burn, but it soothes the itching. She gasps, works her arms and legs faster. She pushes past the breaking waves, into the deep where she knows currents lurk beneath the skin of the sea. The trick is to swim across them, never to fight. But when she feels their pull, she enjoys the dance with them. She twists, swims down, little pebbles whirlpooled against her. The horizon shimmers. That familiar longing for annihilation. When she was younger, she could swim all day, until her fingers and toes were as wrinkled as old apples. Even now, the cold tug of the sea reminds her of the childish stories she told herself. That the sea might pull her into an underwater kingdom, to palaces made of cockle shells and seed pearls, a secret place where only she and Charlie could go. She begins to picture it as she did then: plates of mackerel longing to be eaten, the ring of laughter, the brush of an arm against her own — she swallows a mouthful of seawater, coughs. When she looks up, she finds she is farther out than she realized, the cliffs as small as wheatsheaves.

"Nell-ie! Nell-ie!"

In the gap between waves, she glimpses her brother, standing on the edge of the cliffs, beckoning her in. His fear is infectious. Cold stipples her skin. She feels suddenly tired, worn out. Her arms ache, her dress sodden and pulling her down. Her wrists are wrenched like wishbones. She has a terrible thought that she will never see Charlie again. She pictures her bloated body washed up in a week's time, eyes pecked out by fish, her brother weeping over her. She kicks her legs, beats the current with cupped palms. The sea sucks at her. Each slice of her arms a small victory. The beach grows closer, and she knocks her ankle against a rock, feels the quick score of blood. The boulder is in reach, the waves slurping, the tide rolling her against the pebbles.

"What are you doing?" Charlie demands, seizing her by the arm. His trousers are soaked to the knees. "You frightened me."

She turns from him, to hide how out of breath she is; to hide, too, her satisfaction that he cares.

"It isn't funny," he says, nursing his bruised knuckles. "It isn't funny at all."

She wades back into the water, then dives for his ankle and gurns like a monster. "I'm going to eat you up!"

"Stop it," he says, shaking himself free.

But she sees a grin tugging the corner of his mouth, and soon she is making him laugh again. Before long, Nell has almost forgotten the cut of Lenny's words, the stares of the other villagers. She forgets, even, that Charlie has a child on the way and will soon be married, and that nobody will want her. Right now, it is just her and her brother, larking in the water, skimming stones. Each pebble fits her hand perfectly, as if this beach, this village, this life, were made for her. Charlie fetches her shoes, and she shivers in the cool of early dusk.

"Let's try and catch a squid," she says.

They keep a net and an old rusted lantern hidden behind a rock, and Charlie retrieves them and lights the oil.

"I don't want to go to the show," he says, so quietly she only just hears him.

"Why not?"

"I've been thinking," he says, "and I just . . . I just don't like it."

Her relief is a surprise to her. She rests her head on his shoulder. "Nor do I."

They watch the water for a while, the sun sinking until it is boiling in the waves.

"There!" she shouts at last, the shadow of a squid pulsing in the shallows. Charlie sweeps it into the net, and the creature thrashes, tentacles tangling in the strings.

She grasps its slippery body, as soft as offal. It is so pristine and helpless. She thinks of the fossilized plesiosaurs that men of science dug from the earth thirty years ago, winged and scaled creatures twelve feet long. She tries to imagine a creature like that swimming into her hand, the money men would pay to exhibit it. She has heard rumors of mermaids made of fish skin and monkey pelts, displayed in museums beside two men linked at the waist.

An age of wonder, somebody called it, and Charlie added, *And an age of tricks and hoodwinking.*

Jasper Jupiter's Circus of Wonders.

The squid throbs, its tentacles suckering her hand.

"We can cook it on coals," Charlie says.

Her stomach growls. It is a struggle not to pounce on it raw, to feel the comfort of *anything* in her belly. It has been a slow week with their wages paid late, and they've eaten only vegetables and pease pudding.

But Nell arches her back and throws the squid into the water, as far from their net as she can.

"What did you do that for?" Charlie

demands, and he frowns and hurls the net
across the stones.

JASPER

Jasper Jupiter's shirt is ringed with sweat, the handle of the whip slippery in his hand. It reminds him of those hot days in Balaklava, how they bore down on deserters, the squeak and crack as leather met skin. The man moans, each lash parting the meat of his back. Jasper stops, dabbing his forehead. It gives him little pleasure, but he must keep a grip on his troupe. He recruits his laborers from slums and rookeries, from the dregs cast from the gates of the Old Bailey: wretches who are grateful for any work, any sense of family. It's hardly a surprise that he needs to discipline them from time to time.

"You won't be doing a bunk again, will you?" Jasper asks, cracking his knuckles. "Not until the end of the season. Good man."

The man limps back to the other laborers, cussing under his breath.

Jasper glances at Toby's wagon. Still unlit.

His brother is late. He should be back, helping dismantle the great skeleton of the tent, readying to move the wagons. Jasper sighs, walks through the field, shouting commands. All is activity, and everyone works even harder as he passes them. His own face smiles back at him from a dozen boards, from parasols for sale and a handbill trampled underfoot. He picks up the leaflet and dusts the footprint from his cheek. "Jasper Jupiter's Circus of Wonders." The monkeys gibber more loudly. Huffen Black, his clown and one-armed wonder, scatters bread and cabbages on the cage floor. The triplets are plucking stolen chickens, white puffs of down lighting the air, guts slapped into a bucket for the wolf to eat. Without the king poles holding her in place, the tent's vast belly billows.

"Hold her down!" Jasper cries, and men wrestle with the corners of the fabric, begin to fold segments of white on blue, white on blue.

Forty wagons, ten performers, a growing menagerie, and eighteen laborers and grooms — not even counting their infants. All *his.* They are a village on the move, a whole community at his command.

He spies Toby trotting into the field, and he hurries to him. His brother's hair is wild, his face pinked. Jasper decides to make light of his concern. "Had you written off for dead. You should be careful, out so late. If a troupe of traveling peddlers found you, they'd pull out your fingernails and teeth and sell you as a dancing bear."

Toby doesn't smile. He is fidgeting with his cap, his eyes skittish. With his long evening shadow, he looks even bigger than usual. Their father always said it was God's greatest joke to assign this hulking shape to such a timid creature.

"Come," Jasper says, softening a little. "A glass of grog? Leave the tent to the laborers."

Toby nods, follows Jasper into his wagon. It contains all the comforts of a hotel. Goose-down mattress, an ebony bureau, shelves of books. Every surface is papered with handbills as if the very walls are proclaiming his name.

"Jasper Jupiter's Circus of Wonders!"

"Jasper Jupiter's Circus of Wonders!"

"Jasper Jupiter's Circus of Wonders!"

He presses a thumb to where one advertisement is beginning to peel, and he smiles. The decanter chimes as Toby fills his glass.

"What was the village like?"

"Small," Toby says. "Poor. I shouldn't think we'll fill the tent."

Jasper scratches his chin. One day, he thinks, he'll storm London.

The drink rattles in Toby's hand.

"Is something the matter?" Perhaps guilt has settled on his brother as it often does, weighing down his mood. He reaches out and squeezes Toby's arm. "If it's about Dash —"

"It's not that," Toby says, too quickly. "It's just — I saw someone . . ."

"And?"

Toby turns his face from him.

"You saw who?" Jasper smacks his fist onto his ebony cabinet. "Was it Winston? Damn it. I knew it. He beat us to our pitch again. We can fight him. Send in the laborers."

"No," Toby says, twisting a hangnail. "It was nobody. It was just . . ." He waves his hand. His voice is high, as it always is when he is exercised. "Nobody."

"Nobody, eh?" Jasper says. "You can tell me. We're brothers, aren't we? Linked together."

There is a sheen of sweat on his brother's neck. His leg jiggles up and down.

Jasper grins. "It was a girl, wasn't it?"

Toby looks down at his drink.

"Aha! Who was she, then? Did you have your wicked way with her? Have a tumble in the hedgerows?" He laughs.

"It wasn't like that," Toby snaps. "She wasn't — I-I don't want to talk about it."

Jasper frowns. It irks him, this realization that Toby exists apart from him, that he has his own thoughts and secrets. He remembers when he was a boy and he saw the sketch of the Siamese twins Chang and Eng Bunker and how it stopped his breath. There on the page was a manifestation of how he felt about Toby. A link so close it felt physical. They might have shared a brain, a liver, lungs. Their hurts were each other's.

"Fine," Jasper says at last. "Keep your sordid little secret."

"I-I should help with the tent."

"As you please," Jasper says.

He watches Toby leave, hurrying to be away from him. His brother, a half of him, as closed as an oyster. His drink is untouched on the counter. What is he hiding? The girl can't have been special; he's barely been gone three hours. Jasper will puzzle him out. He always does.

He inhales, pulls a face. The breeze carries a waft of rotting crab, of putrefying seaweed. The knacker's van has arrived to feed the lioness, and he can hear the drone of wasps from here. He fingers the ring in his pocket, runs his thumbnail into the engraved initials. *E. W. D.* It reminds him of what Toby is capable.

"Stella," he calls, because he cannot bear to be alone. He can see her through his small window, pausing as she washes down his elephant. He named his *"famed behemoth"* Minnie, and he parades her alongside a mouse called Max. *"The biggest and smallest creatures in the world!"* Last week, on his thirty-third birthday, he bought Minnie for £300, pleased to liberate her from the traders whose hooks had cut her ears to ribbons. It's curious, he thinks, how he can stand human suffering but not animal. In the Crimean War, it was the wounded horses that disturbed him the most, while he scorned the screaming of the soldiers. "What use is that racket?" he would comment to his friend Dash. "As if elegiac wailing will coax their limbs back onto their torsos."

"Come, drink," he shouts to Stella, and she puts down her bucket. He longs to bury himself in her, to possess and enter and satisfy. To feel that by having her, Dash has forgiven him. When he lifts his glass to his lips, he is surprised to find he is trembling.

NELL

Nell is candying violets in her cottage. As she dips the flowers into the egg white and spins them in sugar, the cat watches her lazily, his ears pricked. All day, in fact, she has felt as though someone is watching her. In the walled gardens, her back aching as she picked hundreds of posies, she felt the burn of other laborers' eyes on her. When she walked home with Charlie, the hedgerows seemed lit with a thousand eyes — pheasants and field mice and a single spider in its web.

Her fingers pause, glittering with sugar. She hears a faint noise, like the air being forced from a pair of bellows.

Oompah, oompah.

"What's that?" Her father, in the corner of the room, startles from his nap.

"Must be the circus trumpets," she says, allowing herself a glance through the window. She can see only the top of the tent, its blue and white stripes. She wishes Charlie were here with her, that he hadn't decided to work the fields this evening.

"I'll cut the throat of that damned lion if it roars all night again." He sits up. "I caught a three-clawed lobster once. Could have pickled the bastard and sold it for a pretty penny."

Nell frowns. The village has been struck with "circus fever," as Charlie calls it. Nobody can talk about anything but giants and dwarfs, pig-headed boys and bear-girls. Piggott, the overseer, even showed them the little cartes de visite and porcelain figurines he'd bought of several performers: strongman, butterfly man, Stella the Songbird. "A shilling each," he announced proudly, tapping his silver fob. But in the morning, he found his hens missing from their hutch, and his smile fell away. Someone had laundry pinched from their line. There are rumors of travelers robbed on the roads, of a girl attacked. When Nell went to bed, she heard shrieking, laughter, the scream of a fiddle. Her heart quickened with fear and excitement.

Oompah, oompah.

Her fingers, dipping, sifting, twirling, pressing the flowers into a cardboard box. *"Bessie's Candied Violets."* A crate waits by

38

the door, marked *"London Paddington"* in thick black script. Sometimes, she traces her thumb across these words, imagines the violets like a set of actresses in puffy purple skirts, hungering to be somewhere else. Their glee as they racket through the country and wake up in a different landscape. Eyes peeping open, scattering themselves out across the city. There, they'll wriggle their purple skirts into towering white cakes, kick their little legs. They might be pinched between the fingers of the Queen herself. Meanwhile, she — who seeded and weeded and cut and packed them — will forever pace the small stone cells where they first sprouted, her hands reeking of the manufactured perfume she spritzes over the petals to make them smell more appealing.

Her father starts to snore, dribble linking his chin to his collar. The sea glass he is sorting patters to the ground. Their cottage is full of these things: useless trinkets he hopes a passing tinker might give him a penny for. Old rusted farm machinery, holed stones, a sparrow skull, mussel shells that he threads on string.

Oompah, oompah.

The other villagers will be gazing at feats so strange she cannot imagine what they are. Magic, spells, tricks. As astonishing as miracles. She feels a twinge of panic, as if everything is changing while she stays still.

Earlier in the day, she heard the showman bellowing from a speaking trumpet.

Step up, step up! Wheezes ever charming, ever new! Step up and see the most astonishing wonders ever gathered in a single show —

Nell glances at her father and wipes her hands on a cloth. It is only three paces to the yard.

It is a surprisingly cool evening for late May, and she shivers a little when she steps outside. The lavender shakes, the nettles flattened by a sudden breeze. She pulls her bonnet tighter around her face.

The large man in the leather jerkin will be there. She wonders if he is a performer, though she could not find him on the handbill. A juggler, perhaps, or a fire-eater.

Oompah, oompah.

It would not hurt to take a closer look. Nobody will see her. And before she can change her mind, she is clambering over the stone wall and racing toward the field.

Wagons are scattered like dropped toys. It smells of burnt sugar and orange peel, of animals and sour bodies. The music grows louder. Outside the tent, it is almost deserted, just a few men sharing a cigar, a three-legged dog pissing against a carriage wheel. The grass is littered with cooking pans, pipe ends, blackened patches where fires were lit. Brackish water the color of gravy. Her heartbeat knocks against her ears.

Each caravan is painted in a different color with a name in looping script.

"Brunette, the Welsh Giantess"

"Stella the Songbird"

"Tobias Brown, Crimean Photographist"

"The World's Smallest Museum of Curious Objects"

It is this wagon that Nell wanders toward. She waits until the men are looking the other way and darts inside.

The walls are lined with shelves. There are glass jars and polished fossils and a tank with a gleaming fish in it. A white crocodile head swims in cloudy fluid, its eye tracking her around the room. She touches a pair of vast trousers, reads the sign beneath it. "Owned by the celebrated Daniel Lambert, fattest man in the world." Beside it, a tiny teapot, "Used by Charles Stratton, General Tom Thumb." For a moment, she thinks of slipping it into her pocket.

Nell knocks her head on the skeleton of something small — a mouse? A rat? — and jumps, steadies herself on a shelf. The creature swings like a convicted soul. All she can hear is her breath, the wet sound as

41

she swallows. She thinks, for a second, that the crocodile is not dead but is about to rear out of the jar and tear out her throat. She puts her hands to her neck, backs away, trips down the steps. The men are gone.

She should return to the cottage and sugar more violets. She could have made a farthing in the time she has already been here. But there, at the back of the tent, she sees the canvas half open. Nobody would notice if she peeped in. Nobody would care.

The fabric is heavy, waxy, and she pulls it to one side.

In a burning circle of light, she sees a tall man in a military suit, a gold cape at his shoulders, a three-foot topper planted on his head. It is the showman from the middle of the handbill, his mouth pulled into a grin. He is sitting on one of those gray creatures, an *elephant.* It is the largest thing she has ever seen, its skin painted with flowers. She bites her lip. His arms swirl, as if he is stirring a vast pot, whipping the crowd into hysteria.

"We present a sight never witnessed before, a sight that will leave you reaching for your spectacles, that will make you question everything you have ever seen or known or heard before. You will *not believe your own eyes* —"

42

The scale of it; the sound; the light. This is louder than storms, than steam trains; brighter than the sun in water. There are hundreds of lamps around the ring, throwing out red and blue and green light. Tallow candles are mounted on hoops and chandeliers, pine knots blazing in brackets. Nell never imagined such a sight might be possible. It is horrifying, enchanting.

"The newest, the best, the strangest." He intones each word, and the crowd shrieks louder, hungry for more. She tries to pick out Lenny's red hair, but everyone blurs together. Someone throws a pot of liquid into the ring, another hurls a rotten cabbage where it bursts like a wound. She has known these people since she was born, Hector and Mary and Mrs. Pawley, and yet they all move as one, a great laughing, snorting mass of bodies.

A crash of cymbals, a thundering of drums, and a loud smack as a woman soars across the tent, gripping a bar on a rope. "Stella the Songbird!" Her legs are creamy and dimpled, and her tiny crimson doublet flashes. Her ruff makes her look as if her face is being served on a platter. All the while, she twitters. She caws like a gull, chirrups like a blackbird. With every turn, she pushes higher, faster, until she is a flash of red, her body twisting like a fish. How must that feel — the rush of air, balancing on a slim bar by a hand alone, as if the rules of weight do not apply to her? And then, Nell sees it — a beard, falling over the edge of her ruff, blond and thick.

Nell gapes, stares. Deep in her belly, she feels the slightest of recoils. It is as if she has seen something unexpected but stunning, like a dead kingfisher in the reeds. She knows, then, how others feel when they gaze at her.

Show us a handstand! Before the other wonders arrive.

She cannot stop looking, cannot draw herself away. She wishes her brother were here, that anyone were here with her, even her father. She watches as a tiny woman in an open coach is pulled into the ring by four poodles, a baby in her arms. A man begins to juggle, loose skin hanging from his shoulders like wings, his back painted like a red admiral. A monkey dressed as a soldier rides a horse, a hunchbacked woman cooks an oyster on hot coals in her mouth, and a giantess slicks beef fat onto a pole and hangs a piece of meat from the top of it. "Who can scale it for the prize?" the showman shouts from his perch on the elephant, and Nell watches as villagers push them-

44

selves forward, as they slip and slide on the grease.

There is Mary, caught in profile, laughing, pushing a boy forward. He must be one of Mary's brothers. But then they bow their heads together, and Nell's heart lurches. It is Charlie. Nell staggers back. As she hurries away, across the field, over the wall, into the cottage where her sugared blooms are laid out by the stove, she feels a shame so sharp it is as if someone is pressing her chest.

Her brother does not want to be around her. He pretended he didn't want to go to the show, but it was a lie, a sham. He wanted to share it with Mary instead. He has already begun to craft his life without her in it.

She spies the violets on the table, candies she spent all afternoon making. She picks up the tray, and the flattened boxes, too. A spike of fury stabs at her. She shovels them into the stove, watching as Bessie the cherub's face catches and shrivels to ash.

Charlie returns an hour later, stinking of beef fat, his eyes bright with all he has seen.

Nell says nothing. She cleans grit from the carrots and slices them into boiling water. She is nineteen, she tells herself, and her brother is twenty. There is no reason why he can't go somewhere without her. Soon, she will have to grow used to it.

"How was it?" she asks at last.

"It was just me in the fields. Everyone else was at the show."

"Oh," she says.

"I don't think we missed anything. I heard their squeals, though, like a sty of badly butchered pigs." He looks around him. "Where's Pa?"

"Trying to sell some old glass and a broken wheel."

"What's wrong?"

"Nothing." She forces herself to smile.

But all through dinner, she cannot look at him. Their father doesn't return, and she ladles his portion to one side. It cools quickly, fat whitening the surface. The carrots are so soft they dissolve between her teeth. The broth is gritty and tastes of earth. Charlie fiddles with his sleeve, his knee hopping as if in memory of a circus tune.

"What is it?" he asks at last. "Tell me."

She puts down her spoon. "I don't mind, you know."

"Don't mind what?"

"If you want to go to places without me —" Her voice catches, sounds too high. "Just please . . . please don't lie to me."

He puts his head in his hands. "I was going to the fields, but I saw the tent and Mary told me to come and . . . and I couldn't resist it."

"Why didn't you fetch me?"

"I-I thought it would upset you."

A thought occurs to her, and she bows her head as if he has hit her.

"You think that I'm like *them*. You think I'm a . . . a *living curiosity. A wonder.*"

Charlie says nothing, and Nell keeps talking, louder and louder. "You think Lenny was right, don't you? That was why you hit him. Because you saw the truth in it."

"What?" he says, hand over his mouth. "How can you think that? You know I see you as just the same as the rest of us."

"The rest of us," she echoes.

Charlie holds up his hands. "I was just trying to protect you —"

"Protect me? I could have a husband and my own children by now."

The truth hangs, unspoken. She can see it, shimmering between them. *But nobody will have you.*

"You're frightened, aren't you, that other people will see me like *you* do? As a-a-a" — she can barely say it — "a freak of nature?"

Her own words land like kicks. She wants to tear them away, to pack them back down her throat. She wants him to say, *You're wrong. You're wrong, Nellie.* But she has made these thoughts real, and when he reaches for her arm, she flinches as if he has burned her.

"Nellie," he tries.

She cannot bear it. She wants to scrunch her fists and bawl; she wants to upend the table and hurl the bowls against the wall. But she can't; she never can. Only once has she lost her temper, only once has she given voice to the rage she has seen others express so carelessly. It was a small thing, a girl who stole the smooth stones she had gathered and then claimed they were her own. Nell remembers the minister's cool voice, the way he said so calmly, *And why would she want to take what belongs to you?* The way he lingered on that final word, as if she had nothing worth having. It all boiled over, slights real and imagined, and she picked up the stones and started to throw them into the fields, her back aching, a roar coming from within — but when she turned around, everyone had paused, more horrified than she had ever seen them. A child began to cry. The girl was aghast, the minister, too, as though they did not understand that they had driven her to it. She realized that she had *frightened* them, her

48

monstrous fury matching the person they believed she was. Ever since, she has tried harder to be good, to be liked, always to appease, to defy their expectations of her.

When she stands — as calmly and slowly as she can manage — Charlie does not try to stop her. She opens the door, and he is still sitting there, hands covering his face.

Outside, she is alone. Her feet are quick, hurrying through the main street, down the coastal path, her tears blurring the hedgerows. Buttercups are flowering, and the last dregs of sun light the yellow buds like candles. A deep puddle gleams, the moon's reflection drowning in it. She raises her skirts and kicks the moon and slices it into a thousand shards, water dampening her legs. She stubs her toe and suppresses a small scream of fury.

She presses on to the cliffs, her breath fast and hard. There is a light bobbing on the ocean: a paddle steamer carving west. Hundreds of people will be tucked inside, embarking on new beginnings, fresh lives unfurling. She picks at the cut on her ankle where the rock sliced her, enjoys the sharp pain of it. Words ricochet — *the rest of us, trying to protect you* — and blood runs down her foot.

Footsteps sound behind her; Nell cowers,

makes herself small, but it is only her brother.

"Another steamer," he says. "To Boston? Or New York?"

He looks so sad that her anger dissolves. "New York, I think."

It is their way of making up with each other: this indulgence in a dream Nell pretends to share with him. America. Charlie talks about it constantly. The farmstead they'll own, the fat harvests just waiting for them to pluck down. It is a harmless fantasy because she knows it will never happen, that they will never be able to save enough money for it. She is safe in this village, with people who know her.

He rests his head on her shoulder. "I'm sorry."

"No need," she says, and he pulls her toward him, so suddenly that she almost stumbles. It is as reassuring as when they were children and slept against each other like piled kittens. Now they have their own mattresses, but sometimes she'll wake in the night and she will scarcely be able to resist reaching out and touching his cheek.

"The old swing's still there," he says, pointing at the oak tree that grows a little inland. Even in the dark, she can see the tattered rope hanging from its bough.

"I know."

Charlie runs toward it and grasps the rope. "I'll go first," he says.

It was their favorite game as children, but as they've aged, they've forgotten about it.

"I'm Stella the Songbird!" he shouts, and he looks awkward as he clings on, too big. He yelps as he swings over the dip.

"My turn," she says. She takes the rope from him and flies much farther than he did, back and forth, the air on her cheeks and in her hair. Her heart scuds. She is filled with that familiar feeling, an inchoate longing to be someone else.

"I'm alive!" she cries. "Alive!"

"Don't go so high," he says, but she doesn't care. She lives for that punch of fear, as heady as gin. She imagines Lenny seeing her, marveling at how she swings farther than he would dare.

Nell links her arm through Charlie's when they walk home, and he chatters about America. "If we work every evening, we'll have saved enough in five years, and then — think of it — us leaning off the back of the steamer, the shores of America coming into view —" She wants to bottle this moment, as if it has already passed. Just the two of them, laughing and kicking stones down the lane.

Soon he will have a baby and a wife, she thinks. *Soon everyone in the village will pair up.*

Villagers are spilling out of the inn. Someone is standing on a chair and hurling out a ballad. "Let's join them," Charlie says. "There's Mary."

"Come!" Lenny cries, beckoning them over. "Piggott says we're to have a dance tomorrow."

Nell stops, heart thudding. She touches her arm where Lenny once ran his hand. Then she notices a man, hunched beside the oak tree. She recognizes the rickety turn of his legs.

"What's Pa doing?" she asks.

"Looking at the handbill."

He is tilted forward, stroking the advertisement as if it is a lapdog.

"The circus's over, you dodo," she says, trying to pull him away. He has been drinking, she realizes, and no longer carries his box of trinkets.

"Don't touch me," he growls, wrestling free.

"He doesn't mean it," Charlie says, too fast.

But he does; she knows it.

His eyes do not move from the bright illustrations. The dwarf in her carriage. The crocodile in the jar. Butterfly man and strongman, the identical triplets and Stella the flying songbird.

"I had a lobster," he murmurs.

"Come, Pa," Charlie says, reaching out his hand.

Their father swats at Charlie, then starts to run, staggering toward the circus. Lanterns dangle from trees like dead moles from a fence.

"Let him go," Charlie says. "He's a fool."

"Jasper Jupiter's Circus of Wonders," she reads, and Charlie puts his arm around her shoulder and pulls her away.

JASPER

Jasper is feeding his wolf scraps of red meat through the bars of her cage. She snaps them from his silver tongs, her teeth blunted and yellow. The hare is curled around the wolf's feet, scratching its ear. They are his favorite creatures; occasionally, as he has done now, he will order a laborer to carry their crate from the menagerie into his own wagon.

"There, girl," he says, picking at a paint blister on the "Happy Families" sign.

These animals were his own initiative, a ruse he saw first in a street seller. The best part is there's no trick. He'll take a predator and its prey and thrust them together when they're babies, scarcely weaned. It amazes him that he can suppress nature and instinct in this way. Only occasionally will the owl exercise its power and eat the mice. The wolf and the hare are as close as if they were the same species.

Jasper looks at his brother, hunched over in the velvet chair. They have always been so different, but here they are, nestled together. Inseparable.

"Who's the wolf and who's the hare?" he asks, barking out his laugh.

"Sorry?"

"Me and you."

"You can be the wolf. You're older."

"You would say that." Jasper bares his fingers like claws, then chuckles. "Do you remember when we found a bag of sheep's wool and made ourselves mustaches? I must have been about ten."

And with that, he is away, shuffling through childhood memories. When he was given a microscope and Toby was given a photography machine. The first time they saw a leopard. When their father took them to see Tom Thumb perform in *Hop o' My Thumb* at the Lyceum Theatre.

He still remembers it so vividly: that humid, velvety room. Patrons murmured around them, their father pointing out Charles Dickens, the artist Landseer, the actor Macready, all sitting in the audience. The curtain lifted, the candles were snuffed. Jasper's heart raced. They watched as the eight-year-old dwarf Charles Stratton rode a miniature horse, was baked into a pie, and fought his way through a lid of pastry with a little broadsword. But Jasper's eyes were only partly on the stage. It was the crowd he watched. Rage, delight, fear. The whole room shrieked with laughter when the little boy declared, "Though a mite, I am mighty!" How would it feel, to hold a thousand people in your grip?

Later, in Lambeth, they watched fifty horses charge around the ring of Astley's Amphitheatre, rifles *pop-popping.* When Wombwell's menagerie wintered in Bartholomew Fair, they sauntered between cages of lions, ocelots, rhinoceroses, and kangaroos. Jasper began to seek out handbills for these shows, and Toby tagged along. They stood on the bank of the Thames when Signor Duvalla tiptoed across the river on a rope. Fireworks crackled in Jasper's ears, his brain fizzing with possibilities. At school, he sold trick cards, firecrackers, and magical hats, all of which he constructed himself, and he spent his time sketching machines and elaborate gewgaws. His purse grew fat. The world was an iced bun, his for the taking. One day, he said, he would have his own troupe, and it would be the greatest show in the country. It was Toby who took him seriously, Toby who said he would own it with him. *Toby and Jasper Brown's Great Show,*

Toby suggested, and Jasper pulled a face. *Brown?* They would have a new name: Zeus or Achilles or — he grinned — *Jupiter. The Jupiter Brothers.*

Their father smiled benevolently at this, convinced that the circus was a schoolboy whim Jasper was bound to outgrow. What Jasper needed was sturdiness, boundaries, he said. His own finances as a merchant were precarious, and he did not wish his child to suffer from the same limitations. When several of his ships sank off Siam and they were forced to move to a smaller house in Clapham, he scraped and borrowed to buy Jasper a commission in an unfashionable rural regiment. Jasper was twenty, he said, more than old enough to abandon foolish notions about performing seals and a hundred rampaging horses.

Jasper's disappointment lifted within days. To his surprise, he found that the military was filled with tricks and showmen, even in the wretched plains of the Crimea. He charged down the hillsides in his uniform with its fringed epaulettes and gleaming badges, Dash beside him. The parades, the bugles and brass bands, the shells like fireworks, the sense of *belonging* — it was circus. Circus was life, desire, amplified. When spring bloomed, ladies watched the battles from hills as they might a play, opera glasses pressed to their brows, a trousered Stella at the front of their petticoated pack. One morning, in those uncertain days before they stormed Sevastopol, he heard one woman say, quite coolly, "The way they flew through the sky when the mortars bore down, they might have been dying birds." Tourist steamers cruised the waters to spectate on naval combats, applauded as shells fell into the sea like fountains. It was said that when the attack at Alma closed in, a host of Russian ladies fled their picnic in carriages, leaving lorgnettes, a half-eaten chicken, champagne bottles, and a parasol. Killing was a show, and sometimes as Jasper speared a Cossack with his bayonet, he expected the man to leap up and take a bow, for an audience to applaud.

When Sevastopol fell in September, and Dash was dead, Jasper received news that his father, too, had passed into the next world. He bought up a dozen Russian horses, a few camels, and discharged himself. *Showtime,* he thought.

Toby was dropped from running the show without discussion, their dreams of shared ownership forgotten. Dash's name hung in the air between them like a fetid scent, never acknowledged. Toby hadn't really cared about the circus, Jasper told himself; but it was more than that, and he knew it. His brother had changed. He was ruined by what he had seen and done. They had never exactly been equals, but now the imbalance had shifted forever. This was Jasper's dream, and Jasper's life, and his brother owed him. It was *Jasper Jupiter's Circus of Wonders.*

Jasper is startled, partway through an anecdote about a schoolmaster and a trick frog, by a knock on the door.

"Come in," he shouts.

Jasper can't be certain if he sees or smells the man first. He is as shabby as a stray dog, clothes so torn they look like mange.

"I've no coins for you," Jasper says.

"I'm no beggar," the man says, wringing his cap between his hands. "I had a lobster once — a lobster with three claws."

As drunk as a Turk. Jasper exchanges a look with Toby, leans back, and smiles. He intends to have a little fun with this man. "And do you have this lobster now?"

"I ate it."

"Oh-ho, you ate it. And you want to sell the memory of it to me as a . . . a curiosity, I suppose?"

The man shakes his head furiously. "Not the lobster. My daughter."

"Your daughter?" Jasper laughs. "You want to sell me your daughter. Well, bring her here, and I'll see if she's to my liking."

"Not in that way," the man says, blushing. "She's . . . she's like your wonders."

"I doubt that."

He turns to Toby to check he is laughing, too, but his brother's eyes are wide, panicked. There is something amiss. Something — he cannot put his finger on it. Toby has never been able to swallow his emotions. As a child, Jasper could sense his brother's unhappiness through the wall at night and would pad through to his bedroom to comfort him.

"Come in. Properly," he says.

As the man crosses the threshold, Jasper sees the wagon as the villager must: the bright handbills, the wolf snuggled against the hare, the fine cut-glass decanters that he wraps in paper when they are on the move. The man bows his head.

"And why is she like my performers?"

"She . . . she has marks on her."

"Marks?"

"She was born with them. One over half her face. Others on her legs and arms. Specklings."

"A leopard girl?" Jasper asks, and his chest quickens. "Vitiligo?"

60

"Not that. It's birthmarks."

"Curious," he says. He has never seen a girl like the man describes, and human novelty is the opiate every showman chases. *An age of monsters, Punch* called the current craze for wonders. *Deformitomania.* But where there's mania, there's money to be made. Jasper smiles.

"You'll ask her," Toby says. "You'll ask her first, won't you?"

Jasper picks up a Havana and presses away the mold that blooms on the leaves. "You saw her on that other evening, didn't you, Toby? That's what you wouldn't tell me."

He tries to swallow the anger, brimming like bile. Hasn't he given everything to protect his brother? He smooths a crease in his trousers, takes a breath.

"How old is she?"

"Nineteen."

"Is she married?"

The man laughs. "No."

"Then she belongs to you."

Toby stares at him, and Jasper knows how to flex his power, how to remind his brother of the debts he owes. Usually he would see the girl first, but it is barely about her any longer.

"How much do you want for her?"

Toby pulls the skin from his cuticles, and

61

Jasper barrels on. The hare shrinks in its cage, its ears flattened. Jasper can smell fresh shit; when the man is gone, he'll have the animals sent back to their own wagon.

"Twenty pounds." The villager says it tentatively, perhaps believing it to be an outlandish sum.

"Very well. And when can we claim her?" The man blinks.

"You'll ask her, won't you?" Toby says again.

The girl's father looks at the floor. "She won't come willingly," he says.

Toby shakes his head. "You wouldn't." Jasper waves his hand to dismiss the old drunk's concerns, his heart pounding. "Won't come willingly? No matter, no matter," he says. "The Carolina Twins have been" — he clears his throat — "*taken* several times. One showman even shipped them from America to England." He adds, "The Two-Headed Nightingale, you know."

"You're a better man than this," Toby says, picking up his hat, and Jasper pretends he has not heard him. The door slams behind him. Who is Toby to preach to him about virtue? He watches the lemon slice bob in his gin toddy, and he reaches for it, downs it in one gulp. He wipes his lips.

"You'll be good to her? She'll be happy.

She'll belong with you," the old drunk says, as if he is trying to convince himself.

"Didn't Tom Thumb's parents sell him to Phineas Barnum at the age of four? And now look at him — his own yacht and a stable of pedigree horses."

Jasper thinks, too, of the Sicilian dwarf Caroline Crachami. Sold at three, dead at nine from exhaustion and consumption. Her skeleton sits in John Hunter's collection. But there are always tales of heartbreak, wherever you turn. He clips the end off his cigar.

"There's never been love between us. Never been affection. She's" — the man pulls a face — "she's got no place here. My wife died because of her. Breathed her last when ushering her into the world." He looks at the wolf, then at the floor. "There were some who said she's a changeling. That I should have left her in the cold when she was born, and the real child would be delivered back to us. They say that, don't they?"

"Folks have all sorts —"

"I never did that," the father insists. "I never believed in that. I never wanted her hurt. Just tell me she'll be happy."

"She'll find her place with us. We'll look after her. You say she won't come easily, but perhaps I could speak to her, try to persuade her?"

The man chews his lip. "She'd never leave her brother."

"Her brother," Jasper echoes. He thinks of Toby, how he kept this girl a secret. And why? Doesn't he trust him?

"I want the money now."

"Not until I've seen her."

Jasper falls into the reassuring language of commerce. They will *complete the transaction* tomorrow evening, when there is a dance in the village. He ushers the man from his wagon, keen to be rid of him. He doesn't like doing business with wretches. If you lie down with dogs, you rise with fleas.

He sits back in his chair and looks out the window. Children laugh as Punch strangles Judy with a string of sausages, as he beats her head against the table. Stella is standing beside a small fire, shrugging off her doublet as villagers watch. He catches a flash of her pubic hair, darker than her beard, her breasts rolling in her hands. One of the triplets is riding a camel in circles. The moon glints like a guinea. Gulls call like hawkers. *Yes,* Jasper thinks, *it is the right decision.* Anything can be bought or sold in this new commercial world. He must grow his troupe; he must be constantly novel. If

64

he scrapes his way through enough rural villages and towns, in a year's time he will have saved enough to afford a pitch in London. And then, perhaps the Queen might even hear about him and request his company. After all, she is known as the *freak fancier par excellence,* who has summoned Aztecs, pinheaded people, and dwarfs to her palace. He imagines himself, arms spread wide, entertaining her in the Picture Gallery as so many performers have done before him, as Barnum has done several times over. Jasper Jupiter's Circus of Wonders. The biggest, the best troupe in the country!

He breathes out, but something snags.

You're a better man than this.

The wolf nuzzles the hare's skull and begins to lick clean its fur.

NELL

The next afternoon, they all pause in the fields as the carriages process down the lane. Camels lumber along, their legs as thin as sticks. A lioness moans. Nell sees Stella the Songbird dressed in trousers, sitting astride a horse like a man. A pipe hangs from her lips.

"Good riddance," Piggott says. "Bunch of thieves."

Soon, the villagers turn back to the field, an army of raised backsides and bent necks. Nell puts a hand to her chest. The relief of it. There will be no more glitter and color. Instead, the only sounds will be metal tools striking gray earth, the crick as flowers are cut from their stems. Her fingernails are clagged with dirt and her shoulders ache. Other girls wear loose cotton gowns, but hers has long sleeves, a high neck. Sweat trickles down her spine, along her thighs. Dust sticks to her, makes her birthmarks itch. The sun is as sharp as a lance.

"Water?" Lenny asks, offering her a flask, but she shakes her head. He stands there as if he is toying with saying something more, but then he returns to laying runners.

Mary begins to sing, and soon the whole field joins in for the chorus. Nell murmurs the words under her breath.

So keep up heart and courage, friends!
For home is just in sight.
And who will heed, when safely there,
The perils of the night?

The day turns and Nell finds comfort in monotony. Her arms work as fast as pistons. Pluck the flower, gather it. Pluck the flower, gather it. Once she is clutching fifty flowers, she ties them with twine and places them in a crate. Sweat drips off her nose.

When Piggott blows the whistle to end the day, Nell can scarcely stand upright. It is earlier than normal, to give them time to prepare for the dance. The men will build a bonfire and the women will make a stew, and they will all dress in their Sunday finest.

On their way home, Nell follows Charlie to where the circus tent was pitched. The grass is trampled flat. It is littered with waste, and she picks up a heel of stale bread. "It would taste fine soaked in broth," she says. Next to it is a scrap of velvet, a long yellow bone that might be a beef shin. The embers are still warm when she scuffs them with her shoe. When she turns to leave, she sees that there is one wagon left, sitting under the shade of the oak tree.

There is no reason for it, but she drops the bread quickly and runs.

The dancers stomp and whoop and clap. The moon is rising, and there is a fire, and dogs lolling in front of it, and old James is sawing at the fiddle. A few people have tambourines, and they rattle them in time to the thrust of their hips. The girls dance, the ribbons in their hair fluttering.

Nell sits on a hay bale at the edge of the dance. Her brother is spinning Mary. She is a whirl of white, her chin thrown so far back that Nell can see the ribbed outline of her gullet. The swell of her bump is already showing, and she pats it every so often, just a small rest of her hand. Lucy, a girl Nell's own age, nurses a newborn, the baby's mouth pursed like a tiny rosebud.

Nell touches her own empty belly. They say she will be a good aunt, a kind aunt, and that should be enough. Already, other girls and boys are beginning to pair off. They groom each other's hair, speak in loud whispers, titter at shared jokes. Nell pulls up her legs and rests her forehead on her knees. She wonders what it must feel like to be on the brink of a life changing, to move from childhood to motherhood, to have her own small room with a stove and pots and a bed. Hers, to clean and tidy and live in. Instead, Charlie and Mary will step over her mattress each morning, and she will scrub the pans that they own, fuss over the children they have created.

Charlie stops dancing and trips over to her, giddy with spinning. "Dance with me," he says, pulling her by the hand. His eyes flash in the firelight. Nell shakes her head; already she thinks everyone is looking at her. She catches Lenny watching her, little glances that can only be disdain.

"Come," Mary coaxes. "Drink this."

Mary holds out a jar of gin, and Nell grasps it and takes a sip, and then another. She drinks until the glass is half empty. She feels the kick of it, as sharp as a slap. The trees fuzz at their edges, but she likes the courage that grips her, as if she might be another girl entirely.

"Easy," Charlie says, squeezing her shoulder.

"Come and dance," Mary says. "What are you afraid of?"

"Go on," Lucy coaxes, stroking her baby's head. Someone else nudges her forward.

Nell touches the ribbons in her hair. The warmth of the drink has started to radiate outward from her belly. She allows her brother to lead her toward the circle.

Charlie takes her arm in his, spins her, and she starts to smile. At first, she is stiff, her feet half-heartedly tapping the ground. She is sure people must be laughing at her, that she is as awkward as a fledgling. Someone passes her another cup, and she drains it in a single gasp, pulls a face, and wipes her hand across her mouth.

"Faster!" Charlie says. They lean back, the world whisking past her. Her joints loosen, and when he lets her go, she twists her arms in time to the drum.

"Yes!" Mary shouts, standing to one side.

Charlie catches her eye, and he begins to dance as wildly as they do when it is just them, alone in the cottage. She joins in, head flung back, hands raised, feet stamping. Her fears are whipped away. Why hasn't she danced properly before, she wonders, to the fiddle and the drum? Why has she always sat at the fringes, hidden herself away? The music thrums inside her, pounding like a second heart.

Nell breaks away from the others, sways her hips, whoops. She casts out her arms and begins to spin once more, leaping from toe to toe. The ache in her shoulders is gone. Villagers are watching her, she knows, but it does not matter. As her plaits flick her neck, she is just like the other dancing, bobbing girls, their foreheads dappled with the thrill of being spun until they stumble. A laugh breaks from her throat. *Free,* she thinks — she is *free.* Her hand is in her brother's again, and he leads her into the middle of the group. Someone says, "Nell!" as if in surprise, or delight. Her palms are sweating, hair stuck to her face. She has lost a ribbon, but she does not care; she does not care at all. As Nell is hurled from Charlie's arms to Mary's, she is one of them.

JASPER

One Christmas, when Jasper and Toby were fourteen and twelve, their father gave each of them a gift. He led them into the drawing room and explained, "A microscope and a photography machine. Each is a different way of surveying the world." Jasper put his eye to the cold cylinder and saw only gray. His father laid down the epidermis of an onion, fiddled with the dials and said, "There, look now."

A universe bloomed before him. There, magnified, Jasper saw a perfectly formed brick wall, invisible to the naked eye.

"How does mine work?" Toby asked, but his voice was muted. Jasper noted the jealous slide of his gaze, how he could look only at the microscope.

It seemed to Jasper, as he squished a small beetle and placed it on the glass, that his father had understood the difference between his sons. Toby was a spectator who was content to observe life from the fringes, rarely to involve himself. Jasper was curious, preoccupied with finding the trick behind every object, dismantling illusion to see the real bones of the world.

To Jasper, the microscope was a portal, a means of beholding the secrets of nature and the way that everything slotted together so neatly, so precisely. He understood the careful design of every creature. He laid out dead ants (monstrous dragonlike creatures with ferocious lacquered pincers), fleas, a fly, a spider. Sometimes he let Toby look through that cold eyepiece, too, and thrilled to share his amazement, to be the orchestrator of it all. They pretended Jasper was an important scientist, Toby his photography assistant, fresh from the jungles of Borneo, where they'd tracked orangutans and rare moths. "You photograph it, and I puzzle it out," Jasper explained. It gave him pleasure to think of his mastery over these kingdoms, that he was the person to make sense of it all. The world could be placed on a small glass pane and made his own.

And Jasper has this same feeling when he watches Nell. When he sees her on the hay bale, he is choked with disappointment. She is so *ordinary,* so plain, just a girl speckled with a few birthmarks, as shy as a cat. He has made his name because his wonders are performers, too, a combination that elevates his show beyond the thousands of human curiosities displayed in back-street shops and at the Egyptian Hall, where freaks stand rigid on podiums. He taught his giantess to juggle, his walking skeleton to jump through hoops. Stella trills melodies and swings on a trapeze. But this girl — she seems to have nothing to her at all.

Jasper knows, at the back of his mind, that it isn't the show that counts but the tale you spin. He's watched showmen pump thousands of pounds into mediocre acts. Jenny Lind, the Swedish Nightingale, could croak an aria no better than a Drury Lane doxy, but Barnum puffed her up so much that she was escorted through the streets of New York by three hundred firemen bearing torches. Still, it helps if the act has *something* you can work with, some nose for performance. Charles Stratton's fame grew partly because he could put on a good show, even if his quips were rehearsed.

And then, the girl begins to dance.

She is ungainly at first, self-conscious, and Jasper lights a cigar. The women around her are dressed in darned frocks, most of them thirty or forty years behind the fashions in the capital. Girls who look as young as fifteen nurse infants. He yawns and doesn't bother to cover his mouth.

But when he looks at her again, he rests his hand on his cane to steady himself. Her hair pounds her back. She is wild yet poised, her arms as agile as an acrobat's. She is magnetic, *alive,* a moth at a flame, joy radiating from her. He sees the other villagers murmuring, eyes on her. If he squints, he can imagine that the fire is a row of gas lamps lining the ring, the fiddle and drum his own band. Beneath his feet, the dirt turns to sawdust.

I present, London, a wondrous sight —

Yes, Jasper thinks. Here is his ticket to the bigger game. She will be brilliant, novel, electric. He has planned his assault on London carefully — it will take a year if he can secure pitches in some of the larger towns like Brighton and Hastings — but with her in his troupe, he might save enough capital within nine months.

"You'll be good to her?" her father asks. "You promise she'll be happier?"

"Of course," he says.

You're a better man than this.

Rot, Jasper thinks. This is show business. This is how fortunes are made, audiences won. He is *elevating* her.

He spent the day furnishing her caravan

to an absurd degree, just to prove to Toby he isn't the monster he made him out to be. He had a zebra wagon cleaned out, sluiced down and painted, and even instructed his butterfly man to take the Turkish coverlets from his own bed. With a pastepot, he glued peacock feathers to the wall. "Even thirty-thousand-dollar Commodore Nutt would be delighted with this," Jasper said, loudly in the hope that Toby would hear.

He chose three books for the girl carefully, remembering how Toby used to treasure their gilt editions, scarcely daring to cut the pages. Even if she couldn't read, she might enjoy the woodcuts and ink sketches. Ovid's translated *Metamorphoses*. Mary Shelley's *Frankenstein*. Charlotte Brontë's *Jane Eyre*. He placed them in the top drawer of her dresser.

When his brother rode off to put up handbills in the next town, Jasper tested the metal bolts of her caravan, rattled them until he was sure they held tight. He knew, as he stood in the wagon and pressed its four walls, that she would be frightened at first. His mouth tasted soaped, a tremor in his wrists. But other showmen would have bought her and treated her like a dog. It was fortunate that he was the one to discover her.

And now, that same wagon is ready and waiting behind him. The horses tussle and clink their reins. One of his grooms is sitting on the box seat and smoking the Indian herb. Jasper will ride on top with him.

"She's never danced before," her father says, and he leans forward, chin resting on his crook. "She's usually the first to leave. Perhaps — I don't know — if she waits for her brother, then . . ." He bows his head, coughs. "She'll come soon, I'm sure of it."

On she dances, faster and faster, a whirl of pale lashing hair, arms thrown out, feet kicked. Jasper cannot stop looking at her. She just *knows* how to move. He wonders if she realizes that everyone is watching her in admiration, that she is captivating, beautiful. It is little wonder that Toby guarded her so carefully.

I present, a leopard girl, a wonder, a marvel —

He would have paid her father twenty times what he asked.

Her face glows with the heat of it. And then, with a final flounce, the girl pulls away from the other dancers.

Jasper's pulse jumps in his throat. Soon,

she will be his. Soon, he will change her life, and she will become extraordinary.

NELL

Lenny tugs her toward him. His hands grip her waist. Nell pulls back, too fast, her elbow clicking. She will not be a joke, will not have his arm around her because others have put him up to it. "What's wrong?" he asks, and she notices other villagers staring, conversations paused, drinks caught halfway to mouths.

"Leave me alone," she says. She stumbles back, slumps on a bale, and Lenny doesn't follow her. The hay pricks her legs. Her limbs feel as if they do not belong to her. Drink: too much of it. She ought to have stopped.

She is sure she catches a small laugh, a smile quickly swallowed. Lucy, the girl with the baby, falls silent, watching her from the corner of her eye.

"What's the matter?" Lucy asks, but her tone seems loaded with mockery.

"Nothing," she says, sullen.

"Fine," the girl says, pulling her child closer.

A wind is rising, racketing the trees around her. The drum thumps, faster and faster.

The music seems to change, to shift to a sharper tenor. The violin shrieks. The straw itches.

The villagers wheel and spin, hard thuds as their feet hit the ground, forearms like fat cuts of beef. Gone are the girls who dance like moths. Nell coughs, leans closer to the blaze. Even the fire seems to rise too high, the flames filled with leering faces.

"Who shall we sacrifice to the angry gods?" one of the fishermen shouts, and then he pretends to wrestle his sweetheart into the bonfire. "Our sacrifice! Our sacrifice!"

She catches a conversation between Mrs. Pawley's daughters.

"They begin with a chain when it's just a calf, just a babe, he told me."

"And then what?"

"It stops fighting, and they replace the chain with string. But the elephant doesn't know how easily it could break free."

"Like breaking horses?"

Nell sees Charlie is in the corner with Mary, his hand twisting the cloth at her waist. Soon, they will sneak away to tup in

80

the long grass. Other girls are being led from the fire, boys promising tenderness in the way they span their waists, press kisses to their cheeks. She brushes her lips, and they are as cold as the earth.

Lenny nods at her, his drink raised halfway to his mouth. She tries to shake her head, to communicate that she doesn't want his company, but he hurries toward her, tripping over a dog basking in the fire's heat.

He laughs out his embarrassment, then sits too close to her. "I brought you something," he says.

She would like to move away, but she is already on the edge of the bale. She feels the helplessness of it, her own limbs tucked tight, his sprawling and spreading like the tentacles of a squid. He reaches into his pocket and takes out a piece of paper. He unfolds it. It is the handbill, its corners torn where the nails pierced it.

"I took it for you," he says. "I thought you'd like it."

Show us a handstand! Before the other wonders arrive.

He grins. The advertisement is a taunt, a reminder that she is different.

"Leave me alone, Lenny," she says. She would like to find words with bite and snarl, words with the power to wound, but she does not dare. The drink has clouded her head. She must leave; she must be at home under her blanket, safe and warm.

"What is it?" he asks, reaching for her arm, but she snaps her hand free with a violence that surprises her and stands. "I just wanted to sit with you —"

She does not look back at him. Out, away from the music, her eyes begin to adjust to the gloom. She stumbles. She can see her cottage at the end of the street. It looks squatter than before, bowed in the middle where the roof is half down.

The trees rustle like skirts. The fiddle ratchets up.

One last dance!

Nell changes her mind. She cannot bear to be alone. She will interrupt Charlie, ask him to return home with her, or she will sit with Lucy for a while.

She is about to turn back to the circle of the villagers when she feels a hand on her wrist.

"I said, leave me —"

Her words die on her tongue. It is not Lenny, but her father, and he is smiling, his lips pulled tight across black gums.

"We don't mean you any harm," someone says — another man, whom she does not know. "We've the most wonderful chance for you."

Nothing makes sense — why her father would grab her like this, who this man might be. Fear grips Nell, and she tries to run, but her feet have scarcely moved before she is pulled backward, a hand across her mouth. A stench of woodsmoke, of oranges.

"Let me go," she tries to say, but her voice is muffled. She struggles, kicks. There is her brother — she can see him, barely twenty feet away. His head bowed, kissing Mary's neck. All he needs to do is look toward her, to understand her fear, even for a second.

"I don't want her frightened. Don't hurt her," the man says, and she notices his upturned mustache, and she knows — she knows what is happening, what they are planning to do. It is Jasper Jupiter — she feels as if a poison is spreading up her arm, across her body.

"I'm sorry, Nellie," her father says, and he starts to sob, and she doesn't care. She would shatter him if she could, split each bone in his body. She would kill him as easily as a pig. She stamps on his foot, tries to claw him. *Her father.* Her skull thunders with the force of a punch. She cowers. The world tips, rings.

She will not give up. With a quick dart, Nell pulls her head free, screams. It comes out choked, but it might be enough. It might be enough for her brother to look up, just for a moment.

And he does; she sees it.

He stares at where the noise has come from, but he is in the light and she is in the dark. Her heart scurries, faster than the fiddle.

Notice me, she begs him.

For the first time in her life she wants to stand out, she wants a dozen eyes on her. But Mary taps his leg, and Charlie looks away.

"I'm sorry," her father says, again and again, as they pull her down the street and her feet scrape the ground. "You'll be happier there, Nellie. There's nothing for you here."

The threshing machine, she thinks, as she's lifted higher, as hands grip her waist, her legs, her hips, as she writhes and kicks and scratches. Her fury is a relief, that she can give into it at last and become exactly what they expect of her. She thinks of pounding metal anvils, blasts of burning steam. She bites her tongue so hard she tastes blood.

"We don't mean you any harm," the man says again, and she roars at him.

"You'll give me the twenty pounds, won't you?" her father whispers, and perhaps he thinks she can't hear him. "Seeing as she's genuine?"

Twenty pounds?

She looks back only once, just before she is pushed into the wagon and the door is slammed behind her. She rakes her fingers against wood, feels the sting of splinters. There was her brother, yellow in the fire-light. He was resting his head on Mary's shoulder in the same way he once did with her, and their faces glowed as unreal as a pair of fairies.

■ ■ ■ ■

PART TWO

■ ■ ■ ■

It is no accident that the photographer becomes a photographer any more than the lion tamer becomes a lion tamer.
— DOROTHEA LANGE,
quoted in SUSAN SONTAG,
On Photography, 1971

TOBY

The last candles are snuffed out in the wagons, and still Toby feeds the fire. Damp wood smokes and pops. As one stick grays, another flares. The animals shift in their cages. The lioness paces.

Nellie, he thinks, and he tries to blink away the thought.

He adjusts the corpse of the zebra. It is an old buck that died on the road. Their menagerie is often thinned by disease or because creatures cannot adapt to the climate. In the morning, the triplets will skin it, and scrape and dry the hide so that Jasper can sell it to a grand London shop. They will roast the good cuts over the fire, stew the rest. Toby wipes the glass plate with egg white and slides it into the photography machine. The light is probably too dim, but it feels important to mark this, to bear witness to the truth of life and its ending, its ugliness and trauma. He ducks behind the

89

cape and counts out a minute. The zebra's mane is cast to one side, its lips black and split. Flies crawl over the creature's eye.

A few miles from here, his brother will be riding over a potholed lane toward them, his cargo a frightened girl. He knows that Jasper will have succeeded, simply because he always does.

Toby stares at his brother's caravan, and he is seized by a sudden impulse to punish him. He wants to tear down his handbills. He wants to set loose the animals. He wants to hurt him as he has hurt this girl. He thinks of the night he smashed his brother's microscope, the dials buckling, glass shattering as easily as ice, the shameful pleasure he derived from knowing his brother would be distraught.

For weeks, they had hunched over that machine, and Toby felt gilded by his brother's attention, as if a very special light were falling on him alone. It had always been the way with them; for as long as he could remember, Jasper's character had been a shelter, a shade. When their mother died of scarlet fever when they were small boys, Toby turned inward, and Jasper turned outward. If Jasper could answer every question for him, and order the servants to prepare the right cakes and dainties, and entertain every guest and busybody, why would Toby do anything but sit back and let him? Soon, he almost stopped talking altogether. When it came to making friends, his voice felt creaky and unfamiliar, his gestures a poor imitation of his brother's. Jasper did so much for him that soon Toby believed he could do nothing for himself: there was an art in knowing the right food to request, the correct thing to say, and it was one he could never master. Sometimes, it felt as if there were air in the room for only one brother, but he did not begrudge it — how could he, when he loved Jasper so absolutely?

At school, he watched Jasper stride through the grounds, making the masters laugh, while Toby scurried with his head down. "Jasper Brown is my brother. My brother, you know," he liked to say, "and we're going to own a show, one day. A magnificent show!" When he sat alone at his desk and walked alone to class and ate alone in the refectory, he thought of the circus they had planned — their matching red capes and silver toppers, how they'd ride into the ring with a blaring of trumpets. It was enough to pull him through the ache of solitude, enough for him to think the future might promise more than his own small present.

One afternoon, when Jasper was out riding with a friend, Toby sneaked into his room and lifted the microscope cover. The metal was so cold, like the pipes of a miniature organ. He polished its brass dials, buffed the tiny slides of glass that Jasper left gummed with squashed insects. He imagined that it was his own, that his brother's whole life was his own; that he was quick-witted and instantly likable; that his father thought he might deserve a microscope as a gift, not a photography machine that made him a mere bystander.

Downstairs, he heard his brother and his friend returning, and Toby ambled into the drawing room to join them. The boys were shelling walnuts, cracking them with a brass hammer.

"Pick that up," the friend said, pointing to a fragment of walnut shell.

At first, Toby thought he must have been addressing their butler, but Jenkins was in the hall.

"Pick that up," he repeated.

Toby jumped. "Me?" he asked.

The boy began to laugh, a harsh *ack ack ack.*

Toby looked at Jasper, but his brother was staring intently at the mantelpiece.

A walnut shell bounced off Toby's shoulder. The second hit him between the eyes. Sugared almonds were next, like tiny silver pebbles.

Toby watched Jasper. He opened and closed his mouth, said nothing.

"He's as fat as a London alderman," the boy said, howling with laughter. "What a fool! A prize fool!"

Toby saw how his brother shifted his gaze to the rug, how he fiddled with the tassels on his red velvet frock coat. Toby thought of how proudly he used to say, *Jasper, he's my brother, you know,* but Jasper's cheeks were pink with shame.

Twenty minutes later, Toby was standing in his brother's room and the microscope was in pieces on the floor. The long brass funnel was bent from where he'd smashed it against the desk, the lens splintered. He could hear the boys laughing in the drawing room downstairs. At him, he was sure. When it was dark, he took the broken machine and abandoned it in a nearby alley.

He did not sleep that night. He was haunted not by fears of punishment, but by the discovery of the violence of which he was capable. In the morning, he waited for his brother to find the microscope missing, for a scolding to follow. Nothing was said for a week, a restless time of long nights, his remorse a weighty thing. At last, their father asked Jasper where his microscope was, and Toby sat at the breakfast table and bit his cheek.

"I lent it to Howlett," Jasper said. "He wanted to examine a particular leaf from his garden."

Toby flinched. Jasper had covered for him so casually, so easily, that it might have been true, that it *became* true. Perhaps Jasper understood that one betrayal had been exchanged for another, and this was his way of making amends. But somehow, as Toby cleared the table and his father lit his pipe, this felt worse than a beating. The truth of his story had been snipped about, suppressed, until he began to wonder if he had imagined the entire incident, and his whole life might never cast a single ripple.

It is hours later when Toby hears the rattle of horses. The sound sets a baby cawing. Toby does not look up. He catches the soft crump of boots on wet grass, the clink as the mares are unyoked and led away.

"Toby," his brother calls. "Drink with me?"

Toby pretends he hasn't heard him. He thinks Jasper will ask again, but the door of his caravan slams.

Soon, even the sounds of the animals fall away. Nothing moves except a barn owl, floating low over the fields. Her wagon is still, a black hulk in the darkness. Faintly, he hears crying.

The sound winds him. He sneaks closer. The crying intensifies, becomes guttural and throaty.

He fingers the long bolt of the lock.

He could lift it from its catch and release her. There are so many things he could do, so many different forks her life could take, if he helped her. They could escape together. He could saddle up Grimaldi and take her home. The horizons about her would contract until nothing stood but a careworn cottage, a tumbled-down wall. Her life shrunk to pin size.

He remembers the yearning in her gaze, that hunger. The scent of the match, as if she herself were that fire.

"Nellie," he whispers, pressing his forehead to the wood.

"Who's that? Who's there?"

Toby touches the bolt, waits. If he lets her go, Jasper will be furious. His brother has protected him when another man would have thrown him to the dogs for what he did. And he scarcely knows this girl; perhaps she does not even remember him.

"Who's there?"

He clears his throat.

"Who's there?" A pause, a thump against the door that makes him jump back. "Let me go."

He cannot do it; he *can't*. He thinks of a hot day in Sevastopol, a city in ruins, a man falling from the battlements, horror written on his brother's face. Toby runs, hands clasped to his ears as her cries grow more desperate. He falls beside the fire, throws on pine needles that crack and pop like gunfire.

The flames form shapes.

Coward.

Coward.

Hundreds, thousands of men might have died because of his deceitful photographs. He was a professional trickster, a liar, creating images that did not tell the truth. Jasper told him to forget it ever happened. Killing was their business out there, the whole damned point of it. "You just took some photographs and made the war look merry," his brother said, "as you were briefed to do. You were instructed by the government. And as for Dash —" He broke off. "What's done is done. You can't bring a man back to life."

Toby rubs hard at his eyes. Tonight will pass. Perhaps sleep will come soon. He is so tired, has slept for no more than five hours every night of the season. In the morning, there will be work to be done — a whole day of raising the tent and setting out the benches and mucking out the animals. He will crack eggs and split out the whites to use in his photography, and villagers will pay a shilling for their likenesses.

Nell is here, in their troupe.

Dawn lifts in a thin red streak. As the circus's morning symphony swells and the lioness growls, he can still hear the echo of her sobbing.

NELL

Nell wakes suddenly, her mouth dry. Her brother is singing in the yard outside.

This is the thief-taker,
Shaven and shorn,
That took up John Bull
With his bugle horn.

The words make no sense. Nothing makes any sense. She blinks. Feathers overhead. No window. Strips of light. The scent of hot fat, of manure and horse sweat.

She remembers it now — the dance and the men and the wagon — and in an instant, she is up and shouldering the door. The wood groans but will not yield. She is alone, torn from her brother. She paces, grips her arms, imagines being paraded through a village. She has no skill except in the picking of flowers, and even then she is nothing but a cog. She cannot possibly perform. And if

98

she cannot perform — she pictures a podium on wheels, dragged by horses. Hands jostling her, prodding her. Stumbling, dust on her knees. Jeers, browned apples breaking against her, the off-key lilt of the organ-grinder. Acrobats turning giddying circles, monkeys heckling, and the meat on its greased pole, fetid and rotten.

Her father sold her.

She has been bought like a cut violet.

Rage boils in her chest, and she claws at the door. Everything is fodder for her fingers, ripping, tearing, smashing. She splits cushions, and feathers explode like a pounced goose. She screams until her throat bruises. She rakes the birthmarks on her arms, itches them until her skin bleeds. Her hands wrench open drawers and three books fall out.

Books.

She has never owned one before. She has held only two books. *Fairy Tales and Other Stories,* its binding scarred and soft. And the Bible, the single volume in their church, as heavy as a stone slab. She learned to read from its tissue-thin paper. Stories of transformation, of genesis, of miracles. Green-stained leather, seams of gold, as precious as breath.

And then her hands remember, and the

books are mere grist for the machine of her rage, and she twists the spines, rips and crumples them in her fists until she is surrounded by little cannonballs of paper.

I am here, she tells herself, her palms cut. *I am real.*

Women's voices, drawing closer.

"Who's in there?"

"A small herd of elephants by the sound of it."

"A new wonder?"

Nell pauses in her rampage, hair slicked to her face, arms scratched from the splintered dresser. A laugh. They move away, and she is alone once more.

She presses her eye to a gap between the slats. The mist and woodsmoke sit low on the fields. The group of women have settled in a quiet circle, as if closing themselves off from the men who scuffle and shout and heave on ropes to lift the tent. The giantess who dived through the knives is cutting red silk and threading a needle. The little woman who rode in the coach is cleaning out a trumpet. The triplets chase one another, weave between the wagons, hands out. *Caught you!*

There is no rustle of drums, no showman telling her how strange and novel these women are. No crowds cheering. Here, they are ordinary, just like the women from her village who sat around the cooking pot or folded narcissi into boxes. Nell presses the bruise on her cheek, pulls her knees under her chin.

Her father sold her.

She thinks of the sea and longs to swim in it, to feel its overbearing power. She remembers the man who watched her swimming and wonders where he might be and if he could help her. There was a gentleness to him, she recalls, a nervousness.

But, she is sure, she will have no need for him; soon Charlie will come. He will have shaken the truth from their father, will have borrowed a horse from Piggott. He will be following the trail they left — spangles falling like breadcrumbs, dried mounds of elephant dung lighting the lanes they took. He will fight them if he needs to, wrestle to free her. A maiden trapped in a tower. A man's quest to bring her home.

On the floor next to her, she sees a drawing on one of the ripped-out pages. She picks it up. A stooped creature made of stitched body parts. She squints to read the text beneath it.

"I was benevolent and good; misery made me a fiend."

Her father —

He sold her.

She will not think of him.

She will *not* think of him.

She balls her fists. She will run, and soon.

The morning passes loudly. Fired commands, a clanging of hammered stakes, the great tent mushrooming into the sky. Through the gap between the wagon's slats, Nell watches the little woman, how she carries a crook that she uses to open wagon doors, to bring bridles to her own height, snapping at anyone who tries to help her. *You'll be hankering to wipe my arse, too, will you?* It kindles something familiar in Nell: a refusal to be pitied, a defiance, and she sets her mouth, almost smiles.

When the tent is up, she smells cooked meat, the smoke thick and greasy. Her stomach growls, and she touches it with her hand as if to silence it. If they bring her food, she will not eat it. She will take nothing from them.

She jumps at the rattle of the door. It is the showman, shouldering his way inside, bearing a plate with two shivering yolks and steak cut into pieces as small as chicken hearts. *Steak.* She can see the fat is crisp and blackened, the meat pink.

He is a tall man, his chin clean-shaven,

102

with a face some might call handsome. His tailcoat is stitched with red sequins, his velvet britches the same pale blue as his irises. His boots gleam like wet stones. He stands in the solid pose of a statue, feet placed widely apart.

"Food," he says.

"I'm not hungry," she replies, though her belly cramps with it. She turns away from him so he can't see the mark on her cheek. She doesn't want his eyes on her, assessing her worth, like a farmer sizing up a prize heifer. She can feel the breeze of the open door, and she calculates, *Could I run, how fast?*

"You can be a success here," he says. "If you allow yourself to be."

She makes a noise in her throat, but he ignores her.

"I'll pay you ten pounds a week, when you're ready to perform. I treat my troupe fairly." He leans casually against the wall, as though these sums mean nothing to him.

Ten pounds. Nell wraps a noose of hair around her finger and pulls it. *Perform?*

"I don't want your money."

He laughs, the tips of his mustache rising. "I'll wager you barely made that in a year. And here, you'll have food, board, friends, and, I expect, fame. Success. Perhaps soon."

He speaks as if this is a speech he knows by heart, as if he assumes fame is something she has dreamed of. He does not understand how hard she has worked to stay hidden.

"My dwarf couldn't even reach the bobbins at the factories where her brothers worked. She was discarded, thrown to one side. Here, I've transformed her into somebody important." He puts the food on the floor. "I can make you brilliant. We can be the making of each other."

His look is distant, as if he is looking past her and at someone else altogether. He speaks with such conviction, the sharp intonation of a man who knows what he is about, his surety almost comforting. Every movement is deliberate.

I'm just a girl, she wants to tell him, *just Nell. You're wrong about me. Put me back where I belong.*

"My brother will come," she says. "He'll take me home."

He laughs, his epaulettes winking. "I'll be sure to expect him. Unless, that is, he wanted a share of the money."

"No," she says, standing. "He'll come. You'll see."

But her words sound like the objections of a child, and he merely shrugs as if he knows something she doesn't.

America. Perhaps Charlie could afford tickets for the steamer now. The farmstead he dreamed of, the house with pillars. Mary with her rising belly, pushing out the space Nell once occupied.

No, she tells herself, *it is impossible;* but the poison of this thought begins to spread, to infect all of her memories of him.

"I saw you dancing," Jasper says, "and I knew. I knew, then, how dazzling you could be."

He takes a step toward her, and she moves back. Another step. She has nowhere to go. The walls shrink. The dresser presses into herback. The wagon is so small, so dark and hot, littered with crumpled books and feathers whose shafts she cracked. He licks his lips, as if readying himself to kiss her. A kicking in her belly, a queasiness. He could overpower her, and easily. All her life, she has grown attuned to the scent of male violence, how to diffuse it, how to make herself small. A look from Piggott that could turn into a beating. A smile from a traveler that could turn into a forcing. Reckonings have shaped her life in subtle ways. Where not to go, the busier paths to take, always home by nightfall. Her brother at her side.

He couldn't want me, she tells herself, but fear cloys her mouth.

Run, she thinks. *Now.*

Nell lunges for the door. He doesn't even have a chance to grab her. She is across the threshold, flinging herself down the wagon steps, past the group of women, Stella the Songbird and the little woman with her crook. Shouts, whistling. The elephant pauses, trunk halfway to its mouth. Out, toward the woodlands. Hot breath, her lungs on fire, propelled by her own daring. She is flying, her footfalls sure. Starlings alight from the branches.

A crack behind her, a shout, the fast pummeling of feet.

"Stop her!"

She swerves to the left, to the right. She is in the woods now, vaulting over fallen logs. To hide in a bush or keep running? They have horses, dozens of them — she dashes on — he is too close. Throat burning, a blazing in her legs. Free. *Free!*

The branches have cut the sky into a thousand shards, and her arm bleeds when she scores it on a bramble. On she races, faster and faster. The gap is widening, his footsteps quietening. She is outstripping him easily. Nell starts to smile. The bloom of heat. The spray from the ocean. Down a narrow path by the shore, flatter here, no cliffs. The sea is brown and glittering. She will be back in her cottage soon, with the crates marked *"London Paddington,"* a place so distant it might as well be the moon. Back with Charlie —

— Her father —

No, she thinks. *No.*

Does she trip on purpose? She saw the tree stump and yet she did not jump or swerve. The pain is quick, grass rising to meet her. As she topples, she recalls his words. *I can make you brilliant.* A sharpness, a twisting in her leg, shoulder jarred by packed earth. He is there, above her. She pulls up runners of ragwort and wild garlic and flings them at the sky.

"Get up," he says, and he seizes her by the arm.

The whip is in his hands. She flinches, readying herself for its quick crack. She can feel the heat of his breath on her cheek.

"Only a fool would prefer that village. Only a fool would throw away what you have."

On and on, the sea pounds the beach.

"I said, get up," he says.

Nell raises her head. He isn't going to hurt her.

She tripped by mistake, she tells herself. But when she sees the first splash of color in the field and it widens — painted wooden caravans, the children stretching their legs and practicing their tumbling acts — something close to relief stirs in her.

There is the photography wagon, set a little apart from the rest. The elephant, a string around its foot. *Like breaking horses.* The scent of frying onions and gingerbread.

The horizon that she knew so well is different here. It is wider, somehow, broken with unknown hills, and everything is new.

JASPER

Jasper drops the iron bar of Nell's wagon.

"I haven't locked it," he tells her, but she doesn't reply. He cricks open the door an inch and strolls away. She won't escape again; he knows that the magic of this world has already dug its fingers into her.

It is a long day, too hot in the tent, and the crowds are in a fighting temper, quick to spoil an act with jeering and hurled fruit. Eventually, Violante is forced to bloody a boy's nose to subdue the audience. All day, Jasper's eyes slide to Nell's wagon and he thinks, *There she is.* He slices off the choicest meat from the zebra they are roasting and instructs Stella to leave it on the top step of her caravan. A minute later, a hand pulls the plate inside. As dragonflies dip in stagnant puddles, he remembers her dancing among that bunch of ragtag peasants. Hair bobbing, limbs neatly turned, the electricity of her.

He knows he might frighten her if he visits her again too soon, so when the evening show is over and the horses are packed in their stalls, he lies on the grass beside Toby and Stella. The laborers have built a bonfire, the establishment cutpurses tipping their takings into a cap. Brunette is stitching a new headdress for Minnie, and when she sees him looking, her fingers quicken.

He turns to Toby. "Put your big paw on the ground."

His brother does it without complaining, bearish hand spread wide.

Jasper darts the tip of his knife between Toby's fingers, faster and faster. There is a tiny silver scar on Toby's thumb from where he missed once before. It is a game of trust. Every day, Jasper plays a similar game with his audience but they don't realize it. Performers catapult over their heads, daggers are hurled, pistols fired, a lion let loose. But the crowds sit there, sucking their toffee apples, because they believe it is all illusion.

"Do you trust me?" Jasper asks, turning to Stella.

She pulls her hand away. "Not a chance. I'd cross you for the price of a bonbon."

"That wasn't always the way with you, when you had Dash," Jasper says, hurling

110

the knife into a tuft of grass.

He sees Toby flinch, the name souring the air. *Dash.* Stella looks at the ground and rips up a patch of dandelions.

"Do you remember when we were boys," Jasper says to Toby, "and father called us *the Brothers Grimm*? The stories we'd make up. The ideas we had." He toys with one of Stella's curls. "I could make up any story about her. I could turn her into anything. A leopard girl."

"Who?" Stella asks.

He points at Nell's wagon.

"Ah, so that's what she is? Where did you find her?"

"Under a rock. Hatched from an egg. Carried by a bird. I haven't decided."

"Where did you *really* find her?"

"That last village. She'll be my star act. I could buy a pelt, fasten it to her. Brunette could stitch me some fronds for a headpiece."

"I don't know," Stella says. "Leopard girls are ten a penny. Make her different."

"I could sell a bloater as a whale."

"But not if every other showman was doing the same."

"Perhaps." Jasper picks up the knife again, presses the tip against his finger. "She has poise, but little skill." He tries to think of

111

other spotted creatures. Hens and dogs, giraffes. Hyenas.

"You could . . . you could make her fly," Toby suggests, blushing. "Or jump. Like a-a fairy."

"A fairy!" Jasper scoffs. "Every girl wants to be a fairy."

But that night, as the moon rises against the springtime sky and the chill sets in, he finds himself pondering the curious marks that shadow her face. He sits on the steps of his wagon, watching as the stars prick the horizon, as silver clouds drift in front of the moon and eclipse it. A sparrow darts in a sharpened V. He sucks on his lip, clicks his fingers.

He can already picture the shifting in the crowds, the murmuring, how the air will snap as he struts out from behind the curtain. Silence, just the crunching of sawdust under his spurred boots. He thinks of the words he will summon, the guises in which he can dress her. *I present* — What does he present?

Toby suggested a fairy. His brother's ideas are often good, but he ventures them so uncertainly that it is easy to dismiss them. *A fairy, flying.* Jasper inspects the idea, as if it is an object he can hold to the light. He taps his fingers against his knee.

112

A Fairy Queen — *no* — the Queen of the Moon and Stars, her marks like a thousand constellations. She could swing, *fly,* across the ring, wings on her back. She could soar ten feet high, with a rope tied around her waist. If only his tent were not so low — she could sweep across a whole field!

Jasper jumps to his feet and begins sketching on any paper to hand — a butter wrapper, a stub of wallpaper — and his mind clicks like the machine it is. He draws the pulleys they will need, the wings themselves. He puzzles out angles and trajectories. He has always had an intellect quick for design and engineering. Even as a boy, he drew horse engines and hydraulic pumps, forges and cranes. He knows which metals should fuse and at what temperatures, enjoys the riddle of fixing an engine. In the war, he built bridges using ropes, poles, and meat barrels, was called upon to fix faults in paddle steamers. In the evenings, men brought shattered rifles to him, and he dismantled them and rebuilt them as easily as a woman might darn a cushion.

As he draws semicircles and bolts, he thinks of all the men who have had great ideas before him. He wonders if this is how Victor Frankenstein felt, sketching his creature on fragments of paper, breaking

113

into charnel houses and cemeteries for scraps of flesh and bone. Excitement fizzing in his fingertips, enraptured by the potential of it all. He thinks of the doctor's needle, stitching the monster together; he thinks of Daedalus imprisoned in his tower, trapping larks and hawks, plucking feathers from pink bodies, the air perfumed with the aroma of melted beeswax candles. The assembly of two great inventions — wings for Daedalus, a monster for Frankenstein. Victor, seeing his creature finished, pride thrumming in his ears. Daedalus, poised on the edge, a spine-breaking fall below him, readying himself to make that leap, not knowing but *hoping* that the sky would lift around him and change his life. As schoolboys, they discussed the moral of both stories. Toby, forced by the master to speak, stammered that the tales were a warning not to overstretch yourself, not to fly too high. Jasper scoffed. To him, they were an exhortation to try, to build. Better to invent a remarkable monster than be imprisoned in a life of mediocrity. Better to fly and fall than to stay trapped in that tower.

When his drawing is complete, Jasper hurries to his blacksmith. The man is gammon-faced with heat, and he puts aside the horseshoe he is hammering. Jasper stabs wildly at the paper, draws shapes in the air. *Here* are the joints to solder, the frame to cut, the spokes that will lever the machine outward, causing those wings to hinge open and shut. They will be huge, yet as ornate as a thrush's.

Jasper shakes the diagram. "I want you to start now, Galem."

His blacksmith stares, wipes a meaty arm across his forehead. "It's late . . ." he begins. "It's dark —"

"Now!" Jasper demands, idling his whip against the man's shoes, and Galem takes the design from him. "I want it finished in two days. I don't care if the horses are ill-shod, if the yokes are broken. I want you to make *this.*"

At last, the man nods, the fire white-hot behind him. Jasper will be made in this forge, too, built higher with Nell's success. As he walks away, he remembers the moment of inspiration not as Toby's tentative suggestion, but when he stared up at the sky and saw the stars arranged there. It was all his idea; all his own making. She takes form in his mind, a carefully constructed machine.

He skips ahead, to a show in London, a murmuring crowd. It does not matter that it might take him a whole year until he can afford a pitch — the months will tick down, and that time *will* arrive.

We present the Queen of the Moon and Stars — the sprite who pulls the show to its close, the day to its end — and tonight, she will fly, unlike any other marvel seen before —

He imagines news spreading, the Queen requesting his company. The draw of his show enough to rekindle her love of circus and the freak show, lost, he has heard, since the death of Prince Albert. He will cheer her, ignite that childish sense of wonder. He can almost smell the halls of Buckingham Palace, where he is sure to be invited afterward. The scents of silver polish and beeswax candles and old books. "What a marvel you are," the Queen will say to him. "What a show you've made."

His troupe is shuttered up. Apart from him and the blacksmith, the triplets are the only folk stirring, their little figures vanishing into the woods to check their traps for hares or pheasants.

Jasper walks to the wagon that is now Nell's. He puts his eye between the slats and glimpses the shape of her hair against her pillow. He is glad not to see the sharp green of her irises, the accusation of her glare. In sleep, her features are so pretty and delicate, her puckered lip almost child-ish. His stomach cramps with desire, with the elation of what she will bring him.

He turns and gazes at everything, at all the individual things that amount to his own glittering spectacle. The wooden poles, the taut drum of the tent. Animals packed into wagons like herrings in a barrel. He knows the name of every performer, groom, and laborer; even the name of the rented baby that they pass off as his dwarf Peggy's il-legitimate offspring. The show is a slickly oiled machine. As he surveys the horizon, he feels so elated that he might own the trees and the hills, too, the ocean beyond it with its split shells and hundreds of mussels clinging to the rocks. He thinks of Astley's Amphitheatre and P. T. Barnum's Museum, burned to ash; Pablo Fanque's, collapsed; and he does not know how they could continue to live after such disasters. Bank-rupts. Nobodies.

He lifts his hand and runs his finger across his wrist. He wonders if everyone else feels as immortal as he does. He has too many thoughts, too many ideas, too many ambi-tions merely to die. When his uncle was buried in Highgate Cemetery, Jasper walked through the Egyptian Avenue with its well-raked paths, its mausoleums with their pulleys and dark tombs, and he heard a man say quite brightly, "This graveyard will soon be filled with men who believed they were indispensable." And Jasper stood there, in the midafternoon sun, and could not move for a full minute.

He rasps a hand over his chin. The moon gleams, and the world shifts fractionally on its axis. He lets himself into Stella's wagon.

"Shift over, my little greenhorn," he says, and she yawns and takes him in her arms. He maneuvers her so that she is beneath him and pulls off his trousers.

When he enters her, he thinks of ink splashing from the pens of Fleet Street hacks, of his name passing from tongue to tongue. *Jasper Jupiter's Circus of Wonders.* The great body of London heaving with his name, pulsing through streets and alleys, tunneling its way into the ear of the Queen. *Jasper Jupiter, Jasper Jupiter.* Tin rattling into his topper.

He pictures Nell swinging above the Queen's head, metal wings beating on her back, arms flung wide. *I designed it all,* he'll tell Victoria in her palace. *I created her. I built the wings, found the girl in a coastal village. It was all my doing.*

"Mmm," Stella murmurs, and he watches her, her eyes half closed in ecstasy. He knows this expression, has seen her pull it for the punters when she strips off her clothes beneath a red-glassed lantern. Head thrown back, teeth biting her lip.

Jasper wonders if she couples with him because she, too, wants to feel the trace of Dash, a closeness that they have both lost.

He shuts his eyes, moans, slumps forward onto her.

"Move over," Stella says, lighting a cigar and puffing on it. "I was thinking," she says, quite casually, as if just picking up the old thread of a conversation, "I might coax out your leopard girl."

"The Queen of the Moon and Stars."

"Who?"

"That's who she is. I've settled on it."

"Hmm," Stella says, blowing smoke from the corner of her mouth. She rolls over. "You dropped something."

He thinks she means money, because she peels notes from his purse every time he is finished and says *Life's a transaction, and I'd be a bigger clown than Will Kempe if I wasn't recompensed for my labor.* But she picks up something small and flashing. The ring. It must have rolled from his pocket. He snatches it back.

"Is that Dash's —" she says, hand over her mouth.

"It's mine," he says, too quickly. "It was my father's. It looks the same."

He pulls on his trousers and is out of the wagon before she can say anything more.

NELL

Two days later, the circus moves in the night. The tent is dismembered neatly, the fabric swept back and folded, the wooden poles gathered in stacks. Nell is aware of performers crisscrossing the grass in front of her wagon — Jasper snapping commands, a little man sanding the claws of a drowsy tiger, the tall woman laughing over a joke Nell cannot catch — but it is Charlie she listens for. Where is her brother? Why hasn't he found her? It would not be difficult to saddle a horse — and the handbills must be plastered to trees for miles around.

Perhaps —

She stops herself.

No, she tells herself, *he could not be in on the money.* He could not do that to her.

She hears creaking, presses her eye to the gap between her wagon slats. The lioness's cage is pulled beside her. It paces, growling gently. Up and down, up and down. Nell is barely an arm's width from it, separated only by her wooden wall and the bars of its cage. Its black eyeball gleams, its teeth shining in the moonlight. She looks at the marks on her arms. She wonders where they caught the beast, how they wrestled it into its small cage.

A thump against her wagon — she startles, leaps back. She sees a person knocked against it. It is Stella, a villager pressing himself against her, her beard in his fist. "Why don't you cut it off, freak?" the man hisses, and his fist swings back.

Everywhere, there is noise — the clanking of yokes, shouted commands — and Nell knows nobody will hear her if she shouts. She looks about her for anything she can use as a weapon — a leg from the chair she broke? A drawer? — but then she hears a quick laugh. The man falls over, hands gripping between his legs. Stella plucks a cigar from her pocket. "And be in the slag heap with the rest of you rats, rather than up on this stage?"

When the man has limped away, Stella turns and says, "Nobody's locking you in there, you know. We've a bowl of punch if you want it."

Nell bites her cheek.

"Please yourself."

She watches Stella's swaying walk, her ease within her own body. Nell used to walk through her village as if on a tightrope, frightened to fall off. But this woman — she swings her arms, takes long strides. She stops to pick a buttercup and pokes it through her beard. How can she do that? Nell wonders: How can she bear to make a feature of her own difference, to stare the world in the eye?

And Stella was right; Nell is not locked in. Stella, she is sure, would not stay hidden inside. It would not take much to go outside, just for an instant. She presses the door. It swings open. Her pulse is quick and heavy in her ears. She lowers herself onto the step, pulls her sleeves over her hands. The lioness paces and paces in its cage, yellow hide draped over narrow bones. A girl runs past with a barrel of cabbages. The strongman and the giantess pack cloth and pans into trunks, heave them into wagons. Nobody points and gawps. She thinks of what Jasper said about the little woman, the factories that did not want her, a person's life discarded because they could not find a place for her. The thought had not occurred to Nell before. She wasable to earn a living in the field, her body still seen as productive. She watches the tall woman leaning against a barrel, rubbing her head as if it is painful, and a curious feeling beats across Nell, something close to shame.

Soon after Nell has returned inside, her wagon jolts forward, the wheels clanking, hooves beating the earth. She lies on her mattress, watches the tall dark hedgerows through the slats. Her chest is tight. She imagines a taut rope linking one arm to home, the other to the circus. With each clip of hooves, her body is racked, bones torn from sockets, flesh split, her mind divided.

When they stop at an inn for water, she hears the name of the village shouted. She has not heard of it. If she ran now, she is sure that she would never find her way home.

Nell is woken by a knock on her door. She did not sleep until daybreak, and now it must be late afternoon. She leaps to her feet. It is Jasper, gripping a brown paper parcel in both hands. He surveys the small destruction she has still not tidied — the torn books, the split feathers — and Nell juts out her chin.

He places the package on the desk. He grips the string. "Shall I?"

He does not wait for an answer, but tugs,

and the paper falls open. "For you to perform in," he says. "You can't wear that old rag forever." Nell planned to say something biting, to defy him, to hurl the gift back at him. But when she sees that it is the blue silk garment that the tall woman has been sewing so carefully, she pauses.

"I knew you'd be pleased," he says. "And this is only half of it. You're to dress in it now. My brother will photograph you. Every performer needs a carte de visite."

Only half of it? she wonders. He waits outside. She brushes the fabric with the back of her hand. It is the same color as the sea in winter. There are shapes stitched on the front — tiny stars, a great white moon, an echo of the shapes on her own face. She thinks of ripping those tiny stitches, but then she sees the pile of shredded books and a quick wave of sadness passes over her. She shakes out the cloth. Two garments: short pantaloons and a sleeveless doublet, just like Stella's. Her legs and arms will be bare. She tugs off her dress, tight with the desire to cry, crouching as if to shield herself from unseen eyes. She spans her birthmarks with her hands. She has always been so careful to hide them, and now they are supposed to be the making of her.

"Hurry up," Jasper says. "Before the sun

turns in. We need light."

She swallows. She is tired of fighting; so tired. But there is curiosity beneath her obedience. What would she look like, dressed like this? Her grimed, patched gown puddles on the floor.

I can make you brilliant.

Nell pulls on the silk, fiddles with its hooks and buttons, then pushes open the door before she can change her mind. Breeze on her bare skin. Soothing, her birthmarks less itchy than before. She steps into the yellow light of the day.

"Yes," Jasper says, drinking her in. "This is just how I pictured it." He beheads a dandelion clock with his cane. "Come."

Dew is already settling on the grass, and she sees the troupe from the corner of her eye. Children are emptying sacks of sawdust on the ground, patching placards all bearing Jasper's face. A stable boy is dicing up dead bullocks with an axe, slinging chunks into the lioness's cage. The beast pounces, tears apart heads and shins and hearts.

"Come along," Jasper says, and she hurries, half running beside Jasper. He stops at a black wagon and pounds the wall. "Toby, shift your hide," he shouts.

Nell reads the looping script: *"Secure the shadow 'ere the substance fades. Tobias*

126

Brown, Crimean Photographist."

"Toby!" Jasper says with sudden warmth when the door opens. It is the bearlike man she saw on the beach. *And he is Jasper's brother,* Nell thinks with a start — though she begins to see the resemblance in their plump lips, their sloe-colored eyes. He is younger than she remembered him — little more than thirty. He looks at her as he did before, with that long, sad gaze, and she finds herself surprisingly nervous, her face hot.

"Wait until you see this, Nell," Jasper says, hands resting on a cloth. "The second part of your costume." He pulls back the fabric with a flourish.

At first, Nell thinks it is a machine to trap animals — foxes, perhaps — jaws built to mince soft flesh. It is a frame made of dull metal with spokes and cogs, strung with white feathers. Three leather straps hang from it. It is as big as she is, a mess of solder and ironmongery.

"You're to wear them," he says, holding them up. He pulls a small lever and the metal creaks, two segments beating back and forth. "Wings."

"What are they for?"

"For?" Jasper repeats. "Why, you're to be my queen. A queen who pulls the moon across the heavens."

She stares at him. He might as well have told her that the sky is green. "Me?" she asks. "How?"

"Here," he says. Jasper smiles, laughs, and she glimpses a childishness in him, as if he has forgotten his place for an instant. "Lift your arms. There. Yes. *Yes.*"

His fingers graze her back, and Nell tries not to recoil. She imagines instead that they are Toby's hands, gentle and careful. Jasper tightens the straps across her belly and under her arms, and she stoops under the weight of the metal. The wings jut out behind her like a butterfly's, the tips sharp and gleaming, four perfect segments. She wishes she could catch her reflection in a puddle, but perhaps she would not even recognize herself.

"Magnificent," he says, breathing evenly. "Magnificent. A wonder. Don't you think, Toby? A wonder. The ropes will feed through here, and you'll be lifted skyward. You're going to fly, Nell. We're going to make you fly."

She wishes he would talk slower, to give her time to filter the meaning from his words. *Fly. Nell. Queen.* She steadies herself on the wagon, remembers how she used to stand on the farthest tip of the cliffs and watch the sea sucking the rocks below her. Charlie would plead with her to step back, not to be so foolish. She kicked earth over the edge and watched it tumble down, until the urge to fall was almost greater than the urge to stand still.

"What do you say, Toby?" Jasper says.

"Very good," Toby says, but he doesn't look up.

"Just bring the photograph to me when you're finished." Jasper claps his hands, roars across the fields, "Round up that zebra or I'll smash your skull in with a spike!" and he is off, half running.

It is simple, being told what to do. Toby tells her how to stand and how long for, and still he doesn't look at her. The wings are heavy. Her arms and legs are so bare. Not even Piggott could afford to have his image taken, and here she is, the box staring at her, the backdrop unscrolled behind her. She has a sudden image of the villagers seeing her — of her clanking into town dressed like this, jangling her wings open and shut. Would they be horrified, amazed? Perhaps they wouldn't believe it was her.

She lifts her arms as Toby instructs, gazes upward, tries to keep the tremble from her limbs. He fusses with her doublet, uncreasing the silk from beneath the straps, apologizing as his thumb brushes her bare shoulder. Her heart hammers in her ears. He steps back, slots the glass into the camera, and ducks beneath a cape, the black eye watching her.

He counts out the seconds.

"Wheezes ever charming, ever new!" one of the children shrieks.

Nell does not move. She is being transferred onto that piece of glass, a carte de visite that people might buy. What would her brother say, if she sent it to him? And Lenny — would he admire her or laugh at it?

"Nine, ten," Toby says, and then lifts out the plate. He unfastens her wings. She can hear his tight breathing, smell cigar smoke on him. He heaves the metal wings onto the ground and casts the blanket over them. "I'll take them to Jasper afterward," he says.

He starts to climb the steps of his wagon, and she wants to stop him, to have him stay with her a while longer.

"Can I see it?" she asks.

He waves the glass. "It's nothing now —"

"Can't I watch you make it?"

He twists his mouth. "I don't know," he says, and he looks across at the fields. "If you're quick," he says, and she wonders who he is hiding her from.

When Toby shuts the door behind her, Nell realizes there is no window, that the gaps between the boards have been sealed. It is so small, so warm and dark. It smells a little like the pills the mountebanks sold, rich and bitter. She stumbles on something soft and a bottle clinks. "Careful!" he says. She can hear the stammer of his breath. He brushes past her and apologizes.

Slowly, gray shapes begin to emerge. A workbench. Pots. Cork-stoppered bottles, tiny images hanging from a line. Fonts of chemicals. A mattress turned on its side. He must sleep on the floor.

He tells her how he wiped the glass with egg white, and she repeats the new words he uses under her breath. *Collodion, silver nitrate,* and then he takes a thimble of liquid and brushes it over the pane.

"What's this?" she asks, picking up jar after jar. "And this?"

"Why are you whispering?"

"Why are you?"

The dark feels as secret and forbidden as the church at Candlemas. She sees books on his shelf and squints to read the spines in the gloom. Titles she does not know. And then, *Fairy Tales and Other Stories.* She pulls it out. An ache in her gut. "My brother and I used to read this," she says. She replaces

131

it, then leafs through a book of cartes de visite. Jasper, hands on his hips, standing on a blurred elephant. A dwarf beside a tall man. A woman with one arm. They feel curiously intimate, the subjects poised but at ease. Their eyes pierce the camera. "You aren't in any of them."

"Why would I be? There's nothing interesting about me."

Nell could contradict him, but within this curious world, perhaps he is right. She looks at the collar of his plain leather jerkin, then down at her own silk doublet.

He turns to the back of the book. "This is where I paste the handbills. Aren't they beautiful?"

"The Greatest Living Curiosity! A Bear-Woman, Never Seen Before!" He lifts the page. She sees him catch his reflection in a glass and pull a face as if pained.

"Extraordinary," she reads. *"Novel. Wondrous."*

The corners of his mouth press down, and then he turns back to the bath of chemicals and says suddenly, "Look, here you are. You're appearing." His hands shake. She wonders if he is nervous because of her. She has a quick urge to hold him, to soothe him. But she doesn't move. Instead, she watches the paper with him.

An apparition. A spectacle. *Tonight, Nellie will appear on the stage —*

Toby lifts the image from the tiny font, holds it — holds her — between thumb and forefinger. It drips. He hands it to her, then lights a match, and she blinks at the sudden flare.

Her edges materialize first, shining from nothing. The triangles of her wings, her bare feet, her hair. The marks on her. Nell's breath catches. Slender arms and legs, toes pointing a little inward. Her chin raised. Eyes wide, a slight downturn to her mouth. Her face half shadowed with the birthmark.

It cannot be her, she thinks; this girl cannot be her. It is a trick. For years, she has avoided her reflection in puddles and panes of glass, believing that she would find something ugly there. The villagers treated her marks like a problem to be fixed, an aberration, even an *omen.* That girl, Nellie the flower picker, made herself so small. She could never have stood this way, could never be somebody a child might long to be.

Toby pegs her image to a washing line, in a gap between a hunchbacked woman and a snake charmer. Nell touches the corner of it. For as long as she can remember, she was told she had little chance of changing her life, that she would only ever be a spinster, her narrative petering out. But here — she could transform herself into anything. A fairy, a queen. A creature flying across the sky. She could make her own money, and a lot of it, too, build a life glossier and bigger than any woman of her status might expect.

It occurs to her that she can never return home. Her life has been irremediably altered. Her father *sold* her; how could she ever resume her place in that cottage?

She tests the idea of it, like pressing a tongue to a tooth and finding it rotten. The leaking roof, the narrow routines and stone-celled farms, the sour smell of pease loaves and boiled vegetables — wasn't it actually unbearable? Wasn't her life, in fact, as small as those walled fields?

The image crinkles in her grip.

"Careful," Toby says, and his fingers brush hers. She does not let go.

This girl with the mechanical wings is *her*, caught in time like an insect in resin. Strangers might buy this carte de visite, prop her on the mantelpiece.

Nell feels a power then, a whisking deep within her, as if she might be capable of anything. As if this girl in the photograph could soar across that tent with its shivering lamps and feel the burn of a hundred eyes on her, and she would not care at all.

NELL

When Nell returns to her wagon, her old dress is not on the floor where she left it. She searches under her mattress, then lifts the drawers. It is not there. It hits her: what must have happened, who must have taken it. She tugs at the doublet as if sleeves might magically grow from it. It upsets her more than it should, the final tie linking her to her past self.

"You can wear some of my shirts. I've a pair of trousers that might be small enough."

She turns, and Stella is standing in the doorway, her pipe between her teeth, one hand on her hip.

"Bonnie's roasting a pig. Now the shows are finished for the night."

The kindness in her voice is too much; for a moment, Nell thinks of stifling it with a snide word, of slamming the door and settling back into this quiet space once more. She grips the floor with her toes as if to anchor herself in place. That overwhelming desire to let herself fall.

"No need to look so terrified," Stella says, and laughs. "You'll eat the roast pig, not the other way round."

"I'd rather stay here," Nell says, and she tries to remember how she looked on that card — the metal wings, the lifted chin — but she can only recall the inward turn of her feet.

"There's power in it," Stella says, twisting a curl of her beard around her finger.

"In what?"

"Performing. You control it. How they see you. You *choose* to be different. Nobody else looks like me, and I'm glad."

Nell cannot meet her eye.

"What are you waiting for?" Stella says.

"My brother," Nell begins.

Stella scoffs, but her voice is still gentle. "You think he's coming to find you?" She cocks her head. "You can spend a lifetime with a family that both adores you and sees you as different."

"He isn't like that," Nell says, too quickly.

Stella shrugs, picks up a broken feather, and toys with it. This was the woman whose figurine Piggott bought, who swung across the tent and chattered and laughed, who Charlie pretended to be when he leaped

137

onto the rope swing.

"Join us," Stella says.

The girl in that photograph would not linger: the Queen, with her sharpened wings. And perhaps Toby will be outside. Nell takes a step forward. It cannot be worse than sitting alone.

Stella smiles, but Nell cannot return it. Eyes down, the wooden steps chilly under her bare feet. The grass is damp, the May evening cold. The sudden warmth of an arm tucked in hers, the squeeze of Stella's hand. She thinks again of what the villagers would make of it — what Lenny would think if he knew this woman wanted to be beside her.

She feels gazes snagging on her skin like fishhooks. "Everyone's looking at me," Nell whispers.

"They're only interested."

Interested. She sifts those stares for pity, for horror, but she can find neither.

By the fire, a few of the performers lounge against carriage wheels, rubbing a tub of grease into their joints. The strongman has a barrel of bobbing apples. He rears up, sodden-haired, apple clamped between his jaws, bellowing his triumph.

"Let me try," one of the triplets cries, and he holds her head under the water until the girl smacks his arms. "Fucker," she shrieks, gasping for air and kicking him in the shins. "Fucker!"

There is the piglet, little bigger than a baby. Its skin is blackened and crisp, a cooked apple foaming between its jaws. Fat drips onto the fire and sends up white jets of flame. The girl who ate hot coals turns the spit. Nell thought there was a trick in it, but she catches bright red blisters at the edges of the girl's mouth, her lips bloody.

"Eyefuls are a shilling each," she says, scowling at Nell.

Nell steps back. "Sorry —"

"Leave her be, Bonnie," Stella says, squeezing the girl into a half embrace.

Bonnie saws off a hunk of pork and passes it to Nell. The crackling snaps. What would Charlie give for a meal like this, for a night of no boiled vegetables?

"Sit here," Stella says, settling beside two women, and Nell is glad to be on the ground where people will not notice her. The giantess pauses in her needlework, the blue silk shimmering in her lap. The little woman stops stroking the baby's head. Nell takes a bite of pork, fat bursting on her tongue.

"We wondered what Jasper had in there," the woman says, dandling the baby. "Huffen said he thought it was a whale in a tank.

But then we saw you, pelting across the grass."

"Is it paint?" the giantess asks. Her voice is educated, like Piggott's daughters. "Or glued hide?"

The woman reaches out a hand, brushes Nell's cheek. Stella swats her away.

"I just want to *see.*"

"How would you like it if she measured your great bones, without asking?" Stella asks, but the giantess only laughs.

"She's Brunette," Stella says. She points at the other performers. Violante the strongman. Bonnie the fire-eater. Peggy the little woman. A wash of other names that Nell cannot possibly remember. Some of them exchange tricks, throwing knives and juggling. She watches them, their hands fumbling, dropping, catching, and to her surprise their skills no longer seem impossible but something she might learn.

"Where did he find you?" Peggy asks, and then Brunette is talking too, questions clamoring. "What's your name?" "What's your act?" "Do I know you from Winston's show?" Faces watching her, waiting for her to speak. Nell draws her legs closer, glances at her wagon. She wishes, suddenly, that she had not come out, that she were safe inside. She thinks of home, the crashing of the sea, the distant lands she imagined when she was swimming.

"Jasper found you in that village, didn't he? The flower farm," Stella says.

Nell nods.

"A flower farm?" Peggy asks. "Roses? Or hothouses?"

"Miniature flowers," Nell says, quietly. "For nosegays and candying."

They ask her more questions, but gently, carefully, as if afraid they will frighten her away. Nobody has ever asked Nell about her life before, never treated her like a secret to be unpicked. At first, she stutters and covers her mouth with her hand, a low fear that she will say the wrong thing, that they will turn her words to taunts. "Narcissi and violets," she says. "That's what we grew."

They wait, and her voice begins to rise, steadier. It loses its quake. She tells them about the circus advertisement, and how Toby saw her swimming in the sea. The show's arrival, how she watched from the back of the tent. There is a liberation in telling it as it was.

"And you wanted to join us?" Brunette asks. "You found Jasper, did you, and he hired you for a season?"

Nell looks down.

The sting of splinters, hands bruising her

wrists. The fiddle, rising in the night. Her brother, glancing away. How to pour these things into words, to give them shape? It is too much to expose, to make sense of; once a story is unloosed, she cannot summon it back. The lie is easier. "Yes," she says. "It was my idea."

Nobody meets her eye, but nobody contradicts her either. On that first night, she pounded on the door until her arms ached, until her throat swelled. They all watched her bursting from the wagon, running across the field. They must know the truth, must have seen it before and now understand what she cannot tell them.

"It was the same for me," Peggy says. "I wanted to work at the factory, to make my own way. But they said I was no good for it." She shrugs, curses at one of the laborers as a thrown knife narrowly misses her. "But Brunette, she had money. The squire's seven-foot daughter. They used to shut her —"

"I can tell it myself," Brunette snaps. She rubs her long shins as she talks. She tells Nell how they locked her in her bedroom when visitors called, in case it damaged her sisters' prospects. "Who'd want to marry them, if they might bear another *freak of nature*?" She explains how they used to

142

starve her in the hope it would stall her growth. They called physicians and forced her to drink sour vials of liquid that made her sick and tired. They bound her feet and legs. She squeezes a daisy between her fingers. "When the circus came to my village, it was my idea. I thought my family would stop me." She falters. "They were glad too. They saw I belonged here."

"And are you glad?" Nell asks, leaning forward.

Brunette is silent.

"I want to be as famous as Lavinia Warren," Peggy interrupts. "Find my own Charles Stratton, and then I can be on the front page of every broadsheet."

Nell watches Brunette. She levers up a scab carefully.

"You liked it here before Abel started sniffing around," Stella says.

"I didn't," Brunette snaps back. "All those people touching me, watching me. To them, I'm a curious spectacle, but this is my life —"

"Abel's her *admirer*," Peggy interrupts, turning to Nell.

"He follows us like the damned plague," Stella says.

"He says he loves her," Peggy adds.

"And she's fool enough to believe it."

Nell stares. Love; it does not seem possible. She glances down at her own legs, at the marks that bloom there.

Lenny once found her alone in the cottage when her brother was with Mary and her father was away selling his gewgaws. Lenny told her that he was looking for Charlie, but he didn't leave when she said he wasn't there. She was sitting on the floor, about to fry an egg, lard spitting in the black pan. He crouched beside her. She rolled the egg in her palm, cool and lightly speckled. He moved his hand over hers. She was so shocked she could not move. This was touch; this was ache, desire, a twisting in the basin of her stomach. His fingers, working their way up her arm, nestling in the hollow of her throat. Tracing the line of her ribs. A door slammed, and he snatched his hand away, appalled at what he had done. "Don't tell anyone I was here, and what . . . what . . . *happened,*" he said, and she nodded, because she knew nobody would believe her if she did. And what had happened, after all? He had merely touched her, which to anybody else would mean nothing at all.

"He *does* love me," Brunette insists.

"I saw him doing a deal with Jasper," Stella says. "For your bones."

"I know you only say these things because

you can't bear me to have what you lost. Because of Dash —"

Stella raises her finger. "Don't you dare say his name."

Nell watches them, the nip of air between them. And then it eases, Stella taking Brunette's arm. A sudden fondness once more. Brunette teases a curl of Stella's beard, presses a daisy through it.

"There he is," Peggy says, and Nell follows where she points. The orange flare of a cigar. A shape, slipping out from behind the trees.

"Just don't let Jasper see him," Stella says.

"Why?" Nell asks.

Peggy laughs. "We're *his*. We're Jasper's, as long as we're in this show."

Brunette hauls herself to her feet, grinning artlessly. She tucks her sewing into a basket. "I knew he'd come," she says. "I knew you were wrong, Stella."

They watch her go.

"No good will come of it," Stella murmurs. "But she won't come weeping to me."

"I think he loves her," Peggy says.

"You notice only what suits you, like a buzzard sees only carrion."

Later, when everyone has turned in, Nell sneaks out of her wagon. She can smell rotting seaweed. The coast cannot be far. She wants only to see the ocean, to feel its chill presence about her.

"Where are you going?"

It is Jasper, darkness shadowing his face.

Behind her, a peewit trills, a smack of bat wings as they flap low from the woodland.

"I wanted to find the sea."

He steps closer. "You can see it tomorrow. Everyone's turned in for the night."

She moves back, nearer to her wagon.

"I won't hurt you," he says. He reaches out a hand, but she pulls away. She can sense it again, that urge to pin down and possess. "There's no need to be frightened."

She tries to hold herself like Stella might, legs apart, chin high.

"Leave me alone."

He laughs, but there is bitterness in it, as if he is not used to being thwarted. "I'm looking for Brunette."

"I haven't seen her."

"Very well."

He whisks his whip against the low grass, turns toward the forest. Brunette will be there, with the man who loves her. She thinks of the sounds her brother and Mary made in the cottage when she was sent to wait in the yard outside. Panting like wild animals. The sound of two bodies moving against each other, fabric rustling. And Toby: the dark peace of his photography wagon.

He says he loves her.

Envy lodges itself in her chest.

She notices that the lamp in Toby's caravan is still lit. She remembers his fingers, the way they brushed hers as she held the photograph. The scents of strange liquids, the book of handbills and cartes de visite he showed her. A room so dark she could not read his expression.

A horse whinnies, and Nell jumps. She runs back to her wagon, hair whipping behind her.

TOBY

Somebody once told Toby that the act of taking a photograph was an aggression. In the war, surrounded by the smell of powder and blood, and dogs feasting on the offal of the freshly dead, the thought felt ludicrous when he seemed to be the only person *not* fighting. But now, whenever Toby hunches behind his camera, he feels as if he is appropriating something. As he unpegs Nell's image from the line, he wonders if he is stealing something that belongs to her.

A moment, caught in time, a girl trapped on paper. The jut of her chin, her eyes that seem both uncertain and defiant.

He should already have carried this photograph to his brother, but he finds himself tidying his wagon, polishing the bottles. Every so often, he glances at Nell's image, as if to check she is still there. Twice, he lifts the card and moves toward the door, but then he stops himself. Instead, he pulls out the book that she looked at earlier. *Fairy Tales and Other Stories.* He could sneak across the grass to her wagon and give it to her. Perhaps it would comfort her. It would be harmless, nothing in it. Jasper wouldn't have to know — but he *would.* His brother can read every small deceit in the twitch of his eye, the downturn of his mouth. He wonders if Jasper would know if he imagined the way Nell looked at him, if he could sense whether the mashing of his pulse echoed her own. He pictures his brother like a butcher, lifting Toby's heart from a bed of brown ice, squeezing it in his fist, placing his ear against it to listen to the quiver of its chambers. Toby shakes his head a little, then weighs the volume of *Fairy Tales* in his hand and casts it to the back of his cupboard. It lands beside a small box, half buried. He pulls the box forward. The wood is swollen, and he has to lever it open.

Inside, he finds photographs of smooth plains, contented men drinking. He sorts through them. Soldiers leaning against guns, their epaulettes winking like stars. This image was printed in the *Illustrated London News,* sent to London in a packet with a general's post. More photographs: troops sitting before a whole roast chicken, laughing in front of their tents. He moves to the pictures at the back, those that nobody has ever seen apart from one officer, who seized him by the lapels and hurled him from the room. A shattered pelvis. The ground littered with fragments of skulls. A dead man, his mouth twisted in agony.

When Jasper joined the military, Toby knew that it spelled the end of things as they'd been before, that this was a place where he could no longer follow his brother. He saw their paths splitting as he knew they always would — one toward glory, the other toward mediocrity. He was not cut out for a glittering military career; instead, his father found him a position at a clerk's office.

Each night, he returned to their new, smaller house in Clapham. The whole terrace felt as if it were fresh from the shelves of a shop. The crisp wallpaper carried the arsenic scent of cut almonds. The banister glared with polish. Each day, Toby wore a small track down the stairs and caught an omnibus to a narrow airless office off Fleet Street, where he filed accounts and filled columns with numbers that meant nothing to him. Jasper visited less and less often, drawn instead to dinners at the barracks and White's, to games of whist and hazard. And so, Toby sat alone in his bedroom, listening to the sad shuffle of his father's footsteps downstairs. The words were on the tip of his tongue. *I can't be a clerk because I'm going to run a show with Jasper.* But it felt like the idle fantasy of a child, one that even Jasper seemed to have forgotten.

Every day, *The Times* was delivered, and Toby scanned it for William Howard Russell's dispatches from the Crimea. He settled on the new cloth divan and imagined Jasper joining this war in only two weeks' time. He could see him, rifle tucked into his shoulder, pulling half-drowned men from rivers, his bayonet shimmering. *My brother, a hero,* he pictured himself saying. *He commanded bravely where others failed.*

The type turned his fingertips ashy.

"Dead bodies rose up from the bottom of the harbor, and bobbed grimly around in the water, or floated in from the sea. All buoyant, bolt upright, and hideous in the sun."

He thought of Jasper, dead. *"Bobbing grimly."* He could not stop reading.

"My sleep was disturbed by the groans of the dying."

"Another night of indescribable agony."

It was horrifying. But so, too, was his own life. Every evening he folded his broadsheet,

151

took the new stairs to his room. Without Jasper, it was as if all the candles in the house had been extinguished, the hall echoing with only his footsteps. Toby saw his life reaching before him like a single-track lane, each day pitted with the same tasks, performed day in, day out. His thick hands, mechanically fixing accounts. His feet, pausing on the creaking step. His body, given mutely to the service of others. His was an existence leached of color.

And then, Jasper announced he would have some friends for dinner, a few days before he was dispatched. He introduced several new acquaintances from the barracks, and he seemed to Toby to be impossibly old — twenty-one with the authority of an adult.

"Excuse these shabby surroundings," Jasper said with a quick laugh. "Lo, how the mighty have fallen! We practically have to serve ourselves nowadays. If you hadn't brought Atkins, Dash, we'd have been roasting our own quails over the candles." He introduced his friends. "And this is Dash," Jasper said, and his voice was filled with the same pride as when Toby would say, *This is my brother.* "Edward Dashwood. His father owns horses at Newmarket. His uncle's making a name for himself in Parliament.

Parliament, you know! He's connected in ways that you wouldn't believe."

Dash's laugh was thick with false modesty. "Really, Jasper, you embarrass me," he said. "Toby, how do you do?"

The man was scattily handsome, his army jacket slung over his shoulder, and Toby said nothing when Jasper placed Dash in Toby's usual seat at dinner. He picked up the glass he had already drunk from and set it farther down the table. He saw how Jasper smiled when Dash did, how frequently he mentioned Dash's *connections*, his estate with a trout stream, his *politician uncle.* Money and social currency seemed to drip from Dash — the silver chain of his fob, the casual references he threw in about *Paris fashion* and *a Florentine greatcoat* and his *grand tour.* Toby, too, leaned toward him, as if they were all plants growing toward the sun.

"I was just saying to Jasper, on the ride here, what a disgrace Russell's dispatches are," Dash said to Toby.

Toby nodded, enthused. He could have recited most of the reporter's articles from memory.

"I agree," he said, and he did. The government's mishandling of the troops *was* a disgrace, a point Russell reinforced in each article. He was about to voice this when a

153

man with muttonchops cut in.

"He's a vulgar low Irishman. A wily creature."

"It was easier, you know, before the damned telegram, when we could handle our wars without this infernal scrutiny," Dash added.

"A disgrace," Jasper repeated.

"He can sing a jolly good song, drink anyone's brandy, and smoke as many cigars as a Jolly Good Fellow. And he's just the sort of chap to get information, particularly out of youngsters," Muttonchops said.

"Valley of Death! Six hundred dead! We didn't lose more than a hundred and fifty."

Toby's hand slipped on the wineglass.

"It makes us look shoddy. All this public outcry. But we've got the antidote for his poison," Dash said.

"Oh?"

Toby saw his brother lean forward.

"Uncle's put a man on the case. Roger Fenton, a photographer. But it takes time, you see. He might only be able to go out in the spring. Doesn't want to shiver through a winter. Uncle was incensed, of course, but what's a man to do?"

"Fenton? Never heard of him."

"He's traveled to Kiev, Moscow, that sort of thing. And we've tasked him with photographing the battlefields. The *Illustrated London News* has agreed to print them. You see, a photograph can speak the truth in a way that words simply can't."

"The truth?"

"Well, the truth as we decide to show it." Dash squared his hands into a mock photograph. "Ordered lines of tents. Laughing soldiers. That sort of thing. None of Russell's damaging tosh. There's more than one way to tell a story." Dash yawned as they stood and moved toward the small drawing room with its ugly new sofas. Toby carried a tray of cigars and port and tiny crystal glasses.

"Are you playing butler?" Dash asked as he grinned. "Very good, sir."

Jasper paused, settling himself beside Dash. He looked at Toby. "Well, what about Toby here? He can wield a photography machine, you know."

"I haven't since I was a boy, and I only photographed foolish things, like trees, or —"

"What?" Dash leaned forward. "You know how all that" — he waved his hands vaguely — "works? It's all potions and humbug to me."

"What about it, Toby?" Jasper asked, swiveling in his chair. "You could travel out after us. Join us on our little adventure. You could be there in four weeks."

For once, Jasper didn't speak for him, but waited for his answer. As the chandelier's shards glimmered, and the candles dripped down, Toby scarcely paused. He saw his brother, laughing over a joke, as handsome as any swell that rode on the Row. He remembered their shared dream of the circus, and he knew his brother would keep him by his side, that he wouldn't leave him to rot in a clerk's office. It was a struggle to blink back tears.

The truth, he thought, but only fleetingly.

There's more than one way to tell a story.

Toby wished, afterward, that he'd given it more consideration than he did, that he'd stopped to reflect on the influence his work would have. But it scarcely occurred to him. He thought only of joining his brother, of his life changing, of this being one of the last times he sat on the ragged tapestry armchair and rested his head against that new lace antimacassar.

"My old photography machine will be quite outmoded by now," he said, the only indecision he expressed.

"Oh heavens, Uncle will buy you another," Dash said. "It's the hobby of every English-man and his dog these days. They're hardly difficult to find."

And it was decided as easily as that.

"Have you seen Brunette?"

Toby startles, slams shut the box, but a few images fall loose. Jasper is standing at the entrance to his wagon.

"Brunette? She was by the fire with Nell —"

"That was an hour ago." Jasper rasps his chin. "Do you think she's run?"

"Why would she?"

"I can't afford to lose her. Why weren't the laborers watching her?"

"I'll look for her," Toby says, standing. "I can't imagine she's gone." When he walks down the steps, he sees her tall shape walking over the fields. "Isn't that her?"

"So it is." Jasper pats his shoulder. "Good man." He looks at the photographs on the floor, with their neat rows of tents. "What's the matter?"

"It's nothing."

"You're thinking about Dash, aren't you?"

Toby gives a small shrug of his shoulders.

"It'll swallow you up. You need to find a way to dam it. To forget."

"It isn't that easy," Toby says.

Jasper pats his arm, then looks around the little wagon, the lamp stammering in the corner. "Is Nell's carte de visite ready?"

Toby bows his head and hands his brother the scrap of card.

Jasper holds it to the candle. "Yes. Yes. It's just right. The way the light is feathered here." He runs his fingernail over her legs. "She looks half real, like a phantom. She will be marvelous. I know it." He sits in the small wicker chair in Toby's wagon, pours himself a brandy. "I've thought of how she'll perform. We can lift her up on ropes, lying flat. Three loops. One under her arms, one around her waist, one across the top of her thighs. If she can balance — if she can do it — well, perhaps we'll be in London next spring, even sooner than planned. My very own Queen!"

"Yes."

"I'm going to winch her up tomorrow, see how she does."

Jasper chatters on, about the wolf's puzzling appetite for fried potatoes, about hiring a new foundling for Peggy as their current baby is almost six months old. But Toby cannot stop thinking about the look in Jasper's eye when he said, *My very own Queen.* He thinks of all the wonders whose handbills he has collected. Charles Stratton, the little man who now owns a stable of pedigree horses. Chang and Eng Bunker,

Siamese twins with their own plantation. Performers who have money, opportunities, that they wouldn't have otherwise. But they are still alive, their stories not yet over. There are others whose endings are well known. Sara Baartman, the Hottentot Venus. Toby read about her when he was a child, his eyes racing over lines that stopped his breath, that made him queasy. How she was sold into slavery in South Africa and displayed in a cage in England and Paris. Bought, at last, by the naturalist Georges Cuvier, who dissected her body after her death and pickled her genitals. Later, his brother told him about Joice Heth, the ex-slave who made P. T. Barnum's name. "Barnum had her teeth extracted so he could exhibit her as the oldest woman in the world," Jasper said and laughed at Toby's wince of horror. "You think that's bad?" he asked, and there was something close to delight in his voice. "When she died, he charged fifty cents for anyone to see her autopsy. It was performed before a thousand spectators!" Jasper's eyes had a distant look, almost wistful. "Barnum's a man who knows how to draw a crowd. He's the greatest showman we've ever seen!" Toby pressed his hand to his stomach and stood up too quickly, the room swinging in and out of focus.

Toby thinks of that small defiant girl on the card, her chin raised up, her metal wings spread behind her. What might become of her? Jasper is not Barnum, not Cuvier. He is not evil. But what happens if Nell does not live up to Jasper's expectations? Would he, Toby, hold Jasper to account? Would anyone?

Toby accepts the drink his brother hands him. He drums the crystal. His eyes settle on the open cupboard, the volume of *Fairy Tales* he thought of taking to Nell.

"In a few months, I might save enough to advertise her," Jasper says with a smile, and his good humor is infectious. Toby clinks glasses with his brother. It is enough for Toby to be in his brother's presence, to be his confidant.

NELL

The ropes gnaw at Nell's skin. They circle her waist, her chest, her legs. The wings are tied beneath her arms and torso. She is bound, crouched on a six-foot platform at the edge of the ring. A laborer fiddles with the cords, tells her that he used to sail on great tea clippers, that he knows which knots will hold. She barely listens. Her mouth is choked, her throat dry. Jasper nods at her. She would like to tell him that she has changed her mind, that the idea is absurd. Above her, the jaws of the pulley click, the rope pulled tight. She is supposed to lean forward, to spread her weight evenly.

The boy snaps his fingers. "Now!"

She cannot do it. She cannot let herself drop. The tent is as hot as an oven, sweat spangling her doublet.

"Why isn't she moving?" Jasper demands, walking closer.

Tears prick her eyes.

"I can't do it," Nell whispers to the boy. "I can't."

"It's no different from the trapeze," Stella shouts. "It's safer, I'd wager."

"Help her off," Jasper shouts.

"No," Nell whimpers.

If she doesn't move, someone will push her. She inches forward, feels the rope tighten across her chest. She gives a little cry as she leans off the platform. The ropes clench, a monster's hand, throttling the breath out of her. She swings, pitches at the highest point, is wrenched back. Her weight is uneven, her head too low. The rope bites into the soft skin beneath her arms. Through half-shut eyes, she can see only faint outlines: the raked sawdust of the ring, the rows of empty benches, the horses that crop sun-baked grass. Her stomach gives a great lurch as she reaches the crescendo of each arc, arms limp, her angel wings stuck out. Commands, thrown from below. "Kick your legs." "Raise your head." "Shift your weight."

She can do nothing but hang there, wilted, ropes smarting. She thinks of how Stella swung on the trapeze, how she soared bird-like, as if she were made only of feather and dander. How she grinned and chattered and twittered.

Performer deaths pulse through her mind. Last night, Peggy was a trove of them, reveling in each account and passing them on in a voice thick with glee. Richard Sands, who walked across theater ceilings with rubber suction pads attached to his feet, but who fell to his death when the plaster gave way. The female Blondin, a tightrope walker who slipped and died when she was seven months pregnant. How must it have felt — the quick slip of air, limbs spinning, hands cradling her taut belly, the hard rise of ground?

"Not so much a denizen of the heavens as a convict at the Newgate gallows," Jasper shouts. "Make her *do* something."

It angers Nell, the guilt she feels — that, after everything, she cannot suppress her desire to please.

I can make you brilliant.

She thinks of that day, standing on the rock, Lenny's taunt hammering in her ears. She kicked off her shoes and fell, pin straight, the cold water sucking at her, arms stretching out, pressing through the currents. The sting of a jellyfish against her thighs, sand churned against her stomach, reaching forward for something she could not name.

Nell shuts her eyes. That long beach with

163

its choppy waves, how she swam through them. She pulls her head higher now, finds her balance as she did in the water, the effort straining her chest, her calves. She is strong, she tells herself, back tightened from bending over flowers, arms scalloped from lifting wooden crates of violets, from digging out trenches. The rope shudders, swings, and she gives a kick, slices her arms through the air.

A sudden silence below, gazes pinned on her. Even the urchins raking sawdust pause. They watch *her.*

You control it. How they see you.

"Open your wings," Jasper says, and she fumbles for the lever, creaks them open and closed.

A rush of air, a jarring as she tops each arc and is dragged backward, the seesaw of waves.

That morning, she tidied her wagon. Levered the drawers back into the dresser, heaped the papers in the corner, straightened her coverlet. When she was finished, she began to feel an ownership over that room, a small piece of space that belonged to her. She had her own door to open and close as she chose. This air, now, is hers — this widening sweep as she kicks her legs.

"Let her down," Jasper calls, and the

laborers lower the rope.

It is over; she has done all she can. The ground wells up to meet her. She tries to stand, but the wings are too heavy, her body too giddy with the endless rocking. She rubs her armpits, her ribs, where the cord has pressed purple welts. Jasper is standing above her, clicking his fingers. His face is distant, difficult to read.

Nell wants to ask, *Was I good?* but it sounds too pitiful.

"Aren't you pleased, Jasper?" Toby asks. "She was wonderful, I thought —"

Jasper does not reply. He is close to fury, his neck pink. He holds up his hand and walks away.

It is Toby who gathers the rope, who unfastens the knots and helps her out of her wings. The pain awakens her body as if it has been sleeping, the sinew and muscle of her, her small breasts where the cord cut in.

"I tried," she says.

"I know," Toby says. He looks at the ground, his large shoulders rounded, his hair in his eyes, and she has to stop herself from reaching for his big hands, from linking his fingers through her own. "I don't know what he wanted."

Someone else, she thinks. *He pictured someone else.*

It dawned on Jasper as soon as Nell steadied herself in the air; he is small-fry. As he walks out of the tent, he can see only flaws, just as a potter notices only where his thumb has slipped and scored the clay. The fabric is scarred with a thousand nicks and patches, stains leaching into the white triangles. His lioness is threadbare and bone thin. Stella's ruff is frayed, as shabby as a Drury Lane actress. Brunette's growing pains mean that sometimes she is too ill to perform, excuses he is certain another showman would not tolerate.

He stalks up and down the rows of wagons, laborers pressing themselves away from him, sensing his mood like the scent of iron. He finds a groom sprawled in the hay with a cigar, and the boy stubs it out quickly, leaps to his feet.

"Isn't there work to be done? The tack is filthy! The saddles haven't been waxed in

166

months." Jasper pulls off his belt and beats him, just to feel the power of it, the crack of flesh, the leather warming to his palm, the boy's side still scabbed from his last whipping. Skin rips as easily as paper.

A year, he thinks, as the belt lands. *A year, a year, a year!*

A year until he can afford a London pitch. A whole twelve months of these scabby villages, playing to a ragged brigade of knife grinders and rural half-wits! A year of unpegging and repegging, a year of ferrying and lifting and trundling!

The boy wails, and Jasper casts the belt away from him, then sees Toby leaving the tent. He hates the way he walks — that slow lumbering, his waist so wide. So dull, so unextraordinary. He runs after him, his voice rising. "Why isn't the tent clean? The wagons haven't been painted in weeks! You're useless, *useless, useless.*" The sight of his brother's sad, wounded face only irks him even more, and he grinds his knuckles into his eyes.

As Nell soared on the ropes, Jasper was shocked by her brilliance. Her arms flung wide, carving through the air as if she owned the skies themselves. There was an ease to her, a rapture — that lightness he glimpsed when she danced. She has moved from potential into something real, something valuable — something that could launch him into London. She could set the whole capital alight! But he cannot afford it; he knows what his ledger says. He crosses the grass and slams shut his wagon door behind him, idling his finger down the columns. There are no surprises. A thousand and fifty pounds, rounded down. That is his worth in the world; that is all he has built. It would buy him a pitch for a week and a few thumbnail advertisements in a periodical.

He fidgets with his mustache. If he had more money, he could plaster the capital with advertisements. London could sing his name from omnibuses, from the sails of riverboats, from every broadsheet. *"Jasper Jupiter's Circus of Wonders presents Nell, The Queen of the Moon and Stars"* — he could build her act higher, have her soar from a twenty-foot platform. From the basket of a great balloon. In that low tent, she looked penned in, almost forlorn.

He picks up a quill, presses the nib into his palm.

If only —

But there is a way.

He thinks of his father's last speculation, two ships wrecked on the rocks off the East

Indies. Crates of tea and silk growing waterlogged, sinking into the sea. A fortune risked and lost.

He thinks of Daedalus in his tower, how he had the courage to jump, to leap into the unknown. Victor Frankenstein, striving for more, longing to make his name.

There is a man, a debtor in Soho, who would lend him far more than any West End establishment. His press agent has mentioned him several times before. A man willing to *share the risk.*

Jasper has never relied on credit, has always felt his troupe is successful enough. And it has been, until now. He has watched Barnum rise, accepting investments, driving himself out of debt. Winston, his greatest rival, borrowed once and was running a hundred-horse show within a year. Perhaps Jasper is the fool not because his tent is shabby or his animals are threadbare, but because he has not seized the chance to make himself bigger.

And perhaps, too, he has not been ready. His wonders might have weathered the quiet lanes of Somerset, Hampshire, and Wiltshire, but country folk will be content with a panpipe and a three-legged dog. The London crowds are different, their palates refined, their tastes discerning. Novelties wilt and rot before they've even flowered.

But now, he thinks, leaning forward, Nell is something unusual, something *truly* new. A *natural.* Her birthmarks like constellations, her poise like that of an acrobat. All she needs is a showman's backing.

Jasper picks up her photograph, raps it on his desk. He steels himself, straightens his cravat. He dips his quill in ink.

"I have lately acquired a magnificent act," he writes, peacock eye bobbing. *"A rare and never-seen-before marvel with performing prowess to boot. I am convinced that, if I can secure the capital to raise her, her name and mine will be on the lips of every kitchen boy, every governess, and every duchess in the country. I would be most grateful if you could pass on my inquiry to the usurer you mentioned when we last met and make inquiries as to a suitable pitch for our show. My troupe currently has eleven performers, but I seek to double that. I seek, in short, to be the greatest showman in the country."*

Risk big, win big, he thinks. That was what Dash always used to say, but he had the cushion of wealth and privilege, each gambling debt waved away by his father. Jasper touches the ring in his pocket. *E. W. D.*

The letter finished, he takes out a new sheet of paper, as fresh with potential as a clean canvas. As the sounds of revelry magnify, and a girl is sick against his wagon, he burns his candles down to stubs. In his mind, the investment is already secured. No; in his mind, the investment is already *paid back*. His pen scratches letters to all the London newspapers, all the omnibus companies, and, last of all, to the Queen herself.

He will take his troupe to London.

Nell will be magnificent, and he will be even greater.

TOBY

That evening, Toby is alone in his wagon again, thumbing through the book of fairy tales. He knows that Jasper has locked himself in his wagon in a fury. How couldn't his brother see it, her power, her brilliance? As she swept across the air, Toby almost forgot to breathe. He felt like a child again, believing that anything was possible — that there were no ropes binding her, that she could truly fly. Perhaps she is sitting in her wagon now, alone and upset.

He taps the book, once, twice, and then he hurries out the door before he can change his mind. He skirts the edges of the caravans, listening for the brisk crack of Jasper's footsteps. The wind whistles like lips on a reed. A clatter of breaking bottles. He jumps. Huffen Black and Violante are drinking by the fire. This is one of the pitches they all treasure, when the shows are full and there's no need to move for a few days.

Nell's wagon is ahead, light spilling through the slats. He hurries up the steps, raps on the door. A pause. He grips the book.

"Who's that?"

The door opens.

Toby clears his throat. "It's just . . . I brought you a book. The one you looked at earlier."

He bows his head. His hands are sweating and will stain the calfskin.

She takes it, doesn't thank him.

"I can read it to you," he says, in a rush, "the book, that is, if you can't."

She laughs. "In my village, we had fire and the wheel, too."

He blushes, holds up his hands. "I'm sorry. I didn't mean —"

But she is opening the door wider, beckoning him inside. He had not expected this. He looks about him. It would be rude, now, to refuse. He crosses the threshold. The room is tidy. His eyes dart from the dresser to the mattress, uncertain where to settle. A small lamp in the corner, a vase of cracked peacock feathers. She is wearing new clothes. Red *cantinière* trousers that must be Stella's. A creased shirt. She tucks a scrap of hair behind her ear, perches on the end of the bed. She pats beside her.

"Have you read it?" she asks.

"Yes," Toby says. He almost tells her how their father called him and Jasper *the Brothers Grimm.* Jasper cast himself as Wilhelm, confident and gregarious. Toby was Jacob, introspective. *I could make up any story about her,* Jasper had said. Toby fidgets with his sleeve. "I liked the story about the hedgehog the best. But I always liked him more as a hedgehog. Imagine magicking away a suit of fine quills."

Nell shakes her head, as if loosening the memory. "Let's read 'The Little Mermaid,' " she says, too abruptly.

He moves to sit beside her, not touching. He wonders if this was a good idea; if it is awkward for them to sit side by side, reading in silence; if they would be better reading aloud. If, even, this is a childish and absurd thing to do. The words swim, and he reads each sentence twice, three times. He can glean only the vague sway of each story. He nods when she asks if she can turn the page. He always liked this book. Its tales of transformation, of magic, of a girl striking a deal with a sea witch who fed toads from her mouth. Her fish's tail cut off —

"In order to be handsome," Nell says. She brushes her cheek. She pauses, repeats it. "In order to be handsome."

He wants to tell her that he thinks she *is* handsome. But she shuts the book, closes her eyes.

"Don't you like it?" he asks. "The story, I mean?"

"I don't know any longer."

She is looking at him, her head tipped to the side. She licks her lips, and they shine in the candlelight. Toby's heart beats so loud and so fast that she must be able to hear it. There has never been a woman before: nobody, a life of not-wanting. His body is a thing of function — he is there to lift and carry and build — and that has always been enough for him. He imagines her reaching out and stroking his cheek. He imagines her slapping him, punishing him for what he feels and knows to be wrong. The claw of her fingernails against his back, her kiss not soft but full of teeth. *She is Jasper's,* he tells himself. *I cannot have her.*

"My father sold me," she says. Her voice is high, on the verge of tears. This is the moment where he should comfort her, put his arm around her. But he cannot do it. He stands so suddenly that his head hurts, his vision blotchy.

"I should — I have to find my brother," he says.

His debt to Jasper is a mountain that can

never be chipped away.

"Wait," she says.

But he is out the door and across the grass. Inside his own wagon, he leans against the wall. His legs tremble, his heart alive. Guilt, eating him. He imagines all the other things he might have done. Eyes shut, he moves his hand against himself, and it is a quiet release.

Four days later, Toby is startled by his brother bellowing through the speaking trumpet, insisting that they must pack up the wagons *now* and race for a pitch in London. He dresses quickly, hurries to Jasper.

"My agent," Jasper says, breathless. "He says there's a place for us. A new pleasure gardens in Southwark. But it's been offered to Winston's show too. The first man there wins it."

Toby stares at him. "But *London.* We can't afford it —"

"We can," Jasper says, grinning. "I've found a way."

"How?" Toby asks, and then it dawns on him. "A debtor?" he asks. He remembers the sunk ships, the risk their father took that crippled him.

"This is different," Jasper snaps, moving

away, shouting that the horses should be yoked, the wagons packed.

It is a storm of preparations. As rain showers pass over them, Toby works with his back bent to the earth. He pulls and twists great bundles of rope, levers iron stakes from the ground, wraps Brunette's juggling knives in paper, forks towering haystacks into the elephant's caravan. Everything he touches belongs to his brother. The dewy fabric that bows his shoulders, even the splinters in his palms. Jasper has built it all from nothing. *But a debtor,* Toby thinks, panic clawing at him. How can his brother have forgotten his father's dank misery as he sat in his new house, his pen patterning looping zeros in his ledger, checking the hall for calling cards and invitations that never arrived? The shame that eventually stopped his heart? His money, his success, all vanished.

"Pick that up!" Jasper bellows, his whips curling. "Faster, faster, faster."

Toby glimpses Nell, working at Stella's side, shoveling sawdust into a barrel. When she passes him the spade, she looks at him and his chest breaks a little. In his wagon, his big hands slide on bottles, wrapping each glass jar in wadding, readying to move.

His brother's voice slices through the

walls, cajoling, alive with the delight at it all. "A snail will beat us to the pitch, at this rate. A limbless sloth! I said, faster!"

They leave in the middle of the night, as soon as they can, riding to the devil down narrow lanes and wider roads, through sleeping hamlets that have little idea of the curious brigade that hammers past. Dawn breaks, and Toby sits at Jasper's side on the bench seat, their weight pressed against each other, the shared warmth a comfort. They will weather this together, Toby knows; he will do all he can to make his brother a success.

Jasper links his arm through Toby's, then raises his right hand and brings the whip down harder and harder. The coaches rattle, the lioness whines. They hit a pothole, and Jasper cries, "Fuck!" He is wearing a tricorn hat, in imitation of Dick Turpin.

Toby clings tight to the box seat. He chokes on the thrown-up dust.

"We'll be there in two days," Jasper says, "if we keep this pace." In his delight, he draws his pistol and fires two shots into the air. The horses bolt, faster and faster, a stream of forty bouncing carriages, zebras mingling with plain bays. They *can* do it, Toby thinks. If anyone can defy expectations, it is Jasper.

"We'll beat the black-coated villain, the lecherous baste of a creature, I'm sure of it," Jasper says, doffing his hat at a shepherd, who gapes as they thunder past. "Doesn't it give you pleasure, to see how the peasants admire us? To see how they want to be us?"

They don't want to be me, Toby thinks, glancing down at his patched leather jerkin, and then up at Peggy in her tasseled coat, and at Brunette the giantess on her designedly too-big seat. Plated mirrors wink and spin, a thousand colors whirled together. It makes Toby queasy, and he tries to concentrate on the gray lines of hills. He is glad that they are moving, as if they are outracing what he has done. He sees a slackening in the tempers of the other laborers, the trail of their own crimes running cold.

"Ahoy!" Jasper calls as Stella rides past, Nell on the back of the same horse. She looks astounded, a little afraid, her hands clinging to Stella's waist. Jasper has mentioned nothing more about his plans for Nell, but he has made her practice whenever the show isn't on, has had her dive from that platform again and again. Toby has watched it, each time her movements easier, smoother. Slowly, they have realized that Jasper is pleased with her, delighted even. His rage has given way to laughter, to shouts of, "Yes, like that! Your arms, move them, too, and the wings — don't forget the wings! Marvelous!"

"Ahoy," Jasper repeats.

But Stella pulls the horse away, does not look at him.

"Did you quarrel?" Toby asks.

Jasper hovers his whip over the veined backs of the drays. He purses his lips. "No."

"It wasn't about Dash, was it?" Toby asks, quiet. "You're sure she doesn't know?"

"I'm certain."

Toby watches them cantering in the scrubland beside the road, Nell's hair tangling. Her feet are bare, toes curled like little shells, trousers turned up around her ankles. He would not recognize her from a week ago.

She must feel his eyes on her because she turns and smiles. He nods, startled. He wonders how long it will be until Jasper puzzles him out, realizes that he visits her each night, even if they only sit in silence and read a book together. Toby winces, touches his arms as though his skin were transparent, his body there for his brother to slice open and delve into. But Jasper is staring straight ahead, eyes narrowed, hand cracking the whip with a casual violence.

"By God, London won't know what's hit

180

it when Nell arrives," Jasper murmurs. "You won't be able to open a newspaper in the country without seeing her face. *'Jasper Jupiter's Newest Act, the Queen of the Moon and Stars.'* " He grins, looks skyward. "My Nellie will set the city ablaze. Everyone will come to my show. She's going to be the making of me, just you see."

My Nellie, Toby thinks, and he remembers the microscope that he longed to possess.

JASPER

London's fog sits so low he can taste it. Sun as pale as a gauze-wrapped lemon. Jasper jumps from his horse, smiles. The pitch is his. All about him, the thump of more boots hitting the earth, laborers and grooms awaiting his command. Their cages stilled at last, the menagerie begin to whine and roar and wicker.

"There," he shouts, pointing to a large clearing on one side of the grounds. "Set up the wagons there." Beside the clearing is a broad circle of lawn where his grandstand will be built.

The tall gates of the pleasure gardens loop in elaborate curlicues. He strolls the other half of the plot, past bowers and follies and pagodas, and a towering replica of an iguanodon skeleton. In a week's time, these grounds will burst with the shrieks of poppets and ladies and frock-coated gentlemen. Lamps will flare like farthing candles.

Patrons will dine at long tables, drink overflowing bowls of punch in its quiet enclaves, and form winding queues for his show.

"Jasper Jupiter's Circus of Wonders, London's Newest Show!"

He sniffs the aromatic Southwark air, and even that feels loaded with potential. It smells of commerce, of a struggle to survive, of bodies vying to outlive, to outsell, to outperform other bodies. It reminds him of the first man he shot, how he watched the Cossack through the eyepiece, clad in a white *beshmet.* He twitched the trigger. *Boom.* That split moment between his finger moving and the soldier falling — the man alive, then dead.

"Shall we build the tent?" a laborer asks him.

"There will be no tent," he says, enjoying the man's surprise.

A tent would only restrict Nell, like a fly butting against a closed window. Jasper's agent has told him about a wooden grandstand, offered for a pittance by a struggling show. Twenty staggered rows of benches curved around the ring, an awning to shield them from rain. But apart from that, it is open, which means — and *this* is the feather in his cap — that he can buy a balloon, tethered so it flies only forty feet off the ground. Nell will swing beneath it, dressed in her blue doublet, her legs and arms dappled like stars.

He glances at his fob watch. It is still early. In three hours, he will plant his topper on his head and cross the bridge and walk to Soho, and he will return with twenty thousand pounds.

It was Dash who began it, Dash whose fingers ripped the first silver crucifix from the dead Ruskie's throat. *Did he?* Jasper wondered. *Could he have — ?* But his scruples passed when Dash sold it and they sat down to a dinner of pork and French champagne. He realized everyone was at it; men sent home Paris-made watches to their mothers, their pockets brimming with crucifixes and lockets of saints.

Their appetite grew, and with it the lust for destruction. Sometimes they stole, sometimes they just enjoyed watching things burn. At the museum in Kerch, they smashed priceless pottery across the floors. "I snatches whatever I sees," Dash cried, wielding a hay fork, and it became the battle cry of their regiment, a way of dealing with the loss they inflicted and incurred daily. These were bonds forged in fire, a kinship closer than brothers. At a great house, Jasper ran from room to room, bayoneting silk pillows and cushions. He waded through goose feathers a foot deep, crunched on shattered mirrors. He hurled physic jars onto the floor, cracked open a grand piano with an axe, lacerating its brass ribs. He stumbled outside, and Dash was firing shots at a coop of peahens with his revolver. He seized Dash's arm, and they waltzed, spun apart, laughed. They were like foxes, killing for the fun of it. At the end of the terrace, they found the storehouse, stacked with dried fish and bags of black bread, and they burned it to the ground. They plunged down into the vineyard, through valleys of brushwood and creepers, eating peaches until their shit was water. In battle, they snatched lives like amulets, robbed the dead before the mule litters and ambulances moved in. How couldn't this much death make them feel alive? They saw the enemy like a monster, a creature to be destroyed. Dash called it the Hydra; cut off one head and another three rear in its place, and they kept cutting and cutting and cutting. They ate well, drank well, bought the finest food from Mary Seacole's establishment. The world was theirs, and it was ripe.

■ ■ ■ ■

Jasper now has the same feeling when he stands outside a skinny brick building on Beak Street, beneath a sign of three balls. "Money Lent." Dander glimmers in the air like gold, windows shining like cut diamonds. All Jasper needs to do is reach inside and scoop loot into his pockets.

"Sir," a man says, bowing, and Jasper follows him up a narrow staircase, candles spitting mutton fat down the walls. "He will see you now."

Jasper recoils when he sees the man. It is — it can't be — Dash is *dead*. And as his vision adjusts, the resemblance fades away. The man's hair is blond where Dash's was dark, his eyes too close together. He merely sits like him, that same easiness, the same pink cheeks and complexion so smooth it looks greased.

"Mr. Jupiter," the usurer says, gesturing to a seat in front of him.

"I haven't long," Jasper says, steepling his fingers. To be busy is to be successful, and to be successful is to be rich. A simple equation that he knows this man will grasp. *I am a serious prospect.* "We arrived in London only this afternoon, and I have much to prepare."

"Yes, yes, your press agent mentioned you might be fatigued." He touches a set of keys. "Well, why don't you explain what you're about? Your agent has given me the bare bones."

"I want," Jasper says, "I want — I am building my show to greater heights. It's already a success. I made five thousand pounds profit last year, which I largely reinvested in stock. Replacing the animals that died, repairing costumes, recruiting two new acts." He waits for the man's approval, but it does not come, so he blusters on. "There's a fair fortune to be made. The public's fascination with living wonders is on the rise. By heavens, it's on the rise. Demand shows no sign of abating. American troupes are beginning to tour here. And with this competition, we must innovate. Barnum made twenty-five thousand dollars a year from Charles Stratton — from Tom Thumb, I should say. And last year he invested fifty thousand in his museum."

"His museum," the man says, stroking his chin, "is ashes now. Nothing but fricasseed crocodile and roasted kangaroo, I've heard."

"But if the fire had not taken hold . . ." Jasper says, then adds, "And now he is out of the game. Now there is opportunity, less

187

risk he will tour here and mop up our crowds."

"And you want to exceed what he has achieved?"

"Yes," Jasper says. "Exactly. Ask any child if they know Barnum, and there's a good chance they will. Or Astley or Sanger or Wombwell or Winston. But my show is still too small, and it's taking too long to rise. I want a menagerie that would have put Wombwell out of business. I want a horse show that would have made Astley weep. I want wonders that would make a physician lose his mind." He flexes his fingers. "I have a new performer, a girl. I've marked her as a sure card, but I must have advertisements. I must make her into a spectacle — an aerial machine, I thought, with her soaring from the basket."

"Intriguing," the man says, smiling a little. "So, tell me, Mr. Jupiter, how I can assist you in realizing this dream."

Assist. Jasper notes it, and he pulls back his shoulders a little farther. "I would like to borrow twenty thousand pounds."

"Twenty thousand?" the man says. "Well, Mr. Jupiter, that's quite a sum —"

"I need to spend on advertising, to build my acts. If we can triple the capacity of the audience by replacing a tent with a grandstand, then that's triple the revenue —"

"Yes, yes," the man says, waving his hand. "I can see how it would work. These sums are simple. But you must bear in mind my rates of interest."

"I expect —"

"Seventy-five percent."

Jasper grips the chair. West End financiers charge fifty percent, and this is a back-street shop, but *still* — seventy-five percent!

"If I lend you twenty thousand pounds, you will pay me back thirty-five thousand pounds. I expect one thousand pounds paid every week for thirty-five weeks."

Jasper nods.

"And say you were to default on your debt. What insurance, what securities, what worldly capital, do you possess?"

"My troupe and fakements, as they stand, are worth twenty thousand pounds. I've built it all steadily."

The usurer sucks his teeth. "I conduct business in the best and fairest way. I don't seek people out. It's their own doing, and their own fault, if they come to me."

"I understand that."

"I am a man of business myself, first and foremost. I am not interested in the causes of the destitute, of the suffering. In short, I am not interested in excuses if you default on a payment." He reaches under his desk and takes out a tiny skull with a silver lid. "Snuff?"

Jasper nods, and he takes a pinch and snorts it. It is stronger than mere tobacco, something else mingled with it. He dusts his nostrils.

"Is that a monkey's skull?"

"I suppose you do run a circus."

The man begins to explain preliminaries, speaking so quickly that Jasper can barely catch his words. He should pay attention, he knows, but the coals are smoking and the room is too warm. He looks at the large eye sockets of the skull, the yellowed teeth, the perfect jagged seam across the forehead. He hears "bill of sale," "worldly goods," "monthly installments," "principal and interest."

"Mr. Jupiter," the man says, at last. "This is no three-card trick. I've been quite clear on my expectations. I've spoken to your agent, who confirms everything you've told me. I can arrange your loan in five minutes if you choose, and then you shall have the money. But the choice shall be entirely yours."

Jasper smiles. He thinks only *money.* He thinks only *fame, success.* The show, triple its size, revealing an array of nature's wonders. Curious animals, human marvels, and Nell — his star act. She swung across the tent as if she were scything through water, as if she were escaping a force that might swallow her. There was fight in her, verve, a yearning that mirrored his own ambition. As he looked up at her, he had thought, *We are alike.* She was Icarus, and he had crafted those wings from iron. He imagined Winston's expression when he saw what Jasper had unearthed. His fury, his envy, his utter inability to compete. Jasper will draw the crowds away from him like sardines in a net.

The man takes the key and places it on the desk. Jasper's mouth is wet.

"Before I attend to your business, I'd like to make you aware, Mr. Jupiter, of my methods."

"Of course," Jasper says, but every moment seems to drag. Every moment, the man might change his mind.

"There are other moneylenders, financiers, usurers — whatever you might call them — who will cart you off to debtors' prison if you renege on your debts. These are not my methods. Holding a man hostage in gaol will not magic coins into my purse, especially if he has no wealthy dependents."

"Yes."

191

"But rattle him, and coins will pour from his throat."

"I see."

"You should know," the man says, quite breezily, "that they call me the Jackal. I'm not to be trifled with. I will secure my return. It would make me happiest if this were through your own success. I am, like you, a man of business, with my own establishment to keep afloat."

"I see that."

"If you prefer, you can visit a gentleman financier in a West End establishment, who drives a four-in-hand, rides on the Row, and for whom moneylending is a mere hobby. A gentleman who conducts his business in a similarly gentlemanly manner. I shall take no offense if you prefer such a gentleman to transact your business. If you find me too low for your liking."

"No," Jasper says, because he knows, and he knows this man knows, that they wouldn't touch him with a king pole. "I am content to proceed."

The man smiles. "Well, Mr. Jupiter, I can see that we are in agreement."

And with that, it is done. With that, Jasper is picking up a pen and scratching his name at the bottom of a contract, and waiting for his money, and shaking the man's hand, and leaving with a fistful of crisp bills and banker's checks. As he steps into the sunshine, his only regret is that he did not come to the Jackal sooner.

The day is blue and white. The cramped Soho dwellings are sun-dipped, the pavements spangled with old wrappers and horse dung. Wasps hover, as if held up by strings.

A boy with a board tied to his neck totters past. *Extraordinary phenomenon! Pearl, the Girl as White as Snow. Now Exhibiting Alive at Regent Gallery, Regent Street —"*

Across the road, a butcher is setting out his stall, his hands purpled from the glossy cuts of ox heart and lamb pluck and the tiny blackened lungs of city chickens. Sliced bits of animals. Jasper presses his own chest, feels his ribcage expand. "Ten kidneys for thruppence," the butcher bellows, and Jasper smiles. A man of business, Jasper thinks, just like him. Doesn't he know that he need only cross the street to discover untold riches? That green door is a portal to another life. Tomorrow, this butcher could open a shop in the finest West London premises, and all it requires is his signature.

A hand tugs on his trousers. He leaps back.

"Sir, sir," a child says, pointing at her leg

stump. She clutches a wooden spoon wrapped in a shawl, in imitation of a baby. "Penny, sir, please, sir."

Usually Jasper would frown and kick the imp away, but this is not a normal day. "What's happened to you, then?" he asks, curious as to what lie the wretch will spin. He can see that the girl's calf is tied behind her thigh, the toes peeping out of the top of her trousers. A classic beggarly trick.

"Machine took it, sir, at the factory, sir, where I earned an honest living, sir, and now I am dest-you-tute, and must nurse my dying sister myself."

He smiles at her. "Here," he says, pressing a shilling into her hand.

The girl snatches it and bolts down the street, hopping on her scrap-wood crutches. Perhaps her instinct is a good one. He looks behind him at the sign with the three balls and hastens his pace. He thinks of Dash, that fleeting moment when he thought it was him sitting behind the desk. But Dash is dead; Jasper saw his body broken beneath the battlements. His fingers, swollen and sun-warmed. Jasper spat on them and attempted to inch the ring free.

Nobody knows, he tells himself, *nobody but Toby.* But he remembers Stella's eyes on his ring, how she has scarcely spoken to him since. He hurries down an alley. Better to be away, and on.

■ ■ ■ ■

Part Three

■ ■ ■ ■

They rush by thousands to see Tom Thumb. They push, they fight, they scream, they faint, they cry help and murder! and oh! and ah! They see my bills, my boards, my caravans, and don't read them. Their eyes are open, but their sense is shut. It is an insanity, a *rabies,* a madness, a *furor,* a dream. I would not have believed it of the English people.

    — A diary entry by B. R. HAYDON, Easter Monday, 1846, upon displaying his paintings in the Egyptian Hall, in the room beside Charles Stratton. Stratton was an eight-year-old child with dwarfism, whose stage name was "Tom Thumb." A month later, Haydon died by suicide.

NELL

"And now, we present the eighth wonder of the world, the most extraordinary display of nature ever seen before, Jasper Jupiter's very own Queen of the Moon and Stars —"

Through Nell's scrunched eyes, everything is blurred: the wooden structure, the puttering gas lamps, the basket of the balloon. Snuffing boys race around the ring, trimming wicks and lighting more tallow candles. Argand oil lanterns blaze in glass chimneys, torches the color of sunlight. A laborer raises a chandelier on a pulley.

The candles shiver. The drums shake. A burst of light. Firecrackers. They are waiting. Hundreds of people, dressed in their crepe and silk and lace, are here to see *her.* They sit in that tiered stand, and soon the balloon will rise from behind the curtain — a velvet sheet that hangs at the back of the ring, and from the sides of which each act has galloped or juggled or swung.

That morning, Jasper showed Nell a pile of newspapers, jabbed his finger at a small bordered box. She was astonished to find a drawing of herself beneath a large sketch of Jasper. Her birthmarks were speckled and exact, her toes pointed, arms stretching out as if her little figure were swimming through rows of type. *"Jasper Jupiter's Newest Exhibit, the Act Everybody Is Talking About."* It could not be true, she thought — how could anybody be talking about *her*? She ran her thumb over the drawing of that girl and it felt as though she were a different person, someone she had met only briefly. An invention, like the characters in the books she and Toby read together.

"Tonight," Jasper said, "might be our biggest audience yet."

The show has been open for six days. Almost a week of soaring above the crowd, basking in the mounting applause; almost a week of advertisements in the broadsheets. The performers do not know how Jasper has done it, how he can be so flush with tin. Peggy whispered that Jasper will sink himself, that the new stand must have cost more than a thousand pounds, the balloon the same, made as it is of acres of silk and fine paper. Perhaps, she added, he will not be able to pay them.

Air squeals so loudly that Peggy's latest hired baby begins to bawl, and the basket lifts. She has practiced this, Nell tells herself, and each evening has run smoothly. She has soared and soared until the wings have made small cuts in her shoulder blades. But still — her stomach lurches as she is wrenched up, feet pedaling air, rope swinging from the underbelly of the balloon. She tries to find that steady balance where her body is held flat. Above her, Toby is in the basket, and he nudges her ropes with his hands, sets her rocking. It is a careful operation; she must not tangle herself on the lines that tether the balloon to the ground.

"Here she is! The Queen of the Moon and Stars is appearing — her very skin speckled with the constellations that exist within her command —"

An ache in her shoulders, the dig of metal in her armpit. Her ears sing. And then, a jolt, as the ropes holding the balloon stretch taut. What would happen if the stakes weakened, if the balloon floated loose? She pictures strings snapping, air rushing about her, landing in a tangle of bone and metal. She pictures herself borne into the night sky, over a whole city, swinging beneath the basket.

A gasp. Nell can see them now — rows of

faces turning to watch her, hands paused halfway to mouths. Some stand on the benches to see her more easily. They make her evanescent, just by looking. There: she has pulled herself flat, her stomach held taut, legs kicking, an illusion of effortlessness. She pulls on the lever and her wings creak, flip-flapping on her back. Toby pushes her rope farther, and then she is soaring in widening arcs, swimming back and forth. She smiles. She cannot help it. A gurgle breaks from her. As wind rushes about her, it reminds her of the pull of the current, how she let herself be sucked along with it. She flies wider, terror in her gut. The crowd shrinks until she can believe it is just her and Charlie, how she'd lark about in the water to make him laugh. *Look at me,* she'd say, turning a handstand, wriggling her toes. The figures she'd cut, the way she'd kick her legs, how she'd stop and check that he was still enjoying her little show. Sometimes she'd jump from the high rocks just to scare him.

My father sold me —

Her gut clenches, and she swallows bile. Her brother was in on the money, she thinks, he is in America now —

"Nellie Moon," a woman shouts.

It is a name she has never heard before.

Someone echoes it, and soon the crowd is chanting it, cheering it.

"Nellie Moon, Nellie Moon, Nellie Moon!"

They pull themselves to their feet, hands slapping like seals. Nell keeps her toes pointed. If she squints, she can see the Thames behind them, the lanterns of night boats and fishermen, church steeples like a hundred masts at harbor.

London lives below her, around her. London: a fairy-tale place, a location she scarcely believed in, and now its great arms cradle her. She wakes each morning to find it shining through her wagon.

It is time for her to speak the lines from *The Tempest* that close the show, and she hurls them into the night, words she doesn't fully understand but that are now as familiar as her own name.

Our revels now are ended. These our
    actors ,
As I foretold you, were all spirits, and
Are melted into air, into thin air:
And like the baseless fabric of this vision,
The cloud-capp'd tow'rs, the gorgeous
    palaces,
The solemn temples, the great globe
    itself,

Yea, all which it inherit, shall dissolve,
And, like this insubstantial pageant faded,
Leave not a rack behind. We are such
  stuff
As dreams are made on; and our little life
Is rounded with a sleep.

Applause, thundering. Someone throws flowers into the sky. A bouquet dips and falls. Nell watches these people, grown fat on wonder. They have seen a giant juggle, a bearded woman chirrup like a blackbird, a dwarf ride a miniature pony, tumblers and contortionists, fire-eaters and dancing poodles, and *she* is the finale. They admire her, want to be her. All her life, she has held herself like a bud, so small and tight and voiceless. She has not realized the potential that lies within her, the possibility that she might unfurl, arms thrown wide, and take up space in the world.

As the laborers pull her and the balloon down, she has the giddying sensation that, for her whole life, the earth has been turning while she stayed still. Now she is in the midst of things. Now her life is beginning.

It is only when her feet are on the ground that she notices the pain, blooming across her shoulders, under her arms. There is blood on her doublet from the cut of the wings.

"You did it again," Stella says, and they link hands, laugh. The clown Huffen Black pats her on the shoulder.

"You should have seen it! The way you rose up there!" Brunette says, her neck held forward as if to shrink herself.

"There's a pig roasting," Violante says, "and sausages and ale."

It is the summer solstice, and the trees around the circus have been decorated to look like a hothouse. Pineapples and watermelons, artificial greenery draped from poles. Now it is dark, the papier-mâché seams are concealed, and the gentle light of candles and variegated lamps hides the trick.

Her body is alive with excitement from the show, her stomach too knotted to be hungry. Nell follows Stella to the shade of the wagons and sits on the blanket Peggy lays out. Brunette begins to plait Nell's hair, hands tugging at her scalp. She closes her eyes briefly, snaps them open to find three boys staring at them.

"Want a brace of lead to go with that eyeful?" Stella bellows, lifting her pistol, and they laugh as the boys run.

"You must have been a fearsome sight in Varna," Peggy says.

"I liked to be in the thick of it. To carry two pistols tucked in my belt." Stella mimes riding, firing her fingers. "I'd sit with the other women on Cathcart's Hill and watch the fighting for days. Dash had this beautiful white charger. I loved watching him. I always sought him out, even before I'd met him. He was a favorite among us." She reaches to fill up Peggy's glass, the barrel just out of the little woman's reach.

"I can do it myself," Peggy snaps.

"I was only trying to help," Stella says.

"I'm not a child," Peggy says, snatching her glass. She turns to Brunette. "Abel was searching for you earlier."

Brunette pulls too hard on the plait and Nell winces. "I know."

"What's that look for?" Stella asks. She begins to tickle Brunette. "You've got a secret. I can tell. What is it? What is it now?"

Brunette wriggles free, swats at Stella. "Stop it," she gasps.

"Tell me," Stella says.

"Fine, fine." She smooths her dress where it has rumpled. "Promise you won't mock me?"

"I'd never mock you," Stella says with faux innocence. "It isn't my concern if your lover is as tall as your armpit —"

Brunette glares at her.

"I promise, I promise," Stella says.

"What is it?" Peggy asks.

Brunette takes a breath. "He wants to marry me."

Stella freezes, Peggy's smile falling away. "What?" she demands.

"Lawks," Peggy whispers. "You won't, will you?"

"He only wants to show you," Stella says. "Turn you into the next Julia Pastrana."

"You're just jealous that somebody loves me," Brunette says, her eyes narrowing.

Stella scoffs. "I wouldn't trade this life for anything. You should be careful, throwing away what you've built."

"Maybe I don't want crowds of people staring at me all day. Maybe I just want a little place to live, a place where I can *be*."

"Are there fairies, too, in this dreamland? And a moon made of cheese? It's easy to say you want a place to live, but who'll pay for it? You think a factory or a fine house will hire you? Look at Peggy. The world decided she didn't fit, that she wasn't *useful*. This is a better life than anything she had before."

"Don't speak for me —" Peggy begins, but Stella talks over her.

"You'll be too tall, and they'll have you out on your ear as soon as you're sick, when your bones hurt —"

"Who's Julia Pastrana?" Nell asks, partly to interrupt the argument.

"The bear-woman," Stella says. She puts on a showman's silky accent. " 'The embalmed nondescript.' "

"She had a beard, just like Stella," Brunette says.

"Stop it," Peggy snaps. "Both of you."

"Who was she?" Nell asks.

Stella sighs. "I forget you used to live beneath a rock."

Nell listens as Stella explains that Julia was a woman with thick hair all over her face and body, whose husband showed her as the Baboon Lady and the Dog-Faced Woman. When she and her baby died in the days after childbirth, her husband saw a richer opportunity — a chance to tour her dead body. *How,* Nell wants to ask, but Stella keeps talking, in a voice so cool she might merely be saying *Isn't the day a pretty one?* Julia was preserved, Stella explains: stuffed, dressed in her old red gown that she herself had sewn so carefully. Her tiny hairy baby was placed in a bell jar beside her, clothed in a little suit. They appeared all over Europe, in London, too.

A pause. Nell swallows. Her *husband* did this.

"I saw her," Stella says. "I went to see her and her baby. I don't know why. At Regent Gallery four years ago. Dickens had visited, and Collins, too." She lights a match and holds it against her leg, singeing the hair. "And don't look like that. *You* asked. I could tell you stories just as terrible about masters and drudges in the factories." She shrugs. "We all chose this life, didn't we, even if not at first?" She turns to Brunette. "You left home for it. And Peggy sought out Jasper when she was barely twelve, begged him to make her the next Lavinia Warren. I'd do it all again. Where else can we be celebrated for who we are?"

"For how we look, not who we are," Brunette says.

"Rot. I was a hungry gutterling, not worth a gentleman's spit. And because of this, the source of all my powers" — she smiles and pulls on her beard — "I've been to Vienna and Paris and Moscow, and done as I please. I've made enough money to make my mother turn in her grave. I could give you a thousand names of wonders whose lives are richer, bigger, brighter, because of shows like this." She reaches for Nell's arm, holds the lit match against it to singe the hairs. Nell watches the woman's hand on her wrist, the white flame. She doesn't flinch. A fizzing, her nostrils filled with sour smoke. "In America, some of the wonders earn five hundred dollars a week. A week!"

"Stella can talk a brave talk," Brunette says, with a quick laugh. "But she's frightened of naturalists and physicians. That's why she mentions Julia all the time. She thinks they want her face. That they'll flay it and float it in gin when she's dead."

"Shut your trap," Stella snaps. "Abel'll have your bones like the giant Byrne's."

They fall silent then, and Peggy hums. But despite the low fear that sits in her belly, and the story she's just heard about Julia, Nell realizes she is happier than she's ever been. Stella casts back an arm and rests it against Nell's leg, and Brunette resumes plaiting her hair. Footsteps; Nell turns, expecting Abel, but it is Jasper, staggering toward them. He smiles, candlelight glancing off his teeth.

"Nellie Moon," he says, holding out his arms. He is drunk, his words melting into each other. "What a show you put on. I've someone you must meet."

"But —"

He grips her arms, and there's no use resisting him. The women move back, watch her go. She smells gin on his breath when he ushers her into his wagon.

"Mr. Richards," Jasper slurs. There is a man inside, holding a notebook.

Jasper's caravan is bigger than hers, floors laid with Turkish rugs, his face looming from hundreds of handbills on the walls. He grins from a lamp, from a cigar box, even from a pipe.

"Ah, Nellie Moon," the man says, putting down his pencil. His eyes take in her legs, her arms. "The eighth wonder of the world."

"Nellie Moon. I came up with that name, you know," Jasper says, and Nell frowns, thinks of exposing his lie. "What a spectacle I've turned her into. I knew it, the moment I saw her dance. Another man might not have realized it, but I've the knack."

"The whole country will soon be floored with a bad case of Nell-o-mania."

Jasper laughs, but his eyes do not smile. "Jasper-mania, I think you mean."

Nell backs toward the door, but Jasper places an arm around her shoulders.

"This man," he says, "is going to turn you into a plaster figurine."

She can feel Jasper's breath on her neck. He holds her tighter.

"But he needs to get the mark of you, to make you up in clay."

"I can see it," the man says, shaping an imaginary lump of plaster with his hands.

He tells her about the celebrity figures his Stoke factory has churned out — little statuettes of the murderer Palmer, and Dickens, and the Queen herself, and Miss Nightingale holding her lamp, all of which now line the mantelpieces of the middle classes in Fulham and Battersea and Clapton.

"I'm envious of any business that runs on machine power. No cursed laborers doing a bunk, or performers begging for more tin," Jasper says. "Oh, and make sure you add the wings, just as they were in the show. Without them, she'd just be another farthing leopard girl."

But the man does not lift his pencil. He stares at Nell. "Was your mother frightened by a leopard in her confinement?"

She almost laughs. *Of course,* she thinks, *it is the mothers who are blamed.* "There are no leopards near Hastings, sir."

"A traveling show. She'll have seen the beast there. Or perhaps a local sailor netted a frightful spotted fish." He nods, warming to his theme. "My father used to study teratology. The science of monsters, you know."

"My little monster is doing very well for me," Jasper says. "I scarcely have time for any other matters. Even today, I planned to visit my debtor to pay him off, but a broadsheet wanted to interview me instead."

A debtor, Nell thinks; that explains his sudden riches.

"A debtor?" the man asks.

"He's a marvelous man. Has a shop on Beak Street. He's transformed my fortunes."

"I had a friend killed by a man who did business there. The Jackal, he liked to be called. Every so often, he'll make an example of a man, when he knows the debt won't be paid. You should be careful."

"Careful!" Jasper cries. "I think the man can wait a day for his payment. I'll have it with him tomorrow." He raps the notebook. "Shouldn't you be drawing her? I really don't know why you can't work from her carte de visite."

"I can offer you matchboxes of her too. Cushion covers. Pianos, even. Umbrellas!"

"On with the task at hand," Jasper growls.

Nell has no choice but to stand there as the man draws long lines with his pencil, as his gaze cuts into her, as he drinks in her bare legs, her arms. The lamp is green glassed, and it gives her the curious sensation that she is trapped underwater. Jasper is the sea witch, she thinks, giving her a new way of existing in the world, which she both longs for and fears. Where she both fits and doesn't.

"There!" the man says, slamming shut his notebook.

When Jasper says she can leave, Nell stumbles outside. She can feel the ghost marks from where he pressed her arm, can still sense the whisper of his breath across her shoulder. She shivers. *What a spectacle I've turned her into. My little monster.* And yet, he has elevated her above all his other acts. He has made her into *somebody.* She even caught Stella staring at the handbill with something close to sadness, a show to which she was once the main draw.

"What's the matter?" Violante asks, pausing as he rolls a great cask of mead.

She shakes her head. "Nothing."

The bushes are fragrant with sprayed scents, the trees hung with oil lamps like spidery chandeliers. Flowers lie in barrels, pulped for their perfume. Sights Nell would never have believed, as if the whole world is enchanted. A man on stilts, pies crammed with live starlings, a bear led by a leather muzzle. She feels tipsy, though she has drunk nothing. Someone sees her and points. "It's her," she hears them say, "Nellie Moon."

The women have moved from their space by the wagon. She looks out for them, as they do her, to check she is safe. There is

Stella, raising an arm in quiet salute. Peggy is riding a camel, Brunette talking to Abel by the trees. Nell knows a human wonder would make a fine prize for a drunken dandy; there are establishments, Stella told her, where gentlemen can go to be serviced by hunchbacks and giantesses, by girls with shrunken hands. All these other lives lurk in the shadows, clicking their teeth, casting out tentacled fingers to suck her in. Existences far worse than her village ever was. It would be so easy to fall. A slip from the ropes, and her life bled out on the sawdust. A slip from her life, and a soiled bed in a dingy street, a man guarding the door. A physician, measuring her skin with calipers. A man who calls himself a *teratologist*. All the while, Jasper holds her life in his palm, strolls through the wagons and knows the power he wields. He *bought* her, tore her from her brother. She touches her side as if to stanch a wound.

Nell runs down a path, gravel spraying behind her. And then she sees Toby, his shoulders hunched forward as though his brother has already occupied his space in the world. Her heart clenches. Toby. His blue-black eyes, his wild hair.

TOBY

The pork skin cracks and blackens, and Toby cranks the spit, bastes the body with a tub of grease. Along with another laborer, he carves slices of meat onto a plate for a gentleman in a frock coat. The man looks through him, as if he has just plucked the meal from thin air, and the pig is rolling itself over. But Toby is used to being invisible; he merely shrugs and takes the man's coins.

There is a sudden *pop pop pop,* and Toby's hands fly to his face. *Fireworks,* he thinks, *it's just fireworks.* They burst against the sky, whistle like mortars. He wants to be on the road again, never lingering anywhere for long, his memories left behind. But they always find him out; always needle their way in, whisper through the slats of his wagon.

Coward. Coward. Coward.

Port bursts like blood down Brunette's dress. Toby holds his stomach. *Just port.* If

216

Jasper were here, he'd soothe him. *I was there too,* he'd say. *And I'm not haunted by visions of what I saw. And as for Dash —* a pause. *It's done. It's simply done. A man can't be brought back to life.*

Toby remembers the day his steamer reached Balaklava, arriving in the aftermath of a storm. Guns boomed from the batteries, vessels with masts snapped like sticks. A harbor thick with debris. A log floating like a corpse. He looked closer, recoiled. It *was* a corpse. And then, he saw Jasper standing on the pontoon, arms tight at his sides, and Toby gave a little cry of recognition.

"Here," Jasper said, and then saw his brother's face and smiled. "This is *war,* what did you expect? Matins sung by flocks of choristers?"

Jasper laughed, and Toby did, too, but his chuckle snagged in his throat as if he had a fishbone trapped there. "I missed you," he said at last.

But his words were lost; Jasper was waving at a man on the bank. "Dash!" he called, and Toby tried to mask his disappointment. "Over here."

The man joined them, scarcely nodding at Toby. Dash walked ahead with Jasper. Toby caught only snippets of their conversation. They talked about men he did not know, scenes he had not witnessed. Toby opened his mouth but found he had nothing to say. A flare of anger darted through him, that Dash did not even try to involve him, that his brother seemed so distant from him. That, in just a few weeks, Toby's place had been so easily assumed by another.

"I'll stay — I need to have the wagon brought in. My horse, my machine, you know," Toby said, expecting his brother to offer to wait with him.

Jasper shrugged. "As you please."

They walked away, and he heard Dash say, "That ambush — the Ruskies! Did you see the chap flung from his charger — ?"

As the mud sucked and pulled at his feet, as Toby floundered past desperate men with the look of starved dogs, he imagined riding a camel into a ring, Jasper beside him. Toby breathed through a handkerchief. Gangrene, half-buried skeletons, the stink of shit and vomit.

Everywhere, evidence of the truth of Russell's dispatches.

On the second day, a general gave him orders to find a pair of healthy soldiers. He found Dash and Jasper, a little drunk. "Did you hear how the storm blew the regimental bass drum into Russian land?" Dash said, and laughed.

Toby felt detached from them, detached from it all. He could not understand how they could enjoy it here, how their spirits could remain so high. Perhaps it was Dash's wealth, insulating them from the worst of it — their marquee was one of the largest, the sturdiest. Perhaps their regiment hadn't participated in the bloodiest battles, and they were still green, sustained by the novelty of it. Or perhaps they just didn't care about the gruesomeness of war; they liked the freedom of it, the thrill and closeness of fighting, a life so different from circling hot London drawing rooms. It was this which made Toby feel even more alone, that he and Jasper could feel so differently about the same situation.

Jasper reached out and patted Dash's shoulder, and Toby flinched. He had been separated from his brother for less than a month. How could Dash displace him so easily?

"Is this right, Tommy?" Dash called.

Tommy? Toby was too surprised to say anything. While he'd lain awake thinking about the man, his jealousy darkening, he realized that he meant nothing at all to Dash. He did not even rouse enough feelings in the man to be irritating. He would have preferred Dash's hatred.

219

"Toby," Jasper corrected him and grinned. "Your memory is utterly dreadful."

It occurred to Toby, too, that Dash couldn't remember his name because Jasper never spoke of him; even the lowest underling at Toby's old office knew all about Jasper. Toby lowered his head and cleared the area for his first photograph. The sky was so blue it hurt to see it. He kicked away a broken cartouche and a human jawbone, handed his brother and Dash fresh boots. He ducked behind the cape, and he saw the way Jasper was not looking at the machine, but at Dash. He gazed at him as if he could not believe they were friends. Toby knew that look; he knew it because it was the same way he himself had always seen Jasper. *My brother, you know.* A thought struck him like a kick between the ribs. *Jasper would choose Dash as his brother.*

When he developed the image into a little square of card, Toby could almost believe the story they were telling. A small scene of contentment. Two merry lads, bonded by the sights they had shared. In less than a month, this photograph might be printed in a thousand newspapers, opened by gentlemen across the country. The situation was fine, they would conclude. Wasn't that tent well cared for? Barely a scratch on those boots, egad! And was that hot whisky? What a jolly time they were having! Russell was the Prince of Humbug, a peddler of lies, no better than a showman!

Below Toby, telegraph lines stretched from Balaklava to Khutor, messages crackling under the earth. A thousand stories could be told and conveyed in seconds, a thousand ways of interpreting a single battle. This was a new war, a machine war, where journalists mingled with troops, where new inventions bore power. Toby's photographs would tell a story in a way it had never been told before. Simpson could paint his watercolors, Russell could spin his words, but the public would trust a photograph most of all.

"It just . . . I don't know, it feels like a deceit," Toby said to Jasper a few days later. "A lie."

"All of history is fiction," Jasper said, dipping a cloth in oil and polishing the barrel of his rifle. "I've said this to you before. Everyone is a liar whether they know it or not. Bias, you know? You might describe life here as untenable and dismal, and I'd say there's a thrill in fighting, and who's to say which one of us is right? Or — I might say Dash is a jolly good fellow, and the wife of a soldier he shot might call him a monster. There are no simple answers."

"A monster," Dash said. "I'll take that."

Jasper touched Toby's arm and said, "You think about things too much." And for a moment it was as it had been before — Toby remembered the circus they had planned together, the closeness that exists only between siblings. In a month, he was sure, their relationship would heal itself.

That evening, in the wavering beam of his lamp, Toby looked again at the photograph he had taken. His gut twisted to see Jasper and Dash laughing like that, while he himself was hidden, invisible. He brushed Dash's chest with his thumb and, for a second, he imagined a Russian bullet lodged in the man's heart. He pictured himself stepping into that blank space beside his brother, filling it once more. He frowned, cast the image across the floor, appalled at himself.

Every story is a lie.

Dash was not a monster. Toby knew he was merely somebody he could not bring himself to like. He hated him because Jasper liked him too much.

And the photograph was not a lie, no more than any other account might be. Dash's and Jasper's contentment was real. Toby was simply following orders. He revolved his shoulders, as if to lessen the weight that pressed on them.

When Nell appears before him, Toby cannot read her expression. She is out of breath, her hair loose.

"What's wrong?" he asks, putting down the tongs.

"Come with me," she says, quietly.

Toby looks around him for Jasper.

"He's in his wagon."

She realizes, then, that he wants to keep their closeness a secret from his brother. He feels a flaring of guilt inside him, not altogether unpleasant. Nobody is looking their way. The triplets are dancing in the middle of a circle as men clap and whistle. Peggy is offering camel rides to drunk soldiers for a shilling, her back turned.

Toby follows Nell, blinking to adjust to the dark, tripping on a shorn piece of topiary. Blood crashes in his eardrums. He can do nothing but stumble after her, down the gravel path, past the iguanodon skeleton with its half-ruined bones. She walks to the edge of the pleasure gardens, to the narrow bower with the wooden benches and a single lamp.

She stops, and he nearly walks into her. Her eyes glint in the moonlight. They are so close, just them and the faint sound of cheering. He wants to ask her why she has brought him here, but his heart is galloping, his tongue too big for his mouth. The ground is damp with dew, and the moon is sliced in two.

He tries to check if anyone is watching them. He has the quick thought that Jasper has put her up to this — that he is waiting in the shadows with a half smile on his face, to see if Toby will betray him.

"Toby," she whispers.

Nell grazes his wrist with her hand. She strokes his arm, tentative at first, and then with more pressure, as if she is tracing vines and patterns on his skin. She shuts her eyes. Perhaps she wants to pretend he is somebody else.

The moment hangs, drawn by a thread. He is afraid to breathe, to speak, as if by doing so he will snap it. If he were Jasper or Dash, he would have her in his arms, would already have reached forward and pulled her to him. But what if he has misunderstood, and she were to push him away? What if he horrified her? And this is enough, somehow; this is all he needs. Her fingertips reach his chest, and he concentrates on the sweep of her hands. Her warmth, which is now pressed against him. She smells sweet, of woodsmoke and cloves.

No woman has ever come this close to him, though he visited a whorehouse with Jasper and Dash in the days before they knew Stella. He paid his fee because it would have been churlish to refuse, and he sat with the girl on a mud-raked floor, a small fire smoking in the corner. It was so cold. She was a timid black-haired scrap of a thing, and when she moved to pull off her shift, he shook his head. He found himself telling her nonsensical things, about the flowers he'd noticed in the fields. Dahlias and anemones, tatty in the closing autumn. Sweetbriar and whitethorn, wild parsley and mint, and how, when the infantry marched, they were crushed underfoot and the air filled with their scent. Of course, she didn't understand what he was saying. He didn't even know the name of her language. He could hear Jasper and Dash whooping at each other through the walls. *I snatches whatever I sees!*

Toby is taken aback by the shock of Nell's cheek against his. His gasp is almost noiseless, surprising to him. The warmth of her, the fear of it. She pulls him closer, their bodies pressed together, and he wants to kiss her but he is afraid he will do it wrong and she will laugh at him. He is so used to being at the edge of things, his head ducked

225

beneath a black cape, a voyeur. He shuts his eyes. The haziness of it; unable to think, to concentrate, the urge to cry. She cannot possibly want him, not when she might have Jasper's affection instead.

He hears his name being called, cast through the arbor. His brother will be summoning him for a drink, or to tell him something new.

He holds Nell tighter. What would Jasper do if he found him like this? It does not matter that Toby saw her first, that he often sees Jasper leaving Stella's wagon late at night. His brother has protected him, and he must give him his life in return. It is a simple transaction.

We're brothers, linked together.

"Stay," Nell whispers.

She does not understand, cannot understand. Toby pulls away. He has to; he has no choice. A dark, glittering fear settles on him that if he stays a second longer, he will not be able to let her go. That he'll always long for this, that years from now, he'll find himself wanting her with a painful sharpness.

As he hurries through the bowers, he feels her touch drawn onto his skin, as if her fingers were paintbrushes. It is a shock, in the light, to see that his arms are the same

226

as ever — milk white and dull and scarcely freckled. He sees his brother ahead, and in that instant, he hates him. He wants to be alone. He needs to make sense of what has happened. The world has sanded him down, left him as frightened as a boy.

"There you are!" Jasper says, staggering over a log draped with manufactured moss.

Toby takes a step back. There is panic in his brother's eyes. He thinks, with quickening fear, *He knows.* He saw them together. And if he didn't, the secret must be written all over his face.

"I'm sorry," he says.

"Whatever for?" Jasper asks. Then he walks closer to Toby, worrying the skin on his neck. He says, "Someone's killed one of the goats."

"How? Why?"

"They slit its throat."

"Who? Winston?"

"No," Jasper says. "I know who it was. I didn't think he'd — Damn it!"

He follows Jasper to the animal. It lies on its side, thick ruff matted with blood, eyes already clouded. Flies and wasps gather on the wound. There is a coin clamped between its jaws.

"Who did this?" Toby asks.

Jasper breathes out slowly. "The Jackal."

NELL

Nell lies on her mattress, fizzing with what she has begun. She presses her fingers to her lips. His body against hers, the warmth and strength of him. She hears Stella, Brunette, and Peggy returning from the pleasure gardens, their voices high and lilting. One of them is playing the harmonica. Often, they will tumble into her wagon and fall asleep on her bed, their limbs tangled together.

"Still alive in there?" Stella calls, hammering on her wagon.

"All well," Nell calls back. Their laughter fades, and Nell pulls the blankets over her head. She wonders what they would say about Toby, if they knew. If they would stop her. If they would believe he could desire her: if, even, she can believe it herself.

She barely sleeps, her mind swinging back to the moment in the trees, her daring. Soon, she hopes, there will be more, bigger memories to replace it. In the morning, they will see each other again. Her heart scurries at the thought. She pictures herself, sitting by the fire, frying bacon, how he will come up to her and take her hand. The book they will read in the evening, the space between them shrinking. The electricity of his hands on her.

But in the bright dawn light, she finds herself frightened, unsure. She stares at the speckles across her legs and arms, then pulls on her trousers. In these new, fresh clothes she finds her marks itch less, her body less hot than before. Outside, the pleasure gardens are quiet. Nobody else is awake, not even the grooms. She knows it is not safe to be alone, that a girl was attacked by a group of drunk militia only two nights ago, but it feels so serene. She strolls up and down the bower — littered now with old bottles and wrappers and a fish skeleton — as if to touch the ghosts of her and Toby, to remind her it was real. She will not seek him out; she will wait for him to find her.

The day passes in fits of hope, of swift misery. Nell watches the queue outside Toby's photography wagon, all the city folk waiting for him to capture their likeness. Is she imagining it, or are there more girls than usual, nudging each other, laughing? She burns to think of him watching them through the lens, taking in their soft, pale cheeks, their bright hair, their unblemished arms.

His eyes slide past her at the show, as he climbs into the basket and she swings beneath him, and she feels wrung out, wretched.

"Nellie Moon," they chant. "Nellie Moon."

After the show is over, Jasper shows her a newspaper. He points to a sketch in the far corner, a girl's head on a leopard's body, Jasper pulling the creature on a leash. It has a simple, docile grin. *"Jasper Jupiter's Newest Exhibit,"* it states. *"A Charming Creature in an Age of Monsters."*

"There," he says, stabbing the paper. "There I am!"

He shows her more articles, spreads out *Punch* before her. "The reviews aren't all positive," he says. "But the point is they're talking about us."

She lifts the periodical to the light.

"In Nellie Moon, the taste for the Monstrous seems, at last, to have reached its climax. She joins a bustling Hall of Ugliness —"

The words blur.

"We cannot understand the cause of the now prevailing taste for deformity, which

seems to grow by what it feeds upon."

She stares at her hand, flexes her fingers.

Monstrous? She is just a girl. A coil of rage tightens around her throat.

"That will bring in the crowds," Jasper says, cutting out the article.

Nell says nothing, ignores Stella's shouts that she should drink with them, and retreats instead to her wagon. She waits for Toby to visit and read with her, but an hour passes, two, and he does not come. To distract herself, she flicks through the volume of fairy tales. Girls are rewarded with kingdoms; deformities are given as punishments. The greedy hunchback is cursed with a second hump on the front of his chest; a spiteful sister is punished by being given a second nose. She remembers that day in the market with her brother and father, the way some people shielded themselves from her, as though she were something to be feared. Could they have thought her marks were a punishment for some evil that lurked inside her? She was a child, she thinks, scarcely four. What power could she have wielded, what harm could she possibly have done them? On she reads. Hans, shucking his spines. The Beast, transformed to a perfect man. The maiden's hands growing back from the stumps on her wrists.

231

Harmony restored, as if being ordinary is the best way to exist in the world, their reward for their goodness. Charlie, waving to magic away her birthmarks. Is she wrong for no longer wanting her skin to be pale and plain, for being glad of her marks? She thinks of all the things she did not do, all the dances she shied away from, because everybody else made her ashamed. Stella's words echo in her head. *You can spend a lifetime with a family that both adores you and sees you as different.* She slams shut the book.

As she lies there, she can hear Toby and Jasper laughing in his wagon. Crystal clinks. Jealousy digs its claws into her. A tightening rage, a fury that has welled in her ever since her father sold her, that, now she thinks of it, she has kept tightly wrapped and buried for years. She peers through a gap in the slats. The moon is full, and she stares up at it. It looks like an eye, watching her, as benevolent as a mother.

Nell's sadness passes and, as two weeks in London turns into three and then into four, she minds it less, accepts that Toby either does not want her or will always choose Jasper. She enjoys, too, the whoop of the spectators, the chants that rise each night.

Nellie Moon, Nellie Moon. The feeling that she is admired, important. Her body aches, fired by the thrill of performing, until she stops noticing how tired she is.

The figurines are delivered, handbills of her face plastered to the boards of omnibuses. A squat man in a gravy-stained suit brings a crate of matchboxes. She picks one up. She is painted on the box, midflight, toes pointed, metal wings stapled to her sides. She thinks of Bessie, the girl printed on the parcels of candied violets.

"Twister's Matches," she reads, and then below it: *"Light Up the Room Like Nellie Moon."*

Nell is about to strike a match when she is startled by a hand on her shoulder. She turns, and in that first instant she does not recognize him. She thinks he is someone from the audience: so ordinary, so plain, twisting his cap in his hands. His trousers fray at the hem like old potato skin.

She drops the matchbox, a gasp rocking her. "Charlie?" she says, and she should embrace him, but her feet will not move. "Charlie," she repeats. Even his name feels foreign, untested for so long. "What are you doing here?"

"We don't have long." He taps a knife in his belt, and the gesture is so helpless that she almost laughs. "Where is he?"

"Charlie —"

"Hurry, before Jasper sees." He looks around him. "Is anyone watching you? I told them I was here to repair a saddle."

She shakes her head. "But . . . but I don't want to leave."

"What?"

"I like it here, Charlie. I'm happy."

He stares at her. There is a snag in his voice, as if he is struggling not to cry. "I spent everything," he says. "I spent everything, all the money I saved — I didn't know where you'd gone." His eyes dart — at the wagons basking in the heat, at the poodles sniffing at the gingerbread stall. She realizes that he was expecting to find a prisoner. A girl in chains, locked in a tower.

"If you were happy, you might have written to me! You might have let me know."

How can she tell him that she thought he was in on the money, that he'd sold her for a crossing to America? She bows her head. "I'm sorry."

"I thought you might be dead."

She can't look at him, can't bring herself to imagine what he has endured. "How did you find me?"

He laughs bitterly. "It wasn't difficult. Pa said you'd run away, but then he told me the truth when he was drunk. The handbills were everywhere, so I followed them, and then they said Jasper'd hurried to London. Your face — I saw it on an omnibus." He scuffs his shoes. "And I came here, where the advertisement said you'd be."

"To take me home."

"To take you home."

He looks at her as if noticing her for the first time. Her red trousers, her shirt rolled up to her elbows. She remembers the heavy cotton dress that she wore in the fields every day, how it soaked to the thigh when it was wet.

She forces a smile. "Come," she says. "I'll show you the menagerie."

They walk among the caged creatures. The tiger shackled by the collar, the llama roped to a stake. They pause in front of the *Happy Families* cage, and the wolf is whining, turning rapid circles. The hare sits low, ears flat.

The animals give her something to talk about, and she speaks too fast, too long, finds herself staring at Charlie's soiled shirt. He smells of manufactured violet perfume, of the dirt and dust of the village. She thinks, *I wish you hadn't come,* and she squeezes shut her eyes at her own cruelty.

"This is my wagon," she says, and she can hardly mask her pride. *"Nellie Moon,"* it reads, in a looping script.

"It's all yours?" he asks, but he does not sound impressed.

Inside, he looks seasick. It is too much, she realizes now. Too gaudy. She wants to dull the shine of the hexagonal bottles, the little mirrors, the silk ribbons. Everywhere, her reflection is cast back at her.

He lifts up her plaster figurine, turns it over in his hand. Its face is daubed with a single sweep of the paintbrush.

"They sell them after the shows." She is speaking too fast. "You can have it. If you want." She stops, realizes she has asked him nothing about himself. "And how is Piggott? And Mary? And the village?"

"The village," he repeats.

They never called it that. They called it *home.*

"How's Mary? Oh, I already asked that —"

"We're married now. Her belly's showing. The baby will come in about four months, they say."

"Oh. That's good."

An aching pause.

"And the flowers — how are the fields?"

"As they always are."

There is disdain in his expression, she thinks, a look that is a little too wide-eyed.

She wants to remind him that *he* was the one who dreamed of escape, that he has no right to judge her. It was he who pointed at steamers carving across the bay and said, *New York,* or *Boston, I'd say,* and he did not look away until they were nothing but white specks. *America.* How they talked about the farmstead he longed for with its field of wheat, the wooden veranda, just like in a photograph he once saw. *Corn just waiting doublet and short pantaloons. for your fingers to pick it.*

Perhaps he wants to contain her in the village, where she is safe in his shadow.

When he looks at her, she finds she has nothing left to say.

After that night's show, Violante takes out the fiddle, and Huffen Black plays the drums. Stella is the first to dance, standing by the fire and spinning until she stumbles. Nell reaches for Charlie's hand, but he shakes his head. She lets the music wash over her. Above them, candles glimmer in trees, and the folly is lit by gas jets. She watches the other women — Peggy, fidgeting with a white hen she has caught; Brunette, smoking a cigar. Nell's eyes snag on Toby. All day, her body hungers for him, as if desire exists outside of her, as primal as the need for food and rest.

"Please dance," she says again to Charlie.

"I don't want to."

"You were always the first to dance. At home." She pulls her knees to her chin.

"This is different," he says.

Charlie was always at the center of their village, strutting through it with a quick word for anyone. But here, it is he who is the outsider, he who does not seem to fit. Peggy kicks her legs in beat with the drum, feet tap-tapping, and Brunette puts her arms around Stella in a rough waltz.

"How can you bear it?" Charlie asks.

"What?"

He gestures at her doublet and short pantaloons. "Everyone seeing you like that. Being turned into a spectacle."

"It isn't like that," she says. "Everyone saw me as different before. Here, at least, they admire me. And I'm not ashamed of how I look. Not anymore."

"I didn't think you were different."

She rips up a daisy. "You noticed my birthmarks, even more than I did. You thought you could protect me."

"That was just Lenny —"

"I think he mocked me because he liked me. I only realized it afterward."

"*Liked* you?"

"He touched me once. Just ran his hand over my arm, when we were alone."

"I don't think so —"

She stares ahead, and the fury is back, working its way under her scalp. What is there to say when he denies her version of events, what she knows to be true?

"I want you to come back with me," he says.

"Why?"

"I don't like it here. I don't like it at all. It feels —" He twists a piece of grass. "It just makes me nervous. Something — I've got this feeling." He takes her hand, and it is the first time they have touched. "I've got this feeling that something will happen to you if you stay. The way Jasper Jupiter looks at you — There's just, there's something about it that isn't right."

Nell laughs, but it is uneasy. She knows where this is leading, and she wants to cut him off, for him not to say things she cannot forget. "You could stay and run seances."

"Stop it." Charlie's finger bones cut into her palm. His mouth curls in disgust. "Please? It's *them* —"

Across the way, Stella is laughing, her mouth hinged open as Brunette pours a steady stream of punch into it. Nell feels a stab of love, of protection. Her fingers rake the marks on her wrist. All those years, being set apart by the villagers. Her brother would have turned his back on her, too, if she had not been his sister.

"These people are my family," Nell says, coldly. "Don't ask me again."

That evening, when her brother sleeps on the floor, she can still hear the drumbeat shuddering in her ears.

I've got this feeling that something will happen to you if you stay.

She thinks of the sketch of the leopard on the leash, Jasper's gaze measuring her, assessing her. The cuts across her shoulders from the folding wings.

Charlie clicks his tongue in his sleep.

Her anger fades. She regrets the slice of her words, his face when she called them her *family.* What did that make him? he must have wondered. Displaced, nothing, all his savings spent to find his sister so transformed.

In the morning, Charlie wolfs down the pork chop and mops up the eggs with his fingers. She remembers the hunger that squatted in their bellies like a stone, years of it, no meat, raw limpets sucked from their shells, sour apples that made them shit.

240

There is a pair of gold-buckled shoes on her floor. A bonnet flung across the dresser. Books. She rubs her eyes. She almost forgot all this, everything she has amassed in little more than a month.

Before she can change her mind, she reaches into her pillowcase and rips the seams. Notes spill out: three weeks of earnings that she has barely dented. When the London shows began, Jasper increased her wages to twenty pounds a week, a sum so large she could hardly believe it. "There's almost sixty pounds here," she says, cramming it into a cloth bag. "For America, when Mary's had her baby. Enough for the steamer, and you can put the rest toward a bit of land."

His eyes are wide, horrified. "Where did you get this money?"

"I'm paid here. I'm paid well."

"But this much —"

"Please. Take it. I'll earn more soon."

He nods, slips the pouch into his vest.

"He sold me," Nell says, softly. "Our father, he sold me. What else could I do? What future did I have in our village?"

Charlie wipes his hand under his eyes.

"I'm happy here," she says. "I didn't think I could be, but I am."

"You know, don't you, that we wanted you

to live with us? With me and Mary? I know you didn't believe us."

She takes his hand and clasps it, because she can't bear to deny it, not when he is leaving, not when she may never see him again.

She watches him go. His bandaged pack slung across his shoulder. His cap, tipped forward, dark hair straggling from underneath it. At the entrance of the pleasure gardens, he looks around him as if he has lost his bearings, a child alone in the world.

Back in her wagon, the plaster figurine is missing. Perhaps he will display it in his new house in America. She wonders if he will be proud of her, if he will tell people she is his sister.

We wanted you to live with us.

She ponders this all morning. She wonders if it is true. There is so much she could say, about how he kept her apart from the other villagers without even realizing it, how he fought her battles so furiously that everyone was uneasy around her. Or did she draw herself apart, did she imagine a distance and then it became real? Lenny, not mocking her because she appalled him, but mocking her to draw her attention. Or was Charlie right — did Lenny actually fear and hate her because of her difference? She could put a new slant on everything, have her whole history recast. But it feels as though she is looking back on the life of somebody else, and it is no longer important.

JASPER

Jasper watches Nell's brother as he turns
the corner and crosses the street, small bag
flung over his shoulder. He was right to let
him in, not to have him thrown out by the
laborers. Jasper knew she would want to
stay, that she would choose him. It is little
surprise after all he has done for her. He
has made her, built her from a rural peasant
into *Nellie Moon,* and now gold streams into
his coffers. Five hundred pounds a night,
sometimes more.

He lets himself into his newest caravan,
where he stores his branded trinkets.

The shelves are stacked with jewelry
boxes, cushions, gloves, all bearing his face.
It is painted onto dishes and snuffboxes.
His name is inked onto tortoiseshell combs,
cameos, the wrappers of cigars. He sifts his
hands through them, laughing a little. He
would emblazon his name on turf, tree,
rock, flower if he could. He heard Huffen

Black joking that only the birds in the sky were free from his advertisements, and the next day Jasper daubed *"J. J."* on three startled pigeons. He tied them to a leash and pulled them into the ring, and the crowd cheered to see them strutting like a pair of strumpets in heeled shoes.

After the evening show, he fills a barrow with a pile of his trinkets and wheels them through the pleasure gardens, hawking them to drunken revelers.

"Do you have any cushions of Nellie Moon?" an old drudge asks, fingering a tasseled pillow, Jasper's embroidered face peering out from behind her hand.

"Ah, but I am the showman." He plumps the cushion. "How delightful this would look, propped —"

The woman tosses it back, pouts. "It's Nell I want."

He smiles, too tightly, and sells a pack of *"Jasper Jupiter"* playing cards to a swell.

Even he cannot deny Nell's magnetism. It pleases him; of course it does. But faintly, too, it irritates him. He always knew that she would be popular, but he never expected *this.* More to the point, he finds himself unable to explain *why;* what quality she possesses, the trick behind her success. The crowds still when she begins to soar, chestnuts paused halfway to mouths. It is true that there is a freedom in her movements, as if she is unmooring herself from something, as if she has left her body behind. Her eyes are always closed, and he wonders if she knows that she has an audience at all. Perhaps *this* is where her magic lies, in her absolute lack of deceit. She is natural, *real*. But success this sudden, he knows, is unlikely to last; he must diversify his troupe, find a new act to rival her. Perhaps that, too, is why they love her. She flies like Icarus, and they are waiting for her to fall.

That night, after selling a few parasols bearing his face and his entire supply of Nell's figurine, he dreams of her. She is transformed into a black spider. She lays eggs around the ring. A thousand fragile bodies hatch and unloose themselves. Miniature aerialists, rope walkers, trapeze artists. Her babies throw down webs. She begins to wrap flies, to paralyze and suck. Sparrows land in her nets. Hawks. A writhing monkey. Jasper raises his hands for the grand finale, but she twitches down to him, fastens his arms to his sides with silken bandages. She clicks her fangs and the whole tent applauds.

He wakes, rigid, a skein of saliva linking his lips to the pillow. He walks to her wagon and watches her sleeping, her golden hair spread across the covers. He cannot understand her. If he puts his arm around her, as he might Peggy or Brunette, she wriggles away. Her shyness disarms him. He cannot think how to bring her in to heel.

The next morning, July breaks, filthy and hot. Jasper knows he must not rely solely on Nell to draw in the crowds; he must build a troupe around her. He opens his ledger, its columns swollen with fat numbers. His hands tremble when he reads them, his heart skipping with possibilities. Profits of two thousand pounds a week, double what he owes the Jackal. He has been cautious, held money back, but now is not the moment for complacency — he must seize the chance, launch himself even higher.

Over the next fortnight, he meets agents, traders, performers. He hires so many interesting curiosities that he must buy new wagons to house them. He is a magpie, snatching anything that sparkles. He auditions Hogina Fartelli, a woman who can fart the "Marseillaise" and extinguish a candle from a meter away. He hires more dwarfs, two mystics, an *extraordinary hermit* who secluded himself in an ice house in Dalkeith for ten years, a *fantoccini* man with marionettes who has performed before Baroness Rothschild; a lobster girl who has traveled all over Russia, America, and France. He places her in a tank and heats it with oil lamps. The audience is in a frenzy, whistling, feet thundering. His circus is pitched to stranger, greater heights.

Jasper builds histories for each new wonder, the fabulous shot through with the scientific. In doing so, he invents them, manufactures them, creates them. The lion woman's mother was attacked by a wild cat during her confinement. The lobster girl's mother fainted at a large catch of the day.

His press stunts grow famous. He rides a rowing boat down the Thames, sitting opposite his tame leopard with its toothless jaws. He saddles a zebra and canters down the Row, and one showgoer later tells him it's all that the swells and ladies talked about for days.

He designs an intricate scheme of gas lights — footlights, border lights, strip lights. He builds a control system with a regulator, branch mains, piping, and secondary regulators and valves. He can brighten or dull all the lamps around the stage with a dial alone, and he dismisses the snuffing boys.

Every week, he writes letters to the Queen,

mentioning every connection he can muster — that Toby was a *"famed Crimean photographer"* and took the likeness of Prince Edward of Saxe-Weimar in Varna at her request. He tells her that he charged Sevastopol, that he built this circus from the carcass of war, that some of the horses are still branded with the mark of their Russian regiment. He tells her that his show is crammed with living wonders, with spectacles she has never seen before, and he begs her to visit. Other showmen say she will not be coaxed out, that she has draped herself in black crepe and sealed herself away, but he does not believe it.

Perhaps, Jasper thinks, he needs to expand his menagerie too; this is the bait that will lure her in. On a sour afternoon, he visits the vaults bordering the Thames where he first acquired Minnie. He is led into arch-roofed cells, the walls damp and dripping, where animals pace and scratch and whimper. He idles beside cages, strokes furs and feathers and scales.

He reaches into his pocket and exchanges mere folds of paper for ten zebras, a giant tortoise, two sea lions, a tapir, four toucans, and a lion, larger than any beast he has seen before. Three hundred pounds for this tallow-colored creature, its muscles wired with pent-up rage. Jasper stares at it, eye to eye. It does not blink. Its eyes are as big and black as plums.

"The king of the plains," he says, "in Jasper Jupiter's Circus of Wonders."

But when he fetches a cage and pulls it across London with a flotilla of trumpeters, it can barely stand, its muscles quivering.

And yet — and yet, even with all his money close to spent, Jasper still finds himself visiting his agent, settling into that mangy armchair and asking if the man has a truly exceptional prodigy on his books. "I still have a little tin left, Tebbit," he says. "And I need another wonder as extraordinary as Nell."

"I've a giant and two living skeletons —"

"No, no, no," Jasper says. "It must be something the Queen hasn't seen before. A true novelty."

"I see," Tebbit says, brushing the cat hairs from his stained suit. "In case you lose Nell to another showman?"

Jasper is aghast. "No!" He mops his forehead. "Heaven forbid. What straits I'd be in if she ever absconded." He strokes his neck and thinks of himself, throat slit like a hog, a shilling clamped between his teeth. The Jackal's calling card, he's heard, a swell killed only last week over five missed payments. But since the incident with the dead goat, Jasper has delivered his payments on time, including only yesterday. He has a week to make another thousand, and he's sure he'll make double that, perhaps even triple.

The agent takes out an album crammed with cartes de visite of "performers all available, all ready, the finest in the trade."

Jasper glimpses stunted limbs, shrunken skulls, human pincushions, and he snaps, "I'm not interested in any of them. I said I wanted true novelty. If I wanted an armless wonder I'd go to a Whitechapel shop."

"And find one of your old comrades?"

"Don't be absurd," Jasper says. The notion sickens him. That somebody close to him, that — he takes a breath — even *he,* had fate dealt him a different hand in the Crimea, might be stared at and ridiculed and plastered on these posters as a *wonder* —

"A real marvel," Jasper repeats, picking up the familiar thread. "That's all I'm looking for."

Tebbit pauses, palms grating on his stubble. There is a girl, he tells him, so newly on his books that he hasn't yet calculated her market value. Her mother has recently begun to exhibit her in a gallery near Piccadilly.

"And what's novel about her?"

"She's an albino. A rare marvel. Exquisite. She's the greatest little mortal that's ever been exhibited, I'm told."

"How old?"

"Four."

"Four! I don't want to take on an *infant*."

"You can control a child. She's *yours*. You can tell her you're her father, if you like. Cleave her to you. Besides, Charles Stratton was the same age when Barnum hired him from his parents."

"Hmm."

"Think of it this way," the agent says, leaning closer. He rubs his hands as if rinsing them with invisible soap. "You don't want to be outshone, do you? There's an albino girl, Nellie Walker —"

Jasper smarts at the name.

"— in America. Nine years old. Exhibited with her brother as the Black and White Twins. Whether he's really her brother — well, it hardly matters. My point is, novelty only lasts for so long. If Nellie's toured here, then you've missed your chance. This is your opportunity to mop up the excitement." He makes a gesture of wiping a bread roll around a bowl.

"And this girl on your books," Jasper asks. "She's genuine? There's no hoax? No mother with a pot of chalk? I can't afford to make a misstep, not now when my show is growing, when my finances are still not assured —"

The agent flicks to the back of the album and presses his thumb to a small image. "There she is. See for yourself. Her name's Pearl."

Jasper adjusts his pince-nez. He tries to ignore the man's choked breathing, the rasp of air through snot.

"Well?" Tebbit asks.

The girl is squinting at the camera, her face set. Pale eyes and lashes. There is a ribbon tied around her forehead. She has a slight underbite, a dandelion clock of white hair. An angel. Acquiring her would be a risk — he's down to his last hundred. It would only take a small fire, a sickness, a week of rain —

There is something familiar about her. He's sure he's seen her before. That's it! He clicks his fingers. A boy carried news of her after Jasper's very first visit to the Jackal. *Extraordinary phenomenon! Pearl, the Girl as White as Snow. Now Exhibiting Alive at —*"

"She's being displayed at Regent Gallery, isn't she?" Jasper asks. The agent nods.

"Why don't I arrange a meeting?"

Jasper pats the notes in his pocket. They sit beside the ring. He pauses. "Don't bother. Most of London will have seen her by now."

TOBY

"I think this is my favorite," Jasper says, picking up a small pipe bearing his face. He lights it, chuckles. "As if my topper's on fire."

Toby watches Jasper as he picks up the other trinkets. Smoke thickens in the wagon, his brother's words and gestures sinking into mist. Toby lifts his glass to his mouth. His ears are pricked for sounds outside the caravan — for Nell's voice, for the quick footsteps of her and Stella returning from the pleasure gardens. He hears her laughter, and it beats through him.

After the night at the bower, he stood in front of the looking glass. He felt the trace of Nell's hands on him, how she had drawn long vines across him, circled his navel like a pollinating bee. He lifted his shirt. His belly was wide but not loose, speckled with dark hair. The skin was pasty. *Ordinary,* he thought. He leafed through his book of performers, his finger pausing on his favorite images. Minnie, whose hide he had covered with flowers. The human painting from Winston's show. He closed it carefully, turned the mirror to face the wall. He could not be enough for her. She was *Nellie Moon*. He had seen her soaring beneath the basket, heard the chants thrown from the grandstand, read the frothing articles about her in every broadsheet. All of London wanted her; who was he to have her? In the days that followed, Toby took a perverse pleasure in denying himself even a glance in her direction. Then, he thought, Dash's death would have been for something; it would reverberate through his own unhappiness.

"I just have the sense she's hiding something. Could she have a lover, do you think?"

Toby startles, a dart of fear in his chest. "Nell?"

His brother looks at him through narrowed eyes. "Not Nell. I'm talking about Brunette."

Toby tries to force a smile. He has that feeling again, that his brother is reading him. He pulls his sleeves lower. "She seems just the same to me," he says, but his voice slurs. He has drunk too much. The candle casts patterned shadows like vines and creepers, an extraordinary rain forest crawling across the walls. He holds his arm up, imagines the shapes dancing over his body.

"I can't afford to lose her," Jasper says. "Not when matters are this precarious. Nell might be the main draw, but plenty of the audience come for Brunette too."

"Precarious? But you're filling the stands, twice a night. The tin's pouring in faster than we can catch it." A thought hits him. He leans forward. "How much did you borrow, Jasper? Five thousand?"

Jasper's smile falls away. "Five thousand?" he repeats with a light scoff.

"How much?"

"Twenty."

"Twenty *thousand*?" Toby's mouth falls open. "Twenty thousand pounds? From a back-street lender?

"Don't look at me like that."

"They're little more than butchers! They'll skin you. They'll kill you over the last penny. They'll sink you." His heart is pounding. "How could you be so foolish?"

"Foolish?" Jasper demands, pulling himself to his feet.

Toby should stop, but he can't, his voice growing louder, more distressed. "When winter comes, what will you do then? There's always a slowing of trade —"

"I'll hire a hippodrome."

"How? Where?"

Jasper slams his fist on the table, his glass jumping. "Isn't my show magnificent? Isn't everyone talking about it? We're filling the stands —"

Toby stares at his brother, and he looks so small, suddenly, so vulnerable. The skin around his throat is pale, tight across his Adam's apple. He thinks about when they were boys, when his brother sneaked into his room and held him. Two hearts, beating together. So close they felt like a doubled flower.

"You wouldn't understand. You wouldn't know what it is to take a risk, how important this show makes me feel."

Toby bows his head. A sharp pain, as if the nave of his ribs is cracking open. The shadow of the candle patterns his arms, and he knows his brother is right.

JASPER

After Toby has left, Jasper cannot sleep. He should be happy, content with his show's expansion, its new performers and animals. But his brother's fear weighs on him; he stares at his ledger, at the outward trickle of pounds and guineas that he had not accounted for. Additional animal food, repaired wagons, wage rises — small expenses that rapidly mount. Something seems unfastened, undone; he imagines his wolf's cage unbolted, his creature slinking across London.

He pulls on his boots and hurries to the menagerie, nodding at the grooms who guard it through the night. Vertigo seizes him, as if a gully yawns beneath his feet, the bulk of all he has built stacked behind him. He has a small and absurd desire for his old show, when he knew the names of everyone in it, when he had so little to lose.

He walks on, past the lions, past the pacing leopards and the sea lions shimmying in their metal tanks. He lifts the curtain covering the cage of his favorite animals, fumbles for the bolt. It is fastened tight. He exhales his relief. *Happy Families,* he reads, written in lilting script. In the sudden lamplight, the hare and the wolf lift their heads, eyes narrowed to slits. He watches the hare rearrange its limbs, shuffling against the wolf. It exposes its white belly. He has a quick longing for the wolf to pounce, to exercise its true nature. All those years of pent-up cravings. It is fat because he must not let it grow hungry.

Who's the wolf and who's the hare? he asked Toby, as if there were any doubt.

And then, with a dart of clarity, he realizes what is troubling him. His show is assured. His finances will recover, and soon. It is Toby; *that* is the piece out of place.

He nears his brother's wagon, its black paint peeling, the familiar scent of chemicals that linger on his brother's clothes. He thinks of Toby, hunched forward, unable to meet his eye. The sadness in his voice. His brother is keeping something from him. But Jasper will pry it out of him, watch him more closely if he needs to. The last time he forgot Toby, his whole world was split in two.

Jasper takes out the gold ring and twists it. *E. W. D.* Edward William Dashwood. He remembers the argument he and Toby had, that cold night when Dash first met Stella.

Word had spread of Stella's soirées, debauched affairs where men woke dressed in women's bloomers, or with their mustachios shaved. Everyone had an incredulous tale about her — "The woman who launched a thousand fibs," Dash quipped. "Thomas told me she wears chap's britches, and her horse died because she fed it too much champagne. Someone even told me she has a beard."

"A beard," Jasper said. "It's not possible!"

"I'd rather like to meet this firecracker and see for myself," Dash said.

Jasper expected rumor had distorted her beyond recognition, when really she was just another ordinary soldier's wife with a taste for depravity. The Crimea was full of women, after all, some with wilder reputations than others. Lady tourists, exhausted nurses with pink-poached hands, sutlers and washerwomen, French *cantinières* in their neat red trousers. Camp followers who'd drawn the white pebble from a bag of black stones and were allowed to join their husbands on the march. Some of the officers' wives sat on the steamers drinking champagne, beating the air with silken fans; others scorned such a way of living and dressed in suits of leather. They had favorites: men that they particularly enjoyed watching in battle.

Sometimes, as Jasper cajoled his men into the fray, he glanced sideways at Dash, and it was as if his own face were reflected back at him — another showman, plunging into those grassed valleys.

Together, they slew Ruskies with exaggerated gestures, slashing and cutting and scything, as if men were hayfields to be cropped. They could feel the eyes of the spectators on them, watching, admiring, and it turned the whole business of killing into little more than a game. If there were no audience, he wondered if he would have seen war differently, as a real thing — if the screams would have echoed afterward, if the bodies would have reared up in his nightmares.

"She's holding a salon tonight," Dash said.

He was eager and puppyish as they ducked into Stella's tent. Toby trailed them, and it delighted Jasper to see how easily he could make his brother smile, just by linking his arm through his.

Her tent was built like a Turkish marquee.

Cocoa mats lined the floor. Benches teemed with silver bowls of hothouse plums and greengages, vases of flowers crafted from tissue paper. They sat and sipped champagne from marmalade pots. Everyone watched Stella, a beard growing at her jowls. She began to sing like a bird.

"Sing like a robin," someone cried, and she performed the perfect warble.

"A nightingale," Jasper shouted.

"A Florence Nightingale?" Stella turned her expression haughty. "Brandy is the ruination of many a good nurse." She seized a lantern from the table. "Now leave me to haunt the wards with my blasted lamp. Nurse! Nurse! Stop your chattering with that wounded soldier or he'll have his fingers stuffed up your cunny before I can say the Lord's Prayer."

"Florence, Florence, Florence," the men began to chant, slamming their glasses against the tables.

It was only here that Jasper realized that the war had begun to wear him down: the winter an ache in his sockets, surrounded always by the reek of choleric men. How badly he needed an evening like this to restore his spirits! Jasper turned to share a laugh with Dash, but he was gazing at Stella. Even when Jasper nudged him, he wouldn't look away. And then he saw that she, too, was looking at Dash, sneaking small glances between her cartwheels and chirruped melodies.

"One day Toby and I'll own a troupe, and she'll be in the center of it," Jasper said, and at that his brother brightened.

"We'll ride in on camels," Toby added. "In red capes."

"I'll build Stella a swing or a tightrope," Jasper said.

"Not if I marry her first," Dash said, biting hard into a bottled plum, wounding the soft red flesh.

"Don't be absurd," Jasper said, and laughed. "Marry her!"

He broke off when Stella walked toward them. Jasper reached out his hand, but she ducked away, settled herself under Dash's arm as if she belonged there. He leaned over and kissed her forehead. It was a gesture of such tenderness that Jasper had to look away.

"You didn't tell me you were already acquainted," Jasper said. "You sly old dog!"

"We aren't," Dash replied.

She'd seen him on Cathcart's Hill, she told them, Dash on his white horse. She liked how he fought. She wished she could fight, too, but she had to content herself with watching through a telescope.

"And me? Did you see me?" Jasper asked, but she didn't seem to have heard him.

Stella and Dash talked for so long that the men began to grumble that they'd been promised a show and wanted to see the end of it. Stella took a slug of wine and snapped that they should find a starved rat in a cellar who'd do them for a penny, because *she* wasn't a monkey on a hot plate, there to dance to their tune. Jasper kept trying to catch Dash's eye as Stella bowed her forehead to his; a lark, he thought — it must be.

At last he gave up. He turned to speak to Toby instead, and there was a look on his brother's face he could not read, his expression turned in on itself. It frightened him, a little. He shook his arm, said, "Toby?" and his brother blinked as if suddenly awoken. He began to talk about the photographs, the lies they were telling — Jasper yawned; it seemed Toby could speak of nothing else — and so he tried to listen in on Stella and Dash's conversation.

"I suppose you want to be alone," Jasper said, expecting his friend would contradict him. But he didn't, and Jasper and Toby walked back to their tent without Dash, drowsy and champagne-sodden. It was cold,

265

frost crisping the ground, and men shivered under thin tents.

"It looks like you're lumped with me now," Toby said, and Jasper saw him hide a smile.

"What?" He chuckled. "Oh, Dash will just be fooling. He'll laugh himself senseless tomorrow. A bearded woman?"

But there was something about Toby's possessiveness that irked him, that Toby could be pleased at the idea of Dash dropping him. The drink had oiled Jasper's tongue, and he found the words came easily, sharper than he expected. "You're always so damned silent, aren't you? So damned *watchful.*"

"What?"

"What do you think about, when you haunt us each night? You just sit there like a stupid bear, not saying a thing." Toby's blank expression only goaded him, and he picked up a stick and threw it at a tree. "It's like you're this great lumbering" — he spread out his arms, searching for the word — "*shadow.* Empty! Nothing there."

It would have been easier if Toby had matched his words with a snarl, had even raised a fist, but Toby merely bowed his head.

Fight, damn it, Jasper wanted to say. *Show*

me some temper! Some life!

But it seemed that his friendship with Dash had only opened his eyes to what his brother lacked, what he wished he would be. They lay on their mattresses and neither spoke.

That night, Jasper dreamed of rotting bodies, of a dead hand on his neck. He woke up shivering, poured himself a glass of hock. He would not succumb to fear, would not be a wreck like so many of the other men. Like Toby. He and Dash were different, he told himself, more resilient; they had *chosen* to enjoy this war, and it was the only way of surviving it. He pulled on his boots, sneaked out before Toby awoke. He found Dash and Stella eating bread and boiled bacon together, their breath forming icy plumes, their bodies curled into each other.

"I'm going to marry her," Dash announced.

"He's going to marry me," Stella said, rouge smudged across her cheeks.

"Of course he is," Jasper said and planted himself between them.

All the next morning, Jasper watches Toby from the corner of his eye, only paying vague attention to his usual business. When it is scarcely ten o'clock, he sees Toby slip out the gates.

It is easy work, following Toby. His brother is a head taller than most people. He crosses the Thames, and Jasper follows. He turns onto the Strand, and Jasper dives after him. Past the Lyceum Theatre where he first saw Tom Thumb perform, through the warren of Covent Garden. And then, Jasper ducks onto New Street and finds his brother has vanished. He runs to the end of the street and back again. There is no sign of him. He peers into the baker's, the knife grinder's, a rag-and-bone shop selling filched wares. All empty. Toby must be in the next building. Dirty lace curtains hang from the window. "Painted Men and Painted Women," the sign reads.

Jasper smiles. A whorehouse! The filthy old dog, and such a low establishment too! That must be why he's been behaving so peculiarly. He's been guarding this sordid little secret, sneaking off here each morning. It's shame that's drawn his eyes away from Jasper's, that has made him fidget and wriggle in his chair.

He could wait for Toby, but he doesn't want him to know he's followed him. Besides, he has a show to whip into shape, and he doesn't like the look of the crowd of children.

"Begone!" he bellows, rapping his ivory cane, and they bare their teeth at him, faces so thin they look like grinning skulls. Everything is in his control, he tells himself; Toby was wrong to be alarmed at the debt — at the *investment* — he has taken on. He has assembled his world so carefully, and it cannot fall.

TOBY

"Through here, sir," the woman says to Toby. She is small and ruddy-faced. She ushers him into a room where smoking bowls of hot oil do little to mask the reek of vomit. His eye is drawn to the soiled divan, the trolley of ivory-handled needles, an opium pipe with burning coals.

"My vivarium," she says proudly. Ferns and orchids sit in sooty glass jars, and there is a tank of tiny striped snakes, lizards, and frogs.

He holds his wrist where his pulse hops.

"Now, sir," she says. "What is it you want?"

Toby opens his mouth, but he cannot find the words. In the dark of his wagon, his idea seemed so simple, but now he blushes, stares at the door, and considers leaving.

"Sir?" she asks, tapping out her impatience with her shoe. "Why are you here?"

"I-I-I want . . ." he says, stammering. "I

want to be painted all over."

"It ain't paint. It don't wash off."

"I know," he says.

"And all over!" She pulls a face. "You're a big man, if you don't mind me saying. A large man. It will take time, and money. At least six of my girls working on you at once, for weeks. More painful than you can imagine."

"Please," Toby says, and when he reaches for his purse, her eyes brighten.

"Very well," she says.

He lies on the bed and the woman begins to trace the outlines of flowers with an ink pen. A garden will blossom across his thighs, an enchanted forest over his back. All his life, he has shrunk into the background. He has nailed spikes and taken photographs and carried boards and fixed wagon yokes, his neck cricked with the weight of the debt he owes. Always, his eye behind the lens, watching and never participating. Resentment has churned in him. But Nell has made him crave more, a different life, a different history. He wants to be equal to her, equal to Stella, to Jasper, to Violante. He is transforming himself into a spectacle, stepping out of Jasper's shadow. It is an act so defiant that it makes him sick just thinking about it. Will Jasper be furious, grateful, horrified? Perhaps he might give him a chance at last. Now he might ride in on a camel as they once imagined, his skin glowing and shifting in the light cast by oil lamps. He could wear a red cape and golden boots, and as the audience rumbles with applause, he might glance across at his brother. There they would be, equals.

The woman holds up a mirror, and Toby twists his head to see. "Peonies and orchids," she says proudly, pressing to the right of his spine, the back of his ribs. "Pomegranates. A thrush. A robin's egg. And a snake for Eden."

After that, she lights the opium pipe and makes him suck it. "For the pain," she tells him. She rings a bell and five other girls appear, bed-tousled. Whores, probably, and he remembers the girl with the black hair in Varna.

When the first spasm of pain fires up his back, Toby groans, legs twitching. This garden will free him. He thinks of the Little Mermaid, her tongue cut out for love, each footstep like stepping on a blade. She exchanged that tail for legs and feet because of *love,* because she ached for something she did not have, because she wanted a new body and a new life with it. The needles rip through his skin. This will make him *extraordinary.*

His head on one side, he watches their alchemy, his mind clouded with the sweet poppy smoke. Ash mingled with bright powder, as delicate as the fluids he mixed in his photography wagon, pristine scenes frozen onto paper.

"A picture speaks a thousand words," a commander said when Toby handed him his fifth packet of images. The public disapproval was abating, the man declared. When they pored over these photographs, any fool could see the troops were having a splendid time, that any concerns were a pile of old rot and nonsense. It was astonishing, he added, what a difference modern machines made. They could offer an exact impression of how things were and have it delivered to thousands of drawing rooms within a fortnight.

Toby nodded, the praise warming him. He had curated his images as carefully as tableaus for soaps or perfume bottles. He had arranged sunny scenes of plump men, well kitted. But instead of slogans like *"Bonnie's Sulphur Soap! It Beautifies the Complexion,"* it might read, *"England's Crimean War! It's Better Than Christmas!"*

But that night, Toby trembled in his tent and heard the groans of the dying, the steady boom of the guns. He shut his eyes and imagined their house in Mayfair where they grew up, how each night Jasper would sidle into his room and climb into his bed, their little bodies hot under the covers.

He jumped at the sound of a shell exploding. His brother's mattress was empty. He was still out carousing with Dash and Stella. They had stopped inviting him; he'd long let go of the sliver of hope that Stella and Dash would exclude Jasper, leaving the brothers together again. In fact, the three were inseparable. He began to wonder if this wasn't just a phase, if it wouldn't pass when the war was over. He turned over, half-asleep. Images flickered across his mind — Dash, killed by a Ruskie sniper. Dash, torn apart by a shell. The comfort Toby could give his brother.

The circus, he reminded himself, to lighten his fear; one day that would happen. He clung to the idea as a drowning man clings to a raft. Every day after that, he imagined the scenes as his brother had described. The sea lions, balancing balls on their noses. A sideshow, with acts like Charles Stratton and the Bunker twins. He and Jasper, linking arms, dressed in matching toppers. For minutes at a time, he was able to forget the sound of the mule litter, ferrying the dead to mass graves. Tiny fragments of light and color and music exploded in his mind, as beguiling as a showman's trick.

On Christmas Day, no cheer, but dull swearing as men struggled to spark their patent stoves, the thin sheet iron too flimsy for their charcoal. Toby kept his eyes down as he walked to Stella's tent, where she'd paid a French soldier to cook a goose. "I shot it down yesterday morning," Stella announced.

"There's my girl," Dash said. "Can you believe my father would have me marry a mute waif with a harpsichord?"

"You don't need to dismiss the charms of another girl just to flatter me," Stella said, tickling him under the chin.

"You haven't met Lady Alice Coles." He pulled a simpering smile, crossed his hands daintily.

"And I don't particularly want to." She poured them flagons of brandy. "Will your father like me?"

"Heavens, no." He said it so forcefully that Jasper laughed. "But I'll be damned if I care."

It was curious, the hatred that spiked through Toby. If Jasper had said this, he would have admired it; but in Dash it seemed like posturing. Always so damned *gallant*. He wished Dash would say something vile; something that would make them all draw back in horror, that would prove him the villain Toby felt him to be. How could Toby despise somebody everyone else thought was so good, so heroic? And yet he did, a feeling so sharp it made his chest tighten.

More troops arrived, paying a shilling to enter. Stella lit the stove, and the tent steamed. *Cantinières* carried tureens of wild duck and a leg of clove-studded lamb. Stella sliced the joint of meat, and it bled gently into the carving tray.

"I've a gift for you," Stella said after the men were served. She handed Dash a small blue box. "To thoroughly ensure your father never speaks to you again."

He unwrapped it carefully. Toby leaned closer. It was a gold signet ring, likely pinched from the pocket of a dead Ruskie. She had carved new initials. *E. W. D.*

"You mean to mark your territory?" Dash asked, and he kissed her on the cheek.

"I can be your witness," Jasper said. "And then you can find a dissolute wench for me, too, beard or no beard. I could do with livening up my father a little."

"I'm not in love with Stella because I want to enrage my father. I can't help it, any more than I could help the setting of the sun," Dash said, and it sounded so much like a line cut from a romance that Toby's jaw clenched, his finger whitening on his fork.

"How very poetic," Jasper said and made a sound of vomiting.

After the meal, there were flasks of wine, ruby port, and sherry, and Toby lay back against the cushions. The others were playing a card game he didn't understand, and he thought he might take a short nap. Someone began to sing carols, and the men rolled about with wine-blackened lips, words slurring. He half listened to the conversation beside him, about telegrams and cut wires. "I don't suppose you'll write home to your beloved *Times* about this feast," one man said, turning to the other.

Toby almost dropped his glass of port. Could this be him? William Howard Russell?

"Abuse me if you will, Thomas — I'm familiar with all the slurs you can level against me."

"No slurs," someone interrupted.

The officer dabbed his lips with a napkin and spoke over him. "I'd hardly say it's a slur to point out that your croaking —"

"Croaking! Is it croaking to state the facts?"

"The facts —" The man wafted his hand. "What on earth are *facts*?"

Russell speared a duck wing and jabbed it at the man. But at that moment, a sergeant took out a small trumpet and began playing it, and everyone fell silent. It was a mournful tune, and Toby found himself beginning to cry.

The room swirled around him, his brother's arm around Dash, Dash's arm around Stella, all these men swaying backward and forward. All of these *friends*. He was alone in the corner. Hopelessness overwhelmed him.

Facts, he thought.

All of history is fiction.

He looked at his brother, and the small patch of rug might have been a ravine between them. He did not know how to make it right, how to find his way out of the dark and lonely maze he was trapped inside.

NELL

Once Nell has been in London for another month, Jasper begins to offer private audiences at houses in Mayfair and Chelsea. A duke writes to her, begging for a lock of her hair. She is sent lavish gifts — silver necklaces, posies, bottles of perfume, a fine champagne with four crystal glasses *shaped from the breasts of Marie Antoinette.*

One evening, Jasper asks Toby to drive Stella and Nell to a party in Knightsbridge. It is almost midnight when they leave the pleasure gardens. Toby sits on the box seat, picks at the varnish while Nell climbs inside. It is only Jasper who watches her, Jasper who touches her wrist for too long when he helps her from the carriage an hour later. He adjusts the smaller feather-and-wire wings that she wears for engagements like this.

The apartment looks identical to those she has visited recently, like an elaborately iced cake. Robin's egg–blue walls, white plastering, a parade of tinseled butlers and tiny morsels of food. Crab on toast and parfaits and miniature meringues, whose names Nell only knows because they are announced to her.

When they walk in, the baron claps his hands, his blubbery lips black with wine. "Here are the wonders! Here they are!"

Everything is pink, from the food to the candles and finger bowls. A salmon is exposed on the table, scaled with sliced beetroot. Ladies help themselves to its soft flesh, knives grazing tiny bones.

Nell tightens her grip on Stella's hand, stumbles forward. Eyes on her, fingers pointing, gasps.

"We had the little monster here," one of the men says. "Tom Thumb. We threatened to bake him inside a pie, even wrestled him down to the scullery." He laughs heartily, and his hands rest on Nell's bare arm, his stubbled cheek pressing against her ear. Stella steps between them.

Over the hours they spend there, titles are dropped like loose hairs — the Duke of Belford, the Duchess of Kinnear, Baroness Rothschild — but they mean nothing to Nell. Stella slips knickknacks into a little bag, and Nell shields her from view. A miniature clock, sugar tongs, a gilded fan, which they'll sell at a rag-and-bone shop tomorrow. "I snatches whatever I sees," Stella whispers and winks.

A woman sitting on a chaise longue snaps her fingers. "Come," she says. "Or ought I whistle for them? You always have such exquisite *lusus naturae* at your parties, Coles."

"I'd like to strangle her with her own pearls," Stella whispers.

The woman clicks again. "Someone fetch Alice more wine, she looks quite out of sorts. Coles, Your Grace, your daughter —"

A pale woman sinks back against the cushions.

Stella inhales sharply.

"It must be the fright of these creatures," a gentleman says.

"There, my sweet Alice, there." A woman fans her cheek.

"Pigs, aren't they?" Nell whispers, but Stella pulls her arm free, hurries across the room, almost tripping over a low table.

"Please excuse me —"

In the hallway, Nell calls after her. "Wait!"

Stella takes the stairs two at a time. Nell follows. They never leave each other alone, especially not when the men are this drunk.

"What's the matter? What is it?"

Stella pulls her into a small room. It is

dark, no candles burning.

"They're fools," Nell says. "Don't you always say not to heed them?"

"It isn't that," Stella says. "As if I'd give a fig for what they say about me." She dabs under her eyes as if expecting to find tears there.

If this were Peggy or Brunette, Nell would wrap her arms around them, would shush them. But Stella is so — *Stella.* She hovers her hand over her shoulder, but Stella knocks her away.

"Don't," she says.

"What happened?"

"That girl," Stella says. "That girl. Her name was Lady Alice Coles."

"Who is she?"

"She was engaged to marry someone I knew. Someone I loved."

"Dash?" Nell asks.

Stella nods. "He was killed when Sevastopol fell."

"Oh."

"He said he'd marry me instead. He said he didn't care for her." She looks up at Nell, and her eyes are brimming with tears. She wipes them away with the back of her hand, slaps her cheek. "Rot, isn't it? Isn't that what men always tell you? That they'll marry you? Perhaps if he'd lived, I'd have realized truths about him that I never knew. He'd never have married such a *freak,* even if I had plucked this out."

Nell stares at her. "Stella —"

"Save me your pity." She pulls at the wisps of her beard. "And I belong to the public, don't I? What business would I have in taking a husband?"

"He might have —"

"You know nothing," Stella snaps. "You're a greenhorn. You're just like Brunette, who believes the world can change. But it's not going to." She looks up. "I thought, once, that I'd have my own show. That *I* could be the showman."

"You could —"

"Don't make me laugh." There is fire in her eyes. "Only men like Jasper hold the reins, and that's the truth. It's only their voices that matter." She leans closer to Nell. "That woman called us *lusus naturae.* I'd wager you don't even know what that means."

Nell blinks back tears. "Please —"

"At first, I thought *lusus* meant *light.* It sounds like it." She pauses. "*Joke.* That's what it means. *A joke, a freak of nature.*" She stands, and there are watery lines tracked through her rouge.

Nell stays in the dark room, her friend's

footsteps thundering away. She kicks at a dresser. She jumps at the sound of it and breathes steadily, trying to calm herself. She slides open the drawer.

Downstairs, somebody is bellowing a poem, a rhyme Jasper adapted from a song composed for Jenny Lind.

All that is monstrous, scaly, strange and
    queer,
Thou hast, O Jasper, brought us here,
Summoned from the womb of earliest
    time
Creatures wingèd, tall, foul and sublime.
Leopard girl and camel, lobster-boy and
    bear,
Monsters spring up, the wolf loves the
    hare.
All brought from thy hand, O thou
    illustrious man,
Now Nellie Moon has joined the caravan.

A roar of laughter, applause.

Who owns me? Nell wonders, hand slipping into the drawer. She remembers what Charlie said, that harm would come to her. She is safe, she tells herself; her life is desirable. Every day, Jasper tells the newspapers more stories about her. She reads how she was hatched from a dragon's egg, spun from

284

moonlight, birthed in a sea of fire and heat. The dull reality of her life — the flower farm and the sea and Charlie — has begun to fog and vanish. Even the truth of how Jasper came across her, the pain of her snatching, is overwritten, a story she cannot tell. *I found her pinching stars from the heavens and extinguishing their tiny fires against her arms.* Jasper has turned her life into his own, his pen distorting her truth. She feels like a pulled flower, its roots severed.

Nell thinks of storming downstairs, smashing the crystal decanters against the wall, upending the table, grinding torn shreds of salmon into the rugs. Would they stare, shriek? How would they tell this story afterward, how would they reshape it? Perhaps they would like it — everything she broke would be replaced with a quick wave of the hand, and she would merely become an anecdote, a tale about a *little monster* and her fit — someone who cannot be controlled or contained. She bows her head. She will not give them the satisfaction.

The drawer creaks. She touches the silks of bloomers, bonnets, and ribbons. Her fingers snag on a small box. It is probably a ring, or a necklace, or money, too great to steal. She fiddles with the clasp. A pocketknife, the handle carved from mother-of-pearl. She flicks out the blade, tests it against her hand.

Before she can change her mind, she slips it into her pocket and runs back downstairs.

Stella acts as if nothing passed between them, as if the scab has already healed and Nell imagined that glimpse of sadness. The dukes and duchesses are drunk, loosened from their stiff poses, as bawdy as rakes and theater girls. A man scorches Nell's arm with a cigar, and Stella seizes it from his plump fist and extinguishes it in his port. Nell expects him to be angry, but he only laughs and leans closer to her. A lady draws out a monkey in a cage, and it chatters, silk leash around its neck. "My darling creature," she says. "Just look at his queer little face."

When the candles are burned to stubs, and dawn is beginning to break, Nell and Stella leave, careering down the marble staircase. "It's a dream," Stella cries, as if she had not just sat in a small, dark room and cried.

"A dream," Nell echoes, and a man chases them, his shirt flapping open. He seizes Stella by the hand.

"Away, beast!" she cries, and he laughs, presses his lips to her hand. Nell pushes him, just gently enough that he will not take offense.

Outside, Jasper and Toby are waiting on the box seat. The man takes a bottle of champagne and smashes it against the wagon, pours it over the backs of the zebras.

"Steady," Jasper says, but he laughs because the man is rich.

Toby looks at Nell, for just a flicker. She longs to reach out, to pull him down to her, to hear his fast breath against her cheek. His lips on her neck, his body curled to meet hers. She wants to knock Jasper from the seat, to ride alongside Toby and feel the gritty London air on her cheeks. But he looks away, his gaze fixed on his shoes.

"Look at me," she shouts, but Stella shushes her. Just as her friend ushers her into the coach, she sees Toby give a small shake of his head.

"Get in," Stella says, giving her a shove. Jasper stares at her, a grin smeared across his face. "And stop bawling like a fox in season. You're drunk."

But Nell slams her hand against the roof, smashing it as hard as she can. Toby does not want her.

"Stop that," Stella says, pulling her hands down. "You need to forget him. And watch yourself."

"Why?"

"If you're stupid enough not to realize, I shan't be the one to tell you."

"What?"

Stella shakes her head, then draws out a rattling bag. "Look what I snatched." She empties out teaspoons and porcelain paperweights and coins.

"Why should I be careful?"

Stella ignores her. She picks up a pair of sugar tongs. "Look what I took," she says.

"Are they silver?"

"I snatches whatever I sees," Stella cries, and she puts her arm around Nell's shoulders. "One day, all this silver will buy me the most magnificent troupe."

Perhaps it is her way of overwriting her upset earlier, and Nell looks at her, decides to play along. "We'll ride in on elephants," she says.

"I'll teach you the trapeze."

"What will we call ourselves?"

The Flying Sisters.

"And we'll belong only to ourselves."

They kick their feet against the padded seats of the carriage, and it is just them inside. Just them as they jolt across the city, past buildings as big and white as the moon. The knot within Nell eases, and they laugh for no reason at all.

JASPER

They thunder toward London Bridge, the wide bellies of the zebras swaying.

Look at me, Nell cried, and Jasper looked at her loosened hair, the edges of tears in her eyes. There was an abandon to her that he had not seen before. He can hear her laughing now inside the carriage. So often, he has found himself on the brink of visiting her wagon at night. And yet, there is something about her that stops him, a quality that resists being pinned down. As if by touching her, he will break her.

It is Stella he always used to visit, but he has skirted her since that night with the ring. He turns it over, the gold dulled. *E. W. D.* Edward William Dashwood. The bruised limbs, the cooling fingers, how he could not slip the ring over the knuckle. He reaches for his brother's arm, squeezes it.

"What is it?" Toby asks, watching the zebras. "What's troubling you?"

Jasper looks at his brother and finds he cannot reply.

Toby pats his arm. "It's the debtor, isn't it?"

"I'll pay him tomorrow."

"How much?"

"A thousand pounds a week." Jasper tries not to notice Toby flinch.

"You aren't worried?"

"No," Jasper says. He taps his foot. "No. My show can only rise."

He knows they are both thinking of their father.

Jasper puts the thought from his mind. After all, he has enough, just enough, to pay the Jackal. In the morning, he will walk to Soho and hand the man the money, as he has done so many times before. The Jackal will flick through the notes, fold them into his pocket, and smile. His teeth, so small in that fleshy face, like lumps of sugar in dough. And then, that green door will close and the sky will swing down to meet him, and Jasper will be safe. Safe, for a little longer.

He wraps his cloak tighter around him and feels the pistol he keeps tucked into his waistcoat. Down, across Westminster Bridge — he darts a look left, then right. They racket past cheap lodging houses, past fake gentlemen in slop-shop clothes. Gin palaces and opium dens, patrons slumped before them. The moon is pinned to the sky like a moth. His brother's leg leans against his own.

Ahead of them, the gates part. Dawn cuts open the sky. A boy runs to meet him, a note in his hand. His face is twisted with . . . what? Panic? Elation?

"What is it?" Jasper asks, and his heart is a weighty thing. *The Jackal,* he thinks — could he have mistaken the date? Could the man want more?

He takes the letter, slits it open with a pocketknife. An unknown crest, thick paper. Neat, looping script. A squeezing in his chest.

"What is it?" Toby asks.

Jasper pauses, tentative, almost afraid to voice it. He coughs. "The Queen wants to see our show." He says it more loudly. "The Queen, Toby. The Queen!"

His brother smiles, and Jasper is brimming with such simple joy that he clasps Toby. He loves this man, loves him as if he were a part of him.

He leaps from the seat, dust rising. "Can you believe it? Can you?" he shouts again. The vindication of knowing he was right to take out the debt — only two months ago he was playing to a small, dirty crowd of shepherds and fishermen! Risk big, win big; and he has won the fattest prize of all.

Jasper thunders the gong, watches as his laborers and performers stumble onto the grass, half-asleep. His body is taut with excitement. They whisper between themselves, wonder what is happening, why they have been woken from their beds. He calls for bottles of wine, orders that bacon is cooked, that a goat is killed and roasted.

He paces up and down, enjoying every eye on him, the tremble in the air. "The Queen," he declares at last. "The Queen will attend our show." Performers grip each other, laugh. Chattering, cheers, Huffen Black thumping his back. A violin starts up. Jasper holds out the letter, shakes it. "It will be the first show she has attended since the death of Prince Albert. My show. Our show."

And as the sun rises and that slanted script blurs with gin and curaçao and champagne, Jasper knows, *knows,* that his fame is assured.

He wakes, dry-mouthed. The wallpaper swings in and out of view. Red and gold and blue. A thousand versions of his face smile back at him. He groans, sits up. He is still dressed in his boots.

The Jackal, he thinks as he staggers to his feet.

It is only then that Jasper remembers the letter, the night of elation, the cups of spirits, how they all danced as the sun rose. The Queen is coming to his show, and yet his heart will not calm. He has the uneasy sensation that her offer will be revoked; that he dreamed it; that it was nothing more than a prank. He fumbles for the letter, reads it more carefully. The soft ply of the paper, that elegant script; it is real. Still, his pulse thunders and his throat feels half-closed. He coughs, spits phlegm into a glass.

You can't do it.

He starts. It is a curious sensation, an unfamiliar one. *Doubt.* He has only ever felt that he has a right to success, to anything he desires. Is this how his brother feels? He laughs drily. Of course he can do it, he thinks, but his mind feels like a room that has not been tidied in months, the surfaces furred with dust. He rubs at his eyes. It must be the payment that is troubling him, the concern at what the Jackal might do. As soon as he's paid the man, his worries will ease. And with that, Jasper dresses, tweaks the tips of his mustache with tallow, and hurries through the gates of the pleasure gardens.

The Queen, he tells himself — soon he will perform before the Queen. It can scarcely be eleven o'clock, the sun not yet peaked. The Thames is the color of tarnished pewter. All about him, butchers whet their blades, and fruit sellers pierce the air with their cries. *Oranges and lemons, oysters, cress cress cress* — everyone fighting, jostling to make themselves seen and heard. He thinks of the woman who wanted a cushion with Nell's face on it, and his breath thickens.

Children watch Jasper, eyes fixed on him as if he is a fish on a line. He should not have worn his leopard-skin britches; he taps his pocket to check the notes are still there. Two children become three, become four, a tangle of gritted hair and filthy limbs. A girl raises her finger and points at him. He is used to being looked at, admired, but this is a gaze which assesses, as if he is a carcass to be carved up, a bankrupt's house to be auctioned off. He pictures them weighing his life in their tiny fists. *How much would such a coat sell for — how much is a life worth?* If they knew he carried a thousand pounds on his person, he'd be killed ten times over.

"Away," he bellows, swiping his cane when a little boy dances closer, but the children only laugh.

The Queen, he tells himself. But last night's joy seems to belong to somebody else.

There are more of them now — ten, twelve — moving like a pack of dogs. They scratch their lice-ridden heads, and he pats the fold of money. It is still there. He shouldn't touch his pocket; it will only draw attention, but only a moment later he finds himself tapping it again.

The children nudge each other, stroke their legs as if imagining that leopard's pelt adorning their own bodies.

There is the Jackal's door ahead, green and freshly painted. He hastens his pace, tells himself not to run. He pictures the man opening the door, those little teeth, Jasper explaining his short breath with a curt laugh. "Of course I wasn't *frightened* of them! I just thought I'd lead them on a merry chase —"

He knocks, sways on his heels. He will make light, too, of the risk of a late payment — *Though if you wish to slay one of my goats tonight, you'd be saving me a task, and I'll never say no to a shilling.* Soon, he will be inside, and safe.

"He ain't there."

He jumps, sees the girl with the wooden-spoon baby, leaning on her crutch. "They don't rise until noon, unless you've an appointment."

Jasper sighs, exasperated. Behind him, the children slouch and whisper, creep closer. He cups his hand and looks through the glass. The shutters are drawn.

He nods at the girl, and then he sets off on his way. On Regent Street, he can hail a cab, shake off the children. He might even duck into a chop-house, wait an hour or so until the Jackal is awake. *Children!* he tells himself with a snort. *Harmless little wretches* — but he remembers the urchins that gathered in Balaklava, how they'd torture an injured Cossack as easily as a tadpole.

He breaks into a slight run. He can hear the patter of bare feet behind him, quick whispering. Sweat spangles his forehead. He touches the notes, then curses. They will know where to stab him, where to grab and steal. What if he didn't sew his pocket tightly enough, and he has already dropped the notes onto the pavement? He would have noticed, surely? He taps his coat again, and the wad feels thick. More children walk toward him, as if to cut him off — he could swear they are the same urchins as before, lank-haired, scratching their fleabites. He stretches out his hand for a cab, but it roars away.

And then, wheeling onto Regent Street, he almost collides with a boy wearing a board around his neck.

"Extraordinary phenomenon! The Greatest Wonder in the World. Pearl, the Girl as White as Snow. Now Exhibiting Alive at Regent Gallery —"

It is the decision of an instant. He ducks into the shop and pays his entrance fee. The children draw to a halt, and it takes all his restraint to stop himself from flashing them a triumphant smile. *Rats,* he thinks. *Penniless wretches.*

He dusts down his jacket. It is a scant crowd, a trio of medical students lunging for each other's noses with their calipers, a few ladies out for an afternoon. He follows them into the next room, and the girl is there, sitting on a podium. She is small even for four. Her eyes are violet-edged, her lashes white, and she wears a dress of dove feathers. It irritates him that she is arrayed like a bird — but really, she's nothing compared to Nell and her great mechanical wings. One of the ladies prods the girl with her parasol, but the child doesn't even blink. The medical students look at her as if they are measuring her for a jar. Her eyes stammer and flicker. He realizes that she is half-blind.

Jasper is glad he didn't buy her. He doubts the Queen would think much of her — he remembers how she condemned the pin-headed Aztecs Maximo and Bartola as horrid *little monstrosities* that *give one the creeps.*

A thought occurs to him. What if she were to condemn Nell? But it is impossible; Nell can only delight. He pictures the Queen's pleasure, bright with wonder, as he presents an array of marvels. His hands, hovering over the lids of imaginary silver cloches. *Your Majesty, I present the Queen of the Moon and Stars.*

If it weren't for the swarm of urchins, he would have left by now. The girl is not particularly remarkable. A crone in a badger hat hands him a pamphlet.

"My daughter," she says.

And if that were the truth, he thinks, eyeing the bashed leather of her cheeks, *she'd* be the wonder, sitting on that podium.

Jasper idly flicks through the handbill. It's the standard second-rate claptrap he usually associates with rural marvels. Birthed from a goose egg (Ha! The old hag contradicted her own literature!), the result of a coupling between a dissolute lord and his

298

pet swan — he yawns, not even bothering to cover his mouth.

If he had the energy for it, he could tell them a thing or two about display. The world is saturated with wonders, these days. Any country maid with a lump or a limp sticks herself in a room at an inn and cries out, *A shilling a view*. And the public are growing tired of it. They need skill, performance, too. They need a showman who can spin a proper story about them. It's no good just to sit there on that chair being swiped at by ladies, or having your toes wrenched by children.

He is about to leave when he hears a voice he recognizes. His agent, Tebbit.

Tebbit is leading a man into the room. Leading — he leans forward — good God, it is Winston. Jasper slips behind a folding screen. He wouldn't be a welcome sight. A few nights ago, his laborers broke into the man's troupe and set loose his zebras. Jasper roared with laughter when he heard the tale.

"She's so newly on my books I haven't calculated her market value," the agent says.

Jasper smirks. Tebbit spouted the same patter a month ago. He just can't shift her, and it's little surprise. The child is as blank as an automaton.

"She's young. Malleable. *Yours.*"

Jasper rolls his eyes.

But Winston seems to be nodding. "Did you know that in some cultures they're known as moon children? Created because their mothers gazed at the night sky for hours during their confinement? I've just the story that could make my name, and hers too. That could, I think, easily eclipse that dreadful hot-air girl."

"No skill in her," the agent agrees.

Jasper touches his neck, finds it hot. *Eclipse,* he thinks. *Eclipse.*

His hard work is not so effortlessly undone. Any fool can see this girl holds little charm.

And yet, what was he thinking only five minutes before? *It isn't the show that counts, but the story you spin.*

What possible narrative could Winston manufacture about this girl? Jasper can think of nothing. Perhaps he means to beat him at his own game, have this child swing from a balloon higher than Nell's — he has the money for it, and thousands to spare!

The girl begins to hum. It is unsettling, like attending a seance with a dud mystic. She is beautiful, he admits, a perfect child. As precious and pearlescent as a shell.

Eclipse.

He's seen it happen before — giants found in distant corners of Scotland, half an inch taller than the current marvel. Trade diverted, halls empty, the only audience a mouse scrabbling across the floor.

"I'll almost certainly take her," the man says. "But let me ponder the sum. I'll have my offer with you by tonight."

Jasper's pamphlet crumples in his fist, the paper torn. He watches Winston leave. Tebbit beams at the crone, balls his fists in delight. Jasper breathes through his nose. He strokes the wad of notes in his pocket.

He has a hundred pounds to spare, on top of the thousand he owes the Jackal. Perhaps Tebbit will take that, and be glad of it.

But what if he asks for more?

Jasper dabs at his forehead. The line, he knows, between success and failure is so thin. Because if Winston does buy the child, the damage might be far worse than one missed payment. Better to renege once more, surely, than to lose everything? The Jackal would understand, if he explained — didn't he say he was a man of business?

Jasper has a small silver knife in his waistcoat. He cuts the stitches of his pocket. The notes are there, thick in his palm. His heart skips. He inches out from behind the screen, pretends he is just entering the room.

"Ah! Tebbit," he calls, and the words slip from his tongue, as smooth as swallowing an oyster. "What a felicitous surprise! I was just visiting the girl, as I mentioned I would, and I find her very much to my liking. I'm to perform before the Queen, as you might have heard. I received a letter late last night."

She costs him a thousand pounds. The agent tells him she will be delivered late that night, after she has attended a soirée at a duke's house. He will not agree to a short-term hire but sells her outright. "Not when there is demand like this. She's yours, or she isn't."

Jasper staggers into the street.

The Queen, he tells himself, but the word sours in his mouth.

He spends a few pennies on port and a hot pie. A woman sidles up to him at the counter, kisses his cheek, her hands hungry for him. When she has gone, he touches his pocket and finds it empty.

TOBY

Toby has pressed his fingers into each flower and vine. He has watched the slow budding of each seedling, each magpie, each leaf, the gradual transformation of his torso. At night, he inspects himself by candlelight, gasping with recollected pain, the skin raised as if insect bitten. A snake wriggles down his calf, its tongue licking his ankle bone. The tattoos stop at his wrists, at the back of his neck, and it is his secret until he decides to reveal himself.

He will no longer be Toby Brown, the dullard brother of Jasper Jupiter, little more than a ballast man. He will be a performer, a living garden, with any history he chooses. He could be a boy who was conceived in a rose bed. The result of a coupling between a woman and a lily, pollen scattered on her skin as she lay naked in a meadow. A child kidnapped by sailors and painted with strange emblems.

He lies on the soiled divan in the shop, wincing with pain, biting hard into a calfskin strap that rests in his mouth. His old leather jerkin is slung over the chair like the discarded shell of another life. He watches a snake in the vivarium, lumpy with a swallowed mouse.

We're brothers, linked together.

He wonders if, somehow, Jasper feels these quick wellings of pain on his own skin. If Jasper looks down at his hips when he is undressing and sees the shadow of a rose blooming there.

"That's you finished," the woman says, standing up. "All done."

Toby thanks her, pays, and dresses quickly, not daring to behold himself, not yet. The bells are tolling two. He must hurry back to feed Grimaldi and prepare the ring for the evening shows.

He limps home, head down, his thighs burning from the sting of the needle. He sees hawkers selling towering stacks of crabs, bawling for attention. Ragged boys turning cartwheels in the hope of a few pennies. Ladies in varnished carriages, paste diamonds glittering on their sleeves like the plumage of a parrot. Everyone is peacocking, fighting to be seen and heard. The thought strikes him as one his brother might

304

have, and a borrowed confidence builds inside him. His fingers linger on his shirt buttons. He twists one, then another, down to his midriff. His shirt billows open. He swings his arms wider. Gazes begin to snag on him. Someone nudges her child and points at him. He feels lit from within. A marvel, a wonder. At school, he hurried with his head lowered, dressed in grays and browns. In the Crimea, he hid behind his photography machine. In the circus, he arranged the scenery, put up fakements. It has always been Jasper blustering forward, Toby trailing behind. He imagines himself on that camel, with that red cape, the crowd stilling —

"Look at him!" someone shouts. "His skin! Did you see?"

He could soar like a kite, turn somersaults in the air. The sunlight catches coach windows, the glinting epaulettes of grooms. A man on his horse slows and stares. Tears prick Toby's eyes. He imagines it is Nell watching him, and desire knocks him so hard that he touches his chest.

When he turns into the pleasure gardens, the benches are still stacked upside down, the grooms lolling on hay bales, smoking thick rolls of the Indian herb.

"What's the matter?" he asks. "The show's in two hours."

Peggy points at Jasper's wagon.

"Is he sick?"

He has the uneasy feeling that he will find Jasper's caravan empty, the man vanished. That his tattoo has performed some kind of magic and written over Jasper's life.

But when Toby knocks, he finds his brother hunched over his desk, his eyes bloodshot. A reek of spirits, of stale bodies.

"What is it?" Toby asks.

Jasper shakes his head, skull rolling loosely on his neck.

"What happened? What about the show?" Toby asks.

A memory flashes — his father stooped over his desk in their cramped, new drawing room in Clapham, his thumbs working his brow like clay.

"I've . . . I've made a frightful mistake." He shields the ledger from Toby.

Toby swallows. "Are you ruined?"

His brother's voice is small. "I don't know." He pauses, draining the last drop of liquid from the bottle. "What will become of me?"

"The Queen," Toby says, desperately. "She's coming to our show. Think of the crowds, the fame, the money —"

"I'm so tired," Jasper says.

When his brother looks at him, the skin is creped about his eyes, his lips downturned. It occurs to Toby that Jasper will die, that his breath will empty as easily as an old dog turning over. He does not know if he could bear his brother's death, if he could live on after him. He clutches Jasper's hand.

"You can't be ruined," Toby says. "Look at everything you've built!"

His brother holds out the ledger for Toby to read.

Rounded zeros. Toby swallows. "There must be a way to trim fat from the show." He studies the page, runs his thumb down the columns. His mind performs clumsy mathematics. He speaks slowly, with more confidence than he feels. "If we can shorten the show, put on a third performance each night, then can't you make up the shortfall in three days?"

"But what if —" Jasper's voice is distant. "You said yourself he's a butcher."

"You haven't paid him today?"

Silence.

Toby closes his eyes. "If you can prove the money's coming, then maybe . . . maybe he'll be generous. What use are you to him if you're dead?" Toby asks, but his heart is pounding. The tendril of a vine is peeping

307

out of his sleeve. He pulls back his hand, but Jasper only stares ahead. He clears his throat. "If you're too tired, I know your show, Jasper. I can be the showman tonight —"

"No," Jasper snaps, and he glares at Toby, breathing hard. There is cruelty in his gaze, a narrowing. "You little imposter."

"It's just —" Toby gestures at the empty bottle of gin, then gives a small shake of his head. "I'm sorry."

"Little imposter," Jasper mutters again, and he picks up the vessel and laughs into it, his voice loud and distorted.

When he leaves, Toby tells Huffen Black to take bread and water to his brother, and he orders the grooms and laborers to ready the show. He watches as the benches are overturned, the zebras let out of their cages. He prepares his photography machine, unrolls the cloudy backdrop. The light is bright enough to lower the exposure time to a few seconds. He calls out to the new performers, photographs them in their costumes, slotting in greasy glass slides one after another. A lobster girl in her wheeled tank, a fat boy, ancient twins, a woman with a curious growth on her ankle who winces with pain. She tells him about her three children, the money she will provide for their schooling.

Already, crowds are forming. He can hear Nell's name murmured, shouted. "Nellie Moon! Give us Nellie Moon." He flinches as he remembers how her chin rested against his shoulder. How she leaped from that rock, and he wanted to reach out and catch her before she hit the surface.

In his wagon, Toby develops the slides in ceramic baths. His fingers seem too big for his hands, and he knocks over bottles, soaks one of the images for too long. He pegs them to the clothesline, palms trembling. Soon, he, too, might shine from the water, wet paper gripped between thumb and forefinger. *"Toby Brown, the Living Canvas."*

He reaches for his book of photographs and flicks through them. Jolly men. Soldiers with flasks of steaming whisky. A man gripping a pair of fresh socks. And then, a skull resting beside a dandelion clock.

After Toby saw the reporter at Stella's Christmas soirée, he began to look out for the man, to *haunt him,* as Jasper said with a laugh. He watched the Irishman playing at cards or sauntering between the tents. He hoped that, if he lingered around him for longer, he might absorb some of his boldness. He watched how soldiers hurled abuse at him, called him *Toad* because of his croaking, but the man did not seem to care. He and Toby were both there with the same task — to report on the war. And yet, Russell's aim was truth, and Toby's was deceit.

All of history is fiction, he thought.

But ever since that Christmas meal, he could no longer hide the fact that each of his photographs told a false story.

One afternoon in early April, he yoked a pair of horses and moved his photography wagon closer to the battle. Along the way, he could hear the groans of choleric men from within their tents, the air reeking of human waste. Already, he was becoming numb to it all, not noticing or caring as he had in the early days. Death was everywhere, suffering and pain a simple fact. He leveled his machine at the scene and ducked behind the cloak.

Camels, he thought, shivering. *We will ride in on two camels with red cloaks on our shoulders.*

He captured a skull with a shred of fabric beside it, half wedged in the mud. A harbor floating with offal and dead dogs.

There will be an elephant called Minnie.

A shattered cartouche.

Our show will be the greatest in the country,

in the world. Toby and Jasper's. The Jupiter Brothers. It will be us together.

He developed the images shakily, saw the truth in the scenes, the abject beauty, how he had pinned pain onto a sheet of card. He felt it again, horror needling between his ribs. It reassured him that he wasn't a monster, stripped of compassion. *This is a record,* he thought, a making of real history.

It was no surprise when Toby handed the officer his photographs a week later, and the man ripped them in two and told him to get out of his damned sight. The strange thing was, as Toby stood there in the honey-eyed light, and a hornet buzzed in time with the military band, he found he did not particularly care.

Crouched in the basket, Toby throws out the bags of ballast, and the balloon lifts slowly. He watches as the ropes binding Nell tighten, and she is hauled up, too, her legs twitching as she finds her balance. The basket rises higher, and when the crowd glimpses Nell, the applause becomes thunderous. He leans over the edge of the basket and begins to nudge the cords that hold her, to swing her back and forth.

She moves as she did in the sea when he first saw her, as if she is only just in control.

She soars across the sky, wings creaking, feet kicking. He nudges the rope farther, and she lets out a *whee* of delight. The crowd gasps, whistles. Perhaps she senses his eyes on her, because she twists her neck to look at him for just a moment. It feels as though a small fish is trapped in his chest, tail beating against his heart. He is emptied by hope, by the impossibility of taking what is Jasper's. If he touched her, it would destroy at least one of them.

Below him, Jasper sings out his patter, and there is only a trace of slurring in his voice. Toby mouths along to every word. "And tonight I — the Prince of Humbug — have presented wonders you never could have imagined —"

Later, when they are pulled down, and the second show is over, and everyone is tired and complaining at being worked to the bone, Toby watches Nell sitting by the fire. She, Stella, Peggy, and Brunette are playing whist, cards smacking down. She glances at him, and there is that look of yearning that he remembers from the first time he saw her.

If she pulled him toward her again, he would not be able to stop himself. She has worked her way under his skin like a knife. The powerlessness is pleasing, as if he has

passed the decision to somebody else entirely.

NELL

When Stella hands her a pot of rum, Nell
shakes her head. She is content merely to
sit by the bonfire and watch as bottles are
handed around, as Violante sings, and the
children fan out the trinkets they have pick-
pocketed. The mood is bright, expectant. In
five days, they will perform before the
Queen, and all their stock will rise a little
higher. The triplets practice their act by the
wagons, spring onto each other's backs,
jump, cartwheel. *Nothing can go wrong,* Jasper has told them, spit gathering in the
corner of his mouth. *Not one mistimed leap.
Not one dropped juggling ball. The show will
be pristine.*

Brunette sits a little apart and, when
Peggy begins to play the fiddle, she clambers
to her feet. Her movements are slow, pained,
her body weighed down with the ache of
growing. Nell looks at the trees, sees Abel
waiting there.

314

Stella raises her head. "Be careful."

Brunette takes her hand, squeezes it, then walks away, limping toward the woodland where the iguanodon bones sit.

"What did you say to her?" Peggy asks, putting down her bow. "If you were being cruel again —"

"Go and boil your head, would you?" Stella snaps, and Nell takes another stick and throws it in the fire.

Stella says quietly, "She married him yesterday."

"Abel?" Nell asks, and she is surprised by her jealousy. "Will she leave the show?"

"Leave?" Stella laughs between her teeth. "Leave the show? Nobody *leaves*. Jasper would find her. She's hardly inconspicuous."

Nell looks at the floor, rolls a painted pine cone under her toes. She wants to ask, *And then what happens?* but she is afraid of the answer.

"Brunette wouldn't be so stupid," Stella says, but she doesn't sound certain.

A wedding, a marriage. Nell tries to picture it — the mildewed stone, the candles wavering in their brackets. In the stories Nell has read, these are moments of joy, the neat resolution to one's life, any difference obliterated by the magic of love. She thinks

315

of Brunette with a dandelion pinned to her frock, two heads taller than the fisherman at her side, wishing not that she would change but that the world would. Simple rings made of tin. The minister stammering through the vows, sneaking glances at the seven-foot bride. A holy sight. *What therefore God hath joined together, let no man put asunder* —

A kiss, where Brunette's dreams should come true, for other people to change themselves and the way they see her. But then stumbling into the gritty air, carriages slowing and fingers pointing. A dawdling return to the show Brunette hates. Could she leave? Would she dare to?

From the corner of her eye, Nell sees Toby glance at her. She cannot bring herself to look at him.

Nell waits until the performers begin to turn in. She walks the empty pleasure gardens alone. The plants are ripe to the point of spoiling: roses brown and crisp and in need of deadheading, damsons turning to mush underfoot. She reaches for a perfect-looking plum, soft and yellow, and turns it over in her fist. It is ripe, ready to eat. A sharp pain in her finger. She cries out, and the wasp crawls, sugar-drunk, from the burrow where it hid itself.

Once she has sucked out the poison, she follows the path back to the wagons. She stops. Brunette is standing beside an oak tree, Abel's forehead pressed to her ribcage. Nell should not pry, but she cannot stop looking. She sneaks closer. Brunette is crying, but the man strokes her back, stands on tiptoe to whisper in her ear. He pulls Brunette's head down to his and kisses her cheek. Nell feels a longing so intense she has to look away.

She tiptoes back down the woodchip paths to the wagons. Something shifts behind her: a laborer. Was he watching her, making sure she didn't escape? Perhaps he, too, was just taking a walk. At the menagerie, the men guarding the animals tip their caps at her, and a monkey beats its chest and shrieks. There are more laborers awake than usual, their eyes on the gates, as if they are expecting something. She treads on a handbill, picks it up. She is at the center of it, beneath Jasper's face.

That girl is her. She has often felt that her life merely drifts along paths set by other people. Everywhere she turns, she is confronted by the dreams of others. Jasper's for a great circus, her brother's for a farmstead in America, Stella's for her own troupe.

317

Nell's own desires have felt trapped, her mind fogged with uncertainty about what she wants and who she is. But as she stares at that picture, her blond hair sailing behind her, the determined arrow of her toes, she is struck by the idea that she is in control of her own life. A wanting for Toby eats away at her, makes her long for his body against hers, a desire so precise and needling.

Toby's wagon is unlit, and yet she has the feeling that he, too, is awake and waiting for something to happen. She hurries to it, raps gently, and whispers, "Are you awake?" He murmurs, and she pushes open the door.

It smells of his photography chemicals. She knocks against a jar, snags herself on the line of hanging images, and curses. Sheets rustle below her.

It is a surprise how fast it happens, how one moment she is her own person, and then she is tangled with another, pulled down beside him, so much touch it is almost unbearable. Hands sliding against her, the rough texture of his back, the muscles rising from each side of his spine. The improbable force of his lips on hers. The power of it; the size of him, a waist so wide she can barely span it with her arms. Her hands nestle in the soft dip above his hips. He winces, as if hurt.

"Nell," he murmurs. "This can't happen — it —"

But he doesn't stop, doesn't pull himself away from her. The clumsiness of him, palms as hard as horn. His cheek, rough against her own. The shock of his hands on her body, slipping between her legs. Her world is shrunk to texture, to the nip of his lip, his answering cry. She pulls him on top of her, pins herself down.

"Nell," he says.

There they are, on the floor of his wagon, the glass bottles rattling. She digs her nails into him as if she is conquering him, testing her power, a fledgling bird assessing the sinews of its new wings. Salt on her tongue, his naked body, his earlobe in her mouth. It is too quick, too fast: time beaten out in swift seconds. She would like to slow each moment to months and years, find a way to live in it.

When Toby stills, she lies beside him, head resting in the crook of his armpit. They are damp with sweat, alive with the knowledge of what they have done.

"I want to show you something," Toby says.

She hears the rattle of matches.

"Please don't," she says.

"It isn't you," Toby says. "I want you to

see me."

Nell blinks in the sudden glare. She gasps, hand to her mouth. His skin is alive. Flowers, vines, fruits, tiny birds with their beaks dipped into peaches. She runs her fingers over him, shocked by its secret, that she has imagined him so differently. He flinches. "Does it hurt?"

"Only here, where it's fresh."

He shows her the most tender patches, where the wound is raised and pink. Violets, like those she used to pick, are pressed into his skin. A whole garden she can trace.

"Has Jasper seen it?" she asks.

A pause. "No."

He cups her chin in his hands and kisses her, and a single tear rolls down his cheek. Outside, the wind twists between the wagons, a shrill whistle.

"Toby?" she says, and he doesn't answer. The sight of his hand, resting on her waist.

At last, there is a finality to the way he holds her, and she knows that she must leave, that it is late and they cannot risk Jasper finding them. There is a small commotion outside, and it is a surprise to remember that the world exists apart from them. She closes the door behind her. Smoke from the yard fills her lungs, and she breathes in that dark, damp air. A noise, a cart arriving.

"What's happening?" she asks a laborer. It is difficult to see, the moon choked by fog.

"New performer," the man says, nodding at the cart. "Jasper's newest purchase."

Many new acts have arrived in the last weeks, the camp swelling with fresh wagons and the litter of juggling apples. She squints to see the latest addition. A tiny girl crawls out from the back of the cart, her feet feeling for the ground. When the laborer swings a lantern closer to her face, Nell sees that her skin is as pale as the underbelly of a fish. The girl cowers at the sudden light, her gray eyes skittering from side to side. She bites on her lip, the toes of her shoes turned inward.

"She's half-blind," the laborer says.

Nell thinks of the wagon, the hands that had grappled her, and she touches her cheekbone where her father hit her. She had wept and railed, clawed at the door, her sobs coming so fast she could barely breathe. And yet this girl is so still and so calm. She merely stands and waits, as if this is what she expects from life — to be bought, haggled over and sold.

"She can bed in with the triplets," the laborer says.

"Wait."

Nell doesn't know why she does it. She

steps forward and takes the child's hand. She assumes she will pull away, but instead the girl reaches up her arms. Nell lifts her. She is as light as a pail of milk. She nestles against her, wraps her fists around one of Nell's plaits. Her breath is fast and rasping.

"What's your name?" Nell asks.

The girl is silent.

"I called her Pearl," a woman says, and Nell notices her for the first time. She wears a tatty badger hat, the tail falling down her back like matted hair. "Here's her clothes. Her feathers." The woman moves forward, and Pearl shrinks into Nell's chest. "Ain't you going to say good-bye to your own mother?"

The child's breath quickens, her fingers clutching tighter at Nell's hair.

Nell walks past the woman as if she does not see her.

"A very nice farewell," the woman shouts after her. "Very nice indeed."

Nell nudges open her wagon door. The child has attached herself like a limpet and can barely be prized free. "There," Nell says, propping her on the bed. What is she supposed to do with an infant?

"You're only sleeping here tonight," she warns, but the girl is already settled on her mattress, pale gray eyes blinking back at her.

JASPER

What is he supposed to do with her? A timid little child? He hears the iron clatter of the cart, the old crone croaking, *A very nice farewell. Very nice indeed.* Jasper shuts his eyes, winces at the memory of that gallery. Those thick, soiled notes, the agent's toothy smile, the cooling in his belly as he knew, even then, that he shouldn't have bought the girl. What could Winston have been planning for her? A cygnet, a moon-gazer, with wings like Nell's? A spirit — the mystic at a seance? But the child, he knows, would weep if attached to pulleys, would stammer and cower if placed in a small dark room with a glass ball and a wall of ectoplasm. Perhaps he could seat her on a podium near the caged animals — but he shakes his head, frowns. His show marries human wonders with the skill of performance; he might as well give it all up and own a tattered shopfront in Whitechapel!

Jasper rasps a hand over his chin, tries to silence the worries that snap at him.

A mistake, the voice murmurs. *Buying the child was a mistake —*

Or is his mistake that he has no plan for her, that he cannot see her potential? Winston had a plan for her; Winston saw a way to raise his own name with hers.

A day of gin has left Jasper's throat dry and tender, his stomach roiling with bad meat. *It's only a thousand pounds,* he tells himself, but he knows it is more than that, that one poor decision might lead to another. He knows, too, that his payment is a day late, and his coffers are almost empty. Should he write to the Jackal, appear at his door, beg? If he showed him the letter from the Queen, then surely the man would understand, would see he was a fine prospect?

He stretches, joints clicking, laughs at himself with a short bark. He will decide what to do with the child in a week; until then, he has greater things to concern him. The Queen is coming to his show, and he is wasting his time worrying over a few lost pounds, over a foolish little girl. He touches his heart as if to unknot the strings that tighten around it. A month ago, he would have sought out Stella, laughed with her.

He taps his pocket, the ring inside. When she saw it that night, she must only have glimpsed it in the half-light; could she have known for certain it was Dash's? Perhaps she lies on her mattress each evening and wonders why he no longer visits her. He will seek her out now, spend himself. It has been too long since he felt that heady relief.

He pulls on a cloak and hurries down the rows of wagons. A groom presses himself out of Jasper's way. A child drops his juggling balls in alarm.

He does not knock on Stella's door but pushes it open. Silence.

"Who's that?" She rolls over, blinks. A candle is still burning in its bracket.

"It's me," he says. He waits for a look of pleased recognition to pass across her face; for her hand on his, pulling him down to her. But she twists the coverlet tighter about her chin and sits up. Her beard catches the light.

"I missed you," he says, taking a step toward her.

He imagines her arms rising to meet him, the warmth of her. She will remind him of his brilliance and hold him as she once held his friend. She will calm him, soothe him.

"Stella?" he whispers.

Her voice is so low he cannot catch her words.

"What?"

"I said, what did you do to Dash?"

"To Dash?"

His friend's name, in their mouths.

"You have his ring."

Jasper has thought about his answer carefully, and the words are as sweet and easy as every story he has ever spun. "Oh, the *ring*. We gambled the night before Sevastopol fell, and I won it off him."

"Liar," Stella says, and her voice is quiet and laced with venom. "Liar. He'd never have given it away."

He blinks. He cannot stand here and argue with her. And what is he to tell her? The truth is, there is no simple answer; he could not say for certain if Dash fell or was killed. He could not say. Jasper opens and closes his mouth, feels a weakening within himself, as if his bones are soft and easily bruised.

So often, he has asked himself what he could have done to stop what happened, if he could have predicted it and intervened. For as long as he can remember, he has secretly provoked his brother's envy. If Toby is jealous of him, then his life is worth something. There were times in the Crimea when he felt so aimless, so cold and empty, when he was haunted by the cut and slump of bodies. But his life brightened when he saw it through Toby's eyes. His growing fame in battle, his gleaming uniform, his friend. Perhaps he teased Toby with Dash; perhaps he needed his brother to be jealous of him. And this is what it has always come back to, every night he has pondered it: Jasper should have known how far Toby would go to make his voice heard, to make himself seen. If Jasper had thought more carefully, he'd have remembered a different day, finding his microscope missing, a small shard of glass glinting between the floorboards. He was confused at first, could not believe that his gentle brother could exert such violence, that he could wreck what was not his.

"I want you to leave," Stella says, each word a quiet stab.

There is nothing for it. Jasper stumbles back down the steps, back between the rows of wagons. Ahead, there is a scuffling, two laborers beside his wagon.

"What is it?" he barks. "What are you looking at?"

They hold out their hands to stop him, but it is too late. He trips on something hard and sticky, rears back. A stench assaults him. How could this happen when he has been gone for only five minutes — how is this possible? The pig's head glints in the lamplight. He steps closer. It is rotten, maggots pulsing through gray flesh. A gold coin is wedged between its teeth.

The next morning, Jasper is determined that things will be different. He will issue commands, repaint the wagons, instruct Brunette to stitch new costumes. He will order in great tubs of macassar oil to brush into the camels and zebras. He will have a bigger curtain made up, stitched from the same stars and moons that dapple Nell's doublet. "Jasper Jupiter's Circus of Wonders," it will read, and each letter will be the height of Brunette. Yesterday was a momentary lapse, a mere slip; after all, he is not an automaton. He bashes a drum and walks between the caravans. "Up, up, up!" he shouts.

Performers stumble from their wagons, stretch. He stalks up and down. Every eye is on him. He can do this, he tells himself; he *can do it*. But the world feels ragged edged, as if his lips are forming bubbles not words, as if his feet are floating on the ground and nobody can see him.

He makes them rehearse the show from the beginning, even though they are tired, even though they will perform before the crowds in only six hours. "In four days, the Queen will see our show. It must be perfect. It must be pristine. Not a duff note, not a dropped ball — this is my moment, *our* moment. The Queen must be spellbound, astonished, stunned with wonder!"

He notices, briefly, that Pearl is not there, that somebody must be keeping her out of sight, and he is glad of it. He makes Stella warble on the trapeze until her voice croaks, and he does not care if she stares at him sullenly. The lobster girl sculls in her tank with her breathing tube, underwater for so long that her skin crinkles. Through it all, Jasper narrows his eyes, asks himself, *Is this any good?* He worries that he is too close to his show, that he has lost any ability to judge it. *The hot-air girl.* If anyone can discern true novelty, it is the Queen, the *freak fancier* herself.

He does not care if they complain or cry or wince. He has given them enough. He thinks of all the wonders that have ever lived before, over hundreds and hundreds of years — the giants, skulls split by their growing bones; the dwarfs, kept in birdcages in royal menageries; the bear-children, baited and stoned in their villages. So many babies just left out in the cold to die. *He* has given all these people a home, board, pay. *He* has given them a platform, a means to raise themselves from a life of ridicule and exclusion. *He* has taught them skills so they don't just rot on podiums as mere spectacles.

"Where's Brunette?" Jasper demands, looking around him. "This is her cue." He pulls back the curtain. "I said, where is Brunette? She'd better not be lying in bed with a sore head again. Fetch her, somebody —"

A shuffling, a rustling of papers, the women drawing themselves away. Nell, Stella, Peggy. He rubs at a patch of sunburn on his neck.

"Is she asleep? Sick? Where is she?"

Nobody will meet his eye. The whip is tight in his hand. A laborer moves forward. It is Danny, the boy he once beat for escaping. "We couldn't find her —"

"Couldn't find her? A seven-foot woman! She's hardly invisible."

The man twists his cap. "I think she's gone. Run."

Jasper stares at him. "How long have you known?"

Nobody speaks. He hears only the squeal of carriage wheels on the streets outside, the creaking of the grandstand in the breeze.

His voice, loud, shattering. "I said, how

long have you known?"

"Since this morning, when you summoned —"

"This morning! She could be halfway to Southampton by now!"

He seizes Danny, wrenches him forward by the shirt. The man falls to the floor. The other laborers pull back, form a wide arc around him. He brings the whip down on the earth with a crack. The ground flinches, dust sent up like smoke. The horizon seesaws, his hands trembling with a violence he cannot swallow. His arm moves with the focus of an anvil, up and down, as smooth as if the whip is an extension of his own arm. The creak of flesh, a suppressed cry from the man, gasps around him. Jasper longs to be back in the Crimea, where anything could happen, where men were killed with the ease of twitching a small nub of metal, where Dash patted him on the shoulder, and they set fire to houses and ran through the hillsides, bags of loot bouncing across their backs, and their kinship was life, breath, everything to him.

Arms bind him, the whip torn from his hand. He writhes, turns, his mouth in a snarl, ready to raise his fist to the man who has dared to intervene. His brother stares back at him. Jasper's hand drops to his side.

He cannot believe it. He staggers, rights himself. Sweat traces a path down his nose, along his spine, and he tries to regain his power, to locate his voice once more. He takes a breath.

"Find her!" he bellows. "Find her!"

They edge back, away from Jasper, his anger burning a fierce ring around him. Everyone moves with steady purpose: to wash the animals, to paint the wagons, to polish the wooden benches, readying the show for the Queen, keeping out of Jasper's path.

"Where did she go?" Nell whispers to Peggy as they cross the yard.

Peggy shrugs.

"What will Jasper do if he finds her?"

"I don't know," Peggy says quietly. "Abel was from a small fishing village. Perhaps they'll find a quiet place, out of the way. They might be lucky." The little woman reaches for a broomstick, dislodging it from its hook with a poker. She fills a bucket, begins sluicing down the paving slabs. "Do something," she hisses, kicking a chicken bone into the grass. "Look busy. When he's in this temper —"

Huffen Black hands Nell a brush and a

pot of red pigment, and she begins to paint the yokes of the wagons, the window frames. She watches for Toby from the corner of her eye, sees him unrolling a new backdrop by his photography machine. Beneath that shirt, he has a whole garden painted across his body. Memories hit her like a kick between her legs. His hand on her thigh. The snag of his teeth against her lip. She does not dare look at him; what if he ignores her again? She cannot bear to feel that small ember of hope peter out for a second time. She tries to concentrate on the easy wash of paint, on Jasper's shouting.

"The giant hunt is beginning," he bellows, lurching between them, and Nell stoops over her work, eyes down. She wonders if he is drunk, or if it is just the excitement of fury. His voice has an edge that Nell does not recognize: a panic. "I'll find her. I'll haul her back like a dog. I'll see to it that she never works for another showman again." He calls for advertisements, rewards, bounties; Nell sees him stabbing his finger at his press agents, boasting of towering stacks of money.

Someone is close behind her; she jumps, expecting Jasper, expecting a command, a rebuke. She puts her hand to her chest, but it still hammers. Her palms are hot.

"You frightened me," she says.

Toby does not speak, does not even smile, just looks at her in the way he did on that first day, as if he is committing her to memory.

"What is it?" Nell asks, and the relief of knowing he wants her is enough to make her laugh, a *tick-tock* at the back of her throat. She runs a thumb over the flaking paint, the brush slippery in her hand.

"He'll see us," she says, her voice rising. "You should go —"

He takes a step forward. She almost moves back, her head filled with distant thoughts. The memory of his naked body, the thrill of her own daring. His hands move across her wrist, hold it. He must be able to feel her pulse racketing there. She wants to speak, to break the silence, to quiet the stabbing in the basin of her belly. His thumb tests the soft skin between her fingers.

"I keep making mistakes," he says. "I can't think."

She is already hungry for more, for whispered promises like Abel passed to Brunette, for her own life to follow the pattern of the romances she has read.

"I can hear him," she says more urgently, and Toby steps back.

Nell breathes out, a slow gust.

They look at each other for longer than is comfortable. His face is so soft and blunt, as if somebody has polished the edges from him. Jasper rounds the corner. Abruptly, she dips her brush in the paint. The shock of the red smear on the old window frame. She hears Toby move back. She finds she is shaking, the horizon unreal, like a glass tipped over.

There is stew for lunch, a viscous gravy swimming with chunks of fat. Nell takes a bowl and carries it to her wagon. The little girl is asleep on the bed, her thumb in her mouth, white hair scattered across the pillow. She stirs at the noise, stares wildly about her.

"Shh," Nell says, sitting down beside her. She strokes her hand, and the child stills, the soughing of her breath like that of a small animal. It stirs something in Nell, something primal, an urge to protect. This fragile child, like a porcelain cup that is so easily broken. She thinks of herself at this age, her imaginary underwater kingdoms of pearls and shells, feasts and companions and dancing.

"Will I have to wear my feathers soon?" the girl asks.

"You're to stay in here for now," Nell says,

and it occurs to her that she must keep the child away from Jasper, must hope he forgets her. "Or close by the wagon. I brought you these marbles." She holds out her hand, and the child's brow is furrowed with the effort of trying to see. Nell takes the girl's palm and closes it over the smallest marble. Pearl laughs, passing the glass bead between her palms.

"Marble," the girl whispers. "Marble."

Outside, she hears Jasper shouting. "I said to clean those lions, not dust them like damned knickknacks!" Nell wonders how long she has until he misses her, until he notices that Pearl is not amid the troupe.

Soon, the sun will set, and Nell will be tied into her ropes, the harness reaching under her belly, thighs, and shoulders. A thrill runs through her, the thought that soon it will be the Queen herself who casts her eye over her, who watches her flying across the sky. She longs, suddenly, for that blind moment in the air when her mind empties, as she flies, drunk on applause. The burn of a thousand faces turned toward her, a reassurance that she is worth something.

"Do you like stories?" Nell asks, and the child nods. Nell picks up the book of fairy tales, weighs it in her hand. She remembers Charlie's wafting hands, trying to fix her, to make her ordinary. She puts it back, takes a breath. Instead, she tells Pearl about a mermaid with a blue-scaled tail. "Her tail was so beautiful," she whispers, "that if men caught her, they'd dry her out and place her behind a sheet of glass, and thousands of strangers would pay to see her." She tells her how the mermaid swam in the deep waters where nobody could find her. "A little like you in this wagon," she says. Pearl smiles, and Nell carries on, explains how a prince's ship was blown off course, and he fell in love with her. He longed for his own tail so much that he visited a witch who ripped his legs from his body and stitched on fish scales with a sharp needle.

"Did it hurt?" Pearl asks, wide-eyed.

"Oh, very, very much," Nell says, and the child grins in delight.

"But when the mermaid saw him, flailing through the water with his silly mackerel tail, she laughed at him and swam away."

Pearl giggles, a tentative exhalation. She looks at Nell as if to check whether this is allowed, that this is the right response. For the first time, Nell understands what was taken away from her when her mother died, what she didn't know she'd lost.

This child, Nell knows, can never be safe. Jasper bought her. To him, she is nothing more than a novelty to be traded. And yet, Nell realizes, the same could be said of her.

"And now, we bring you Nellie Moon, the eighth wonder of the world, a marvelous sight who will soon be soaring before the eyes of the Queen herself —"

There is that jolt, her legs a little too high, a struggle to find balance. Her belly stirs as she swings. She can smell the burnt sugar of toffee apples, the reek of animals kept too close together.

Nell hears the racket of applause as she is lifted. The approval of the crowds pulls on her, as strong as opium. But tonight, something shifts; perhaps it is the thought of the child sitting in the wagon with her little glass marbles, of Toby's hand on hers, of Brunette, hiding in the countryside. A blueness settles over her. She can no longer spy faces in the roiling mass. The crowd roars as one, its thousand limbs flailing, eyes devouring her. She imagines them with glinting cutlery, carefully filleting her, sucking her bones until there is nothing left.

What if she slips before the Queen? What if she cannot find that steady balance, if her ropes tangle? What if she falls that night? She pictures it with the clarity of prophecy. All it would take is one bad knot for the bags of ballast to shift. The sudden rush of air, the iron clatter of her wings, the Queen watching with her hand over her mouth. And her name, blazoned on newspapers, whispered across firesides, savored and turned over like sweetmeats.

Did you hear how she died —
Did you hear, Nellie Moon —
Did you hear —
Did you hear —
Did you hear —

To steady herself, she looks up at Toby, leaning over the basket. Love hits her with the buzz of performance, a longing to carve out a small space with this man, a place that is *theirs*. A child; Pearl with them too. She sees the curve of Jasper's nose in his, the likeness of their too-close eyes. It only excites her. Jasper took her from her own brother, and now she is doing the same to him.

TOBY

On the day before the Queen's visit, Toby is woken at eight o'clock in the morning. The fakements shine like wet rain. Newly painted wagons. Buffed pathways. Jasper no longer sends the performers to lunches in private apartments, but holds everybody back, allowing only Toby to leave to deliver the Jackal his late sum. As soon as he returns, there is more to be done, more orders given.

Toby does as his brother commands, and yet he finds his aches are gone as he lifts and saws and ferries. The Queen's arrival means little to him; she will not see *him* perform. Instead, Nell occupies his thoughts so absolutely that he wonders if he has any life left of his own. Each night, she sneaks into his wagon, fingers tiptoeing across his skin. They read together, a candle balanced on Nell's chest, pages shuffling like feathers. Their love is sometimes quiet, sometimes furious; sometimes he nurses a bleeding lip, a scratch down his back. In the books they read, love recurs again and again. On the pages it seems amplified, predictable. But what he feels exists outside language. He senses a kinship in each story, but a distance, too, as if his own experience is unique and he is the first person ever to feel this way. When he wakes up and finds that Nell has returned to Pearl in her own wagon, he stares at himself in the mirror. Writhing vines, yellow snapdragons, a striped snake twisting up his arm.

Small things move him. A flower, half trodden. The way the light falls on a chipped teacup. A pristine imperfection he never noticed before. When he lies on his mattress and wavers between sleep and waking, he imagines a thatched cottage with a blue door. It is surrounded by forest, strawberries in wild beds, chickens in the yard. Nell stands by the hearth, children tripping about his feet. "Lift us, Papa," they beg, and he spins them round and round until they cry out.

But sometimes, his joy curdles. As her lips linger on his cheek, he imagines her discovering what he has done, and his breath catches in his chest. He finds himself unable to look at Stella, an understanding dawning on him of what Dash's loss might have meant to her, what he himself might have caused.

"What is it?" Nell asks, the night before the Queen's arrival, and Toby merely shakes his head. She is weary from the show, her shoulder blades cut from the wings. He kisses them, inhales the meaty scent of ointment.

"Something's the matter," she says.

He wants to tell her about the cottage, the future he hopes will be theirs. But he is afraid she will find him possessive, that he will realize his affection is stronger than hers. "I just had a foolish idea," he says.

"Oh?"

Falteringly, he tells her about the blue door, the brick hearth, a forest where nobody could find them. She does not speak for a while.

"It sounds like a fairy tale. A girl shut away."

"You won't be shut away," he says.

"And what about Pearl?"

He pauses, thinks of the girl they keep out of Jasper's sight. He likes her, of course he does. But he knows, as Nell must, too, that with no purpose in the show, Jasper will sell her on. How can Toby tell Nell, without sounding callous, that she must not grow too attached to the child, that it is cruel, too, to allow the girl to depend on her?

"Pearl," he repeats.

"She'd have to be there too. In our forest prison."

He forces a laugh. "If not the cottage, how do you want the story" — he cannot bring himself to say *us* — "to end?"

"Stella might want me in her troupe."

She is making light of it. Toby turns into the pillow to hide his disappointment, his shame at wanting too much. Nell wraps her arms around him, tells him she's sorry, and for a moment he feels moored. Her hands map his back, the vines that are no longer raised and swollen, the bird on his shoulder. Excitement stirs in him, and he reaches for her, astonished by his power to please, to give pleasure. A momentum builds in him, an unsettling thought that he could not be without her, that his life meant nothing before she arrived in it. He shuts his eyes to close it off, hates her for how cleanly she has undone him.

As they lie there, he thinks of the city, spread out around them. Tens of thousands of lives being eked out. Mudlarkers on the riverbank, stumbling across a gold ring once shaped in a Roman smithy. Old men breathing their last, girls frying silver herrings on the hearth. Nell turns a kiss to a bite, and

344

he pushes himself deeper into her. A city teeming with pain, with joy, with dark and light. Lives burning themselves out.

Soon, Nell will be gone, back to the little girl, a child she fills with stories in which girls like Pearl are heroines; where children with pale skin or hunchbacks or birthmarks are not to be feared or transformed.

And then they hear it, Jasper calling Toby's name. They still, and he puts his finger to her lips. He does not know what his brother might do if he found them together. A few weeks ago, he is certain his brother would have read it on his face. Now, he brims with secrets his brother has not discerned. Nell's love, his painted skin. Either Toby has found a way to make himself opaque to Jasper, or his brother's grip is loosening.

"I'll be a moment," Toby calls to Jasper.

He does not wait to see Nell's expression, to understand if she minds. He pulls on his shirt and trousers, leaves Nell lying on the mattress, her face in the pillow.

"I'm in need of a drink," Jasper says when he sees him.

"I'm tired," Toby begins, but Jasper is already leading him toward his wagon, and Toby trots to keep up with him. Toby sees how intently the grooms watch his brother as he passes them, bodies curled forward like question marks, how eagerly they want his approval. How must it feel, to hold people spellbound like that? Toby shifts his sleeve just a little. The pink edge of a flower. He imagines it is he who feels the attention of the troupe, he who surveys a world that he alone has built. Many think it is easy to grow a business, that you need only capital. They do not understand, as he and Jasper do, the difficulty of managing an operation of this scale. The careful planning, the risk, the fear every day of disaster. Stands toppling like those that killed Pablo Fanque's own wife. Rampaging fires that turn a lifetime's work to ash. Performers slipping and plummeting to their deaths.

"Two fingers of gin?" Jasper asks, and Toby nods, settling into the chair in the corner of Jasper's caravan. They clink glasses. "I won't be able to sleep tonight. I know I won't." Jasper fans himself. "It's hot. It reminds me of that humid weather before the bombardment. That anticipation." He sits back, lights a cigar.

Is Jasper toying with him, reminding him of what he did? Toby takes a long gulp of gin. "Yes," Toby agrees. "Too hot to sleep."

"I lived for those days, you know," Jasper says.

"I know."

"Sometimes I miss the fields. We were supposed to have been miserable there, but I wasn't." He squares an invisible rifle to his shoulder, aims it at Toby, and pretends to fire. "I knew I was fighting for each man beside me. It felt good. Important. You liked it, too, I remember."

Toby cannot bring himself to agree. There are times when he wonders if his brother lived through a different war; if he had a different childhood too. Jasper has retold everything, obscured small betrayals, taken snippets of their lives and sewn the wrong flesh together. It has made Toby question whether his own memory can be trusted, if his way of seeing the world is faulty. Perhaps it is easier this way, pretending that life is rosier than it is, that theirs has always been a relationship of contented equality, that Toby was happy. But still, it makes him feel as if he is being silenced, overwritten — *what happened to our circus,* he wants to ask, *the show we would own together?* But he cannot admit one truth without admitting all of them. The microscope shattered. Dash, his body broken.

All of history is fiction, Toby thinks.

His brother reaches for his hand and squeezes it. His nails cut in. "The show will be a triumph, won't it?"

"Of course," Toby says. "You always are."

"There'll be no rampaging lionesses."

"Not a single one."

Jasper smiles at him.

Toby could unbutton his shirt now and show him his body. He could stand before him, a living garden. But what would Jasper say? Would he shout at him, throw him from the wagon? Would he smile, clap his hands? He pulls his sleeves over his thumbs, touches his collar to check it is high enough.

"I was thinking about the girl," Jasper says.

"Nell?"

A cloud passes across Jasper's face. "No. Not Nell. Pearl."

Toby's heart scuds. "You aren't thinking of selling her?"

"I'll wait until my success is assured. Maybe in a few weeks. By then, I'll be so renowned, I could risk selling her to Winston."

"She can't stay?"

Jasper laughs. "Don't be absurd. She cost me a thousand pounds."

Toby's mouth falls open. "What?"

"I know. I know." Jasper takes a drink. "It was an impetuous decision. But soon, I hope to scrape it back. Winston wants her, after all."

Toby nods. He bites the inside of his

cheek. The reek of gin makes him queasy.

"Drink up," Jasper says, but his own drink is untouched and his hand trembles.

"Tomorrow will run like clockwork."

Jasper pulls a face. "I don't know."

"It *will*. It always does."

They sit there, and the silence is warming. Eventually, Toby stretches and says he needs to sleep. He walks to the menagerie to check the animals are shuttered up for the night. When he reaches the cage in the corner, he finds the wolf whining.

Happy Families.

The hare must be hiding in the straw. But when the wolf stalks to the back of the cage, its yellow eyes narrowing in the lamplight, Toby sees the white curve of bone. A tiny skull, picked clean.

JASPER

Jasper wakes early, surprised that he managed to sleep at all. He reaches for his camel-skin boots and begins polishing them. He dusts his cap, inspects his glittering red tailcoat for any loose buttons. He is certain that the Queen will summon him to Buckingham Palace afterward. As his hand glides over each pin, he practices quips he might deploy. "Of course, I am sure my performing poodles make far fewer messes than yours —" A wink at her lords-in-waiting. He mouths the words in front of his mirror, then crumples his face.

Weak.

Or, perhaps, with a wry little look, "All my acts are genuine, unlike Winston who'd put a smoked herring in his waistcoat and call himself a mermaid."

He frowns. Something will come to him in the moment. He buckles his shoes and imagines strolling the same corridors trodden by pinheaded people, by Aztecs and giants and dwarfs, and all their showmen. He has read so much about the Queen's Picture Gallery that he has already imagined himself inside it. The murals, the silk-covered divans, and her spaniel against whom Charles Stratton drew his sword and pretended to duel. When Jasper moves to put on his shirt, he finds a rash on the insides of his elbows.

In the mirror, his face is ghostly. He pastes it with white lead, rouges his lips with dyed whale fat. It clags between his fingers, a fishy scent. He takes a quick sip of gin, and it steadies him.

It is scarcely light. Outside, the trees are bickering, but no rain drums the roof. He sits on the steps of his wagon. Nothing else stirs, not even the canary. In an hour, the barrow boys will begin rounding up the messes spilled by the pleasure gardens the evening before — pools of vomit, lost petticoats, beef and chicken bones. They will scrub the paths with buckets of water.

He stretches, sighs. The dew shines in perfect little globes. He picks a blade of grass, drowsed forward with the weight of its droplet. He touches his finger to it, watches it break.

This is his day, the moment when his

name will rise higher than ever before.

All morning, Jasper buries himself in preparations, bellows at the grooms to muck out the cages, to buff shoes and buckles and toppers until they shine like mirrors. He wheedles and threatens, his whip flicking at his side, longing to give a beating. But everything is done as he commands; the tack is as clean as if freshly bought, the petals from hydrangeas scattered on the paths to greet the little Queen's feet.

The day scarcely seems to turn; it feels as if it is nine o'clock forever. He watches the thickening clouds and prays the rains will wait. He bites his fingernails until it is painful to hold the whip, instructs his press agents with last-minute requests for tomorrow's broadsheets.

"You must say my name until they are sick of writing it. *Jasper Jupiter.*" He taps his temple in time to it. "Jasper Jupiter, Jasper Jupiter. Crimean hero, circus owner, it must be *me* at the heart of it," and they nod, pens scribbling. "All my acts are my own invention."

In the midafternoon, he gathers his troupe in a semicircle, assumes his place in the middle of them.

"We have the finest show in the country," Jasper says. "*I* know it. *You* know it. And soon the Queen will know it too. Every night, we soar. Every night, the audiences grow."

He makes them laugh, and Jasper sees how his brother watches him, admiration in his eyes. Even the animals, the birds, the rustling trees, seem to fall into silence.

"I've consulted meteorologists at Greenwich. Rain is blustering in, but we might be fortunate. We must pray that it holds off," Jasper says, and they all look up, as if his hands have lifted their chins. There is an uneasiness in the atmosphere, a dull scent of metal. The clouds are low, heavy-bellied, the color of tin, and they all know that storms are coming.

At five o'clock, Jasper prepares the small procession that will accompany the Queen on her journey to their show. She will sit in her own coach, but he will ride his finest pony beside her, Peggy following in a tiny papier-mâché carriage shaped like a walnut. The dwarf wears a pair of wired wings draped with gauze, a hired newborn clutched to her chest. It shrieks pitifully, lungs working as furiously as a pair of miniature bellows. Three laborers will follow at the rear, armed with pistols and knives.

"And make sure the globes are lighted the instant you see her coach," Jasper says as he leaps onto his horse. Its mane has been dyed with powdered paint, its flank and legs colored in red and blue. Huffen Black hands Jasper his standard, and it flutters in the breeze.

"Jasper Jupiter's Circus of Wonders!"

As Peggy's carriage pulls out of the gardens, and Jasper trots beside her, he stands, balancing on the saddle just as Dash taught him. Fishwives pause, hands caught midgut, their baskets squirming with silver herrings. A girl shouldering a crab pot pauses, the shelled beasts click-clacking over one another. Cress sellers, sutlers, footmen, ladies with great ostrich feathers — all pause and stare as they trot past. The trees rustle their applause, the Thames clapping against the wharves. Jasper shifts to one leg, arms stretched out.

"Jasper Jupiter's Circus of Wonders!" he cries out. "By royal decree!"

He imagines his name bellowed in every side street, hawked in every alley, murmured in every drawing room and office in this glorious, belching city. Urchins scramble back to pull in more crowds. "Look, look, come see!" For a moment, the gray clouds lift, and the light is so bright he has to shield his eyes.

"Jasper Jupiter!"

At the palace, Peggy releases the cage of painted pigeons, each marked with an elaborate *"J. J."* They hop out, stubby clawed. Soon, they will be mince for a cart, for a fox, but now they are his little ensigns, pecking at the gravel, careering as if drunk.

And then, the carriage appears — Jasper squints to catch a glimpse of her, but her curtains are drawn. It does not matter. It is enough to know she is in there, that he has caught her attention at last, that he has been the first showman to draw her out in years. The little Queen, with the stature of a child. *The freak fancier.* As the miniature ponies turn and follow behind her, it seems that this day has been built with the exactitude of machinery and nothing can go wrong.

Before each show, there is always a rustling of wrappers, a low murmuring, a tension as sharp as a held breath. The performers shuffle from foot to foot, shake the last shred of stress from their toes, exchange half smiles. The animals paw at the sawdust, heads swinging.

Jasper stands solid, legs planted a shoulder's width apart. It is almost dark, the lanterns about the stage winking like little eyes. He peers between the curtains. There she is, dressed in her black widow's weeds. She holds a satin bag, embroidered with a gold poodle. She is waiting for him.

He nods at the trumpeters, and they inhale, instruments pressed to their lips. His elephant, Minnie, lies down, and he vaults onto her back, adjusts his red cape, his glittering topper. He clicks his fingers, gently.

And with that, the trumpets are sounding, and the curtains are drawn back, and Minnie is stumbling into the ring. "Welcome," he bellows, his voice as sure as it ever was. "Welcome! Your Majesty, it is my honor to present the greatest show on earth, Jasper Jupiter's Circus of Wonders! Today you will see acts that will make you question your own mind, that will have you fumbling for your spectacles. You will hear sounds that you've never even dreamed of —"

This, he thinks, as he whisks up his arms, as he whirls a long whip about his head, is the greatest moment of his life. He has built this show from nothing but a few stunned Russian horses. He has taken risks, tracked down every act and every animal, and trained them with the meticulousness of an artist. He stands at the center of it. He, Jasper Jupiter, exultant, *extraordinary.*

When the balloon rises, and Nell swings

beneath it, Jasper knows he has been a success. Squibs, crackers, and Catherine wheels squeal and hiss in his ears.

We are such stuff
As dreams are made on; and our little life
Is rounded with a sleep.

A thundering from the pleasure gardens. A crowd has built behind the grandstand, and they are all waiting. They flap their wallpaper flags, chorus their applause. Jasper can almost smell the fresh ink on tomorrow's broadsheets. They will be flooded with new patrons, will fill the stand four, five times in an evening. He need only hold out his top hat to catch the stream of gold.

He bobs his hands as if conducting the pens of a hundred Fleet Street hacks.

"Jasper Jupiter entertained the Queen in a triumph of a show —"

When Nell lands on the ground and the basket of the balloon is secured once more, Jasper orders a laborer to bring champagne. They drink from old jam pots, clinking glasses. He feels a sense of belonging so acute it is an ache. Tonight, they moved as one body, outflanked all their rivals.

It is no surprise when a courtier appears. He delivers the invitation to come to the

357

palace with a quick bow. Nell is to accompany him.

"She's magnificent, isn't she?" Jasper says. "I built her myself."

"Her Majesty is most keen to make her acquaintance."

"As I am hers," Jasper says. "I'll summon us a coach. Shall we come now, or at an appointed hour?"

A pause. The courtier fidgets. "Ah, you misunderstand me," he says. "Her Majesty enjoyed your show greatly. But she would like to receive Nellie Moon." He looks at Jasper as if he might be simple. "Only Nellie Moon, at the palace."

TOBY

The storm arrives with a snap. The great bowl of the sky splits with lightning. Thunder rolls, thick and low. It is biblical, God's fury unleashed. Rain falls as if poured from a pail, spits out candles, turns sawdust to pulp. The animals shiver, the lion drawn to its haunches. Toby seizes their leashes, drags them back into their cages. All about him, puddles are boiling, water dripping from his nose, his chin.

He works steadily, with none of the haste of the dispersing crowds, gentlemen dashing for cabs and coaches, ladies so wet they look as though they have been sucked into their frocks. He pulls the tarpaulins over the benches, tries to rescue some of the papier-mâché ornaments. They turn to mush in his hands. The ring is little more than a well. There is no use trying to save the curtain; it is so waterlogged that not even Violante could lift it. Thunder simmers. Jasper's shouts echo in his ears. *Fetch that, bring that, put that away, I said, away!* His brother stands in the middle of the ring, benches arced around him. His hair is slicked to his face, his finger jabbing the air. Nobody nears him. In the wagons, Toby sees lamps striking up, Stella hurrying Pearl from Nell's wagon into her own.

He skirts the grandstand to check the animals are more settled, that somebody has fed them. He leaps over a widening stream. Foul-smelling water is bubbling up through the drains. He shudders, lifts the boards onto the menagerie wagons, throws a few dry blankets over the leopards.

Grimaldi is in the stable, pawing at the ground. Toby hushes him as he used to do when the guns roared in Varna, rests his cheek against the horse's soft nose. "Shhh," Toby says, and the animal begins to settle. Toby presses Grimaldi's warmth to him, so cold in his wet clothes. On winter nights, he often sleeps beside his horse, head resting against his belly. He considers it tonight, but he needs to check his wagon hasn't leaked, that his photographs are safe. Rain hammers the roof.

"Settle now," Toby says, and his horse lifts its head and nuzzles him. "There's my boy."

Out again, crossing the ground, filthy

water swirling around his ankles — a sudden split of lightning. The painted script of his caravan illuminated. *Secure the shadow 'ere the substance fades.* The wood of his door is swollen, and he has to put his weight behind it. Inside, it is dry, and he exhales his relief, lights a lamp. The little room swings into view — his mattress on the floor, his rows of chemicals, a book that he and Nell read together the evening before. He can smell her on his bedclothes — lemons and oil paint and something earthier — and it irritates him briefly, that she has taken up so much of his life, that he can think of little but her.

He is about to peel off his wet clothes when his door is flung open. His brother stands there, dripping on the floorboards, wringing rain from his hair and cloak. Fury lifts from him, as white and hot as steam.

"That little bitch," Jasper hisses.

Toby has a sudden fear Jasper will catch Nell's scent too; that he will work it out, that this will tip him into something uglier. But his brother's look is wild, eyes unable to settle, a reek of gin lingering on him.

"How could she? How could she?" Jasper demands. He takes an empty bottle, weighs it in his hand as if about to break it.

"Perhaps —" Toby says, but he falls silent.

He has never seen his brother like this, never felt the weight and gust of his anger.

"Didn't she know it was my show? Didn't she see me, my name, everywhere?" He twists the glass in his hand. "*Nellie Moon!* I created her! I made that little monster. I built her from *nothing* — from a filthy little hovel! How couldn't the Queen see that? How couldn't she see that Nell is *mine,* that she's little more than a puppet on a string, that I am her damned *creator* —"

Toby opens his mouth, closes it. His objections are swallowed. He touches his lips in the hope of finding words there, an easy defense of Nell. Another man would have pinned Jasper to the wall, would have stopped the torrent of Jasper's fury. But Toby merely blinks, his big arms heavy. He does not have the courage to defend her.

On and on Jasper paces, his hands flexing with rage, insults cast and spat, and Toby tries not to listen, tries to let them wash over him.

Coward, he thinks. *Coward.*

He looks up only when his brother falls silent, when his footsteps stop. Jasper is looking at him strangely, mouth half-open.

At first Toby does not understand.

"What have you done?" Jasper whispers. "What have you done to yourself?"

"What?" Toby touches his head, thinks perhaps he has cut himself.

It is only then that he sees his shirt is torn at the neck, that it has turned transparent in the rain. Faint shapes peep through. The pale lace of vines, a crimson peony breaking across his chest like a second heart. He tries to reach for his bedclothes, to cover himself, but Jasper smacks his hand away.

"What have you done to yourself?" Jasper repeats, louder this time. He seizes Toby's shirt and tears it to his midriff, buttons skittering across the floor.

Roses and lilies spill over his torso as if dropped from the back of a Covent Garden barrow.

"What — What *are* you?"

"I-I thought you'd like it —"

"Like it?" Jasper spits. "You've turned yourself into one of *them.* A freak. You'd choose their lives?" He is staring at Toby as if he does not know him, as he might look at an animal. "You'd choose to be on a podium, prodded and ridiculed? You'd *choose* it?"

Jasper raises his hand, and even though his brother does not touch him, Toby stumbles. He falls to the floor, pulls in his legs as if expecting Jasper to kick him. He turns his hands into a small fist. He *could* fight back if he wanted to, ground Jasper with a single blow. He *could* —

Jasper's voice is choked, and he turns away. "After all I did for you, everything I saved you from, after Dash —"

"Wait," Toby begs. "Please —"

But Jasper is gone, vanished into the dark.

Toby is alone then, alone as the rain thunders on the roof. He pulls off his trousers, the legs thick with muck and stink. He stares at his trunklike thighs with their flowers and vines, and something bristles within him. He remembers that pride he felt, pushing through the crowds, the scent of fresh baking in the air, gingerbread stalls and chestnut barrows, how everyone saw him and marveled.

He pictures a cottage and a thick forest; a wife and their child. He might curate an exhibition, fill a room with neat frames bearing small truths, histories he alone has recorded. A dead man, a broken rifle, an army in disarray. Tents like crumpled paper. He imagines himself at the center of it, clicking his fingers like a showman, revealing the trick that the world has conspired to conceal, a making-good of the lies he told. Then he remembers, too, what he has done, what he has kept hidden. *Dash.* He pulls his cover over himself, his cheek still wet with rain.

NELL

Nell is led down halls as wide as houses, ceilings supported by pinkish pilasters. The footman moves at a fast clip, and she has to half run to keep up with him. Up a marble staircase, banister rolling like seasickness, down more corridors, wider this time, hung with striped green satin. As they walk, the attendant clips out commands — "Never address the Queen directly, do not turn your back" — and Nell stumbles on a loose rug. Everything has been rinsed in gold, polished to a sheen, and Nell sees hundreds of miniature versions of herself reflected in doorknobs, in the glossy cornicing, on the mirrored walls. Her birthmarked thighs, the doublet and pantaloons with their moon and stars. She tugs at the seams, tries to pull it lower down her legs. If only she were wearing a dress or trousers; if only Toby or Stella were with her. She had no time to change after the show, had barely lifted those heavy mechanical wings from her shoulders, when Stella told her to hurry into the carriage, to leave before Jasper saw her. Something was shuffled out of order, though she did not understand what or why; she asked Stella to find Pearl, to give her supper.

Into a room as large as the grandstand itself, sculptures leering like an army of decapitated enemies. Nell takes a breath. Fireplaces thunder. She notes hipped vases on podiums, cravatted courtiers who scurry like frightened mice. She turns to face the wall, uncertain where she is supposed to look. There is a frieze, a bas-relief of pygmies and tiny people with stick-thin legs, giants — *"Brobdingnagians,"* she reads, though this means nothing to her — and dwarfs, meadows as smooth as ironed sheets.

And then an arm is on hers, and she finds herself propelled forward. There, at the end of the gallery, is the Queen. As the formalities are run through — a bow, an introduction — Nell feels as if she is being observed through a sheet of glass. A few months ago, her back was bent to the clod, trowel digging at soil. She touches her wrist as if to feel the comfort of her own solidity, to remind herself that she will not shatter.

"And you are the Queen of the Moon and

Stars," the Queen says.

Nell nods. She wonders if she is expected to say something entertaining, to dance a little jig, or tell a joke, or pull a flower from the Queen's ears. The nonsense ramblings of Huffen Black fill her mind — *the barber shaved bald magpies at twopence a dozen, he did, all rubbed down with cabbage-puddings, but still they caught the collywob-blums in their pandenoodles —*

"Your face," the Queen says. "May I touch it?"

Nell does not reply. She cannot find her tongue. But the woman is already stretching out a hand, soft palm against her cheek.

"I can see there's no trick." She sits back, satisfied, a small smile on her face. "I'm wise to humbugs." She turns to the footman. "Fetch me my little beast. I believe she and Nellie Moon share the same tailor."

The courtier returns with a spaniel on a pink ribbon. The dog is white, spotted with large liver marks. Its docked tail swings like a pendulum.

A dog, Nell thinks.

"They are quite twins! My pets of the palace." The Queen leans forward, claps her hands. "Oh, how amusing! If only Vicky and Bertie could see this. Shake her paw."

Nell reaches forward as if she is a puppet,

as if she can do nothing but submit. She grasps the dog's tiny foot.

"How do you do," the Queen says in a curious high-pitched voice that, Nell realizes, is supposed to belong to the dog. The animal whines, squirms, itches with discomfort. Everywhere, eyes on her, as if she is a pilchard on a plate. Something to be *devoured.*

"Wondrous! Simply wondrous," one of the ladies-in-waiting says. "What an entertaining little monster she is."

She means the dog, Nell tells herself, and yet everybody is looking at her. She has still not uttered a word. She pats her chest, as if hoping to find the words tamped down there, ready to gurgle up. She hears only the racket of her pulse.

Jasper has taken my voice, she thinks, but she shakes her head as if to rid herself of such an absurd thought. She thinks of the sea witch, her house built from the bones of shipwrecked sailors. She cut out the Little Mermaid's tongue with a gutting knife.

I belong to the public, Stella said.

Nell's shoulders are raw from the dig of the wings. The mermaid's feet bled as though she trod on sharp knives.

"You must visit me again," the Queen says. "I should like that."

And with that, Nell is dismissed, left to retrace her footsteps down that staircase and along those long corridors. The pillars have the speckled look of manufactured meat. She pictures flesh fed into a grinder, turned to mince. Feet bleeding. Bonnie the fire-eater's mouth, singed with hot coals from where the leather mouthpiece has worn thin.

A carriage is called, and rain smashes the roof, as biting as hail. Nell can see nothing through the steamed-up window. When the horse stops at the pleasure gardens, she jumps down, dodges streams. The grounds are turned to quagmires. A sharp slice of lightning. Her hair sticks to her face. There is a candle burning in her wagon, and when she pushes open the door, she finds she is not surprised that Jasper is waiting for her.

Nell is knocked to the side. A smack as she hits the floor, wind forced from her lungs. And then Jasper is above her, pinning her hands to the ground. The meaty reek of his breath, hot on her neck.

The wagon blurs. She does not think of the pain on her wrists; she does not think of how she should be fighting, how leaden her body feels. But her mind reels back to a small pebbled beach, a lamp and a net and a slippery sea creature pulsing in her hand. You have to stun a squid to kill it, drive a skewer through the gap between its eyes. It doesn't fight or thrash, not like mackerel. Those are dispatched easily, with a thumb placed gently in their mouths and pulled back, the dull crunch of a broken spine.

This is what the girls felt, she thinks, those seized by peddlers in the lanes. Pinned down like moths, like squids on rocks. This is a fight women have always fought, their soft bodies turned to battlegrounds, slim bones crushed beneath the solid weight of men.

She realizes, with a fleeting sadness, that this is all Jasper has ever wanted — to bring her body under the control of his own. That she has overstepped herself without meaning to; that he has accidentally raised her higher than himself.

"I created you," he spits, fingers fumbling for her doublet. "How can't she see that?" A sound of ripping fabric, and it is curious to Nell that this is what snaps her from her stupor, the thought that her outfit will be torn open and ruined. Without it, she is nothing — she is just a freckled girl in a dress. She bites, kicks. She is a mackerel, breaking free. Her elbow meeting cheekbone, her head butting against his chin. Her hands, her knuckles, a knee, driven up. He cries out in pain, and she is free, scarcely harmed, and she grasps her side, finds her costume is only a little torn. Her legs remember how to run, and she dashes down the steps, between the rows of wagons. He does not follow her.

She could go to Stella, tell her what happened, have the woman stroke her hair. But she does not want sympathy, does not want to be told how to feel, for her body to be touched like a fragile pot that might break. She fears, too, upsetting Pearl, the child seeing her so frightened.

There, ahead, is the black wagon. *"Secure the shadow 'ere the substance fades. Tobias Brown, Crimean Photographist."*

Toby pulls himself up when she bursts in. "What is it?" he asks, and she shoves him, seizes him. It is a collision rather than an embrace, as if she is trying to rid herself of what has just happened, to push him away rather than draw him in. Teeth and hair and nail. She wants to share her hurt, throw it onto somebody else. She grips him with her fingernails, scores them down his back, bites his shoulder. The power of it, as if she is felling a giant; the relief of it too. Oblivion — that is what she wants, to lose herself, to find herself, to *feel.* She would like to hold something in her hand and see it shatter.

"What's wrong?" he asks.

She realizes she is crying, tears silent on her cheeks.

"What's happened?"

He wraps his big arms around her, binds her tight.

A sudden sound, just outside the wagon, the door pulled open. It sways on its hinges.

"What was that?" Toby whispers, but he does not let her go.

"Just the wind."

"There was someone there. I heard it."

"It might have been a branch, or the rain," Nell says, though she is certain who it was. She presses a hand to her ribcage. Tendrils of anger root deeper within her.

■ ■ ■ ■

Part Four

■ ■ ■ ■

Is it possible you are Barnum? Why, I expected to see a monster, part lion, part elephant, and a mixture of rhinoceros and tiger!

— P. T. BARNUM, from an encounter with Mr. Vanderbilt in *The Struggles and Triumphs: or, Forty Years' Recollections of P. T. Barnum,* 1869

JASPER

Jasper remembers it as if through fog. The rain, as sharp as bullets, the water that trickled down his spine, the cold that lodged itself in his bones. Standing in the middle of that sodden ring, the curtain sagging, the sawdust wet beneath his boots. Fast breath, his palms tight and sore.

The courtier, his apologetic pause.

Ah, you misunderstand me.

He has lost control of his story, has watched as it has spun and built and gathered without him in it, no longer about him but *her*. Everywhere he turns, she is there. Her name, in the courtier's mouth. Her bite and kick, her refusal to submit to him. And then, that light glimmering in Toby's wagon. He stumbled toward it, and there they were. Four legs, four arms, writhing. The sickening pulse of ecstasy, its gasping breaths. Toby's patterned arm, moving across her waist. His brother's allegiance made clear.

A cold understanding settled on Jasper. He tried to mop his forehead, but his hand was too heavy. He was tired, so tired. He slumped to the ground, and he could not pull himself up. A heaviness, a curious calm. He was alone, adrift, and everyone had peeled away from him.

He should have been prepared for this — Icarus, that moment of soaring amid the molten heat of the sun, the slow drip of melting wax. Victor Frankenstein's ferocious ambition, his monster living outside his control and dismantling his life. Stories echoing through time, of men who have strived too hard, built towering bastions that can only fall.

Jasper passes in and out of consciousness. He knows only that days are turning to nights and the rains are not stopping, that there are no shows, and without shows, there is no money. How long, he wonders — how long can they live on nothing? Every day, he must pay rent, he must buy food, he must pay his troupe — every day a drain, and nothing coming in! The fever of it, white-hot. Throat parched, eyes filmed, cool linen on his forehead.

A man he does not know prizes apart his jaw and forces a cold instrument between his teeth. He spits, tastes bitter powder on his tongue.

"Away," he cries. They are going to take him to pieces, to pickle him, to display him in a bell jar — they are going to strip flesh from his bones! The names of doctors swim across his closed eyelids. Cuvier, who dissected Sara Baartman, the Hottentot Venus. John Hunter, who ignored the wishes of the giant Charles Byrne and boiled his great yellow bones and displayed his skeleton in his museum. Dr. David Rogers, who dissected Joice Heth as spectacle, proving Barnum's trickery about her age. Professor Sokolov, who turned Julia Pastrana into a specimen of stuffed taxidermy —

"No," he cries, thrashing his arms, hitting small silver dishes, glass bottles, powders. "You've made a mistake —"

"A chill," someone says. "He caught a chill —"

He feels his skin lifting, his bones pulled from their sockets, catches the scent of preserving fluid. Hears the Jackal's voice. Little teeth, a smile that shows too much gum.

"Shh," a man says. "Shh."

At night, he dreams of Nell, her body splitting and growing, filling the whole grandstand until the benches scatter like matchsticks. No room for him; no room for anybody else.

He thinks he wakes, but when he opens his eyes, he looks at his hands and finds them shrunk, the size of mouse paws —

Is this madness, he wonders, *the inability to distinguish between what is real and what is illusion?*

He hears murmurings. "Don't tell him; he can't hear; he's insensible, can't you see?"

But he hears it all the same. The wagons are robbed, one overturned. A zebra has been found dead, a coin under its tongue.

The Jackal, he thinks, another missed payment.

"How long?" he mumbles. "How long?"

Seven days of rain, they tell him. Too wet for the crowds. No money. Hunger, the performers restless, impatient to be paid. They have fed the sentient sheep to the lion, as they had nothing else to give it.

"Shh, shh," Toby says.

Jasper realizes his brother has been there all this time, that he has not left him. He grasps Toby's hand, holds it to his cheek.

Shh, shh, shh.

Waves brushing against shoreline. Toby's chest, beating for him.

Shh, shh, shh.

Jasper reaches for the ring in his pocket.

The night stretches. Light, bright pronged, and when he wakes, he is in the Crimea. He is there, in Dash's tent, with his friend and Stella sprawled beside him, Toby in the corner. He flicks open a knife in rhythm with the *tu-whit tu-whit* of canister, round and shell. There is a low beat of fear, the knowledge that tomorrow they will continue the assault on Sevastopol, that they might not survive it. That many men will not. It sharpens their laughter, the novelty of being alive. They rustle their hands through their small chest of chains and watches. Stella presses a crucifix to her throat. "What do you think? Would this appease your father? Have him believe me an angel?"

Dash laughs and kisses her.

Jasper looks away. "You might spare me this sight —"

"On our last evening on earth?" Dash says. He pulls Stella down beside him, and she lets out a whoop of pantomime horror.

"The masons can wait a little while to carve your gravestone, I think," Jasper says, laughing into his cup of porter.

"You don't know that." Dash's expression is suddenly grave.

"Pfft," Jasper says. He swallows, thinks of how his regiment has been named the *verloren hoop.* Forlorn hope. He forces a smile and turns to Stella. "I beg you, snap him out of this. If he carries on any longer, I'll be begging for a sniper to finish me off."

"I just have a feeling about it. An uneasiness." Dash taps his chest. "Here. As if I can't quite breathe."

Stella pulls his hands away, kisses his knuckles. "Enough," she says. "I won't hear another word of this morbid prattle."

"Would you miss me?" Dash presses.

"Terribly," she says, with a strained lightness, but Jasper sees how she turns from him, how she wipes her eyes on her sleeve when she thinks nobody is looking. She stands and gathers Dash's uniform and begins to polish the gold buttons with salted lemons, to scrub at old stains on its fabric. Jasper has never seen her perform any domestic function before; she leaves any cleaning, any washing, to her charwoman. She takes an oiled cloth to his discarded boots and rubs them in slow circles. Dash watches her, his hand resting on her ankle. It is in this moment that Jasper feels that he is intruding, that this is a ritual as private as if Stella had taken a bowl of water and begun to soap his friend's feet.

Outside, horses are being packed up, commands issued. The hasty crump of boots on earth. A man is crying, a humiliating *caw-caw* that digs between Jasper's ribs. An army readying itself, a cat about to pounce. Stella takes a thread, sucks it, and begins to repair a hole in Dash's trousers. Jasper would like to say something to shatter this sudden somberness, an intimacy he has never seen before between Stella and Dash. For the first time, he believes that Dash truly loves her, that he will marry her, and he will not care if he is disowned. But it is the sight of Toby that tips Jasper into the relief of irritation, to the beginnings of rage. His brother is lying there, his knees pulled into his chin, a look so pathetic that Jasper almost laughs.

"I'm tired," he says, standing, because he understands that Dash and Stella do not want him there. Toby trails him back to their tent. Jasper has a longing to needle him, to thrash out their differences in the open, to demand why his brother does not worry about him like Stella does Dash.

"Why don't you say anything?" Jasper asks, turning on him. "Why do you always sit in the corner like a damned fool?"

Toby scuffs his shoe. "You brought me here," he says, miserably, "and now you wish I was gone."

"Why do you glare at him like that?"

"Who?"

"Dash. Like he's some sort of villain!"

Toby juts out his lip, ducks after him into their tent.

"Well? Or are you going to stay silent as you always —"

Toby looks at him, his voice choked. "He thinks he deserves everything he's given. That he can take whatever he wants."

Jasper stares. It is a struggle to see how anybody could be so mistaken about his friend — how Toby can fail to see Dash's generosity, his utter lack of deceit. "Takes? He gave you this position, Toby! He found it for you. After everything, I think you'd be a little grateful —"

There is a spot of color in Toby's cheeks. "Grateful? You're just blinded by his money and connections. You can't see him for what he is."

"You're wrong," Jasper says, tugging off his shirt. "It's pitiful how wrong you are."

They lie down on their mattresses, facing away from each other. He cannot sleep, cannot bear the snotted sift of Toby's breath. *Verloren hoop,* he thinks. After a few hours, his brother speaks, his voice small and contrite.

"We'll have our show, won't we?" Toby whispers. "We'll still have it?"

Jasper does not reply. There are spiteful things he could throw back, but he finds he is tired of it all. He wants only to be back beside Dash, to be galloping down the hillside, saddles creaking, hooves pounding as sharply as their hearts. He wants to see this war won, the Ruskies crushed beneath his weight. He wants to be able to say he was a part of it. He dresses quickly, fingers twisting the unpolished buttons of his jacket, and the morning air is cold and sharp. Stella and Dash are already up, a pan of water on the boil, their legs entwined. The sun is not yet risen, the fortress of Sevastopol gray and ghostly in the early light.

"Will we take it, do you think?" Dash asks.

Jasper raps his temples. "Easy," he says, and Dash laughs at his bravado. "Shouldn't have emptied that bottle of rack. My skull feels like it's breaking in half."

Stella excuses herself, turns into the tent. Jasper can hear the sound of her piss hitting the pan.

He sips his drink. "I think Sevastopol's ours. I really do."

Dash is quiet, disassembling his rifle, dipping a cloth in oil. "If something happens to me, you'll look after her, won't you?"

"What?" Jasper is so surprised that he spills his flask and curses quietly.

"If something —"

"I heard you," Jasper says, with a quick laugh. "If anything happens to you! Really, I don't know what's brought on this somber turn. Should I arrange a few mutes, too, to gurn outside your tent?"

Dash runs a cloth on a wire down the barrel. "I know it's easier to make light of it."

"One thing's for certain, Stella's the last person who needs looking after."

"She's softer than you think."

"Ha," Jasper says. "The Ruskies would have surrendered within the hour if she'd been in charge. It'll be yesterday's drink."

"Yesterday's drink?"

"Knotting your chest."

Dash pulls himself to his feet. Jasper squeezes his shoulder, and they walk into the rising dawn, the smell of rot wafting over those low green hills. Stella follows them, straightens Dash's jacket.

"Dash thinks he's going to die today," Jasper says, because he wants to turn it into a jest, to unravel the anxiety that has settled about him.

"Never," Stella says. "It's impossible."

"That's exactly what I told him."

Dash smiles, kisses the tip of her nose.

Before they saddle up their chargers, Jasper looks for Toby, but his brother must still be sulking in the tent. He shrugs, checks his rifle. There is a restlessness in the air, as raw as the scent of rust. Some of the soldiers have tied tickets around their necks, marked with their name and address so their families might be informed of their deaths. The iron smell of fear. The horses, muscling forward. The men silent and watchful, awaiting his command. He's craving it already, almost as much as he's dreading it, the rush and thrust of battle, that feeling of detached oneness with the men around him.

It isn't until dawn the next morning that they occupy the Great Redan, the Ruskies retreated, the city lit with bright flashes. Terror and chaos; a city smoking and burning, explosions splitting the air. *The Great Fire of Sevastopol.* Three days later, they sweep into the shattered shell of the city, ash hot under their boots. Standards blaze. Everywhere, the roar of infantry, the quick step of the regiment's brass band. Dash is at his elbow, and together they clamber over the remnants of the dead, rush into that broken fragment of a fortress.

"It's ours," Jasper whispers, and then he says it louder, a cry that is lost to the roaring of the guns. "Ours!"

From afar, the walls looked so white and pristine, but the illusion is short-lived. It is a place of split churches, buildings pocked with shell holes, twisted green cupolas. No roofs; most of the walls destroyed. A city crushed like an insect. Bodies so broken they look like they've been crushed in a machine. The city is still burning, cloaked in black smoke. Torsos shattered like wine casks, faces flayed from skulls. When Jasper sees a dead man, he notices only the gold chain at his neck. He sees a watch in a pocket. Money, loot. His chest pounds as they race down the narrow streets, littered with fallen masonry. The Ruskies have fled or crept into holes where they will die like poisoned rats.

"Sevastopol is ours!" Dash cries, echoing his shout, and a smile lights his face.

"How disappointed Stella will be, to find you still alive. She needn't search for a new husband after all."

"I feel quite the fool," Dash says, and laughs.

There is so much to take, it is difficult to know where to begin. They see other officers carrying antique chairs, porcelain services, sabers, all of which they will send home. Someone bellows that they have found a supply of brandy. As the sun glazes the buildings and an old bell strikes ten, the ambulances and mule litters roll in, and Jasper catches sight of Toby's black photography wagon, the horses stumbling over shattered bricks.

Jasper and Dash watch as he jumps down from his van, as he settles his machine in the ruins and ducks behind his cape. Jasper cranes to see what he is photographing. A dead soldier by the looks of it, crushed beneath masonry.

"I can sense his sulk from here," Jasper says. "Let's leave him alone."

They ride away from him, ignoring his calls, dismounting to pull crucifixes from sun-blackened necks. Beside a small ruined wall, Dash stops, stretches. Beside them is a small green garden, miraculously unscathed, its trees in full leaf.

"Doesn't he tire of it?" Dash asks.

"Doesn't who tire of what?"

"Your brother. Watching the whole battle through a small eye?"

"Not being in the thick of it, you mean?"

"Not being in the thick of anything at all." Dash twists his jacket. "I just — I wonder. Will he always follow us everywhere? To every battle, to every damned war?"

Jasper looks at Dash, at his dark hair curling around his neck, his easy way of standing. "I had an idea," Jasper says, "that we would discharge ourselves now this is over. That we could own a show. You and me." His words are easy, smooth, revealing nothing of the uneasiness he feels. The betrayal of it, what Toby would say if he heard.

"A show?"

"A circus, you know. Horses and pantomimes. A menagerie. Stella was made for it."

Dash sets his mouth. "Because of her beard?"

"No, no," Jasper says, though that is what he meant. "Because she's a performer. A natural. You've seen how she entertains the men." He leans closer. "Think of it. Jasper and Dash's Great Show."

"A circus."

"A circus, yes!" He grins at Dash. "Do you know how much Barnum makes? Thousands each month. And Fanque too. It wouldn't matter if you were disowned. We'd be magnificent. We were born showmen."

Dash laughs. "I suppose my father has horses. He can sell us some before I tell him about Stella."

"Easy."

"We could perform before the Queen."

"It will be the greatest show in the world!"

Jasper laughs, feeling like a child again, plotting his outlandish dreams — but this time it seems tangible, a thing they might really do.

A pause, and Dash chews his lip. "What about Toby?"

"What about him?"

"What on earth would he *do*? He'd suck the atmosphere from any tent. He's a dullard."

"A dullard?" Jasper echoes. He stiffens.

"Come, you've said it yourself."

"He's my *brother,* Dash. I'm allowed to say it." He brushes a hair from his eye. "I don't know. He's always admired me. You never had brothers. You wouldn't understand."

Dash throws a brick at a wall and watches it split open. "I know, but it's just — the damned man never speaks! He doesn't even look at me." He shrugs. "I'm not suggesting we just *abandon* him, but can't you find a different occupation for him? A clerk, or something? A dullard's profession." He must grasp Jasper's expression because he adds, "If he had to, he could help us build the show, I suppose. Carrying, lifting, that sort of thing."

Jasper is silent. Now he has planted the idea, he cannot take it back. He thinks of

Toby arriving on the steamer, the relief, the hope on Toby's face when he saw Jasper waiting for him on the jetty. As if Jasper could fix everything simply by being there.

At the next house, Jasper peels away from Dash, says he'll find him later. He blinks to adjust to the gloom of a cottage. Sunlight pours through the open ceiling. He begins rifling through drawers, emptying cupboards, cramming his pockets full. A slight movement in the corner of the room. His hand is on his pistol, then he laughs. It is just a canary in a cage, wings beating against the bars. Beside it, a music book with a woman's name on it, a vase of flowers.

He holds out his finger. The bird flies against it, whistling. He smiles, lifts the cage. He will keep it as a pet.

As he moves to the door, he sees a man's shoes, a man's legs. One hand grips the canary and the other finds his bayonet.

Outside, his face spattered with blood, Jasper tramps through the streets of the broken city, cobbles glittering with bullets and fragments of lead. Vultures, kites, and buzzards circle. He sees Dash clambering over loose stonework, heading toward the battlements.

"Dash!" he calls, and the man turns.

"There'll be a magnificent view from up there. Perhaps we could salute Stella on

392

Cathcart's Hill."

They pick their way up a shattered staircase.

"No show without Punch," Dash says, and Jasper turns and sees Toby following them, his head down, feet stumbling on torn masonry.

— when he led us into the drawing room and we saw the two machines —

Jasper opens his eyes. He is in the Crimea, he thinks, his mouth parched; with Dash —

It is Toby, his broad shape hazy, a glass of water in his hands.

Jasper is back in the wagon, back in his show, his handbills flapping on the walls. His breath is loud and sore.

"Jasper? You're awake?"

He cowers, grips his throat as if to find it slit, moves his hand to his lips. He is surprised to find no coin clamped between his teeth.

"You've been asleep for so long."

Jasper blinks, and just before those skeins tighten about his lungs again, just before the aches seize his limbs, he thinks of the Jackal and how he will manage to pay him. His show is growing stale. Soon it will be winter, the crowds smaller. He is sure that his mind can only falter in the footsteps of

393

those before him, that none of his thoughts can ever be original, that every story has already been told.

He sinks back. Easier not to strive, to feel only the hitch of tiny, dry breaths. He reaches out his hand, grips only air.

TOBY

Toby squeezes the sponge over his brother's forehead. Jasper mumbles, spittle gathering at the corner of his mouth.

"Shh," Toby says, dabbing his brow. "Shh."

Outside, he can hear Nell's laughter, Pearl's delighted scream. He left them playing in the drizzle, Nell swinging the child by her arms. Toby sleeps in Nell's wagon each night now, the three of them tucked together as rain pounds the roof. In the green morning light, they read books, or crouch by the fire under a tarpaulin.

"Look at our girl," Nell said as the sun rose that day, as Pearl chased after a marble, and it broke something in his chest. *Our girl.* Toby thought of all the things he had ever wanted and could not have. Now he can put his arm around Nell, unafraid of anyone seeing, and it feels miraculous to see his hand there, resting in the dip between her shoulder blades. A small claiming of territory, a thrill that they are each other's.

It is not always easy — their days of rich meats and cheese are at an end, and they must thin out cheap butcher's cuts with carrot and cabbage. The elephant shudders against the bars. Nobody has been paid in two weeks. The troupe is restless, on edge. But he is surprised, too, by the little pocket of quiet they have found together, as if the rain has slowed the whole world. He thinks of the cottage with a blue-painted door, wisteria clinging to its window frames. Sometimes, when he sees Nell looking at Pearl with that softness in her eyes, he thinks of telling her what Jasper said about selling her. But he bites his tongue, cannot bring himself to break this small piece of happiness.

He sits back, blinking at a sudden spear of sunlight. He turns his head away from Jasper. He realizes he can no longer hear rain drumming the roof. An eerie quiet. He peers through the window. Children emerge from wagons, holding out their hands as if they cannot believe it. Nell is carrying Pearl on her back, and the child is pink with laughter as Nell pretends to jog her off, careering this way and that. Huffen Black has let out two zebras and is beginning to exercise them in the ring. Toby watches them cantering in circles. They might have a show tonight, if this weather holds, and bring in a little money; but then Jasper shifts in his sleep, and Toby puts the thought from his mind.

Toby's sleeves are rolled up, revealing a blackbird just below his elbow. He remembers Dash's taunt. *Dullard.* And yet his brother will not let him have the life of a performer, either, cannot allow him to encroach on his territory.

What if they hadn't grown like two linked boys? What if they had grown like two plants in a vivarium, Jasper taking all the nutrients, all the light, Toby wilting beneath him?

What would happen, Toby wonders, if Jasper were to die? He would commission a mason to carve a lavish headstone, arrange a funeral with black-boxed advertisement in the papers. But once the fanfare was over, there might be a way for *Jasper Jupiter* to live on, just as shops and businesses pass through several hands and keep the names of their original owners. Jasper has turned himself into a construct, a patchwork quilt stitched from a thousand different stories.

Toby reaches for the cushion to raise his brother's head. Jasper's breath snags, stops. Toby waits. It begins again, choked. Goose feathers prickle his palms, the pillow so soft.

Vines strangle Toby's arms, as if pulling his hands down against his will. He rests the cushion against Jasper's nose. A thought crackles, lightning fast. *You could —*

Toby lifts the back of Jasper's head gently, tucks the pillow behind it.

"There," he says. "Now you can breathe more easily."

But the thought was there, and he cannot forget it.

NELL

Nell watches Toby leave Jasper's wagon. He raises his hand in greeting, and yet there is something unsettled about him, something enlivened too. The sun is piercing, exposing, like a match struck in a darkened room.

"Is something wrong?" he asks, but it is Toby who bites his fingernails, who cannot stop glancing at Jasper's wagon.

"It's just this." She gestures about her. The owner of the pleasure gardens is unrolling tarpaulins from the chairs, readying to open the grounds again that evening. "How long can we sit here and wait?"

Peggy and Violante must have overheard her, because they put down the basket of wet laundry and join them. "Do you think we could?"

"Could what?" Toby asks.

Peggy pauses. "Put on the show again. Tonight, perhaps."

Nell looks skyward. She wishes, almost,

that they were back in those endless days of rain, when there were no possible answers to the questions of hunger, of quiet, of no shows, when doing nothing was the best they could manage.

"There's no showman," Violante says.

Toby holds his chin a little higher.

"Stella could," Peggy says. "There's nobody else."

"She wouldn't do it to Jasper," Violante says.

"How long are we supposed to wait? With no money to feed the animals, no money for *us,* time passing since the Queen visited —"

Toby coughs, gently, and they look at him, then away. They all fall silent, contrite at having voiced the idea. She sees Violante glance at Jasper's wagon, its curtains drawn, its paned window observing them like a narrowed eye.

"I'm sure he'll be well again soon," Nell says, with a warmth she does not feel.

"You don't understand," Toby says. He scuffs a mound of dirt with his shoe, and she wonders if he is about to cry.

Later, Pearl is grizzly, and Nell and Toby put her to bed early, blankets heaped around her. She and Stella trapped a mouse in the afternoon, and Pearl insists on keeping its cage on the floor. It unsettles Nell to hear its panicked scrabbling, the quick flurry of feet from one wall to the other.

"Can you tell me a story?" the girl asks.

"What about?"

"About me. Where I came from."

Nell pauses. "I can't tell you that story. Only you can."

A look of fear passes over the child's face. She wants a new history, Nell realizes; she wants to wipe away what has passed before.

"You were born in a walnut shell," Toby begins, "in a land where they ate nothing but —"

"Cream," Pearl supplies. "And there were baby mice everywhere. Hundreds of mice. Mice, mice, mice."

"Yes," Toby says.

"Mice like Benedict." She adds, "That's his name. Stella told me."

"Very well," he says.

Nell listens to Toby's story, knows it by heart. The cottage with the blue door. The hens pecking. Newly laid eggs breaking in a skillet. Her chest stirs with a fretful longing, a sudden desire for him. The heat of him. How each day she learns his body, as if he is a country to be mapped, a continent to be spanned with her fingers.

"She's asleep," Toby whispers.

The talk of stories makes Nell want to read. She lies against Toby, hungering to tip it into something more, but aware of the child, too, and content just to be held by him. They turn the pages of *Fairy Tales*. Pearl's breath is quiet, her mouse sleeping in its cage. Her girl is safe. They are safe. *There will be a show soon,* she tells herself; they will find a way. Only briefly does she remember the shock of Jasper's hands on her wrists, and she places her head in the crook of Toby's shoulder. He turns the page of "The Little Mermaid," and there is a woodcut with a line beneath it.

"I know what you want," said the sea witch. "It is very stupid of you, but you shall have your way, and it will bring you to sorrow, my pretty princess."

Nell rests her head on Toby's chest. "Who would you choose?" she asks.

"What?"

"Me or Jasper."

He stares at the ceiling, then whispers something so quietly she can scarcely catch it.

"What did you say?" she asks.

He takes her hand, grips it. There is fight in his eyes. "I said, would you leave? Now? The three of us?"

She pictures packing a bag and walking through the gates, Pearl clinging to her back. A cottage in the trees, years slipping away quietly, just like before. Leaving Stella and Peggy. A life like the one her brother wanted for her, ostracized in small ways. Her body, hidden away like a secret. "I can't," she says. "I need this. I need to perform."

Toby grips her hand more urgently. "One day, we'll have that cottage, won't we?"

They rest their foreheads against each other, noses touching. "Perhaps," she says.

As he begins to drift into sleep, Nell looks at her birthmarks, each telling a story, her own story. And yet it is Jasper who has crafted tales and histories about her. She unhooks Toby's arm from around her and sits on the floor, bare legs pulled into her chest. Pearl's mouse shivers, makes itself small. Nell opens the cage door. She remembers that day by the sea, hurling the squid back into the water, her relief as it pulsed away. The mouse moves forward, nose twitching, but then scurries into the farthest corner.

Go, she wills it, giving the cage a little shake. But the mouse will not move, whether out of fear or choice, she is not sure.

JASPER

The world shifts in and out of focus. In some moments, Jasper can see clearly — a glass catching the light, his brother's hands rinsing a sponge. Other times, it clouds and fogs, and he is back in Sevastopol, back on those streets. Once, he opens his eyes, and Stella is sitting there. "Stella," he says. He blinks. "Forgive me."

"What do I need to forgive you for?" Her voice, chilled.

A tear slides across his cheek, pools in his ear.

"They say you're dying," she says. "They say you won't live."

He is surprised by how little this news surprises him, how little he minds. "Are you glad?"

She sits there, biting on her lip. "I want to know what happened to Dash."

"I don't know."

"You do. You have his ring!"

404

"It isn't that easy."

"Tell me what happened," she says, again.

And he tries, falteringly, because words are elusive and swim in the air before he can grasp them. He tells her about the birdcage and wiping clean the end of his bayonet. A smell of rising rot, flies in angry clouds, clambering over the battlements with Dash, because his friend wanted to salute her on the distant hill. He tries to articulate all this, but perhaps he only murmurs nonsense, because she says, "Did you . . . did you do something to him? Did you *hurt* him?"

He shakes his head. "Me?" His voice, so small. "Hurt him? How could you think —" He tries to grasp her hand, but she pulls it away. "You have to believe me. He was my *friend.* I'd never have —"

She pulls at the skin of her hand like it is a piece of cloth, her nails leaving ugly marks in the flesh. "If you won't tell me what happened to him, what am I supposed to think? Tell me, Jasper. Tell me!"

There is a pulling sensation in his skull, as if an insect is gnawing his brain. He opens his mouth, and a spit bubble forms. He wants to tell her the truth, to tell her everything, but it isn't his story.

We're brothers, linked together.

405

He tells her all he can bear to impart. That Dash was balancing on the edge of the battlements and he slipped and lurched forward, and it happened so quickly that he could not grab him. How Jasper heard the sound of him hit the ground before he had even understood he had fallen. He does not tell her that Toby was there, too, that there was a strange beauty to it — the sun low and slanting, glancing off the broken rifles and cartouches and epaulettes of dead men. That for a minute, neither of them could move. His breath is rasping and short.

Stella is crying quietly, teeth working the tender skin of her bottom lip.

"I thought —" She takes a breath. "When I saw the ring, and you wouldn't tell me what happened, I thought perhaps —"

"No," Jasper says, and it is a relief that he does not need to lie. "How could I? He was the dearest friend I ever had."

He keeps talking, tells her how he stumbled down the slopes and found him, still and crumpled, how he was surrounded by a thousand other men. He heard the steady rumbling of cacolets, the mule litters that ferried the injured and dying to the hospitals, but Dash was gone, and what could he do? He could not take a dead man back to camp. He dragged Dash to a cave blown into the walls by a mortar, and he placed him inside, out of the day's heat.

"Why didn't you tell me? Why did you hide what happened to him?" She leans forward. "I could have returned for him, buried him. I could have known and grieved him then."

Sobs roll from him. "I don't know," he says. "I was ashamed of what I'd done. I robbed him, Stella. I robbed a dead man. Robbed my *friend.* I wanted to forget it. I couldn't bear it." Jasper tries to sit up, but his head reels. "I wanted the ring. I wanted it so much." He looks at her, says almost angrily, "He was my friend too."

Dash's hand was puffed and swollen, the metal sparkling. Jasper spat on the ring to oil it, but the thick gold band wouldn't move, wouldn't even slide to the knuckle. He moved as if freed of thought, his body deciding for him. He reached into his pocket, and the knife chilled his hand. He began to hack through flesh and sinew and bone. He told himself that he was taking it to give to Stella.

Did he keep it because he wanted to remember his friend too? Or because he saw only gold, a thing to be possessed? The canary twittered in its cage. He slipped the ring into his pocket, and he could not bear to stay there a moment longer, could not bring himself to dig a hole and lift that broken body into it, to acknowledge that Dash's life had played itself out. He ran, cage bouncing against his legs, Toby lumbering after him.

"I could have buried him," Stella says again, head bowed.

"I'm sorry," Jasper whispers, and his throat is dry and aching.

They returned to camp, and Jasper cooked the canary like a songbird, drowning it in a vat of brandy then roasting it over hot coals. "Where's Dash?" Stella asked, but he calmed her, said he had left him carousing in the village. He could not meet her eye, and beside him Toby trembled.

The canary was tiny, scarcely bigger than his thumb. He cracked its little ribcage against his teeth. As he swallowed the last sharp piece of it, he felt a rush of horror, a dawning awareness of his own monstrosity.

"Take it," Jasper says now, the handbills in his wagon dimpling in a sudden breeze. He reaches into his pocket. "It's yours, isn't it? He'd want you to have it." He holds Stella's gaze. "But I didn't touch him. I swear it."

She accepts the ring, fingertips running into the little grooves she once carved.

E. W. D.

The door shuts behind her, and fatigue overwhelms him. He shivers, sinks into a tunnel as black as pitch, its walls cold and slippery. He allows himself to fall. Light recedes to star pricks.

When Jasper stirs, he finds himself in the Crimea again, rifles discharging all around him, ladies and journalists cheering from their vantage points on the hillsides. The crash of steel, mortars thundering, the scream of horses, the beat of drum, fife, and trumpet. A lion roars —

He blinks.

Applause, shattering.

He rubs his cheek.

A lion? There were no lions there.

It roars, louder this time.

He opens his eyes. His face shimmers back at him, a thousand times over. Powders and glass jars sparkle into view. His bureau, his cabinet of gin and curaçao. A tin of brandy snaps. But still, the sounds of war continue. The martial beat, the bright fife, the trumpet —

His insides turn.

He must be mistaken. A crowd is roaring. Music spins. He looks down at himself, dressed in his linen nightshirt, rimed with sweat. His sheets are damp and yellowed. And yet, he can hear himself in the tent, the pitch of those words he knows so well.

And now, ladies and gentlemen, I present the final feast for the eyes — a sight never before witnessed —

He swallows. When they were boys, Jasper once walked into his bedroom and caught Toby wearing his blue velvet britches, his eye pressed to the microscope. He sneaked up on him, meaning to surprise him, but in the moment before Toby could arrange his face, his brother's mouth was a snarl. It was a look of thwarted desire, of bitter ambition.

It is the greatest act you will ever see. The most wondrous, the most dazzling. Nellie Moon will eclipse the heavens themselves —

Jasper picks up a tumbler and hurls it at his dresser.

He stares around his wagon and he sees her, arcing across the latest handbill he has plastered to the wall. He made her. He *created* her. And now she and Toby have eclipsed him, have gorged themselves on his fame, on the show he has spent a lifetime building.

He runs a thumb over the advertisement, over that body which bucked underneath him, that threw him off. The knee that

410

punched between his legs. He tears her from the wall. The paper quivers in his hand. He reaches for his lucifers. She is even on the matchbox.

The edge of the handbill flares. He watches her legs, her arms, her face, curl and blacken. He drops the paper and scuffs it with his slipper. All that is left is white ash.

The crowd applauds, roars, whistles.

It is enough to rouse him, to draw him to his desk. He touches his brow, overcome by giddiness. He is ravenous, and his hands shake as he sketches out rudimentary plans.

In this age of wonder, epiphanies are born in the ecstasies of dreams and fevers. Mary Shelley dreamed up *Frankenstein.* Alfred Russel Wallace conceived the theory of natural selection while raving with fever. Keats and Coleridge birthed their greatest works in the throes of opium. And now he, Jasper Jupiter, has settled on the invention that will immortalize him. He will tell this story for years to come, the tinderbox moment when the idea struck him.

He has the answer; he knows he has it. *This* is what will set him apart. *This* is what will make him. He dips his quill into a brimming inkpot, and his vision sharpens.

TOBY

The crowd is in a frenzy. A thousand limbs lift and sway. A thousand mouths hinge open in laughter. Do they laugh harder than they did for Jasper? Do they thunder their feet more loudly than any audience before? Toby can turn gasps to jeers, jeers to sighs. He draws back his shoulders, stands taller than he has ever done before. He clicks his cane, and poodles dance on their hind legs, their pink bonnets bobbing. A smile splits his cheeks. When he catches his reflection in the glass-paned tank, he startles. He thought, for a second, that he was his brother.

While Nell flies, Toby hides behind the curtain and takes off his boots, his shirt, strips down to a pair of blue trunks. He strolls back into the ring, his cape wrapped tightly around him. As the balloon is lowered and Nell lands on the ground, he feels the audience's attention turn back to him.

The oil lamps hiss and flicker. Time stretches. The crowd waits. He must act before boredom settles.

He fumbles for the ribbon fastening the cape, pulls it away.

A gasp goes up, fingers pointing. His body is richly patterned, a riot of color and shapes.

"And that," he shouts, "was the greatest show on earth, Jasper Jupiter's Circus of Wonders."

His voice rises, louder and louder, until he might even *be* Jasper. He looks down at his painted skin, and he feels alive. Important. He has assumed his brother's life with the ease of stepping into a pair of varnished boots. He has strengthened while his brother has waned. Two hearts pounding in a vivarium, and the weaker organ has begun to suck back its half of the blood. He wishes his brother could see him, could realize the spark he has buried for more than thirty years.

"I am Jasper Jupiter, and this is my circus!" Toby bellows, and even he believes it. He raises his arms, and the audience screams.

When the crowds have departed, Toby sits on a bench and flicks his whip in the dust.

413

The fronds of the pine tree look illuminated, each leaf pristine. He could do anything, be anyone. He could live in a cottage with Nell and Pearl. He could run this show forever.

A murmuring; he sees Stella and Peggy glancing at him, nudging Nell. They cross the grass and sit beside him.

"Let's have a look," Stella says, giving his shirt a small tug.

He shows them the vines on his arms, the blackbirds and pomegranates, the adder inching across his chest. "Isn't it magnificent?" he asks, but Peggy's lip is curled in an expression close to disdain.

"Magnificent to have a choice," Stella says. "To look like this when you could have done something else."

Toby laughs, thinking she might be joking, and at least there is no malice in her voice. She flicks a bird with her fingernail. *She could cut off her beard if she wanted,* he thinks, but then he notices Nell itching a birthmark on her arm. She does not look at him. Peggy leans on the crook she uses to dislodge high buckets, to open high doors.

"We've got to make this life work, don't we, Peg?" Stella says, with a smile.

"I'm going to marry a man like Charles Stratton," Peggy says, but her voice has a glazed, rehearsed edge to it.

"I should see Jasper," he says, wrapping the shirt around himself. "See if he's well."

As he crosses the grass, he sees a boy pointing. "It's him! Look, look," the child shouts, and there it is again — that new, fluffed pride. Toby casts Stella's words from his mind. Remarkable; that's what he is. *Important.*

He forces himself to hope that Jasper is alive, though he is already imagining touching his forehead and finding it cold and damp, picturing himself informing press agents and cemeteries. A great plot at Highgate, a funeral cortège with ostrich-plumed zebras.

Outside Jasper's wagon, Pearl is playing with her mouse. He stops and plucks a daisy and hands it to her. She squints, cannot see what it is. "A flower," he says, "for Benedict the mouse." She accepts it carefully, tucks it between the bars of the little cage.

"There, mister," she whispers to the little creature. "For you to wear like a bonnet."

Toby smiles at her. Peggy and Stella are still looking at him. He swallows, then pushes open his brother's door without bothering to knock. Jasper is hunched at his desk, his spine as prominent as a row of pebbles.

"Jasper?" he says, taking a step back.

"Are . . . are you well?"

There are ashes on the floor, a wound on the wall where a handbill used to hang.

"It doesn't suit you," Jasper says, without looking up.

"What doesn't?"

"Me. You always wanted what was mine."

Toby fidgets with the hem of the cape. "I didn't."

Jasper says nothing, but his pen creaks across the page and spritzes little mists of ink into the air.

"You're . . . you're better?" Toby asks.

Jasper doesn't give any indication he has heard him.

"I-I-I —" Toby stops, curses the stutter he hasn't had for more than a week. "The pleasure gardens were closed, you understand. The rain — it almost ruined them. It almost ruined us too." He tries to sound authoritative, as if he has done nothing wrong. "I paid the grocer. The chandler. But the rent and the Jackal . . . I didn't know what the arrangement was. Tonight and yesterday, you see, the rains lifted — it made sense — we filled almost every seat." The words jar. If only Jasper would speak. "Wasn't that the right decision? To make some money for the . . . the . . . the debts? And with you so ill, and dying even, we

416

thought —"

Jasper keeps writing.

The cape is limp on Toby's shoulders. He feels as small as he did when he stood in the ruins of Sevastopol and heard Jasper and Dash talking about him. He'd gone to find them, and there they were. A *dullard,* Dash called him.

They were planning the show without him even playing a part in it, with him, at best, as a mere *mule.* Perhaps if he'd heard their plans back in London, it wouldn't have mattered to him. But there, on those scarred plains, when his brother was all he had, when the circus had been the strings holding him together —

Can't you find a different occupation for him? A clerk, or something?

That soulless new house in Clapham, identical to all the others on the terrace. His hand wearing a groove in the banister. It was all he was good for. And in the place he'd once thought was his would be Dash, standing on the saddle of a camel. Dash the Crimean hero, the brother he was sure Jasper would have chosen. Toby was tired, so tired, of wanting and not being wanted back. A cannon sounded, and a group of soldiers pushed past him. He drove his fist into the wall. The pain only sharpened his rage.

Jasper's pen scratches the page.

"What are you drawing?" Toby asks.

His brother's wrist clicks as he works. His cheeks are hollowed. This man, scribbling furiously, feels little more than a stranger. Outside, Toby hears the stable boys exercising the animals, the benches being put away. New roads, new fields, new audiences.

Toby walks closer. "What are you drawing?"

But Jasper shields the page with his arms. When he looks up at him, Toby backs away, frightened by the hatred he finds there.

NELL

In the shadow of the rose bower, Nell and Pearl scoop Benedict a palace out of dirt. She hands the child oyster, mussel, and scallop shells, discarded from the nights when great silver trays were ferried through these paths. The child turns them over, feels their edges, presses them to her ear. Benedict is asleep in his cage.

"You should be careful," Stella said to Nell the evening before. "She isn't yours to have."

But Stella is wrong, Nell thinks as Pearl plants a shell on the top of the mound with a smile, as she steps back and claps. She is Nellie Moon, isn't she? She has visited the Queen. She has a wagon crammed with gifts and dried flowers and perfumes; why can't she keep this child too?

Pearl places five mussel shells around the dirt castle. "Mussel shells. Stones. Oysters," she announces. "He's a mouse prince."

"With the finest castle I've ever seen."

Nell has learned this girl. Pearl likes patterns, shells arranged in size order, marbles in long rows. She sticks out her tongue when it rains, and she prefers wet weather to sunshine, which makes her scrunch up her eyes. She counts her steps as she walks, tries to hide how she shuffles her feet to check for branches, for anything that might trip her. When she falls asleep, she clutches Nell's hand in hers, and it gives Nell a liquid feeling, of knowing she is needed. Nell's heart pounds when the girl vanishes behind the wagons, for just a minute. If she could, she'd bind the child to her, never let her go.

"What's that?" Pearl asks.

A dull, rhythmic beating. It is the drum Jasper uses to summon them. Nell stands. Her heart quickens with hope and fear. Her life will resume as it was, and she tells herself that is a good thing. "Come," she says to Pearl. "You can make another castle under our wagon."

"But Benedict wants *this* castle," Pearl says, pouting, but she follows Nell, promises not to move until Nell fetches her.

Performers hurry from all directions, laborers hauling themselves to their feet. She finds Toby, Stella, and Peggy, and they settle on the grass near the back. Jasper is there, standing in front of the bonfire ashes. He is thinned by fever, his face little more than a skull. Nell remembers the weight of him, pinning her down, how she writhed and fought and kicked. Rage stirs within her; that he can recover so quickly, behave as if no harm has been inflicted. Toby takes her hand. Jasper sees it. A flinch, rapidly concealed. She is glad to see him flustered, even briefly. She would hurt him more if she could, would snap that smile from his cheeks.

"I have a way out of this," Jasper says. "But we shan't put on another show for a week."

"A week?" Peggy whispers. "But how will we live?"

"We want our pay," a groom shouts.

A shuffling, a rustling. A week ago, nobody would have dared to speak up like this. Nell looks behind her, and the laborers are barely listening. They whittle grass into whistles, nudge each other.

Is this the man, Nell wonders, who once stood on the back of an elephant and held a thousand people spellbound? Is this the man who tried to suppress her will beneath his?

"We will need to make changes before we rise again. You will need to be patient."

"Our pay!" A chorus, building.

He takes his whip, cracks it. There is Jasper Jupiter once more, electric, a snarl on his face. The men fall silent. "Our show is not at an end. My idea will bring us to greater heights than ever before. Our show has become dull, a mere imprint of the thousands of other shows across this country. My idea will make us different, unique, a *true* novelty."

"How?" a man demands, but others shush him.

"It will make all your names, just to be associated with it." He looks skyward, and Nell cannot help sharing that excitement, his energy passing around this circle of battered performers and laborers.

Jasper must sense the attention shifting to him because he speaks quieter, everyone straining to hear him. "We will have to sell some of the animals and fakements to tide us over, to fund this venture. Anyone who wants to leave is free to do so. But anybody who stays will be paid double when the new show opens."

A whispering.

"Tell us your plan," a man shouts. "What if you're all bluster?"

"It's your decision," Jasper says. "Wait and see, or leave and read about it in every broadsheet in the country."

Nell looks at Toby. He shakes his head. He does not know either.

They drift away, uncertain what to do with the evening. She wonders what Jasper might be planning, what her role will be. Usually, Nell would be rising in the balloon around this time, the crowds roaring. How long will her fame last without a performance, without a mention in the newspapers?

She returns to her wagon, thinking the child might be hungry. Pearl has built a new dirt castle, decorated it with dozens of mussel shells, the mouse in its cage above it. She looks up at Nell and grins.

"Mama," Pearl says.

It is the first time she has called her that. Nell touches her belly as if to find the trace of her there. A queasiness rises at the thought that she might lose the child, that Jasper could sell her alongside the fakements and animals. She remembers Stella's warning. *She isn't yours to have.*

When Pearl busies herself once more, prodding mouse tunnels into the palace, Nell whispers to Toby, "I've been thinking. I could buy her."

"Buy her?"

"From Jasper. I have a little saved. Eighty pounds. I could offer it to him."

Toby shakes his head. "That isn't enough."

"What do you mean?" In her mind, it is an absurd sum. Her own father was paid twenty pounds for her. "He can't want more than that."

Toby lowers his voice. "She cost him a thousand pounds."

Nell takes a breath. "No —" A wave of panic swallows her, her heart thundering. She pictures the girl, torn from her, sobbing on a podium, prodded by passersby. She did not know how big a love could be, that she would do anything to protect this child.

Perhaps the girl senses her fear, because she looks up at her. "What is it, Mama?" she asks.

Nell reaches for Pearl, kisses her head with sharp pecks. Her skin is so soft, her hair as fine as a dandelion clock. The child begins to wriggle, sudden sobs rising. "What's wrong? Am I going to be sold?"

"No, sweet," Nell says. "I won't let you go."

The next morning, the bones of the show are pulled apart. Men take axes to the benches, hack them back one rib at a time. The curtain falls like a jaw. They watch it, Nell and Peggy and Stella.

"Where will we perform?" Nell asks.

424

"Huffen Black said Jasper was going to use the old tent," Stella murmurs.

"What if he doesn't want us?" Peggy says. "What if we have to find a new showman?" She sucks at a bleeding fingernail. "I don't want to be put on a podium. Laughed at and mocked and —"

"Stop it," Stella interrupts. She puts an arm around Peggy's shoulders, squeezes. "He'll keep us. The crowds say they want novelty, but they don't really. Any showman worth his salt knows that."

"It's easy for you and Nellie to say. I'm not the main act," Peggy says.

But Nell watches the destruction of the grandstand with a growing unease. How will she fly? Her balloon will not fit in that low, domed tent.

"I'm sure he's thought of us." But even Stella sounds distracted, nails raking a fleabite on her elbow.

She is not afraid of Jasper, Nell tells herself; he is just a man. She crosses the grass, and her footsteps creak in the dew. He has his back to her, is ordering wagons to be towed away, marking a sheet of paper. She touches her chest as if to remind herself that she is powerful. *Nellie Moon,* the audience used to chant, their applause fanning across the city.

He does not look at her, not even when she is standing beside him.

"Jasper," she says, in a voice quieter than she hoped for.

He turns, eyes narrowed.

"How will I fly in that tent?"

He does not reply but looks past her as if she is someone who does not matter.

"I will still fly, won't I?" she asks, more forcefully this time.

And then she sees it, the wicker basket being lifted into a caravan, the folded silk sheet.

It does not make sense; why would he do this to her? Nell runs toward it, hair beating her back. "That's my balloon," she cries. She tries to pull a corner of it, but the men push her away. There are footprints on the soft fabric, a small tear. Her ropes are wound into a ball.

"Yours?" Jasper asks, and his face twists into a smile.

She sees a trace of Toby in him, a sharper curve to his lip. His eyes are hard and watery. She remembers his hands on her wrists, pinning her to the floor, and she takes a step back.

"Nothing is yours."

"But the crowds," she insists, unable to keep the desperation from her voice. "What

426

about the crowds? They want to see me."

"I told you, my new show will be different." Jasper looks at her. "Did you know they call you the hot-air girl? That they say there's no skill to you. Just a puppet on strings."

His words might be branded into her skin; Nell is so taken aback, so hurt by them that she cannot find a retort. *It isn't true,* she tells herself. What she does requires agility too. But she feels as if he has a needle and is slowly unpicking her. She would like to thrash and kick as she did on that first day, to rend the silk in two, to smash her fists against the wagon until her palms are stippled with splinters. But she cannot bear to let him see how much she cares; and what's more, she *needs* him. There is nothing to do but walk away, walk back to the wagon, to where Pearl fits herself into her arms and shows her the seeds she has dried for Benedict. Toby is sitting in the middle of the bed, carving her a whistle from a piece of wood.

"What's the matter?" he asks. "What's happened?"

He is Jasper's brother. He is there in the line of his nose, in his eyes. Nell turns away from him.

When she hears the wagons process

through the gates, she does not join the milling grooms and laborers. Her balloon is gone. She hopes only that Jasper has a new idea for her, a different way for her to rise.

Overhead, she watches geese leaving for winter, skimming low over the city. One of the triplets aims a pistol at them. Nell jumps at the crack.

"What was that?" Pearl asks, reaching for her hand.

"It was only birds," she replies.

Geese plummet like rocks. Someone screams at the triplets to stop it.

JASPER

It is the departure of the animals that Jasper cannot stand. The sea lions meant little to him, but he turns away when the largest leopard and the bear are sold. He feeds Minnie five cabbages, laughing as she reaches her trunk behind his back and plucks them from him. He pats the thick bristles on her head, strokes the ears the traders shredded with hooks.

"One day I'll buy you back," he tells her when she is loaded into the wagon, door slamming shut. She bucks, whinnies, and he feeds her another cabbage. He watches her go, standing at the entrance of the pleasure gardens, hands on his hips. The bright caravan, bumping down the road, his little elephant inside.

Beside Jasper, laborers lash the container of reptiles to a van, the sea lions barking in their slopping metal tank. His grandstand has been dismantled, the wood sold to a shipbuilder in Greenwich. His old tent is stretched out on the grass, and men are on their knees, scrubbing it with beeswax and pitch to make it watertight.

If he had known this would happen two weeks ago, it would have broken him. To his surprise, he finds he is curiously calm, almost relieved. Tomorrow, the shipbuilder will pay him, and this will give him enough to reimburse the Jackal. He wrote to the debtor yesterday, assuring him that his installment would be delivered, just a little late, explaining his illness. He has heard nothing. No letter in reply, but no threats, either. Still, he finds himself flinching at the slightest movement, and he has even fitted a lock to his wagon door.

"I'll look after Minnie," Winston says, and Jasper straightens. "She'll be the star of my show."

"Heaven knows, you need something to entertain your audiences of three peasants," Jasper replies, watching as the llamas are herded into a small caravan.

He has a few animals left — some monkeys, a lion, a snake, some of his birds — but only because Winston doesn't want them. His show will be different, Jasper reminds himself, better. It will be unlike anything anyone has ever seen before.

"I've recently acquired a pair of leopard twins," Winston says. "Vitiligo. It's a shame for Nellie Moon. My heart breaks for her, truly it does."

"Good," Jasper says.

"Good?" Winston asks, surprised.

"I don't care for her any longer," Jasper says.

"How curious," Winston smiles. "You pipped me to that albino girl. It was very sly of you."

"She's yours, if you pay me enough."

"Truly?"

Jasper has barely seen the girl since he bought her, just a glimpse of her disappearing behind wagons, sitting quietly by the fire. He is vaguely aware that she sleeps in Nell's wagon, that they have formed an attachment to each other, that Toby dotes on her too. Their own little *happy family.* Jasper suppresses a grin, remembers the courtier's polite smile, the moment his world tipped over.

"How much do you want for her?"

"A thousand."

The man laughs. "In your wildest dreams. Only a clown would pay that much."

Jasper is so very tired. "Very well. Five hundred."

They shake on it.

431

"When will you pay me?" Jasper asks. "I can come to your show tomorrow and collect it."

"Not for another week."

"A week?" Jasper is aghast. "I need it sooner than that. You can't empty my menagerie and half my wagons and —"

Winston shrugs. "Show me another man who'll buy them sooner, but by then I shan't be interested."

It's bluster, Jasper tells himself; *it's all bluster.* But what if Winston means it? He's right; he'd struggle to find another buyer, and it might take weeks to arrange. If only the Jackal would acknowledge his letter, would forgive the delay — the shipbuilder will pay him only tomorrow, and then he'll have enough, just, for another payment —

"Very well," Jasper says, unable to look at Winston. An idea forms. "You can come to my new show, pay me, and fetch the child afterward."

"Your new show?"

Jasper smiles, savoring the panic on the man's face. "You'll see."

"The suspense is unbearable." Winston yawns, but his eyes dart to the side, as if to discern a clue in the paltry animals Jasper has kept.

Once Winston has gone, Jasper begins to

pace. He must concentrate on his future. He thinks of the intricate ink drawings that wait for him on his desk. Metal lungs, patchwork bodies. Tomorrow he will have enough to pay the Jackal; today, even with Winston deferring most of his payments, he has enough money to begin work.

He binds his plans into a tight bundle and saddles his horse. He pushes her into a trot, leads her down narrow roads toward Battersea. It is a hot day, and thirst only tightens his anxiety. Dirt sticks to him, and he chokes on the fumes of burning tallow and a thousand roadside fires.

What if the Jackal isn't content with the delay? What if he is following him, even now? He digs his spurs into his horse's side, checks behind him.

Up ahead, Jasper sees the wide workshops that his blacksmith told him about. He jumps from his horse and rings the bell, the papers gripped in his hand.

The owner takes a while to arrive, wiping his palms on a scrap of old leather. He ushers Jasper inside. There are carriage yokes scattered on the floor, a box filled with metal candlesticks, blades and axe ends and machine cogs. It stinks of hot oil, of woodsmoke. Iron clangs like the tolling of a great bell.

Jasper smooths his plans on a workbench, and the man grunts, traces his thumb over each part. His fears retreat, a certainty settling in. He thinks of Victor Frankenstein and the monster that ruined him; his problem, Jasper realizes, was that Frankenstein's creation was endowed with a soul. What if that lightning bolt had never animated his beast, what if his patchwork creature existed within his absolute control?

"And that wing is yoked to that socket," the man says.

Jasper corrects him, gestures and talks quickly, at home in this language, in this world. If he'd been born poor, he'd have worked in a place like this, where things slot neatly together and machines are built. He might have raised himself as an engineer, a bridge maker, a rifle manufacturer.

"It'll take two weeks," the man says.

"Impossible," Jasper says. "I've already sourced the bones from Smithfield, and the fish hides from Billingsgate, so you need only make the structure. I require it in a week, sooner if you can."

The man shakes his head, begins folding up his notes for him.

He needs to be making money soon to pay the Jackal again, and the tent's capacity is smaller than the grandstand. "Please," Jas-

434

per begs him. "I can pay you double. Anything."

More money, promised away. Jasper runs his thumb across the ridge of his gullet.

The man cocks his head. "Triple," he says. His eyes have the dull, glazed look of a partridge. At last, Jasper folds the paper into his pocket and agrees.

The moment Jasper leaves the workshop, he is set upon. Arms bind him. A fist smacks his teeth. A rush of blood in his mouth. Pain, searing, his wrist wrenched back. He is hauled down a narrow street where there are cinder heaps and old ashes.

This is how it ends, he thinks, and the sun gleams and dances in elaborate patterns.

He is shoved to the ground, and kicks land with a force so sharp he feels only their impact, the air crushed from his lungs, a low crunch that might be his nose or a tooth. A seam of a boot, the stitching loose, the leather rimed. A foot on his neck. He waits for the gleam of a blade, tugged across his throat. He tells himself he will stare death in the eye, as he did every day in the Crimea. But as he lies there, the knife twisting and flashing in the man's hand, a desperation grips him, and he finds himself beginning to cry.

"Shall we slit his squeaking pipe, then?"

"No," Jasper gasps. "Please, please." Here he is, face in the dirt, begging for his life.

Every second, he expects the slide of a coin on his tongue, a cool metallic taste.

"The fucker's pissed himself," one of the men laughs.

The Jackal crouches to his level, his little teeth punctuating a smile.

"The money," he says. "You *assured* me you would have it. You *promised* me you would be a success."

"Tomorrow," he croaks.

"We agreed," the Jackal says, "that you would pay on time. And this is the *third* payment you're late on."

Jasper spits out a tooth, sucks blood from the cavity. "I have a way of making more. An idea. More than an idea. I have the answer."

"Let's hear it."

He tells the Jackal about his plans, the instructions he has just delivered to the blacksmith, a task too great for his own smithy to take on. A leaner show, an easier one, almost empty of human wonders. No performers absconding or fighting or demanding more money, no animals to feed and water. He tells him about the showmen who've pulled themselves back from the jaws of ruin. He tells him he can do it too. He tells these stories with a yearning that cuts into him, as if their lives are his own.

The Jackal nods and says he will wait another day, but if he defaults once again — he pauses. Jasper sinks forward. The ash is as soft as a pillow. His horse is gone, run off or stolen.

He breathes in thick, life-giving gasps, touches his heart where it thunders. *Alive.*

He cleans the blood from his nose in a barrel of filthy water, dabs at his damp britches.

TOBY

Everybody, it seems to Toby, has a secret. The trees rustle messages to each other, birds pass titbits of gossip. The laborers seal themselves in tight packs. Everyone is brittle and fractious. A tumbler breaks her arm when practicing forward flips. Huffen Black drops a tray of dishes. Scuffles break out with scant provocation, children beaten for doing little more than talking. Whispers pass, *The show, what's his show?* A few performers leave. Jasper keeps only five laborers, a slim pack of those most loyal to him.

Once again, Toby ferries and lifts. He secures those old king poles, just as he has done for years, pulls the tent as taut as a drum. He hammers stakes into the ground, and each lift of the mallet drags his shoulders down, as if he is being pulled beneath the surface of the sea. He wears his shirt tightly buttoned, his tattoos concealed. His brother weaves between the laborers, bellowing instructions. *Lift, pull, yes, there.* Less than a week ago, Toby stood in the middle of the ring, his skin rippling and flashing as the crowd roared. Already, it feels as though it happened to somebody else, that he could never have done it. He is a dullard, he tells himself, raising the hammer above his head. The iron sings. A dullard.

"Faster! I want the tent secured by dusk!"

Toby narrows his eyes, casts the stake to one side. His brother cannot force him to work, cannot wind him up like a tin toy. He unfastens the top buttons of his shirt, walks to where Nell is slicing cabbages. She looks at him as though daring him to do it. He wraps his arms around her, and she makes a small, contented sound. He feels the scorch of Jasper's gaze, but Toby only draws her closer. "What are you thinking about?" he whispers. "You were smiling at something."

She taps his nose, pulls free. "Nothing."

"Tell me," he says, and even he can hear the ugly desperation in his voice.

He aches to think she has lived before him, that she exists apart from him. He has a crazed urge to understand every detail about her, to be at the core of somebody else's story for the first time, to be the hero of her life. Recollections rise, his days spent on the fringes of Jasper's existence. Sitting in his bedroom and listening to his brother laughing downstairs, his eye stinging from where a sugared almond hit him. Snorts of amusement between Dash and Jasper, a bottle of grog passed from lip to lip, Toby trailing them. *What was the joke? What was it?* A small shake of the head. *Nothing that would entertain you.*

Toby glances at Jasper, his face a patchwork of bruises, his arm cradled like a bird's broken wing. What happened to him? What is *he* hiding? He watches Jasper limp toward the gate.

He dithers for a moment. Why should Jasper know everything about him and yet keep himself opaque? Before Toby can change his mind, he slings a saddle over Grimaldi and canters after his brother. He rides so far behind that he almost loses sight of Jasper, but he cannot risk nearing him. He has a new horse, Toby notes, a ragged bay. Every few seconds, Jasper glances around him, takes quick turns, doubles back on himself. What is he working on that he must be this secretive, this wary? There was a time when Jasper might have confided in him.

His brother dismounts at a blacksmith's shop. Thick smoke billows. Clanging comes from within. Toby cannot understand why he isn't using his own smithy, what reason he could have for employing a workshop this large. He is in there for hours, so late that Toby begins to wonder if he has left through another door; but when he creeps closer, he hears his brother's voice, barking commands. Jasper doesn't emerge until it is almost dark, leaping onto his horse and pushing it into a quick gallop. Somebody shouts at him to slow down, but he is gone, dust rising like mist.

Toby waits and waits. His belly aches with hunger, and the moon is as thin as a wishbone.

It is late when the clattering stops. Beefy men file out. The last man locks the workshop with a thick chain and crosses the road to a small stooped cottage. The yard is quiet. Toby leads Grimaldi to the wall, ties him to a metal ring. There is a window at the back, shuttered, the wood split. With a quick jab of his elbow, Toby cracks the frame of it, brushes away loose glass. He scrambles inside. The coals from the fire are white-hot, and he blinks at the sudden brightness. Lanterns hang from the ceiling. The horse puts his head through the window and harrumphs.

Toby tiptoes past all of it. Pokers and

knives, anvils and cogs. An open piano with tiny hammers. In the corner, he sees what looks like a printing press, its levers poised. He shuffles across the ash-carpeted floor. How will he find what Jasper is working on?

But he recognizes it the instant he sees it. The microscope slides have come to life. Jasper has formed those creatures — magnified and colossal — in metal. Five of them in a row, nestled in wooden coffins. Iron beasts with jaws and teeth, long gleaming bones and scales made of beaten tin. Each has a lever, a careful system of cogs. One is a vast wood louse, its body upholstered with leather, built like a miniature steam engine. There is a fly, too, with wings like Nell once wore, its visage stitched with fish skins. Feathers are stuck to it, fine ribs that might be a hawk's or a rabbit's. Toby's fingers slide down their spines, span the edges of their wings. His palms are creased with black oil. He brushes his hand against the spider with its long crab-leg limbs, horsehair stippling the joints. It creaks. These patchwork creatures; he stares at the oven, still hot, the forge where they were made from a hundred assembled parts. Victor Frankenstein robbed graveyards, dug up motley pieces of flesh and skin and bone, and sewed them together. *A monster,* he thinks, staring at the spider's mouth, cow's teeth mingled with the metal.

He steps on a nail and stumbles. He wants to be away from here; he wants to be back in his wagon, Nell's arm tucked around him, Pearl asleep on the floor. He turns, lunging for the window. Glass scatters across the ground, but he is scrambling into the yard, blood on his arm. He lands heavily, pulls himself to his feet, unties Grimaldi's rope with trembling hands. He mounts his horse, and his boots aren't even in the stirrups before he urges it forward. "Go," he whispers. And he is on the street, flying even faster than Jasper did.

Everywhere, there are eyes on Pearl, laborers watching her. After dark, Nell sees only the burning tips of their cigars, knows that they are close. She is certain it must mean Jasper is selling the child, that he has her worth in mind. Nell's fingernails are shredded, the skin around her lips dry and flaking. Sometimes, in that blue hinterland between sleep and waking, she thinks of the knife she stole from the apartments and imagines dragging it across Jasper's throat. She thinks of Julia Pastrana, her and her baby's stuffed bodies shown around the world, dressed in the red frock her hands once sewed. She thinks of Charles Byrne, his bones stripped and displayed against his will. It is so horrifying her mind numbs. She cannot imagine how such existences must have felt, cannot grasp the texture of these people's lives beyond the rudimentary facts. If Stella were here, she knows her friend would tell her about other acts — those who enjoy performing, or at least its spoils. Chang and Eng Bunker, the farmstead they bought, their many children. Lavinia Warren and Charles Stratton, married with a mansion and a yacht and a stable of horses. But still, Nell cannot stop thinking of Pearl, alone on a podium, a physician circling her. She pulls the girl tight against her.

One evening, when the tent is raised and the sun is low and Jasper has ridden out, she and Pearl wander through the pleasure gardens. The sky is gray like chewed gristle. Pearl swings on the ribs of the iguanodon. Nell flicks her finger against its bones. Toby told her that the creature that gave rise to this mold died thousands and thousands of years ago. Its skeleton was picked clean, rain eating away at the soil, exposing the glossy bowl of its pelvis, a black jaw. And then pickaxes and scalpels prized away the rocks around it, unsettled it from where it had slept for so many centuries. A body laid bare. Gentlemen cataloged it, named it after themselves, tied labels to bones, wadded it into wooden crates, all seventeen feet of it, their miniature hammers knocking at clavicle and skull.

Nell imagines a bolt of lightning, a lowering storm. The grass, lit white. She pictures a stone finger flexing, concrete splintering, the cries of alarm as the creature breaks free of the metal pins that hold it in place. A monster, lumbering through the park, shucking Jasper like an oyster. It would pounce on her and Pearl and gather them up, embrace them, carry them away.

"Did you see me jumping?" Pearl asks, shuffling over tree roots. She hops and skips, hops and skips, and Nell claps. Behind them, the square-jawed laborer kicks the earth.

"Am I the newest spectacle you've ever seen?"

She takes the girl by the hand. "You aren't a spectacle at all," she says. "You're a girl, a perfect little girl."

Pearl frowns, uncertain what to do with this sudden earnestness. She lowers herself onto Nell's lap.

Should they have run away when Jasper was sick, as Toby suggested? But Nell could not bear to flee, to feel hunted as Brunette must. And in doing so, she would be turning herself into only a mother and a wife. Toby wants her to be those things, and she wants them too; but she also wants to perform, to feel that hum of brilliance as a crowd watches her and cheers, to be *some-*

446

one. The Queen of the Moon and Stars — anger snaps through her, but it has nowhere to go, no way of being let out. She relies on Jasper, cannot confront him. It retreats into her, brims in her chest.

Nell sits there, rocking the girl, playing with her toes. Pearl smells of boiled milk, of fresh hay. *A miracle,* Nell thinks. *This child is a miracle.*

There is a sudden commotion, raised voices, the blast of trumpets.

Nell grips Pearl's hand, and together they take the woodchip path back to where the tent sits. It squats among the trees like a giant toadstool, wagons lined close beside it, newly made papier-mâché fruits dangling from the branches. Two caravans roll through the gates, stop in the mud where the grandstand once was. Jasper sits on the box seat and, in the sunset, his topper blazes.

Wagon doors and discarded pans clatter, performers and grooms and laborers pressing forward. She finds Stella and Peggy and does not release Pearl's hand. She cannot see Toby; he must still be in the city, carrying out the errand Jasper sent him on.

"Can I stay?" Pearl whispers, and Nell nods, keeps the child close to her where Jasper will not see her.

"What's inside?" Peggy asks.

"I heard it's a mermaid," Huffen Black says.

Stella snorts. "Those fakeries barely duped the masses a hundred years ago."

"Is it a new performer?" Nell asks. She pictures a girl bound inside each caravan, fighting to free herself.

"I want to see," Pearl whines. "I can't see."

"Wait —" Nell says, but the child has snatched her hand away and wriggled forward. Nell moves to find her, but the crowd is too tight, elbows beating her back when she attempts to push through. She tries to breathe evenly.

"She just wants to see," Stella says. "Let her go."

Nell glances at the wagon, and Jasper is grinning, conducting the trumpet with a wide swing of his arms. She wonders again what is inside — people? Animals? A magician? The wagons are padlocked with chains. Perhaps the creature is dangerous. Perhaps it is a real plesiosaur in a tank, netted by fishermen.

"The hacks are desperate for novelty," he bellows. "And tomorrow they will discover its true meaning."

"What's inside?" Violante shouts.

A murmuring of agreement, feet shuffling, necks craned.

The call, louder. "What's inside?"

"I'd wager it's a giant. A real giant. Bigger than Brunette ever was," Huffen Black says.

Every eye is on the wagon, as if expecting the creature to buck free of the wood, to cast the iron struts aside.

Nell forces herself to look away. She cranes her head for a flash of white hair, that little blue frock.

Stella squeezes her hand. "You can't watch her forever. I warned you not to get too close to her."

The truth of it stings Nell's eyes.

"She'll be fine," Stella whispers, linking her arm through hers. "I'm sure of it."

"Tomorrow you will see my newest trick," Jasper continues. "Tomorrow, the world will see these creatures for the very first time. You will be startled, amazed, incredulous. We will be the greatest show in the world!"

Pearl will be with the triplets, Nell thinks. Stella is right; the child will be safe.

"I've printed handbills, notices, taken advertisements in *The Times*. Hacks will flood to our show tomorrow."

Jasper talks on, and Nell watches him, the fire globes now lit beside him. He speaks with the confidence of a man who is imagin-

449

ing an audience greater than the one laid before him, who expects, even here, for his words to be recorded and remembered.

She thinks of the books on her shelves: all their tales of transformation, of joy, of death. A monster hunted across the world. A mermaid caught in the liminal state between girl and fish. The yearned-for feet that bled whenever she stepped on them. But these characters are not real. No book could capture the truth of what she feels.

"My creations are marvelous, magnificent, the most extraordinary thing you will ever see —"

Every writer, Nell thinks, *is a thief and a liar.*

Jasper's machines will not do a bunk, or demand more money, or fight or die. They will not eat their way through crisp piles of pounds and guineas; they will not be pursued by the law. He need only run an oiled cloth over their joints, tighten their couplings, polish their skin. And most importantly, they will not eclipse him, because *he* is their inventor. They exist within his outright control.

He balls his fists, punches the air. "Our show will be the greatest in the world!" he bellows, and they all cheer, all raise their arms as if he is turning a great lever. Bats fly low like sparrows, scream in the trees.

He stands on that wagon, and he sees the hungry eyes of his troupe — laborers, performers, grooms — and he feels a fleeting stab of sadness that soon he will require so few of them. But this is the machine age. Steam engines belch their way across the

451

country, printing presses churn out identical journals, cotton mills spin bobbins the size of cartwheels. And human beings are the collateral of progress — jobs lost, skills fallen away. Soon, there will be no need for most of mankind, the world ruled by those who have had the ingenuity to innovate, to evolve.

His press agent wrote to say he had found Brunette living in a small cottage near Whitstable. She was married to a fisherman, he said, no longer wanted to show herself. The agent expected Jasper to drag her back, to force her before crowds with threats of debtors' prison and blackmail, but he waved his hand and said to leave her. There will always be a stranger person to be found, a show eclipsing his own. When he heard that the Queen had declared Winston's leopard boys a finer sight than Nellie Moon, he felt nothing but satisfaction. Nell's career will end with the abruptness with which he began it.

When Victor made his great monster and it grew too strong, he had to destroy it.

He searches for her, sees her standing there with Stella, her eyes on him. His stomach tips, queasy with triumph. It is easier than he thought possible; the child is not even beside her, but standing at the front with the triplets. He gives a slight nod, and a laborer pushes through the crowd, coaxes Pearl away with a brown mouse in a cage. Soon, Jasper will show Nell what it means to be eclipsed, what it means to be forgotten.

"Let us see," they cry, clawing forward. He cracks his whip. The wagon shudders.

"Tomorrow," he shouts. "Tomorrow."

Tomorrow he will unveil the creatures as the finale of his show. He has ordered fireworks, Catherine wheels and hundreds of twinkling candles. In their reflected light, the machines will gleam like oil. The tent will fall silent. Mouths will gape, eyes widen. A hush will descend. Jasper will stand there, his arms raised, as the monsters begin to flap their iron wings, to open and close their mandibles. A man will stagger to his feet, and then another beside him, and the tent will roar with the force of their wonder. He will rake in the money then, pay off the Jackal in weeks.

P. T. Barnum owned whales captured near Labrador. He stored them, alive, in fifty-foot tanks in the basement of his museum. The walls were lit with gas, but the light frightened the creatures and they skulked at the bottom of their containers, rising only to breathe. A woman told him that she knew it was humbug — that the sea monster was fabricated from India rubber. It was a machine, operated by steam, she said, the bursts of air blown by bellows.

How much better, Jasper thinks, to create actual machines, to have the crowds look not for the seam or trick, but to marvel in what is real, in what he has created. To stare as they stared at the first locomotives.

Jasper Jupiter, they will cry, and he wishes only that the machines might speak, that they, too, could proclaim his name.

"Tomorrow, you will all perform as usual, and then I will unveil my new act," he announces. He watches Nell carefully, struggling under his gaze like an insect beneath his microscope. She looks about her, eyes landing where the child was an instant before. "With a single exception. *This* finale will replace the one that ran before it."

A pause, as the troupe takes in his words. He watches Nell's expression change. A murmuring.

"You may surmise," Jasper intones, his heart quickening with daring, with delight, "that this means Nellie Moon is gone. Faded. Vanished."

She is beginning to panic, he sees. She can sense the net tightening around her. She is forcing her way through the crowd, searching for the child. She almost knocks over one of the triplets. This is the sort of spectacle he craves; those who fly too high will always be brought low.

"The truth is," Jasper says, "that the public have grown tired of Nellie. She has been eclipsed by Winston's leopard boys."

He sees Stella shake her head at him, and the shame is hot but fleeting. *You're better than this,* he thinks, recalling Toby's words of more than two months ago, back before any of this began, before he had even seen Nell.

Jasper nods at the laborers, and three of them move forward, seize Nell by the arms. She gives a small cry. He wonders, for a moment, if he has misjudged this, if this is excessive even for him. If, perhaps, his troupe will side with her. He jumps from the wagon, carves his way through the crowd. He speaks more softly now, his lungs choked with a feeling he does not recognize.

He watches as her eyes search the crowd for Pearl, as she sees the triplets standing alone. "Pearl?" Nell calls, and then she looks at Jasper with an expression close to terror. "Where is she?" she demands, fighting against the men who bind her. "What have you done to her?"

"I don't want to make a spectacle," he

says, trying to keep his voice steady. "I just want you to leave."

She snaps her head up. "Leave?"

"You can join any other troupe you choose."

The grass makes a ripping sound under her feet.

"You *bought* me."

"And now I can dispose of you."

"Where is she?" Nell's voice, rising.

"You'll only frighten her if she hears you."

He is stunned by how helpless she looks, how lost. Can this be the girl who held London spellbound? She looks nothing more than a gutter wretch — He tamps down the nausea that rises in his chest.

"Pearl," Nell shouts, and the laborers grip her by the waist, by the arm. She thrashes, kicks, bites. "Pearl!"

"Send her out," Jasper says, clicking his fingers.

"Pearl," Nell calls, frantic now.

Hatred simmers in her eyes, a loathing so acute that Jasper looks at the sky instead, at the narrow smirk of the moon. He remembers when he desired her, when he was bursting with plans for her.

"Help me," Nell cries. "Please."

Stella turns to him, and he has never seen such disgust on her face. He takes a step back. "What are you doing, Jasper?"

He cannot look at her, cannot meet her eye. He thinks of the early days when Stella was the star of his show, the moments of quietness that they shared together, something approaching love. Something approaching what Dash had enjoyed and he had wanted.

"Get away from her," Jasper says, circling the whip.

Peggy steps forward, forcing herself between Nell and a laborer. The women will not move, but they do not raise their fists, either. Perhaps they know that battle is futile, that their bodies are too soft and small and easily outflanked. Stella dabs Nell's cut lip, whispers to her. When Nell tries to buck free, Stella grips her cheeks, says something that Jasper cannot hear. Hands on her back, murmured comfort. *Love,* he thinks, and there is a catch in his voice again.

And then Toby is there, back sooner than Jasper expected, elbowing his way through the crowd. Jasper curses under his breath. "T-T-Toby," he stammers. His brother's shoulders are drawn back, fury and determination written on his face. Jasper feels his grip loosening, the thread of power slipping away. He has the curious sensation that he

457

is playing a part badly, that this is somehow not him at all.

"What's happening?" Toby demands. "What are you doing to her?" He collars a laborer, hurls him onto the grass.

Jasper moves his weight from one foot to the other, his chest tight. His brother seems larger than ever before — those trunklike legs, those arms that hang like butcher's meat.

"Pearl," Nell says, clutching at Toby's shirt. "He's taken Pearl."

"Where is she?" Toby demands.

"How heroic," Jasper sneers. "Look at what you've become."

There it is, laid between them, as clean and horrifying as a body on a slab. Toby's disdain. How long has it been since his brother looked at him with admiration, with awe?

"What I've become?" He tries to steady his voice, to add grit to it.

"Let her go," Toby demands, and the laborers shift back. He is strong, Jasper realizes, his chest as hard as a ship's hull; he could scatter these men like a flock of fine-boned birds. Jasper has never witnessed Toby's fury before, has only ever discovered its aftermath. The shattered microscope, the broken man. His brother's neck is pink, a vein trembling in his temple.

Jasper lets out a small laugh to indicate he does not care. He is having trouble focusing. He can taste blood. He touches his nose to check if he is bleeding. The pistol is cold against his hip. He struggles to keep his mind clear. "Nell is to leave this show, and if she returns, I will kill her."

The threat feels too big, like that of a floundering child, so mighty it is empty of any meaning.

"If she leaves, I leave," Toby says.

Jasper stares at him. Toby's eyes are dark, wet with fury, like staring into a looking glass. "W-What?" he stammers.

"If she leaves, I leave too," Toby says. "You're nothing without me."

Jasper's mouth opens with a snide retort, but the words are not there.

He watches as his brother takes a step toward Nell. He pulls her to him. The women link arms, as if in a chain against Jasper. Stella is whispering to her, squeezing her hand, nodding assurances.

When they were children and Toby couldn't sleep, he would sneak into Jasper's room and lie down on the mattress beside him. Jasper would wake in the morning and see his brother's curls spread on the pillow, his chest rising and falling. It was enough to send him into a second slumber, their hands joined in a tiny fist. They were everything to each other.

We're brothers, linked together.

"Get out," he says, quietly. He raises his whip, cracks it down. "Get out!" he bellows. "Get out, both of you!"

He is the wolf, Jasper tells himself, the wolf; he thinks of the neat bones Toby found in the *Happy Families* cage, polished clean of meat. The wolf, licking its paws.

Toby turns to leave, Nell pressed against him. Jasper stares at his brother. He cannot be leaving; he cannot possibly be leaving. After all he has given Toby — his fist moves as if he has no command over it. It lands on his brother's ribs with a sharp smack. Pain flowers up his arm, an electricity seizing hold of him. He pummels harder, sweat stinging his eyes, his shirt damp with it. The irresistible urge to hurt, to make another person suffer as he does, to exert his mastery over the situation. And then, Jasper stumbles back, the world swinging down to meet him. What has happened? He is sprawled on the ground, the taste of coins in his mouth, Toby standing above him, rubbing his knuckles.

No, he thinks, *this is not how it goes.*

He tries to stand, but the wagons are rocking like boats unloosed from their moorings. He can think of only one thing that will stop Toby, that will signal his triumph.

"What did you do to Dash, Toby? Why don't you tell everyone what happened to Dash?"

His brother turns, his mouth open.

He has him, he thinks. And with it a curious relief, that this secret no longer binds him, that he is free too.

Jasper expects Stella to turn on Toby, for that confrontation to bubble over at last. But she hasn't heard him, his words lost to the wind. And Toby; he thought he would fall to his knees, would grovel, beg for pity, reminded of how Jasper protected him. But when he looks up, Toby is gone, vanished into the crowd.

■ ■ ■ ■

Part Five

■ ■ ■ ■

Altius egit iter.
He drove his journey higher.
— OVID, "Daedalus and Icarus" from
Metamorphoses, Book VIII, AD 8

NELL

Nell sits in the corner at an inn, the table scarred with spilled wine and hundreds of little cutlery nicks. Opposite her, Toby splays his hand and stabs a blade between the gaps, faster and faster. Part of her longs for the knife to slip, to watch the frantic blossom of red. There should be blood, ripped flesh, the chaos of physicians and black-plumed horses. There should be mangled bones and screams and cries. Could her brother have sensed this coming; is this what Charlie tried to warn her about?

In the middle of the room, a woman laughs, and Nell digs her fingernails into her thighs.

She wonders if Pearl is asleep, her thumb in her mouth. She wonders if she is frightened, if Stella has found her or if she is already with another showman, alone in an unfamiliar place. When Jasper threw Nell from the troupe, Stella whispered that she would find Pearl or discover where Jasper had sent her, that Nell should return tomorrow just before the show begins. Jasper will be distracted, Stella added, and she will bring the child to her if she can. Nell shuts her eyes, tries to imagine kissing the peach down of Pearl's cheek, hearing her chatter about Benedict and the seeds he likes best.

It is nearing midnight, and the innkeeper yawns, clinks the glasses against each other in the hope they will understand his hint. Around them, chairs are upended. She thinks of the animals shut in their cages. She thinks of Stella and Peggy and Brunette.

Toby grips her hand to stop it tapping against the table. Her rage, so sharp it feels combustible. It tightens her jaw like a bolt. She has been bought and spat out. Turned into an outcast, taken away from everything that matters to her.

"Come," Toby says, and Nell can do nothing but follow him.

They didn't have time to take anything with them. No money, no fresh clothes. The innkeeper and his wife have allowed them dinner and a bed with the horses if they clean the stables in the morning. As they leave, Toby touches Nell's arm in quiet protection, and she realizes that the innkeeper's wife was laughing at her.

The stable is small and grimy, the hay soiled. Nell sits on an old horse blanket, and Toby rests his chin on her shoulder.

"I won't sleep," she whispers. Her heart pounds. "What if he's already sold her? What if he hurts her?"

Toby breathes out slowly. "You have to wait until tomorrow. There's nothing you can do now."

She should be finding a way to Pearl. She should be *doing* something, rocking the wagons, setting loose the animals. How can she just lie here? Horses shift nearby. Toby tucks his body around hers, and the comfort is fleeting. There was a time when this would have meant everything to her, when she wanted only for somebody to love her. Through the tiny window, she watches the moon sharpening itself like a polished scythe.

A recollection rises. That first night after she was sold, hands ripping pages out of books. An anger that felt fresh and new. Spines cracking in her fist.

"What would you think," Toby whispers, "if I told you I'd done something terrible?"

She shuts her eyes. "Is it about Pearl?"

"No," he says. "Of course not." A pause. "Would you forgive me?"

Nell pulls the blanket up to her chin. She

doesn't want to hear it. She wants to concentrate on Pearl, to will her into being until she becomes real again. She cannot be burdened with anything else, an incomplete story that she will be forced to make sense of. "Don't tell me. I don't want to hear it."

Quiet, just the rustle of straw, a horse kicking. The gap between their breaths seems to stretch, growing more and more distant. She scratches the birthmark on her wrist. The skin is thinner, and she can feel it beginning to break.

"Nell?" he asks.

She doesn't reply. She catches the trace of Jasper in Toby's voice. Their noses, alike; their eyes, so similar. She puts her hands over her ears.

Above her, she watches a spider sewing its careful web.

TOBY

They work all morning in the stable. Nell flinches at the rustling of leaves, at the clatter of hooves. "We just have to wait," Toby tells her. "I'm sure we'll find her." She pulls away when he tries to hold her, a coldness that is close to fury. That familiar feeling, of being unwanted. His mouth presses downward, and he turns back to scrubbing the tack, the leather grimed with dust and horsehair.

"Let me clean the floor. You can rest," he says, and it is not kindness so much as a need to feel useful. "Please."

But Nell swats him away as easily as a donkey shakes off a fly. She works as if she is a storm unleashed. Her hair flies about her, mouth tight, a narrowing in her eyes. She hurls metal buckets at the wall, scrubs the cobbles until her trousers are torn and her knees bleeding. Fetid water clots the gutters. He can do nothing to comfort her.

"Nell," he tries, but she doesn't answer. *Dullard,* he thinks. *Half bear.*

He longs to please Nell, to make her smile. If he could, he would find Pearl, carry her on his back, return like a hero fulfilling a quest. Perhaps, then, she would love him with the same ferocity with which she loves the child.

He bows his head, tries to lose himself in the brushing and rinsing. This is all he has ever been good for: his body not his own, but a mat to be trodden on, a scraper against which boots are cleaned. His life will always settle into the same grooves. He can escape it no more than the wolf could forget how to kill.

"Nell," Toby tries again, and he finds he is close to tears.

At noon, the innkeeper brings them a small pie of sour vegetables, and Toby chews each mouthful for minutes, can barely swallow. Nell doesn't even pick at the pastry. The man returns, hands in his pockets.

"Are you Nellie Moon?"

Nell does not reply.

"I saw you in Jasper Jupiter's Circus of Wonders. We all did."

The man brushes the marks on her hand. She doesn't flinch. Toby would like to push him away, but the moment passes, and he takes another bite of the pie.

"I bought a figurine of you. It's on my mantelpiece, beside Chang and Eng Bunker. They were a marvelous sight too."

When neither of them speaks, he coughs, nods, and retreats.

Toby wants to say something to comfort Nell or make her smile, to induce any reaction in her. The chewed food sounds loud in his mouth, the wet crunch of his teeth. He picks at the crust, his knuckles swollen. He cannot remember the swing of his arm, the flash of impact. Just his brother floored, the look of disbelief on his face.

It was the same with Dash, that instant of falling clouded. He has run over it so many times, and he is still unsure what he intended, what happened.

Nell links her fingers between his. She does not tell him to stop crying.

"I did a terrible thing," he says. "A monstrous thing."

But she says only, "We have to find her."

He kisses her hair. "I know."

The day is scorching, as sharp as a needle. It is one of those late summer days when the world feels overripe and ready to burst. Dogs pant in the shade, their ribcages vibrating. Earthworms are baked to shoe-

471

laces. A candle, left in the sun, liquefies to milky fat. At least there is a breeze, sifting through the doors, unsettling the hay in the manger. When he is too hot, Toby pulls off his shirt. The colors ripple, gilding him. He sees Nell watching him.

Their life could be an ordinary one. A farm, perhaps, with a field of corn that he tends each day. A cottage with a blue door. A happiness that is particularly his to give. He has never needed power like Jasper. Love, he thinks; that is all he has ever wanted. To matter to somebody. He steps closer to her. She is so near. He can feel the promise of her breath on his chest.

She shuts her eyes.

It happens whenever she stands close to him. A pulling within him, impossible to deny. He wants to possess her, to kiss every part of her, to tease moans from her throat.

Nell turns away from him and begins forking hay once more.

Shame cools him. "I'm sorry," he says.

She touches his arm in quiet forgiveness. Perhaps it will be fine again; perhaps they will find Pearl and a way back to where they were before.

"Here they are!"

The innkeeper is there with four ladies.

"Do you want your horses?" Toby asks,

and Nell looks at him as if he is a fool.

The ladies peer in, lifting their shoes from the swirling muck. They are looking at him, he realizes, at his patterned chest, at Nell with her rolled-up sleeves.

"Quite something, aren't they?"

Laughter, beating round the stalls.

"She used to be famous, didn't she?"

"Come here, girl," the innkeeper says, clicking his fingers.

Toby moves closer to Nell, and perhaps they understand the threat, because the man scampers back. They walk away, laughing. "Finer freaks than you'd find in the Egyptian Hall. Just arrived here — We couldn't believe our eyes!"

"Nell —" Toby begins, but she looks at the floor, kicks mud into a little pile.

"Don't," she says. "Don't say anything."

All afternoon, the innkeeper brings small parties of guests to view them. Toby stares anywhere but at them: at the iron troughs, the wooden mangers, the hooks and ropes hanging from the walls. He is a beast, paraded about, put on display.

He can hear a bell being rung in the street, a shouted patter. "Freaks of nature! Human wonders! A penny a peek —"

You've turned yourself into one of them.

Toby did not imagine that it would be like this. The burn of eyes, laughter held behind hands. Staring at him as a *thing*.

At last, he hurls down his bucket. "I can't bear it," he says.

"Where will we go?"

"We'll wait in the trees by the lane, near the gates. Anywhere's better than this."

The innkeeper tries to stop them, tries to wheedle them into standing on two tables in his upstairs room, offers them five shillings each. Toby pushes past him. They walk back to Southwark through crowded streets, not touching. Their anger rubs against each other like flint. Clouds wound the sky. Crickets rasp and shiver. In an hour, his brother will begin his show. Perhaps, even now, he is preparing his mechanical creatures.

Toby pats down a patch of weeds under an oak tree. Through the railings of the pleasure gardens, they can see the corner of the tent, the wagons around it. He takes Nell's hand. "We'll find Pearl, and then we'll have a family," he says with a conviction he does not feel. "We'll live in a cottage near a forest, and we'll only need each other."

She stares between the fronds of long grass, as if willing the child to appear.

"A house with a blue door, and white

474

roses. I could work in the fields. It would be a peaceful life, a quiet one."

"A quiet life," Nell says with a snort. "I had a quiet life once." Her eyes are blood-shot, her lip trembling. "You don't know what it's like. I'd rather be up on the stage than in the slag heap with the rest of the world. I'd rather be *someone.*"

She fumbles in her pocket, pulls out a little object. It is a plaster figurine, wings on her back, toes pointed. "This is me."

"But you'll always belong to someone else."

She says it dully as if she cannot believe it. "Stella and I will have a troupe —"

"It won't happen," he says. "You know it won't."

She moves away from him. He has the mad notion that this is his punishment for what happened to Dash; that he might earn her love if he told her the truth about it.

Coward. Dullard.

He opens his mouth, but he cannot find the words.

NELL

The sun has set fire to the clouds, their bellies smoking like braziers. The grass is scorched, leaves wilting on the trees. When Nell cannot wait in the copse any longer, she crosses the lane and grips the railings. There are crowds outside the tent already, smells of burning chestnuts and hot sugar. She can see Bonnie's torches flickering as the girl juggles them higher and higher. There is a gasp, a roar of light. The spheres flare. Somewhere, among the scattered wagons and stalls and baying animals, Pearl might be waiting, if Jasper hasn't yet sold her. Nell plucks a dandelion and twists it. In her village, they will be laying the violet runners for winter, heaping the beds with piles of manure, repairing any cracks in the stone walls.

She hears Toby's footfall beside her. She lets him lace his fingers through hers. She remembers the thrill she once felt when he held her hand like this, the warmth of it, passing through her body.

"Can you see Stella?" Nell whispers.

"Not yet."

Hours seem to pass before she sees a figure hurrying toward her. Nell waves at her, beckons, but her heart is a stone in her chest. Stella is alone. Pearl is not with her.

"Perhaps she'll bring Pearl after the show," Toby says, and his voice is so aggravatingly calm that she hates him.

"Where is she?" she shouts.

Stella shakes her head, runs the last few paces.

"Where is she? You'll bring her later?"

She shakes her head again. "I'm sorry, Nell —"

"What? What's happened to her?" She grips her friend's hand, squeezes it. "What's happened? Tell me."

Stella looks at her with such pity Nell has to glance away. "He's sold her."

"No," she says, and she writhes free when Toby tries to hold her. "Who? Who to?"

"Winston isn't a bad showman. There are worse."

The words zigzag through Nell's head, re-arrange themselves. *Sold. Winston.* A child. Passed from hand to hand like a trinket. What is she supposed to do, to say now?

They are staring at her, as if waiting for an answer. She would like to find a sureness in her voice, to dig inside herself and discover something other than emptiness and fury. It is too much. The railings slice into her fingers.

"Has he taken her already?" Toby asks.

"No. Winston's here. I saw him. He'll take her after tonight's show," Stella says.

"She's in there? She's there, now?" Nell leans closer.

"Jasper has her. He won't allow her out of his sight." Stella takes her hands. She is too kind to tell Nell that she warned her this would happen, that this is simply how things are. "I have to be back. Before I'm missed."

Nell watches her, that proud march, her chin held high. The trumpets sound, and she hears the distorted hum of Jasper's patter.

"Wonders —"

"Sights —"

"The newest —"

On any night two weeks ago, Nell would be fastened into her ropes by now. The balloon would be behind her, and she would feel the prickle of anticipation. The others would be alive with nerves too — Stella, stretching her calves; Peggy, hopping from foot to foot. Even the lion would be fidgeting in its cage, Huffen Black feeding it another slab of meat to sate it. They would all be waiting for the twist of the curtain, the sound of the trumpet. Tiny cues, rotating their shoulders, shaking their feet, ready for the moment when they will strike out and sense the scorch of a thousand eyes on them —

And she feels this now, standing behind these railings. A fizzing anticipation that something will happen. Pearl is still there, within reach. She will find a way to her. The sun lowers, its long light cast like a torch. The dried grasses glimmer like tinsel. Fabric rackets in the breeze.

When Nell scrambles over the railings, nobody sees her and shouts. She takes the path by the pagoda and the iguanodon bones. It is empty of patrons; they are all in the tent. She nears the wagons, her heart kicking, feet flying out behind her. Jasper has released most of his laborers, and nobody is even guarding the caravans. They will all be inside, settling the crowd.

"Wait," Toby calls after her, but she does not stop. She cuts a quick line to the wagons. She hears galloping from inside the tent. The air thickens with late pollen.

"Wait," Toby says, but he is slow, lumbering. "What if he sees you?"

"I don't care."

Jasper's wagon is beneath a tree, close to the tent. Nell puts her shoulder to the door. It is locked. "She might be inside," she says, bashing it with her fist. "Pearl?" she shouts. "Can you hear me? Pearl?"

"I can do it," Toby says. He throws his weight behind it, and the hinges buckle. She steps inside.

What is she doing? What is she looking for? Of course, Pearl is not here. Nell stands there, blinking in the sudden gloom. A thousand Jaspers stare back at her, their mustachios perfectly curled, their mouths twisted into half smiles. A neat bureau, a ledger. Letters. A monocle and cakes of face paint. Bottles of spirits and crystal glasses. She lifts the decanter, sniffs it.

The audience roars. Jasper's voice rises and falls, a crowd held in his grip. She touches her wrists where he gripped her, where he hurled her into the wagon on that night with the bonfire and the dance.

"We should leave," Toby says. "If he finds us here —"

"He's in his show. He won't come."

She holds out her arms and spins round, knocking her hands against the walls, against the dresser. A smile rises to her lips, a gurgle that is close to a scream. Glasses shatter. A globe tilts and cracks. She claws at the handbills, paper bucking in her grasp, and Toby is beside her, ripping and tearing, hurling the advertisements into a great pile on the floor. Things are building and building and building and she could not stop them, even if she wanted to. The evening slips through her fingers like a wet fishing line.

JASPER

There is a child sitting in the front row. He has orange hair, a rash of freckles on his arms and cheeks. His fingers split the hot shells of chestnuts. He chews them carefully, his jaw working so mechanically that Jasper wonders if he even tastes them.

Usually, Jasper does not watch the crowd, but he cannot draw his eyes away from this child. He sees the show as the boy must. He remembers Tom Thumb fighting his way out of the pie, and the laughter that rumbled through the theater. Later, when they went to see Signor Duvalla tiptoe across the Thames, Toby reached for his arm and squeezed it. Standing there, in the tarnished city light, it seemed that all of London held its breath. Even the clouds were still, the wind fallen to nothing. One day, he longed to pinch a crowd between his fingers and hold them there.

And now, as he introduces act after act —

"the wondrous," "the marvelous," "the world's greatest living curiosity" — as he drops heavy hints at the "astonishing" finale, as he stirs the wonder of the audience — he thinks, *I have done it.* It does not matter that the show is half its original length, that he only has a paltry menagerie, that a debtor snaps at his ankles, that he is back in his old tent. Stella sits on her trapeze and kicks her legs and twitters like a swift, like a rook, like a sparrow, and the red-haired child widens his eyes.

Jasper's life falls to a hum. It is just him and the crowd; that is all that matters. He loves this small tent with its scent of mildew and sawdust and oranges and animal dung. The show is running so well, building so deftly to its climax. Citric oil burns in ceramic pots. The evening light has a pinkish glint. The lanterns are lit, snuffing boys ready to extinguish them when he clicks his fingers. Chandeliers burn with a hundred candles, wax dripping down into silver dishes. Jasper stands on his horse and bellows, "This is nothing, *nothing,* compared to the wonders I will unveil for you tonight —"

Stella lights fuses in her beard, fireworks spiral into the crowd, and the orange-haired boy claps his hands.

Behind the curtain, his machines wait, blank-eyed. He has brushed their furs and feathers, neatened their stitches, oiled their joints. They are ready. He is ready. He wishes only that the Jackal were here, that he could see what a sure prospect he is, how right he was to invest in him.

Jasper nods, and Huffen Black blows a long note on the trumpet.

The curtains are pulled back, and there they are. His machines.

As he stands there, he feels his throat closing with the urge to weep. He touches his gullet where the hog's neck was slashed. He can smell hot sugar, thinks of the molten wax that dripped from the tips of Icarus's wings.

The red-haired child leans forward, squints to look. The bag of chestnuts drops from his lap. Little brown shells scatter across the ground. Jasper has lifted his worries and his fears, turned his mind only to what is in this ring. He has *entertained* him. Jasper raises his hands, and a laugh breaks from his chest.

TOBY

There is always a point when the mood shifts. When a finger, held too long over a candle, begins to burn. When a joke sharpens, and a boy throws sugared almonds and another child laughs. When a microscope is shattered. When a story tips into a lie. When a man helps himself to too much —

I snatches whatever I sees!

Nell twirls Jasper's cigars, inspects the box of matches.

"That's me," she says. "It's me."

Her pointed toes, the great mechanical wings strapped to her back. Toby remembers sitting on bags of ballast in the quivering basket, carefully controlling her ropes. He could hear her, whooping into the night. Occasionally, he dared to pull himself to his knees to glance over the edge. She swung below him, feet kicking, arms pedaling. The lamps and candles guttered beneath her as though she were swimming through flame.

A match was struck, and there she was. *Nellie Moon.*

She touches her shoulder where the cuts have scabbed.

"Light Up the Room Like Nellie Moon."

He has grown used to her in such a short time. He has adapted his life to fit around her until, without even realizing it, he can no longer see a future apart from her. And yet, he still feels out of place, in danger of saying the wrong thing.

It has been the same all through his life: at once settled but also an imposter.

In some ways, Toby grew used to the Crimea, the sight of looting and the bodies and the stink of it all. On the day Sevastopol fell, he rode over the battlefield and scarcely noticed the litter of jawbones and purple intestines and scraps of tattered uniform. When he saw a hawk rising into the sky, clutching a hand in its talons, he merely spurred on Grimaldi, his photography wagon plowing through the mud. Ahead of him, a woman turned and pointed at the bird and cried out, "Heavens!" He wondered how these ladies would fit back into normal society, how they would sit in scalloped drawing rooms with pincushions and harpsichords and be silenced and forget what they had seen. He did not think of Stella often, but he thought of her then, wondered what Dash's politician uncle would make of her, if Dash would still love her when she did not belong in his world. He could not picture her away from her small marquee and its silver bowls of fruit, its beeswax candles. In Toby's mind, she lived only in the Crimea, just as he was certain that Dash and Jasper were only friends of circumstance; away from the war, they would drift apart. The circus burned bright in his imagination, nourished him as he jolted over a half-buried man. Once this was over, he and Jasper would be everything to each other. Racing from place to place, surrounded by novelty. A new village, new acts, the tent rising in the dawn mists.

In the gray ruins, he set up his camera on its wooden tripod and tried to shock himself into caring. The torn trunk of a man's body, arm curled into his chest like he was merely sleeping. Maggots writhed in his stomach. Toby stared at him as though to pinch himself. But it seemed that the world had shifted fractionally on its axis, that nothing had the power to surprise him any longer.

He saw his brother and Dash ahead, riding away from him. The memory of the argument was sour in his mouth, but he still shouted out to them.

They did not hear him. The rubble was too thick to allow his wagon through, so he dithered for a moment before leaving Grimaldi. "Jasper!" he called again. "Wait!" He hurried down the ruined street, but he could not see them. He ducked down the lane they must have taken. And then he heard them on the other side of a wall, Dash's laugh rising. He was about to shout again when Dash said his name. He stopped.

Toby heard it all, the words crashing over him.

Can't you find a different occupation for him? A clerk, or something? A dullard's profession.

It felt as if someone had wrenched apart his ribs and was squeezing hard on his heart. He thought, *Dullard, dullard, dullard. The* camels shimmered to nothing. The bright wagons rotted and splintered. All that was left was a doll-sized office with a high window, miles of papers just waiting for his hand to fill them. Horizons shrunk to the size of a ticking clock on the wall, a narrow partition between offices. He stepped back, his breath thin.

Dash would take his place in the show.

Walls were pulverized, houses abandoned, mortar holes ripped in masonry. The whole earth, shattered. Even the blue sky was knifed with smoke trails like scored pigskin.

He wished Jasper had never met Dash. He wished Dash did not exist. He wished Dash had died, that a Russian bullet had settled in his heart.

They did not see Toby as they walked down the street, as Jasper ducked into a cottage, and Dash strolled on, his rifle clattering against his side. Toby tried to imitate that carefree way of walking, the easy slouch of his body. He tried to see the city as Dash might, dead men glinting in the rubble like specks of gold.

Jasper emerged from the cottage, and Toby followed them, across a pile of debris toward a staircase, blown open by a shell. They turned and noticed him. Was that a crease of irritation he saw on Dash's face, of resignation?

Toby could have left, but to leave would be to admit he had nothing or nobody, so he marched on, his head bowed, heavy feet thudding on stone. He could not accept that his place had been usurped, that they did not want him; if he followed them for long enough, he reasoned, they would have to let him in. At the top, the rampart was half destroyed. Guns were abandoned. A giddying drop, a blue sky, and Cathcart's Hill on the distant horizon. Dash planted his hands on his hips.

"To the victor belong the spoils," Dash said. "Do you think Stella can see us from here?" He waved with a broad sweep of his arm.

Toby tried to see it again through Dash's eyes, to view a landscape as if he himself had won it. Thousands of lives pulverized for this small patch of territory, and to feel that as triumph! He shook his head. They scrambled on, and Dash slipped on a piece of scree and Toby's heart thundered. The man laughed. "Close," he said. Rocks plummeted off the edge, landed a few seconds later with a sharp crash. "Watch your footing," he said, but it seemed that he only said it to Jasper, as if he did not care if Toby tripped and fell.

Dullard, he thought. *Dullard, dullard, dullard.*

He caught his reflection in a puddle and pictured himself as Dash, staring back at Toby. A dismal lump of a man, trailing them like a bad smell. He began to imagine the worst things Dash might think about him, how he might laugh about him with other soldiers.

Why won't he leave us alone? We're sick of him, can't he see it?

Dash's voice ricocheted across his skull, the deep pitch of it, the easy rise at the end of the sentence in expectation of laughter.

He's worse company than a lame carthorse. A drab beast of a man.

The curious thing was that he could see these words pouring from Dash's mouth as if he had really said them.

He's as dull as a parish priest on a wet Monday morning —

He pictured a roaring of approval, Dash breaking into a laugh, smacking his thigh.

Did I tell you, he thought he'd own a circus! That dullard, in the circus!

He imagined screams of laughter.

The only thing he'd be good for is if you dressed him in gray and called him your elephant.

He followed them, tripping over the stones, his breath sharp in his lungs. He watched them slashing the pockets of a dead Ruskie, shoveling trinkets into their pouches. They moved over the casements, and Toby climbed after them, queasy with vertigo. The battle plains were laid below them, grass charred and pocked with mortar wounds, dead men spread like the debris of a ruined picnic. It was probably not safe here; the mortars had shattered these walls, and they might topple with the lightest of footfalls. Dash jumped onto the edge, tiptoeing like a tightrope artist, holding out his arms. He tilted his chin upward, closed his eyes.

"Don't be a fool," Jasper said. "Step down from there."

Or — ! Or — ! The only thing he'd be good for is if we lashed him to the wagons and had him pull us from town to town.

Toby moaned, as if to shut out real words. He could picture his brother laughing, uneasily at first, then louder, admitting the truth of what Dash said.

Imagine his shows! I'd rather have a London alderman say grace in Latin for twelve hours than watch him for five minutes in the ring.

Dash paused, a monarch surveying his kingdom. It was so *unfair.* A childish thought, a pitiful one, but it brought the beginnings of tears to Toby's eyes. Dash believed that the world was a feast spread before him, that he could pluck and discard Toby as easily as a sour fruit, that he could quickly displace him. And he had; Jasper preferred him, Jasper had moved Toby aside so carelessly.

Or a harlequin, a harlequin — hand him a tricorn hat, a goose, and a string of sausages, and the tin would pour in. He'd assume the cap and bells as if he'd been born wearing them —

Perhaps it was carelessness. Perhaps it was the tears, blinding him to the rock that jutted out at shin height. Perhaps it was deliberate, calculated in a tiny nook of his brain that he didn't recognize. Toby did not know then, and he does not know now. He took a step forward, and there was the rock, the rock that he had not seen. That he did not *think* he had seen. He found himself falling forward, arms spread out before him. Why was the angle at which he fell so exact, his hands finding so precisely the center of Dash's back? The man did not teeter, he did not reach out. He was there, and then he wasn't.

It was strange, in that moment of suspended time, when a bird crowed and the sun continued to shine, that Toby felt a scrap of gladness within him. The stories he had read often ended with the villain killed. Harmony restored. Jasper's old words cut across him. *I might say Dash is a jolly good fellow, and the wife of a soldier he shot might call him a monster.* In Stella's mind, might it be Toby who was the devil, who deserved to be punished? But how could he help it? Misery had driven him to this, had rubbed the soft edges off him.

493

The sound of a body breaking on the stones below, a life cut short. Toby was on the ground, sharp pebbles cutting into his palms, the knee of his trousers torn.

He could not have done it. A man could not be alive and well one instant, and then dead the next, because of him. It was simply not possible. He was a bystander, wasn't he? His life affected nobody's.

A purple iris sprang from the stones, bathed in golden light. A starling was whistling on a tree trunk, crickets rasping. And he could not bring himself to see the look on his brother's face. Could not bear to read the horror in it, to understand the fiend he had become.

In the tent, violins saw, the same pitch as when Nell would rise beneath the balloon. This must be the finale when Jasper will unveil the machines, when they will creak and flap their wings and blow great puffs of smoke. Toby has a sudden desire to see it for himself, to hold those ropes in his hands and hear the hushed silence of the audience.

He should be attuned to the roll and swell of a thousand small incidents, the finger-click instant when a river breaches its banks. But he finds he is surprised to see Nell take the match and strike it against the paper. That smell of camphor, the quick curl of smoke. A marbling in the air. She holds it in front of her eyes. The flame lowers and twists. She drops it. It falls like a girl, pale hair flung out behind her.

NELL

The match drops. It settles on the pile of handbills they have gathered on the floor. For a second, nothing. Nell thinks that is it, that the moment will peter out, that her anger will shrink inside her once more. The papers blacken in growing waves. The edges are red. And there it is: the first dance of flame.

It unloosens something within her. There is her music, the sound that once carried her into the sky. She thumps her feet. Toby cries, "Stop," but she doesn't, she can't. All those years she spent making herself small and harmless, swallowing her anger, defying what people expected of her. Toby reaches for a glass of water but she snatches it from him, hurls it at the wall. Doesn't he understand that this is what is left of her life? That this is all the power Jasper has allowed her? Flames lick the walls. Nell raises her hands above her head and twists her hips, kicks her legs. Storms hammering the rocks, waves thrashing pebbles, a current that tugs her under like a great fist. Glasses crack and burst. Shards pierce her shoes. The heat rises, irresistible. Her feet are bleeding. She catches the heavy lip of a decanter and smashes it on the floor. A laugh brims in her throat. She spins wildly, faster, an eddying whirlpool that she cannot fight. Briny fingers twisting her under the surface, a man's hands on her wrist and waist, hurling her into a wagon, metal wings splitting the skin of her shoulders, a perfect white-haired child, squinting as she prods seeds into a mouse's cage —

Toby is scrambling for something to throw on the fire — a blanket, another pot of water — but can't he see it's too late? The flames are thirsty, their white tongues dancing. They lick up the bonfire of torn handbills, run their fingers up the sides of the bureau, swallow the books in a single gulp. As he pounds the walls with the blanket, he only fans the fire, only presses it higher.

The smoke bites Nell's eyes, stings her lungs like a swarm of bees. Low and black. She cannot see, cannot breathe, cannot hear. She could stay here in the dark, could feel the smoke closing about her, sink into it like a lover's bed. She coughs, splutters.

"Toby," she tries to croak, but no sound comes out.

Arms about her, bundling her outside. Sunset, splitting open behind her. She hawks black phlegm onto the ground, pounds her chest. Her hands are as sooty as an urchin's. When she looks up, the wagon is ablaze, wood spitting and cracking.

"Toby," she murmurs, and he pulls her toward him. "Where's Pearl? We need to find Pearl." She leans into him, his big arms wrapped around her. She shuts her eyes, and flames still beat there.

"We should hide," Toby says. "We should wait in my wagon. Then we can find her."

Her mind clears for a moment. There will be chaos, the surprise of Jasper's burnt caravan. Then she will find the girl, and they will slip away.

It is only then that she notices the straw the laborers heaped on the muddy earth, dried from three days of sunshine. The crisped leaves of the tree between the wagon and tent are already alight, papier-mâché fruits little more than kindling. Flames twist along the branches. The tent, newly waxed, waits like a candle.

JASPER

The silence descends, just as he imagined it. Mouths fall open. The red-haired child shifts on the bench. Jasper watches a hack, his pen piercing the page, ink blooming at the nib.

Ropes creak as the machines are lifted from the ground. The fly's wings shudder open and closed, the creature spiraling in a slight breeze. Violins scream. He sees the metallic tail swatting from side to side, just as he designed it. A single crow feather breaks away from the body and drifts down. It is time for the wood louse to inch along the track, and there it is, steam torrenting from its belly. The tent is filled with the reek of industry, of oil and boiling metal, of things being invented and built and powered. A child coughs on black smoke.

Nobody moves. They sit, stunned. Jasper flexes his fingers. He thinks of the broadsheets, whirring from black-hammered presses, rolls of paper as large as haystacks. His name, filling every column inch — *"Jasper Jupiter's Mechanical Marvels, Jasper Jupiter's Mechanical Marvels"* — ink poured onto tiny stamps, the pages regaling readers with the glory of his inventions. The shimmering scales, the feathers, the claws made of an eagle's talons — a patchwork of life and industry and machinery. *"The machine age is here, welded to the Romantic age of nature and the sublime."*

Time ticks. The tail thumps. Fish scales drop like confetti. He waits for the applause, for the crowd to stumble to its feet, whistling. He waits to be hailed as magnificent, as the greatest showman in the world.

Time, he realizes, dabbing at his forehead, is stretching. His white-painted face begins to sweat, rouge leaching down his cheeks. Low murmuring, a shifting. He surveys the crowd. It dawns on him. It is not fascination that stills them. He touches his chest, does not want to believe it.

They are disappointed. *Bored.*

He stands, frozen.

A woman begins to laugh. It is just one person, a single stifled giggle. But she is laughing at him, at everything he has built. Other people begin to whisper, to murmur. Somebody yawns.

He blinks in the candlelight. He has broken the spell of the show. He has lost his audience. Behind him, Stella coughs, wills him to do something.

But as he gazes around the tent, he sees it all anew — the pain that sits beneath this shimmering illusion of ease and magic. Behind each cartwheel is a child, sobbing as her mother presses her legs into the splits each morning. Heavy beams lugged in the rain, elephants straining on chains, sick animals with little meat to feed them, stables to muck out endlessly.

He sees Winston, sitting there, watching the show and waiting for Pearl. The man's lips curl into a smile. Shame creeps up Jasper's throat. Winston has not ruined him. He has ruined himself, sent a Trojan horse into his own camp. Pearl, and now this. His mechanical spider spins helplessly on its rope.

He should, at the very least, leave the stage. But he stands in the middle of the ring, the monsters creaking above him, his hands loose at his sides. The smoke of the engine is building, filling the tent with the scent of burning. A woman jumps to her feet. The little boy with orange hair looks about him, trips forward.

"Fire," somebody bellows, and he turns

and sees it behind him. A flash of yellow, racing up the side of the tent. But he is ready. He has planned for this, how to extinguish a blaze before it grips the tent. He knows what to do. He keeps a barrel of water beside the ring, two buckets to be filled and slung on the fire.

He does not move, cannot move. He watches the spreading flames as if it is happening to a different showman, as if it is merely a scene spinning on a Japanese lantern. He is vaguely aware of panic, screams, shouting. Benches are overturned. Horses cower, canter here and there, toss their heads and scream.

Jasper walks toward the barrel and dips a bucket in it. He flinches at the coldness of it, as sharp as a burn.

He has tried to hold the parts of himself together, tried not to let the quicksand close over his head. His dream has gripped him in a stranglehold. He has bucked and struggled and fought. He should have known how it ended, should have gleaned warnings from every myth he ever read. Those who strive for more will be punished. So many books, so many poems caution against it. *My name is Ozymandias, king of kings —*

I am just one person, Jasper thinks, staring around the tent as the sides are torn open, as screams rise. *I am just one person trying to get ahead, trying to make my name.*

He has taken too much, from too many people.

He remembers how Toby tripped, his hands landing squarely in the small of Dash's back. He'd said it was a mistake, but Jasper knew better. The strange thing was, Jasper was not angry. He wanted only to protect his brother, to suck the poison from his guilt. As Toby lay on the ground, Jasper fitted his arms around him as he had when they were boys. He had always been able to understand him, as if he were a line of neat type, a heart living outside his body. "We're brothers, aren't we?" he had whispered. "Linked together."

As Toby quivered beside him and repeated, *A mistake, I tripped, it was an accident,* Jasper was stung only by his own remorse. He realized then as he realizes now, how careless he has been, how cheaply he has held Toby's affection. The show they planned together, the two camels and the capes, how much it meant to Toby. Breaking their dream meant little to Jasper because he knew that his brother would forgive him. Toby would stay beside him, as meek and loyal as a shadow. *I was benevolent and good; misery made me a fiend.* Those walnuts, flying through the air; the flurry of words that mocked him. It was he who had driven Toby to it; he who had goaded and pushed and lavished affection and then withdrawn it. As if Jasper were a great scientist, testing human nature, Toby his specimen, wriggling on a glass slide. How powerful it made him feel, how *important*.

When Toby crossed that field with Nell, he could not believe it.

The fire is before him, the barrel of water in his hands. His skin tightens at the heat of it. The fly clatters to the ground, the ropes dropped. Metal crumples. Scales split. Its head is twisted at an unnatural angle. *Dash,* he thinks, broken on the rocks, the ring that glinted on his finger. He wonders how long it will be until the Jackal hears of this. He touches his throat.

He would do it all differently, if he could. He would start again. He would give everything to Toby freely and expect nothing in return. He would be nobody, ordinary. He would live a decent life and find contentment in it. He would not strive.

No, he thinks. *That is a lie.* He would do it all again; he could not do otherwise. A wolf cannot stop being a wolf. Instinct cannot be suppressed. This fire will make his name, even if he does not live to see it. The conflagration of a man on the cusp of greatness.

The bucket of water is so heavy. Jasper throws it to the ground, tips over the barrel. In its place, he seizes a bracket of candles and hurls it against the tent wall.

NELL

A brick-red triangle lights the sky. The fire is a monster with a hundred tongues, a thousand fingers, licking and spitting and panting. Its great lungs heave. Nell made this. It is here because of her. She puts her hands over her ears. Screams rise.

She shouts Pearl's name, again and again, ramming her way through the crowds. She seizes soot-blackened children, turns them to see their faces. "Pearl," she bellows, her throat cloyed with smoke. "Pearl!"

The mob heaves past her, a searing mass of bodies, their skin sizzling with droplets of burning wax. A trumpet, pressed into the mud. A scent of molten fat, of wood, of a whole world eating itself up. She stands among the wagons and rocks back and forth. The fire spreads along the grasses, touches her feet. Toby's caravan catches, and she can hear bottles bursting like baubles. *Secure the shadow 'ere the sub-*

stance fades. Those lines, obliterated at last.

"My photographs," he cries, but there is nothing he can do.

A grating, symphonic boom from within the tent, and she shields herself with her hands. Fire rips a hole in the sky. The whole tent is lit.

What is a half-blind child supposed to do in a fire? Where would she run? Nell zigzags across the fields. A tank of rattlesnakes is split open, and they writhe through the grass, their scales seared and splitting in the heat. The lion hurls itself against the bars of its cage, roars. The monkeys are wailing, tiny fingers clawing at their ears, at their chests, hammering at the locked gate of their pen. Already, the fire is gripping the wheels of their wagon. It is too late to yoke horses and pull it to safety. She seizes the bolt, and the monkeys spring out, scamper into the trees.

"Pearl!" she shouts, and her hair is stuck to her face, each step a blade of pain. "Pearl!"

Would Jasper have kept the child in a caravan, guarded her until Winston collected her? She breaks into wagons, searches up trees, in chests half turned to charcoal, all the while calling the girl's name. The flames writhe like bodies. She trips over dropped hats, coats, a woman's shoe, scattered chestnuts and discarded bottles. The child cannot simply *disappear.*

"Pearl!"

There ahead, she sees Stella and Violante, their shoulders bent to the lion's wagon, trying to pull it away from the fire. The heat stops her as fast as a wall. She seizes Stella by the arm, rattles her. "I can't find Pearl —"

And when Stella points to a small girl, hunched in the shade of a tree, Nell lets out a cry that is scarcely human. The child is safe. She kisses her on the arms, on the cheek, grips her so tightly she worries she will hurt her. "Pearl," she says. "You're safe. You're safe."

"I can't find Benedict," she cries, her lip wobbling. "They took him away."

"They'll have set him free," Nell says. "We'll find you another mouse."

"Not — the — same —" Pearl wails, and Nell clasps her, breathes in the scent of her hair.

Behind her, the tent burns. Screams, sobs, names hurled into the night. "Laura" and "Beatrice" and "Peter." She and Toby could leave with Pearl now. They could slip away, build a life together.

But she cannot leave what she has created, cannot turn her back on this. The flames, the choking smoke — it is all because of her. Jars of oil pop like bullets.

Nell joins Stella and fits her shoulders to the lion's cage, drags the animals to safety, Pearl beside her. Dry earth crumbles under her feet. "Open the birds' cage," she shouts to Pearl, and the girl fumbles with the catches. Parrots and hummingbirds and mockingbirds fly upward in a dense cloud of feather and wing.

The show crowd has gathered in the road, massed with more people, passersby who have come to watch the fire. The roofs of nearby houses are crammed with spectators. Men and women climb trees for a better view of the tent, faces basking in the glow of the flames. A great gasp as the tent creaks. It is impossible to pull the animals any farther, impossible for any firemen to drive their wagons through.

Nell screams, "Get back!," but the eyes of the mob do not move from the fire.

A groan of awe. Arms rise, pointing. A man is lumbering toward the tent, pushing past those who try to stop him. His shoulders are stooped, his chest wide.

She throws herself forward. The heat beats her back. The crowds will not part. Someone smacks her across the head, elbows her in the side. Pearl is crying, and she lifts the child onto her hip.

"Jasper's still inside," Stella shouts at her. "He won't leave —"

She realizes, then, what Toby is doing. She surges forward, but arms bind her, haul her back. Stella and Peggy cradle her as she fights and thrashes.

His name echoes in her skull and chest and mouth, screamed again and again, but it is swallowed by the roar of the crowd.

Just before he ducks inside the tent, he turns and looks back. He does not see her.

"Toby," she shouts, but he is gone.

TOBY

We're brothers, linked together.

How can he explain how deep their roots are, that they are formed from the same tree?

One Christmas, Toby was given a photography machine and Jasper was given a microscope. His brother's excitement was feverish, and Toby was infected too. "Look through there," Jasper said, tapping the metal circle at the top of the machine. He hopped from one foot to the other. "Through there, *there.*"

Toby did as he was told. He reared back. He saw glossy pincers, as large as his fist, twine-thick hairs. "What is that?"

"A beetle," Jasper said. "And look. Look at this spider."

He looked again, through all the slides his brother prepared. Worlds bloomed before him. They trapped wood lice and fleas, ladybirds and flies. They tried to force the cat's paw beneath it. They laughed and dreamed up stories about trekking through Borneo, how Jasper would make scientific discoveries while Toby cataloged it all with his photography machine. They were *the Brothers Grimm,* one quiet, the other genial. Were they content, or was Toby jealous, even then? Has the way Jasper relayed these memories twisted the truth of them? When he remembers the war now, he mainly recalls the images he took, printed on wet card.

All of history is fiction.

Jasper had held Toby as he lay on the ramparts, as his knee bled from where he had fallen. "Nothing happened," he whispered. "A mistake. You just tripped, didn't you?"

He said it as if he believed it, as if it were a simple fact, as if it were his right to replace a true history with a false one.

"Yes," Toby said. "I tripped. A mistake." He didn't know, though; he didn't know what really happened, what the truth was.

For the first time, it occurs to him that Dash was just one man among thousands who were killed in the war, their slaughter legitimized by the simple equation of where a man was born. Russian, English, French, Turkish. Another dead soldier was not a story worth investigating. And yet, he believed this was different, that the puzzle of Dash's death sat at the heart of his life, that it would undo him. In every book he has read, crimes build toward moments of revelation, of discovery and punishment. He has exhausted himself with fearing it, has allowed it to shape his life in innumerable ways. But what if Dash's death meant nothing, if that time of reckoning never arrives?

Toby stumbles forward, tripping over split beams and ropes and overturned benches. The wet horse blanket steams in his hands, his eyes stinging.

"Jasper?" he calls. He folds over in a fit of coughing. "Jasper?"

A breeze twists through the tent, and in the second before the flames rage with even more fury, there is a break in the smoke.

His brother is standing in the middle of the ring. His arms are cast upward, as if this is all part of the show. Toby pushes toward him, flames searing his shins, his shoes useless, hot ash frying the pads of his feet. Oil has spilled into the grass, and the ground is on fire. Sawdust lit like kindling. Pain as sharp as an axe. It is so dark, the smoke so thick. Toby coughs into the blanket, stumbles on debris.

"Jasper," he whispers.

We're brothers, linked together.

Something crashes behind them. One of the king poles buckling. The fabric swings down. Toby screams, shields his face from a curtain of hot sparks. He holds out his arms.

"Jasper," he tries to say, but his throat is too dry.

Love swells in him, bucks at the nails of his chest. His brother. His *brother.* Their lives are small echoes of each other's. Home and Sevastopol and the show; a lifetime of shared stories, their feet propped on crates as they smoked pipes and drank gin and laughed.

A sudden lance of pain; he cowers, his eyes creased. Just two more steps and he will be there, beside his brother. He reaches for him. Heat. But Jasper moves back, and suddenly Toby realizes why he is still here, what he is planning to do. His brother is poised, ready to throw himself into the fire. Toby tries to speak, but his voice is lost, his throat choked with smoke.

"Leave . . . me," Jasper says.

Toby can do nothing but watch as his brother reaches out his arm to the tent wall. Jasper does not break eye contact, his mouth in a small smile as if to say, *You can-*

not stop me. His hand, reaching forward, his body about to follow, a man on the brink of annihilation — and then Jasper flinches, darts his hand back, nurses it. Horror on his face, an understanding of what pain means, of what he cannot bring himself to do. His mouth is crumpled, and he begins to keen, to low like an animal.

Toby reaches for his arm, seizes him in a clumsy embrace. It is easy, then, to still Jasper, to roll him in the blanket.

Who would you choose?

He knows the answer, as he lifts Jasper onto his back as easily as a beam, as he hunkers low to the ground and lumbers through burning benches and pools of melted tallow. His brother's heart beats against his own, a half of him.

NELL

Nell strains, thrashes in Stella's grip.

"Let me go," she shouts, again and again.

The great body of the tent swings down, crashes to its knees. A ripping sound, as if the sky is being torn in two. Screams tear her throat, her hands turned to claws. Sparks billow like fireflies.

"Toby," she cries, and even Stella loosens her hold for an instant. But Nell finds she has no fight left. Her arms slump to her sides. Peggy takes her hand, grips it. Her friend does not speak, does not try to find words to console her.

But a great cheer is rippling through the crowd. A man blocks her view. She beats forward. "What is it?"

Stella and Peggy lift her, and she sees Toby ambling forward, a weight on his back. Her hand covers her mouth. He keels over, a hunched figure placed on the ground, curled like a child in prayer.

Applause, cheering, as if this is the finale they have all been expecting — as if a man in a glittering red topper might ride out on an elephant and bellow, *Encore!*

Figures descend, blanketing Toby, concealing him from view. They wrap the body in cloth and sling it on a horse.

"Is he dead?" Stella asks quietly. Nell is surprised by the sadness in her voice. "Is Jasper dead?"

"I can't see."

There is a bellowing for water, for the crowds to move aside so the dray can pass through. Nell thinks of Charlie, those empty early days without him, how she would wake in the night and expect to find him there. That glimpse she had of him just before Jasper snatched her away, his forehead bent to Mary's. She is weighed down with all she has lost, all she has had taken from her. The silence between them when Charlie visited, her life changed from what he knew. But still, for all that, she has always had the power to make choices of her own.

When Stella takes her hand, Nell does not resist. Together, they weave through hundreds of people, cheeks orange with reflected fire. Her friend barters with a man with a cart, nods at Nell. She lifts Pearl onto it.

"Horses," the child says.

The cart moves slowly through the crowds. Pearl snuffles against her, whimpers as the horses move, cries for her lost mouse. Peggy lies against the wood, her eyes black and fearful. They turn down streets lined with rickety houses, down lanes with darkened hedgerows. The bright sphere of light dwindles to nothing.

Stella hands Nell a bottle of ale and a cloth, and she sponges the speckled burns on the child's arms.

"Where are we going?" Pearl asks.

Ahead, it is dark. No lights, no houses. It is a blank future on which she might inscribe anything.

■ ■ ■ ■

Epilogue

■ ■ ■ ■

And let there be
Beautiful things made new.
　　— JOHN KEATS, *The Fall of Hyperion:*
　　　　A Dream, an epic poem that was
　　　　unfinished at Keats's death in 1821

It is a damp Wednesday afternoon when Toby sets off on the road to Oxford. He carries a flask of water, two salted beef sandwiches, and a leather purse. He walks with a slight limp, the leathery burn on his thigh tightening with every step. It is a humid day, and sweat gathers at the back of his neck. He rolls up his sleeves. His tattoos have smudged over time, flowers blending into each other, pinks turned to purple. The green apple looks more like a bruise.

He walks past yellow fields of oilseed rape, ramshackle cottages, farmers herding their cows with sticks. He sits by a river and scoops more water into his flask and drinks thirstily, then sets off again. In his pocket, there is a faded handbill. *"The Flying Sisters."*

It is his charwoman, Jane, who brings him news of passing tent shows. She has given him the handbills of Astley's and Hengler's, Winston's and Sanger's, and the big American circuses that Jasper once dreaded. Toby has read his brother the advertisements and watched his face for a flicker of joy or resentment or sadness. Nothing. He has continued to draw and mutter, barely raising his head.

All these troupes have passed within a whisker of their cottage. As Toby has sat by the hearth, boiling potatoes and mashing turnips, he sometimes swore he could hear them riding past. The roaring of a lion. An elephant, distressed. Perhaps Minnie was among them. Perhaps she was dead. He closed his eyes and imagined their bright coaches and caged beasts and sequined performers, all passing the towering oak by the turnpike, bouncing over that pothole he always keeps topped up with gravel.

And then, one afternoon, Jane pressed a new leaflet into his hand. "All women in this one. All women!" She sniffed her disapproval. "A *very* dignified life, I'm sure, flaunting themselves."

Toby thanked her and crumpled the paper into his pocket without a thought. But a few days later, when Jasper was sleeping, he went for a walk. The crab apples in the churchyard were ripe, branches bent with their weight, and he scrumped a few. He moved to put them in his jacket and found the balled handbill. He opened it.

It felt as though someone had punched his insides out of him.

There she was, in the center, as steady as a flame.

"The Flying Sisters!"

She looked the same, as if time had not touched her. Golden hair loose on her shoulders. As beautiful as she ever was. Her legs, bare and dappled. He had kissed every inch of them. And there was Stella, perched on a trapeze, Peggy juggling, and other women he did not know. A pale girl with white hair dressed in a doublet, mice tiptoeing down her arms — he smiled. Pearl.

It was quite simple; he thought of Nell all the time. He thought of her when he peeled vegetables for his brother, and when he walked out to the river in the mornings and saw the mists steaming like milk, and when he sat in his old pew and tried to summon prayers that would not come.

At first, in the days and weeks and months after the fire, it had distressed him, as if something essential had been severed from him. He thought of seeking her out, abandoning his brother. But how could he? They were brothers, linked together, beating with one heart, breathing with a single pair of lungs. His penance was to stay with Jasper. They had each saved the other once, but rather than freeing Toby, it had only forged them closer. He learned merely to live with Nell as a comforting presence. They conversed constantly in his head. He often imagined a chance encounter, an acknowledgment that she thought of him too. *That would be enough,* he told himself.

But the sight of this advertisement had jarred him, disrupted these steady thoughts. Ten years had passed, and yet she wormed her way into every alcove of his mind. He felt bilious. His heart rose in his throat, in his ears, at the thought he might go to her show and see her. Lust sickened him.

He had to go. He asked Jane to look in on Jasper, and he packed a small cloth bag. He wore the same old jerkin, scrupulously cleaned, dyed again with woad. He would not look at himself in a mirror to see how badly he had aged.

Toby keeps walking, nods at farmers and ladies and boys in ragged trousers. He can see the spires of Oxford in the distance, blue in the haze. Fat bumblebees drowse on wild poppies, legs dusty with pollen.

Ten years have passed, he reminds himself. *Ten years.*

She might have married. She might have forgotten him. Her life has moved forward, while his has stayed in a rut. Her world will have been filled with colors and wondrous sights (*"a European tour,"* he read on the handbill; *"Paris, Berlin,"* and *"America and Moscow," "Performances before royalty"*), while his life has shrunk to a single cottage with a narrow dirt track. He painted the door blue. It is as he always pictured it, except without her in it. And in a way, he has been content. He has enjoyed giving himself to the service of another. He has found the extraordinary in the ordinary — the sweet scent of a dog rose, the way the light knocks the chipped table first thing in the morning. Things he would never have noticed or understood if his life were not so small. Occasionally, he catches himself looking at the world as an observer, squaring his fingers like a photograph, and he always plunges his fists into his pocket and keeps walking. He pushes his old wagon from his mind, its looping script. *Secure the shadow 'ere the substance fades.*

It helps, of course, that his brother does not complain, does not criticize. "Look at this," Jasper will say each afternoon, and he will push another drawing toward Toby. Even Toby can tell that it is nothing but a mash of lines and cogs, endlessly looping. "It will make my name. The greatest in the world," he will mutter. He will grasp Toby's hand, a pleading look in his eye. "You'll send it, won't you? You'll send it to London."

"Yes," Toby will say, accepting it and tucking it into his pocket.

Perhaps Jasper knows that Toby secretly uses them for kindling, because he never specifies an exact address or a recipient, never asks about a reply. Each drawing is forgotten about instantly, a new idea taking its place. In the evenings, they will sit by the fire, and Toby will relieve his guilt by talking about their childhood, just as Jasper always liked. He will say, "Do you remember when we first read *Frankenstein*? Do you remember when you were given that microscope, when you caught me trying on your clothes? You always used to laugh when Father called us *the Brothers Grimm*." Sometimes, Toby will look up and see tears dripping from Jasper's chin, and he will calm his brother like an infant. Remorse and grief follow quickly, until Toby cannot bear to look at Jasper, and he has to busy himself with scrubbing the hearth or turning down the bed.

Sometimes, he imagines it differently; that

he'd told Nell about Dash and what he'd done. That Stella had found out. That it had boiled over into a fight, that Nell had left him because of it, that what he did to Dash had had some *meaning*. Dash's death felt like casting a stone into a pond and no ripples showing.

There, ahead, is the circus with its striped tent. The honk of trumpets, the sawing of a violin. All is chaos, laughter, entertainment. His chest constricts. He stops at the stile to regain his breath. He searches the crowd, tries to shed his limp. If anything, it seems to worsen.

He sets his mouth and walks on.

A girl is juggling apples, her face whitened with paste, peacock eyes painted on her cheeks. He passes the snuffbox stall. Hawkers flog baskets and tinware, girls sell tickets for the lucky-bag swindle. He notices Stella, lifting a child so that he can see the elephant. He raises his hand in greeting, but she does not see him.

"Tickets, sir," a girl says, and he turns, and Pearl is in front of him, a topper in her hand, rattling with coins. Behind her stands a muscled woman, to guard it from thieves, no doubt. Ready to give chase if she needs to.

"Pearl?" he whispers, but she does not

respond. She does not know him.

"Family tickets a shilling."

"Just me," he says, quietly, taking out his purse and handing her the coins.

She is grown, a woman now. She must be fifteen years old.

He imagined, somehow, that it would be easy. That Nell would see him instantly, and they would chatter. He would link his fingers through hers, run through reminiscences. But what would they talk about? His small life, her great one? He would have nothing at all to share.

Toby walks toward the tent. And then, he sees her, through a gap in the fabric. She looks just the same as she always did. That mouth he has kissed.

She leaps onto a trapeze, laughs at someone below her. Her smile is as artless as ever, but her movements are surer. He slips inside and stands at the back. The seats are not yet filled, the audience still outside. It is as hot as a forge. A horse is plucking at tufts of grass.

Nell begins to flip her body. It sets the rope swinging. She has learned trapeze, then. Even Jasper would say she is skilled. She gains momentum. Toby recalls the old collision of their bodies, nails scratching his back, teeth biting his earlobe. He shivers.

"Has someone checked the ropes?" she calls, and then she drops backward, hangs from her knees.

As Nell flies across the tent, her hair spilling beneath her, Toby has an urge to stand up, to seize the reins of one of the horses, and to fly beside her. To gather the fragments of their old life and piece them back together. To leave his life as he knows it. That dripping house where they eat pottage each morning. Circus has always made him believe that anything is possible. But he knows, too, that it is illusion, that life does not share its boldness, its neat stories.

Because what would happen to Jasper, then? Who would care for him? Toby's dream comes to a stuttering halt. He was wrong to think he could come here. He belongs with Jasper in that quiet cottage.

We're brothers, linked together.

A sudden thought strikes him: she will not want him here.

He should have known how these stories end. But with all his love of books, he was blind to it. For all that, he thought they were mere fantasy, that his reality would somehow be different. Edifices burn down, and then they are regenerated. People destroy each other, are punished, transformed.

When the tent burned down, Nell's life

began, Jasper's ended. And Toby — he trapped himself somewhere between the two of them.

He frowns. Outside, he can hear laughter. "Wheezes ever charming, ever new!"

He looks down at his old jerkin. His worn shoes, tied together with string. The blurred edge of a tattooed vine peeking out of his sleeve. He does not fit here. He never did. The purpose of his life is to give comfort, to repent. An ordinary, quiet existence. He always made a pitiful hero.

Nell is clambering down from the trapeze. She has not seen him. And before Toby can change his mind, he slips away, through the gap in the tent, and then he is blinking in the bright sunshine. He will take that little road back home and forget he was ever foolish enough to visit. He will tell Jane that the show was stupendous, marvelous, incredible. He will thank her for looking after his brother, and then he will resume his usual duties. They will sit by the fire, and Toby will tell Jasper stories about microscopes and clothes and gifted books.

He gives his ticket to a child, who grins in delight, and then he limps back through the meadow, toward home. It is a narrow path, hewn at the edge of a stream.

For the next few weeks, he knows the

memory of Nell will be unbearable. He will not sleep tonight. He will pace and shred his fingernails. He will think, *What if, what if, what if.* But those feelings have passed before, and they will pass again. Soon, her imagined presence will become comforting, and he will find small but constant contentment in his life.

Just once, when he is halfway over the stile, does he turn and look back. Crowds like milling ants around a sugar cone. The cries and shouts are audible even from here. He waits for the hush. The show is about to begin.

Nell sits in her wagon, a cake of red face paint discarded beside her. She knows they will be looking for her, knows that the benches are full and the audience is ready. She hears the gong being beaten, summoning the last of the performers. She reaches out and touches a glass wind chime, listens to its quiet reverberations.

It can't have been him, she thinks. A glimpse was all she caught, his hunched shoulders, his dark hair, and then the curtain of the tent swung shut behind him. She has seen him in so many places. In Paris, she once followed a man for five minutes until he ducked into an inn and she saw his nose was the wrong size. In Barcelona, she glimpsed him across a crowded ballroom, but when she hurried toward him, she saw his movements were too fluid, his figure too neat. Often, as she swings across the ring, she'll find herself searching the crowd for him. After, Stella will tell her off, scold her that a lapse in attention means a broken neck.

"You left him," she'll say, "don't forget that," and Nell will shrug and say, "I don't know who you mean."

Nell rubs her face, her hair drawn back in a tight plait. Perfumes are scattered about her, tortoiseshell combs, a silver looking glass. Tiny animals carved from amber, gifted to her by Danish royalty. She took the steamer across the English Channel, hung over the back of the main deck and watched the water churn behind them, Stella's and Peggy's arms linked through hers, Pearl shrieking with laughter. Nell picks up a miniature leopard, weighs it. *It won't have been him,* she tells herself again; *it is not possible.*

The gong sounds more urgently. They will be wondering where she is, Stella cussing under her breath. Nell stands, stretches, bounces on the balls of her feet. She shakes her head at herself, smiles. This is her room, her show.

She crosses the grass. There they are, fretting, searching the crowds for her. They have not seen her yet. Her women, with their soft, strong bodies. Pearl and Stella and Peggy. They belong only to themselves.

Nell quickens her pace. The audience is waiting for her. Her friends are waiting for her. She feels the familiar crackle of power.

AUTHOR'S NOTE

By the 1860s, the Victorian freak show, which peddled physical difference as a form of entertainment, was booming. "Deformitomania," as *Punch* called it, swept the globe with an unabated fury. Queen Victoria, dubbed the "freak fancier," was the industry's biggest fan and helped to popularize it, entertaining countless "human wonders" and showmen in Buckingham Palace. For the performers themselves, the industry might have offered some opportunity and freedom, but it could also take them away with devastating effect.

I wanted to shine a light on the individuals involved in this world. As with most fiction, the question I wanted to ask was: *How would it have felt?* How would a young girl like Nell have experienced and navigated such coercion, opportunity, fame, and objectification, while also retaining a sense of herself? Was there such a thing as choice when this industrial society refused to adapt itself to the needs of people like Peggy? More than a hundred and fifty years later, a handful of the era's most famous personages are still known, the most prominent example being Joseph Merrick, dubbed "The Elephant Man" for a still-undiagnosed medical condition which produced growths on his body (he is not mentioned in this book as he did not appear publicly until 1884). But there are countless other stories that have been lost to time, a few faded cartes de visite the only sign that the performers ever lived at all.

Before I started *Circus of Wonders,* I considered writing about real historical figures, especially those who are lesser-known. However, when I sat down to write, it felt like I was invading their privacy — these were real people about whom so many outlandish stories had already been spun by media and showmen, their voices silenced and their histories overwritten by those who profited from their lives. While, up to a point, all of history is fiction, the imagination of the gray areas of these lives — impulses, desires, reactions — seemed like a trespass. Therefore, I decided it was important to make my characters and their stories entirely fictional. However, echoes of real people and performer's narratives can be found in many historical accounts, and I felt it was important to acknowledge the wider context of their stories, too. All of the information about individuals such as Julia Pastrana, Joice Heth, Charles Stratton, Charles Byrne, and Chang and Eng Bunker is correct and derived from my research.

Julia Pastrana, a singer and performer from Mexico, had hypertrichosis and was sold to the circus by her uncle. She toured in life and was then was toured in death by her husband, Theodore Lent. He had her dead body — sewn into a dress she herself had made — and that of her newborn baby embalmed and displayed around the world. Julia and her child were widely shown as late as 1972, and finally buried in 2012 in a cemetery in Sinaloa de Levya, a town near her birthplace.

Joice Heth was an enslaved African American who was bought by P. T. Barnum in 1835. Slavery was illegal in the north of America at this time, so Barnum negotiated to "lease" her. She was blind and almost entirely paralyzed, but Barnum had her remaining teeth extracted to make her look older. He marketed her as "The Greatest Natural and National Curiosity in the World," alleging that she was 161 years old.

Upon her death, he sold tickets to her autopsy, which was attended by 1,500 members of the public. When it was proven that Joice Heth was not as old as Barnum had claimed, he spun many different tales, including one suggesting that Heth had escaped and that they'd performed the autopsy on the wrong person. Alive or dead, it seems Barnum did not care, as long as he made a profit. It was on this "success" that P. T. Barnum, the so-called Greatest Showman, launched his career.

Charles Byrne measured between six feet seven inches and eight feet tall, according to various sources, his height caused by a then-undiscovered growth disorder known today as acromegaly. The fictional Brunette has the same condition — it would have caused severe headaches and joint pain, among other symptoms. Byrne became a celebrity in London, entertaining large audiences and even inspiring a stage show, *Harlequin Teague,* but he was constantly hounded by those who wanted to examine his body against his will, and it is widely reported that this caused him to sink into depression. Aware that the surgeon and anatomist John Hunter wanted his body upon his death, and falling ill due to medical complications and excessive drinking,

Byrne made detailed arrangements to avoid this fate, including the instruction that he should be buried at sea in a lead coffin. However, Hunter bribed Byrne's friends and obtained the man's body. Charles Byrne's skeleton was displayed until 2017 in London's Hunterian Museum. There are ongoing debates as to whether his skeleton will be exhibited when the museum reopens in 2021, as many petitions have called for his body to be buried in line with his wishes.

The very fact that the remains of Charles Byrne and Julia Pastrana were displayed until so recently highlights their treatment as medical curiosities rather than real people who deserved the dignity of a burial. Whether alive or dead, they have been objectified for the entertainment of spectators.

While this abuse is undeniable, there were many performers who sought out, benefitted from, and appeared to welcome the fame and financial security offered by the industry. Chang and Eng Bunker, conjoined twins from today's Thailand, toured the UK and America. They played badminton and discussed philosophy before audiences and, after three years, decided to dispense with a showman and manage themselves. In fewer than ten years, they had made $10,000, with which they bought a large estate. They married two sisters and fathered twenty-one children before dying quietly at the age of sixty-two.

Charles Stratton was a little person, acquired by P. T. Barnum at the age of four (unlike his character in the film *The Greatest Showman,* who is a fully grown man at the time he chooses to join the show, a rewriting of history that downplays the power imbalance and exploitation of the freak show). Stratton's rise to fame was stratospheric. Newspapers sang his praises, a Parisian restaurant changed its name to *Le Tom Pouce,* actors begged to be associated with him, and between fifty and sixty coaches of the nobility were seen outside his exhibition rooms at any one time. He married another little person, Lavinia Warren, in a lavish ceremony witnessed by ten thousand people, as reported in newspapers from the *New York Times* to *Harper's Weekly.* Queen Victoria gifted them a miniature coach. They earned vast sums of money and came to own several houses, a steam yacht, and a stable of pedigree horses.

With so few firsthand accounts from these performers (which is, of course, telling in itself), it is impossible to know how they felt about their careers, especially considering how limited their options would have been due to a deeply prejudiced society. Lavinia Warren once said, "I belong to the public," a sentiment that I attribute to Stella in this book, and which has always struck me as heartbreaking.

Circus of Wonders is, among many things, a book about storytelling. There are no simple answers, no easy ways of reading a deeply complex and problematic piece of history. I wanted merely to highlight how this industry could both exploit and empower, and to put Nell at the heart of her own story.

Elizabeth Macneal,
November 2020

ACKNOWLEDGMENTS

I owe so much to so many. Countless books have inspired and educated me, and without them it is difficult to imagine writing this novel. Historical fiction, of course, is as much about the time in which it is written as the time when it is set. Therefore, I am indebted to many contemporary accounts about disability and physical difference, spanning essays, memoir, poetry, and fiction. I recommend these wholeheartedly and encourage anybody reading this to seek them out. In particular *Marked for Life* by Joie Davidow; *Beyond the Pale* by Emily Urquhart; *Dwarf* by Tiffanie DiDonato; the poetry of Sheila Black (especially *House of Bone*); *Disfigured: On Fairy Tales, Disability, and Making Space* by Amanda Leduc; *Disability Visibility* edited by Alice Wong; and *The Girl Aquarium* by Jen Campbell, as well as her Instagram account (@jenvcampbell) and YouTube channel (jen-campbell).

I have spent many months immersed in books on Victorian circus, the freak industry, and the Crimean War. In particular I am grateful for *The Wonders* by John Woolf; *Freakery: Cultural Spectacles of the Extraordinary Body* edited by Rosemarie Garland Thomson; *Crimea: The Last Crusade* by Orlando Figes; *No Place for Ladies: The Untold Story of Women in the Crimean War* by Helen Rappaport; *The Life of P. T. Barnum* by P. T. Barnum; and the Crimean War dispatches of William Howard Russell.

There are many individuals who have helped to build this book. I am filled with gratitude:

To my astonishing editor, Sophie Jonathan, who has shaped this novel with such sensitivity, intelligence, and care. I know how lucky I am; thank you. To my agent, Madeleine Milburn, for supporting me in innumerable ways. You are a powerhouse and a true friend. To everyone else at her agency — it is a pleasure to know you all.

To everyone at Picador. It is a rare and precious thing to be able to call your colleagues "friends," but this is my particular joy of being published by Pan Macmillan. My gratitude for Camilla Elworthy is boundless — I hope there are many more road trips to come, though I'm not sure if my stomach muscles can take much more laughter. Katie Bowden, you are magnificent! Thank you for all of your incredible marketing ideas and enthusiasm. Katie Tooke designed the UK book jacket, a work of art in itself. There are so many others I long to thank, for everything from marketing to sales to book design to finance to editorial to postroom, but I am afraid I will forget somebody. But you know who you are, and I hope you also know how grateful I am.

To everyone at Emily Bestler Books, and my international publishers, for continuing to make my dreams come true. Emily Bestler and Lara Jones, I am so glad to work with both of you.

To the booksellers and book bloggers who have supported *The Doll Factory,* I appreciate it so very much.

To those who generously shared their own experiences with me when I was planning and writing this book, and for talking so eloquently about the representation they'd like to see. In particular, thank you to Sarah Salmean.

To Jen Campbell for the sensitivity read. Your thoughts and ideas were invaluable and I hope I have done justice to your edit.

To Philip Langeskov for being both tough and encouraging about the first iteration of my opening chapters.

To John Landers and Diana Parker, Sophie Kirkwood, and Lydia Matthews and Aneurin Ellis-Evans for friendship and a place to stay when I couldn't concentrate at home.

To Kiran Millwood Hargrave for reading my first draft and being so thoughtful and generous with your feedback (and many more bowls of noodles and weird cocktails to come, I hope).

To all of my friends — thank you for the delicious meals, for the endless moral encouragement, for reminding me "it's just a book" (ha), for the jokes and beach swims and the best of times. You all kept me sane, and I promise the third novel will be a less arduous journey for all of you (or at least I'll be less insufferable).

To my family. It was a lucky, lucky day when I wound up with all of you in my life. I cannot thank you enough. Support, laughter, distracting hikes, pep talks, and endless love. Mum, Dad, Peter, Hector, Laura, Dinah, and — as always — Grandma and Grandpa. I love you all so, so much.

And to J & A, for everything.

ABOUT THE AUTHOR

Born in Scotland, **Elizabeth Macneal** is a writer and potter based in London. *The Doll Factory,* Elizabeth's debut novel, was an international bestseller, has been translated into twenty-nine languages, and has been optioned for a major television series. It won the Caledonia Novel Award 2018. *Circus of Wonders* is her second novel.